PRAISE FOR

"Piper Bayard's FIRELANDS is a harrowing and cautionary tale of a world in strife, of men and women struggling to survive amidst the fiery, apocalyptic ruins of modern society. Thrilling, moving, and ultimately hopeful, here is a novel to be savored long after you turn the last page."
—James Rollins, New York Times bestselling author of *Bloodline*

"With great characters and an amazing world that both mystifies and terrifies, FIRELANDS deserves to be mentioned with the other great dystopian novels of the past three years."
—Jeff Ayers, *Author Magazine*

"FIRELANDS envisions a terrifying and prescient future of a United States lost to the worst extremes. Piper Bayard's wonderfully relevant and beautifully realized fantasy tale would make George R. R. Martin proud, as it combines the best of *Children of Men* with Stephen King's seminal *The Stand* . . . the result is a major debut that is not to be missed."
—Jon Land, bestselling author of *Strong at the Break* and *Betrayal*

"With echoes of *Under the Banner of Heaven* and *The Hunger Games*, FIRELANDS is a sprawling adventure ranging across a world racked by post-apocalyptic want, denial, and prophetic dictum. Equal parts heroic quest and morality play, it races forward on a current of deftly woven characters and breakneck action, never failing to deliver what every reader wants—a helluva good story."
—Ryne Douglas Pearson, screenwriter of *Knowing* and bestselling author of *Simple Simon* and *Confessions*

"Piper Bayard explodes on the scene in FIRELANDS. Creative. Imaginative. Chilling and reassuring. A captivating tale well told."
—Vicki Hinze, bestselling author of *Duplicity*

For David—
You are my home.

FIRELANDS

PIPER BAYARD

This is a work of fiction.

The characters and events portrayed in this book are fictitious. Any similarity to any actual persons, living or dead, is coincidental and not intended by the author.

Shoe Phone Press
2770 Arapahoe Road #135-229
Lafayette, CO 80026
Print ISBN: 978-0-9915692-0-5

Multi-format eBook editions of this book and a trade paperback edition were published by StoneGate Ink in 2013.

Cover design: V.K. Hinze

Layout design: Jessica Lewis

ACKNOWLEDGEMENTS

THEY SAY IT TAKES a village to raise a child. Forget the child. It takes a village to write a book. My deepest, abiding gratitude to my village:

- My family, who continued to encourage me long after I discontinued cooking for them in order to write.
- Kristen Lamb, my editor/mentor/friend who adopted me from the Writers Shelter and taught me the difference between writing a book and playing with my imaginary friends.
- Jay Holmes, my BFF, violence consultant, and constant source of humor and determination.
- Ellie Ann, world's best beta reader and author support.
- Susan Spann, publishing attorney extraordinaire.
- Neil Pugh and Kerry Meacham, bow hunting advisors.
- My local friends, Maria, Suzzette, Jenni, Iain, and Pat, for sounding board services and comic relief.
- My amazing friends in cyberspace who encouraged me with their interest and presence.
- Anthony and the ladies at Mojo's Coffee House, who provided a warm and loving home for my muse.
- Every person whose eyes lit up when I said, "I'm writing a book."

Thank you.

THE GOSPEL OF JOSEPH
Chapter 3, Verses 1–7

1. Famine was rife across the land, and man cried out for the bread of mercy. But iniquity was in abundance. And God said, "Let there be fire."
2. The great volcano Taupo brought forth man's atonement from her bowels, blanketing the earth in the fire and ash of Apocalypse.
3. And as the earth shook, and the anguished wails of man split the firmament, I cried out to God, saying, "Send me your champion."
4. The Archangel Michael appeared in a cloud of fire, his flaming sword held high. "Prove your worth, and God shall spare your people."
5. Forty days and forty nights we battled, before the Lord God called us to cease.
6. I fell to the earth as one dead, and the Archangel Michael held his sword above me like a cross raised to the heavens. "Be thou not afraid, Joseph. With thee, God is greatly pleased. His Kingdom is come to this earth, and thou shalt be His prophet."
7. And the Archangel Michael struck his sword to the ground and revealed the Seeds of Life. "Take these seeds and with them feed thy people. Feed only the righteous, for all but they are this day damned. Keep thy people pure with the fire of Atonement, even as God has this day purged the earth of iniquity, and they shall never hunger again."

CHAPTER 1

MY STOMACH GROWLED, AND I begged it to be silent, afraid the sound would spook my prey. I had followed the majestic buck since the full moon was high above me, and now with dawn breaking, I nocked my arrow for my shot. Daisy, my shepherd mutt, crouched, ready to fly at the buck's throat with my release. Forcing the importance of this kill from my mind, I consciously slowed my heartbeat. In that moment, it couldn't matter that it was Reunion. It couldn't matter that my people hadn't tasted fresh venison in two months. All that could matter was that shot.

I drew my breath to whistle his head up, victory surging beneath my skin. Suddenly a bullet whizzed past me, clipping a branch off the tree beside my ear. Reverberations shattered the morning silence.

The buck shot from the glade, and I dropped, motioning Daisy to freeze.

I heard one man stomping through the forest, and my blood ran cold. I knew it was a man because I was the only woman of my people who would brave the forest alone. But was he one of us? A Sec? Or was he a Josephite? Was he aiming at me or the buck? More importantly, was he alone? I crouched behind a nearby juniper tree, ready to shoot if necessary.

Daisy whimpered and wagged her tail, and then the man came into view. I watched him kneel to search for a blood trail, and both relief and fury flooded my veins. I knew him. From the feather on his plainsman hat to his long, black braids, beard, and hemp clothes, I knew him.

When he rose and stretched, I didn't stop to think. In one swift movement, I stood and took my shot, pinning his hat to the ponderosa pine behind him.

He dropped and rolled behind some deadfall. The cleaved feather from his hat gracefully rocked to earth on the breeze, its serenity a surreal contrast to my racing heart.

Gradually, he hazarded a peek, his rifle at the ready. With a quick glance, he took in the arrow. Shaking his head, he lowered his rifle. The sound of his fury echoed through the glade. "Archer, dammit, it's me. Don't shoot."

With my nod, Daisy bounced across the distance to greet him, her joy of reunion with her pack member grating on the anger in my heart. My stomach rumbled, and all I could taste was bitterness. Our people would go hungry again.

Pulling the camouflage scarf back off my face, I stepped from behind the juniper and followed my dog, determined to rise above the situation and hold my tongue. That didn't last long.

"That was my buck, Quinn. I had him, and then you came along with that crappy excuse of a shot. Not two inches from my head, by the way." I held up my fingers, showing him how close he'd come to killing me.

"Me? What about you?" Hands clenched at his sides, he started pacing a short, quick line, his braids flying as he turned. "I can't believe you tried to shoot me. Of all the stubborn, impulsive things you've done—"

"Tried to shoot you? If I were trying to shoot you, you'd be dead. You know what that buck would have meant to us. Just be glad I only killed your hat."

Stopping abruptly, he shoved his finger at me, his face red, and a wrath in his eye that called to mind a wounded mountain lion. "Back off, woman. That was too far. Too. Far."

I batted his finger away, crossed my arms, and glared. He was right. "No blood, no foul" was understood between us, but his shot had been an accident. Mine had been deliberate. And he only wanted the same thing I did. To feed our people.

Biting off my anger, I lowered my gaze. "You're right, but at least it was an easy shot."

I glanced sideways toward him through my lashes. His blue eyes flashed warning, and I quickly looked back at my feet.

"But mostly, it was irresponsible," I said, "And I'm sorry. I'm glad I didn't kill you." I peered back up, waiting for his forgiveness. Hoping, anyway. He took his time about it.

Finally he turned and wound his way through the deadfall to wrench my arrow from the tree. After inspecting the new holes in his hat, he whacked it against his pants to clean it off. Shoving it onto my head, he said, "Fix it. And I want your best feather."

"Fair enough." I tipped the brim to him.

"And Archer . . ." He reached down to scratch Daisy behind the ears. She groaned with pleasure and leaned into his hand.

"Yes?"

"I'm glad I didn't kill you too. I would have missed you." He gave the dog two quick pats on the head and turned away to retrieve his gear.

I smiled. Shrugging out of my pack, I put the hat inside and pulled my camouflage scarf off my head. It tangled in my long, mahogany braids but then released them with a gentle tug. I wished I could cut them short, like the rest of the Sec women, but I didn't have that luxury. My safety depended on looking like a man any time I left my meadow to hunt. If the Josephites ever caught me looking like a woman, they would surely brutalize me. I'd even heard of them setting stray Secular women on fire down in the Border Regions.

"What are you doing out here, anyway?" I asked, pouring a bit of water from my canteen into the hollow of a rock for Daisy. I held my filter straw, ready to finish off whatever she didn't drink.

"Granny sent me to find you. You said you'd be home by noon yesterday to finish digging the new outhouse. You know how she worries."

"Oh, no. I forgot I told her that." I sighed. "I can hear it now. 'Deena. Your mother didn't walk through the Valley of the Shadow of Death to give birth to you to have you mauled by a Dixie bear.'" I untied a scrawny squirrel from my pack and gave it to Daisy. "Truth is, I didn't want to come back empty-handed."

"Your pack looks pretty full to me."

"Nah. Nothing but a few marmots and Daisy's breakfast. That was the only deer I'd seen all week, and now . . ." My stomach protested its emptiness. I ignored it, but I couldn't watch as Daisy devoured the kill.

Quinn reached into the pocket of his hemp cargo pants for some venison jerky and handed it to me.

"Thank you." I tried not to attack it like a ravaged animal. I'm not sure if I succeeded.

Spotting his machete where it had dropped on the ground, I picked it up and handed it to him. "Here. Don't forget your lady friend. You might get cold at night without her."

"Thank you. I can't lose Clarisse." He inspected the machete and then pulled a cloth from his pocket and lovingly wiped the blade before tying it back on his belt.

I rolled my eyes. "Honestly, Quinn. No wonder you're not married. There's no room left in your bed for a wife while you've got that thing."

"Hey. At least Clarisse doesn't try to kill me like some women do." He winked at me.

I smiled. "You want to talk about killing people with that lame shot of yours? Tell you what. You stick to trading, and

I'll stick to hunting."

Quinn chuckled. "Deal. Now pass me half your load and let's get home."

I pulled the plastic bags full of marmots from my pack and handed them to him, and he re-arranged his items to accommodate.

"Shortcut through Gap?" I asked.

"No, it's safer through the woods."

"I know, but the forest will take all day. We'll be back by noon through Gap, and there won't be any patrols on Atonement Day."

"There are sometimes. You've just been lucky so far. Do you want another beating like the one you took last year?"

I looked down at my crooked pinkie. He was right, again, but the excitement of seeing my friends and family after the long winter got the best of me. "Come on, Quinn. It's Reunion, and I've been out for three days. I really want to get back in time to clean up before dinner."

"Well, I don't like it. But it's true, you could use a good scrubbing." His eyes twinkled mischief.

"Hey." I punched lightly toward his arm, and he dodged. "That means if we do run into a patrol, I'll stink so bad they won't want to get close enough to thrash me."

"Okay, but if we do, you two stay back and let me handle them."

"No worries. I'll shoot their hats off."

I dug out my prized Maui Jim sunglasses that I'd scavenged from the dump a few years before. We set off at a traveling jog, Daisy forging ahead, surveying the forest smells.

The crisp April breeze brushed my cheek, and I breathed deep, glad there was no ash in the air where we were that day. Folding my scarf in a tidy square, I tucked it into its pocket on the side of my pack.

When we reached a spot with a clear view of the plains, I took out my binoculars to check the movement toward the east. Miles of tall, white windmills stretched to the horizon through the endless gassplant fields. Only the ominous towers of Promise City, the Josephite capital, shadowed the vast expanse beneath us.

It was hard for me to imagine, but cities had thrived on those plains before Ash Wednesday—the day a supervolcano on the other side of the world ended the Age of Plenty. The Josephites called it the Apocalypse.

"Have they started?" Quinn's voice was tense, and he looked away when I glanced at him.

I knew it was a bit early, but I also knew what it meant to him, so I looked back toward Promise City and checked for the pillars of smoke from within its walls that would tell me if Atonement had begun. "No. No Godfire yet."

I lifted the glasses to the wider horizon. "Ash and smoke coming up from the south, though. Still down by the Borders, but it looks thick. Capulin must have blown again." The volcanoes to the south, west, and north were a constant source of air pollution, even though the closest one was over a hundred miles away.

Quinn shrugged. "We should be okay if it's up from the south. It'll stay down in the plains."

We started back down the mountain, but this time at a walk. Without stopping, Quinn slung his rifle over his shoulder, took out his kinnikinnik pouch, and rolled a cigarette. We shared it as we wound our way toward the ruins of Gap.

"Did anybody get here yet?" I asked, passing him the smoke.

"The folks from North had just started setting up when I was leaving yesterday evening, but the Tinkers' people from Iredale weren't in."

He took out his scissor clamp from his smoking pouch and handed it to me. I crunched it onto what was left of the cigarette we shared and passed it to him to take the last drag. Then he carefully extinguished the nub and threw it on the ground.

"Seriously?" Shaking my head, I pulled out the small tin I

always carried and picked up the tiny scrap.

He laughed. "I just wanted to hear you holler."

When we reached the ruins of Gap, we slowed in respect for the dead. Even playful Daisy lowered her tail. Navigating the flowing waves of colorless rubble, I pondered the world of Granny's childhood with its parks, schools, and cars everywhere. She'd shown me pictures in her smuggled books, but I had trouble imagining what those places actually felt and smelled like. I had only ever known life in the foothills where my people lived scattered in small meadows and towns.

Glancing at a long, low, gutted building on a hillside, I could barely see the tilted sign on the ruins that gave the place its name. "Gap." When the Josephites leveled the city, the final pocket of the Western Resistance, they forbade us to ever speak its true name again, so we called it after that sign.

Quinn stopped and shook off his pack by some flat slabs of fallen concrete. We sat down to rest a moment, and he took out his canteen while Daisy settled at my feet.

"Quinn, do you think it's true that people used to die from eating too much?"

He offered me the water first. "Well, that's what they used to teach us back at the work camp. I know I saw a few seriously fat Josephites when I lived in the city, and the Joe girls were a lot plumper than Sec women. But so fat they died? I suppose it could happen."

I poured a small drink for Daisy and took a short swig for myself. "I wonder what it would be like to be fat?" I took off my pack, pulled out my techcloth blanket, and shoved it up inside my camouflage turtleneck.

Waddling around as I had seen pregnant women do, I asked, "What do you think, Quinn? Don't I make a pretty Josephite girl?"

He laughed. "With your braids wrapped in leather like mine and three days' dirt on your face? No. But I expect you'll clean up well enough for Reunion. You might stick that blanket under your dress, though, if you want to catch an eye. Puts a little meat on your bones."

His comment roused the mischief in my heart. "Ah, so you like me like this, huh?"

"Me? No . . . I mean . . . I meant . . ."

I could swear he blushed. Encouraged in my orneriness, I was about to tease him further when Daisy jumped up and barked, her alert echoing through the ruins. With a rush of adrenaline, I jerked the blanket out of my shirt and jumped back to back with Quinn. Everywhere I looked, I saw a Josephite soldier. We were surrounded.

CHAPTER 2

WITH A SLIGHT SIGNAL from me, Daisy dropped to the ground, a low growl rumbling in her throat. I was terrified they would shoot her, but, to my surprise, they ignored her.

Their leader, a short, stocky blonde man, stepped forward, and the sunlight flashed off his captain's insignia. I fought to keep my knees from shaking. The last time I'd seen a captain was the night they took my father. "Drop your weapons," he said, his revolver trained on us. We did.

Quinn nudged himself between me and the officer. "Please. Let him and the dog go. You can do whatever you want with me."

"Don't flatter yourself, Sec." His voice was calm. He holstered his gun, hardly needing it with ten more trained on us. "We have no interest in you. We're looking for a Josephite girl. About this tall." He held his hand as high as my shoulder. "Early twenties, long, red hair, blue eyes. Have you seen her?"

"No," Quinn answered. "We've been in the forest. We were going home. We don't want any trouble."

The captain glanced at Quinn as he might a bug and then took out a holowafer and tapped it. Instantly, a six-inch, floating image of a beautiful woman hovered above the small card. "Her name is Tamar Dobbins. If you find her, detain her and report her to your field monitor or a city gate guard. We will reward you with an extra twenty-five pound bag of hemp seeds if you bring her to us unharmed."

My jaw dropped. Twenty-five pounds of hemp seeds. We could expand our field. We'd be sure to meet our quotas for the Josephites. It would even give us some extra to trade for fuel. But all this for a girl? I glanced at Quinn and saw he was as baffled as I was.

The captain tapped the card again, and the woman disappeared. He tossed the holowafer at our feet. At the sudden motion, Daisy jumped up and snarled. A soldier raised his gun to shoot, and I dropped to my knees, wrapping myself around her to shield her.

Quinn grabbed my arm to pull me back, but the captain put his hand up. "No. No need. It's a good dog that protects its master." He turned to me. "You have it under control, don't you, Sec?"

His icy stare unnerved me. Unable to speak, I nodded, afraid to move anything but my head.

"Remember. Twenty-five pounds of seed to the Sec who brings her in. Spread the word. To the truck, men."

Quinn and I stayed put while the sound of the Josephites receded until Daisy's low protest was the only thing we heard. Then Quinn pointed across the ruins toward the forest and mouthed the word, "Go."

Quick as a shot, we raced through the ruins to the trees and ran until we reached the old pine carved with with the symbol of our meadow, three arrows forming a triangle with a sprouting seed in the center, which indicated our outer boundaries to other Secs.

Slowing to a walk, we caught our breaths. I recovered first. "What just happened?"

Quinn took his beaded amulet out from under his shirt,

kissed it, and put it back before he answered. "Well, it seems they're looking for a girl named Tamar."

"Oh, thank you, Captain Duh. But why would they look for a lost Joe girl out here?" A rabbit broke near us, kicking up dust, and I signaled Daisy to make chase.

"Well, she's not lost. That much is sure."

"How do you know that?"

"If she wasn't high class, they wouldn't care, and high class Joe girls don't get lost. They've got somebody watching over them all the time. Besides, didn't you catch the name?"

"Tamar Dobbins. What about it?"

"Dobbins. That's Joseph's last name. With a captain on the patrol, there's a good chance she was from his house. Granny will know."

I nodded. I knew Granny was somehow related to the Prophet's clan, but she didn't like to talk about it, them being on opposite sides of the war.

Daisy returned with the rabbit and relinquished it to me. I put it in a tan plastic sack with a big red "s" on the side that I'd scavenged from the dump. Then I tied the bag to my pack. "Why would some high class Joe girl come here? Wouldn't she get someone to take her on to Mexifornia?" The Josephites' reach didn't make it to the coastal land across the glaciers and the Western Desert.

"She might," Quinn said. "Who knows? Maybe she left in a hurry and thought she'd find water here in the hills." He shifted his pack to the left.

"If that's the case, she'll be sadly mistaken." I turned to face Quinn and grinned, walking backwards. "Think of it, Quinn. Twenty-five pounds of seeds. We'd be rich."

"You know, I hate to be the one to tell you, but you can't trust Josephites. They'd stiff us and throw her in the Godfire. As far as I'm concerned, Joe girl is Joe business, and we're better off staying out of this one."

"I know we can't trust them, but why wouldn't they give us

the seeds? It's nothing to them. They can always clone more."

"You keep thinking that."

"Do you really suppose they'd burn her? I thought that was only for their criminals and whores." His face darkened. I quickly remembered his mother and added, "And widows. Criminals, whores, and widows."

"Joseph'll burn anybody. Rumor has it the first Atonement was his own mother back on Ash Wednesday." Quinn took out his canteen and passed it to me. His voice became low and flat. "You've never seen anyone burned to death. I have. And I see them again every night when I close my eyes. I don't care who she is or what they'd pay, I won't turn a girl over for that."

I shrugged. No, I hadn't seen anyone burned to death, but I had seen them starve. Dead Josephite, maybe one of Joseph's own, and we'd get seeds. I didn't see the downside to that one.

We angled toward the overgrown jeep trail below us where the low, narrow canyon widened into Middle Meadow. Touching our hands to our hearts as we passed the cemetery, we skirted the edge of the hemp field toward the cluster of buildings at the west end—three houses, a barn, and two long, low greenhouses for the seedlings. Apart from them, across a dry creek bed, the old stone house I shared with Granny hugged the north cliff, along with an outhouse, her kiln shed, and an old dog run where we put out racks of meat to dry in the summer.

The windmill at the barn corral rotated gently in the breeze, pumping our well while one plough horse and several Angora goats grazed lazily away from the trough beneath it.

Three tents dotted the field near the houses, and I saw another half a dozen hide and hemp cloth structures in various stages of completion. In a large, open area near the corrals, a fire pit exuded tantalizing aromas that seasoned the air in the meadow. I salivated at the thought of the goat, an annual treat.

Goats were precious for the mohair they produced, and we slaughtered only one each year to celebrate our Reunion with our family and close friends. Unfortunately, I had no venison to add to the bounty, and I knew the goat wouldn't go far. But the smell of cooking food buoyed me up with anticipation of the evening ahead, sure to hold dancing, drumming, laughter, and storytelling. Leave it to Quinn to bring me back down.

"Granny sure was mad at you when I left," he said. "I don't know what died under that outhouse of yours, but she was counting on you to finish the new one and help her with the cooking today."

I glanced toward our home. Granny was out by our small fire pit with one of Tinker's boys, supervising him while he dug up her slow-roasted squirrels.

Tension knotted in my stomach, and my stubborn side rose up in defense. "Hunting food is just as important as cooking and outhouses, right? I mean, without hunting, you wouldn't need cooking or outhouses anyway, would you?"

Quinn snorted. "Leave me out of it."

I released Daisy to go greet Granny, hoping a few puppy snuggles would soften her up before I had to face her. Granny stopped her work when she spied the dog running toward her, and her face lit up with joy. She pulled Daisy's favorite deer bone from the pocket of her overalls, ready for the dog, who wagged her tail and licked Granny's hands before taking the favor.

The old bridge over the dry creek bed creaked its greeting when Quinn and I crossed. He slung his pack and rifle off his shoulder and set them on the bench in front of the house, saying, "I don't know about you, but I could eat a Dixie bear about now. Hope Granny's got some gruel on the stove and wasn't just waiting for dinner tonight."

A bone-deep hunger urged me on while Quinn and I hung the marmots and rabbit outside. I saw Granny head toward the back door of our three-room house as we worked. I was none too eager to face her, but my stomach gave me no choice.

Once inside, I hung my traveling pack and bow on their

pegs at the hearth without looking at her. She didn't look at me either while she set the table with two bowls of cold gruel, the hemp seed concoction that was our dietary staple. I washed my hands and pretended I didn't know what was coming, focusing instead on how good it was to clean up for the first time in days.

"Hey, Granny." I gave her a quick hug and sat down at the table.

Daisy settled onto her favorite spot and began gnawing her bone, savoring it, admiring it, and rolling it about between her paws.

I glanced up. "How's your hip today?"

Granny crossed her arms and stared at me, her left eyebrow climbing up her forehead into her fringe of silver hair. The Eyebrow of Impending Doom, I called it. Her head only came to my chin, but we both knew she was the bigger woman of the two of us, and I cringed. She said nothing.

Fighting the urge to wilt under her gaze, I started woofing down my meal.

"Great batch," I mumbled between bites.

She picked up a broom and started sweeping around her pottery wheel and shelves without glancing my way.

I turned an imploring gaze to Quinn for help, but he only smiled and put his hands up defensively, letting me know I was on my own. I glared at him.

Finally I could take the silence no longer. "I'm sorry. I should have come home when I said I would, but I really wanted to bring back a deer. Granny, you know what that would have meant for us."

She stopped and leaned heavily on her broom, as she did when her arthritis troubled her. Her slow, pleasant, Southwestern singsong did nothing to alleviate my feelings of guilt at her words. "Deena Sprague, your mother did not walk through the Valley of the Shadow of Death for you to be mauled by a Dixie bear, nor did I raise you to die at the hands of Josephites. How was I to know I wasn't going to be burying another child?"

"I know. I'm sorry."

"Not only that, there's no new latrine, and you said you'd be here to help me with the cooking. Freefall had better things to do than to dig up my squirrels for me today."

"But there was this buck. And he was huge. He had to be at least two hundred and fifty pounds. That would have been fresh meat for the meadow for the whole month and then some."

"When people love you, you don't live in a vacuum. Besides, if he was that big, how would you have gotten him home alone?"

I shrugged. "I'd have found a way."

Quinn snorted, and Granny shook her head, fighting off a smile. "Nothing's too big for you, is it, child? Now give me a hug, and don't scare an old woman like that. My heart can't take it."

Relieved, I fell into her open arms. I was always amazed that anyone so old could have such strong arms. "I'm sorry I worried you, Granny."

"Well, I'm glad you two got home without any trouble, but don't do that to me again."

I tucked a stray strand of her short hair behind her ear.

Quinn finally spoke. "We did have trouble. We got caught by a patrol at Gap."

Granny anxiously looked us over. "On Atonement Sunday? That's odd. And you're not hurt?"

"It wasn't a normal patrol," Quinn said and then filled her in on the encounter. "And get this. The girl they were looking for? Her name was Dobbins. Tamar Dobbins."

Granny's brow knit with worry. She shook her head. "This is trouble. Gather everyone at the fire pit immediately. We need to cancel Reunion."

CHAPTER 3

IDROPPED DOWN IN my chair, aghast. "Granny, you can't mean that. We've waited all year for this."

"You think I don't know that?" Her eyes flashed, and she looked away, but her voice was softer when she spoke again. "I'm sorry, but it's for the best." She put the broom in its corner and started for the door.

"Why?" I asked.

"Tamar Dobbins is Joseph's granddaughter. My sister's granddaughter. She's your cousin, Deena. They're sure to come looking here." Granny turned through the door and headed toward the meadow.

I was flabbergasted. I knew her baby sister married a Dobbins, but I didn't know it was *the* Dobbins. No wonder she didn't want to talk about it. Quinn and I jumped up and hurried to follow her.

Soon we were all gathered around the fire pit. Some of our visitors had made camp the day before and had been occupied in games, gossip, and dinner preparations. Others were eager to finish setting up their tents and getting ready for the festivities. All forty or so were perplexed at being interrupted for a meeting.

"We have trouble," Granny said. "The Josephites stopped Quinn and Archer this morning down at Gap."

Several people gasped. Others turned and whispered with their neighbors. I noticed a young man in the Iredale group whom I didn't recognize. He knitted his brow under his deep auburn hair and leaned forward.

Granny continued. "They're fine. No harm done, but the Joes are looking for a girl, and I have reason to think they will come here. As some of you know, I have an unfortunate connection to Joseph by marriage. The girl they seek is none other than his granddaughter, Tamar Dobbins. My niece. They seem to think she came this way, and it's only logical they would look for her here where I live. I think we'd do best to cancel Reunion, and you should all pack up and go home while you can before they get here."

A round of protests rose from those gathered.

Darryn, the Doman of Iredale, held up his hand for silence. "Wait. With all due respect, Granny, it took us two days to get here. My people are in no shape to go back over the hills tonight, and the Joes might not even show up. If you don't mind, I'd like to hear a little more from Quinn and Archer before we decide."

Granny nodded toward Quinn.

Quinn told the group about our encounter. When he spoke of the twenty-five pounds of seeds, they fell so silent I could have heard bugs crawl.

I watched the reactions of our meadow families. Tinker and Makenzie shared a look of concern over the heads of their seven children. Across the circle from them, Arys, his face troubled, reached an arm around his young wife, Charlotte, and their infant son. Beside him, his dark, wiry little brother, Bane, whispered with his blonde bear of a friend, Greagor, whom he'd brought with him from South. But it was the brothers' mother, Harmony, who caught my attention.

She squatted like a finger-painted toad on the stump beside

them, her homemade makeup a poor attempt to recapture her supposed glory days of beauty. Suspiciously heavy for a Sec, many of us wondered if she had been stealing food from our stores, but no one had caught her yet.

Her permanent scowl almost lightened at Granny's news, and she broke the silence. "We have to find her. Twenty-five pounds of seeds? Do you know what that would mean?"

Bane's foxlike face perked up like he'd sighted a bunny. "Let's go now before Reunion. That will give us something to celebrate."

Greagor gave him a nod and a fist bump, but Tinker's oldest, Freefall, glowered. "This is no matter of yours, food thief."

Bane glared. "You didn't prove that."

Zander, Freefall's brother-in-law, stepped forward, his six and a half feet of solid farming muscle overshadowing those around him. "Let's focus here, people. We're talking about seeds in the here and now, not wrongs past."

"Ain't nobody getting any seeds." The deep voice had a ring of authority. A tall, strong man with curly, close-cropped gray hair stood clenching and unclenching his fists in a way that made the raven in his Army tattoo shift back and forth on his chocolate-colored bicep as if it were nodding its agreement. The tail on his coonskin hat danced his agitation. It was Flynx from North, a former Josephite who had defected toward the end of the war. A good friend of Granny's.

"I'll say it again. Ain't nobody getting any seeds. I don't care what that captain said. Joes don't part with seed if they don't have to, and they never have to give seed to Secs."

Harmony put her hands on her hips. "Then why didn't they thrash Quinn and Archer? Huh? I say we look for that girl. Our men know these hills better than any Josephites. We're sure to find her first, and we need those seeds."

Arys stood and put a hand on his mother's shoulder, speaking low to her. Harmony shrugged him off, and Bane and Greagor glared at him.

"I'll say what I please," she said.

Bane and Greagor moved between Arys and Harmony. Arys took hold of Charlottes shoulders and distanced his family from the trio.

Quinn, his calm voice a contrast to Harmony's belligerence, said, "They'll Atone her if they find her."

"I don't care. Her burning is better than us starving," she said. "A dead Joe, and we get seeds? Sounds like a good deal to me."

I flinched to hear my own thoughts coming from someone I considered a waste of food even in the best years.

Flynx stuck his chin out. "Granny is right, and so is Quinn. I'll stay here to protect anyone who isn't able to go, but I'll have nothing to do with a burning."

Zander chimed in. "I've found it's always good to listen to Granny, but the girl's not here, and from what Quinn says, that captain wasn't interested in messing with us. So how about this? We put a guard at the jeep trail down by the cemetery to warn us if they come, and we go ahead and have our fiesta."

Harmony stomped her foot. "What about finding that girl?"

Granny cast a withering gaze at Harmony, and her low voice held more than a hint of threat. "I'll remind you all it's my niece you're speaking of." It was clear that anyone who was going to burn her niece, seeds or not, was going to have to go through Granny.

Doman Darryn spoke again. "That sounds like a fair compromise, Zander. What do you say, Granny?"

"It's reasonable, but I have a bad feeling. Be sure to secure any contraband now, and we'll go ahead and post a guard."

Several people nodded their accord. Harmony crossed her arms and harrumphed. Bane spit on the ground, and Greagor shook his head, his face sour with disappointment.

I smiled to myself. Reunion was on, and Harmony was thwarted—two things that always warmed my heart.

Granny sent one of Tinker's boys to the meadow entrance

with an electronic device that keyed into alarms in our houses, a system we usually only used in the summer when the field monitor was likely to stop by for inventory. Then I opened up the kiln shed tunnel where we stored our hemp bales. We hid our remaining food stores with them. We didn't want to take the chance of any Josephites finding our food and deciding we had too much.

When that was done, Quinn took Daisy up the dry creek bed with her favorite bone to stay at his house for the night. Then I packed up our deepest secrets—the few books we'd scavenged from the dump, my three full journals, some first aid supplies, and blinkers, the small, plastic cards that held money credits. Secs were not allowed money credits except when trading on special cards at the Big Box, but somehow Quinn always managed to drum some up with his trading business.

I stashed the loot under the floorboards in my room, pausing only to caress the cover of my favorite book, *Watership Down*. It was a story about refugees, like us, who beat the odds and triumphed over their enemies.

Granny brought in a few more books and set them on the floor beside me. I sighed. "Ah, Granny. I sometimes wonder if I wouldn't be better off ignorant."

She laughed. "Don't worry. You're plenty ignorant enough." When I didn't laugh with her, she put her gentle hand on my shoulder. "Have faith, child. Josephite rule is unnatural, and unnatural rules must always fail. Even God couldn't make humans obey an edict against knowledge."

"It's so unfair." I sighed.

"This, too, shall pass, but until then, we'll make our own fair."

I didn't know if I had faith that anything would pass, but I had faith in Granny.

"Here," she said. She reached into her pocket and pulled out a heavy necklace of woven gold studded with diamonds. It caught the afternoon light and scattered stars across my bunk bed, washstand, and little chest of drawers. "I wanted to give this to you to wear tonight, but with the Joes on the prowl, we'd best pack it away. Still . . ."

I didn't know what to say as I looked at the priceless Buccellati heirloom in her hand. Literally priceless. The Joes would kill her if they knew she'd smuggled it out during the Secular Exile, or she would have sold it long ago. The only person we could trade it to was Maverick, and even he would never risk the torture and Atonement for trading us the one thing that would match its value—seeds. So there it was. A relic from her past too valuable to keep and too valuable to sell.

I had a sinking feeling when I thought about the timing of this gift. "Why now?"

"Well, you're the age I was when your great grandmother gave it to me for a wedding gift. You're not getting any younger, and neither am I. I'd rather give it to you than have you inherit it."

An old darkness opened in the pit of my stomach. I knew where this was going, and I shoved her hand away from me with a bit more vigor than I intended. "No, Granny. Please. Don't speak to me of this."

CHAPTER 4

"**D**EENA, IT'S BEEN THREE years since Faebin died. It's time you moved on. I'm not saying forget him, but it's no betrayal to love again."

"You never loved again."

"I was sixty-five when I lost my Charles. We had a good, long life together. You're a young woman in your prime, and it's not right for you to be alone. Faebin wouldn't want this."

She was right. Faebin had grabbed life with both hands, and he had wanted the same for me. Still . . . I shook my head. "That part of me died with him."

Granny took my hand. "Your heart isn't dead. It's only dormant. Let the spring back in."

My pulse began to race, and my mind threw up walls. "No. I'm not ready. And besides, the only suitable man I know is Quinn, and he doesn't count. Freefall drinks too much, and his brothers are much too young. And you surely can't mean Bane or that dog of a South Doman's son he brought with him."

"Heavens no. The sooner they're gone, the better. I was a soft-minded fool to ever say he could visit his mother for Reunion." She shook her head, regret furrowing her brow. "But what's wrong with Quinn?"

"He's Quinn. That's what's wrong with him. He's been my foster brother too long to be anything else. He would never see me that way."

"Pshaw. Why do you think he moved out so long ago?"

I snatched my hand back from her, my cheeks burning. "No more Quinn."

"You're right. I'm sorry." She patted my shoulder. "But promise me this. At least meet that young man who came with the Iredale clan. He seems like a likely fellow, and they say he's a talented farmer come up from the Borders to find a wife. His farming and your hunting could build a good foundation for children."

I started at the word. "Children . . . Granny, please. I promise I'll talk to him if you promise to stop. And keep the necklace. I'm not ready to think of you not being here to have it."

She took me in her arms and stood on her toes to kiss my forehead. "All right, child. I didn't mean to upset you." Her bear hugs always filled my soul. "Now put this in there, nail down that floorboard, and get on down to the party. We'll be setting up the table soon. Makenzie made a big pot of marmot gruel from those critters you brought in today."

When I'd finished nailing, I threw my men's clothes over the bearskin at the end of the bottom bunk and poured some water into the washbasin on the stand. I loved that little stand. Granny had painted it with mountain daisies, a flower that went extinct after Ash Wednesday. I liked to look at their sunny, hopeful faces and pretend I would see one someday. That somehow, some way, there was a seed out there lying safe and dormant for the right time to take its chance at life.

Unwrapping the leather from my braids, I rubbed my hair with Crust N'Brush, a waterless shampoo that bound with the dirt and oil to form a crust. With a fair amount of elbow grease, I combed it out, leaving clean, shiny mahogany waves that fell to my waist.

I cleared the dust and ash from my nose with a neti pot and

washed my face and body from the basin, careful to recycle the water through the filter in the top. Relieved to finally be clean after days in the forest, I put on my one dress. I had traded three deer hides for it at the fall Gathering down at South Meadow the year before. It was green. A hemp and mohair blend, fitted and "cut down to there," as Granny said, giving even me a show of cleavage.

I took a belt from my dresser, one decorated with bone and pottery beads, and wrapped it around my hips in a way that emphasized the slight curve of my waist. As a final touch, I tied on my lion claw necklace—the claw from the lion that had killed the Tinkers' youngest in Kingdom Year seventeen.

Turning to the small mirror above my dresser, I was surprised to see a woman looking back at me, and I was not displeased. Though I was too tall and had none of the plumpness that Sec men found so attractive, I had stormy gray eyes, high cheekbones, and a pretty face, and my long hair, so mannish in braids, was oddly feminine when I let it down.

I liked shedding my hunting clothes and being a woman. It was a privilege for me. I would have loved to have a whole closet full of dresses. With a final glance, I gave way to my excitement and headed down to the party.

The board bridge sang my anticipation as I crossed. A pavilion and several tents wove a loose web around the large fire pit, and a few hammers still resounded on tent stakes, not quite keeping rhythm with the drummers warming up for the night's festivities. Children played sack ball, old people sat and gossiped, and women bustled about their camps, breaking out their goodies for the evening meal. It would not be a feast, but rather a sharing of what was left at the end of the long winter, now that our spring crops would soon be sprouting in the seedling sheds.

"Hey, Archer." I turned to the familiar voice just in time to see a sack ball coming at me on the ground.

"Hey, Thomas." Kicking it back toward the kids, I grinned.

An adolescent left the game and wrapped me in a warm hug, his head barely reaching my shoulder.

Thomas was a kid from North Meadow whom I adored. Cecilia and her husband took him in a few winters back when his parents starved to death during a Correction Year. To me, he was the little brother I always wanted.

"You ready to lose that slapjack game tonight?" His cocky tone matched the tilt of his chin.

"You wish."

"Double or nothing. Three rounds."

"You're on. Just get ready to give me the next puzzle box you carve."

"Oh, yeah? Say good-bye to your bear skin." He winked and jumped back into the sack ball game.

A half-naked toddler scurried past me toward the fire pit. Scooping him up, I returned him to his exhausted mother, who was chasing five steps behind, her arms full of infant twins.

"Cecelia. Oh, look at you. You had two."

"Maria and Benito." She glowed with maternal pride, introducing her newest additions.

"Does that make five now?" I asked, reaching out to take little Maria from her.

"Yes, and surely these are Mary's last blessings upon me." She passed me the infant with the pink hemp bow around her head.

I chortled at the baby, barely old enough to hold my gaze, and admired Cecilia for making the trip so soon after their births. Stretching, tiny Maria closed her eyes and yawned, settling into the crook of my arm and instantly winning my heart.

"I'm so glad Granny let us stay," said Cecilia as we walked to her tent. "You don't think there'll really be trouble, do you?"

"Well, the captain didn't seem to be interested in beating the crap out of us like the Joes always have before. They didn't even hurt Daisy, and she was growling at them the whole time."

"That is odd, but I guess we can't stop living." Cecilia studied me as if she'd noticed me for the first time. "Look at you. All grown up and pretty. You be careful." She winked and nodded toward her children. "It's looking like you that got me chasing after these. But then again, it wouldn't hurt you to get on with it. You're not getting any younger."

"Uh, thanks. You know, I told Makenzie I'd help her out with some cooking tonight. You take care." With a little kiss, I passed Maria back to Cecilia and made a speedy exit. Fielding the marriage talk from Granny was bad enough. I certainly didn't want to get into it with our friends.

While I passed through the outer tents, I called out greetings, returned smiles, and made plans for the games the next day, looking forward to the shooting and goat shearing competitions. I only participated in the shooting, but the goat shearing always made me laugh. Makenzie Tinker had come up with that competition as an easy way to get her herd sheared each year, and now adults and young people alike wrestled the animals down and harvested the mohair.

I waved to Quinn, who nodded back from under his small pavilion near the fire pit where he turned a brisk business trading his moonshine and ganga. Both were valued among Secs for their medicinal benefits as much as for their recreational qualities.

I noticed he'd taken time to let his long black hair down and had changed into his leather pants and vest, the ones he only wore for celebrations. He glanced up and saw me, and his eyes lingered. I felt my cheeks start to flush, and, confused, I looked down. When I chanced to peer back at him from the corner of my eye, he was busy with his customers, and I wondered if I had imagined his appreciative appraisal.

The drums paused, and I heard men's voices to my right. Turning, I saw several young men from North and Iredale sitting on the hood of Tinker's ancient pickup truck. They were pointing and smiling at me, nodding their approval.

Thrilled, I tossed my hair and pretended to be fascinated with Sally the plough horse that studied all of the activity from behind the board fence of her corral. The men's attention didn't bother me like Quinn's glance had, and even my closed heart enjoyed feeling young and pretty.

Then I saw Bane standing off to the side with Greagor, drinking and staring at me with a special interest that made my skin crawl.

"Hey, Archer," he called.

I pretended not to hear.

"Did you really shoot Quinn's hat off his head, or is he jerking us?"

At that, I turned. "What? Don't you think I could?"

"That's pretty good, even for you. Let's see you do it again."

"Sure," I said, giving him a look that I hoped showed my disdain. "As long as it's your head and his hat." I jerked my thumb toward Greagor, who wore a stocking cap.

The other men laughed and raised their mugs.

Zander said, "To Archer, Hat Slayer."

The rest followed suit. "To Archer, Hat Slayer." I acknowledged their salute with a gracious nod, but passed by Bane and Greagor without another glance.

I felt a hand on my arm. "Come along, Deena, there's someone I want you to meet. Remember, you said you'd try."

"Not yet, Granny."

"Now." Granny steered me toward the fire where the handsome redheaded man I'd seen at the meeting sat on a log, playing a drum. My heart pumped faster, and I regretted telling her I'd give it a chance.

"Deena, this is Iain. He's here from the Borders to help out his family in Iredale for the year. Iain, this is my granddaughter, Deena. Now you two young people get to know each other." With a pat on my back, she abandoned me to my promise.

Iain stood to greet me, and I was pleased to see he was my height. Close enough, anyway. He shifted his drum to hold out his hand.

I stopped him. "No, that's okay. Please go on with your drumming. It's very nice." I didn't want him to know how sweaty my palms were.

I sat on the log a good three feet away from him, and he offered me a shy smile as he played. I noticed his rhythms became more elaborate, and I suspected he was showing off. He was good. That still didn't mean I wanted to talk to him.

Finally the dreaded moment came. Iain went into a furious drumroll, and with a flourish and a slap, he completed his performance. I clapped and smiled, wondering how soon I could get away.

"Deena, was it?" he asked, holding his drum between us as if he were afraid of getting too close to me. That suited me just fine.

"Archer, actually. Everyone calls me Archer. Only Granny calls me Deena."

He smiled, and I noticed it started in his green eyes. It was a sweet smile. An innocent smile. I couldn't help but like him.

"I see," he said. "And why does everyone call you Archer?"

"I'm a bow hunter. I bring in the meat for the meadow."

"Really? It's the men who do that down in the Borders. How is it that it falls to you?" He set the drum down in front of him, but made no move to close the space between us.

"My father taught me, and it seems I have a bit of a gift with it. I love the freedom of it, too, and being on my own in the forest. No one to answer to, and no one to judge me."

"Ah. An independent woman. How is it the Joes haven't killed you yet?"

I laughed. "I hide from them. I dress like a man. You know—camouflage shirt, cargo pants. That's why my hair is so long. I usually keep it in braids."

"I can't imagine even Joes are stupid enough to think a pretty woman like you is a dude."

He locked eyes with me, and I felt the heat rising in my

cheeks. He was a nice man, and he was clearly attracted to me, but I just didn't know if I could go there.

I broke Iain's gaze and glanced away, only to see Quinn, his face clouded and brooding, staring at us from under his pavilion and leaving his customers to wait. Guilt flashed through me and then anger. Who was he to disapprove of me?

Iain shifted closer to me on the log. "I hear you have a pet dog. How did that happen?" Pets were rare among our people. Animals were usually food.

"She's a shepherd mutt named Daisy. I raised her from a pup after I killed her mother down at the Gap dump about three years ago."

"What? You killed the mother and felt sorry for the pup?"

"Something like that. I tried to use her den to hide from a gang of Joes. She attacked me."

"Check you out. How did you get away from a wild dog and a gang of Joes?" His voice and eyes held genuine admiration. I was a bit surprised. Quinn was usually the only Sec man who appreciated my wilder side.

"Well, the bitch surprised me the first time, as you can see." I pulled up my sleeve to show him the scars from her teeth. "When she came at me at me the second time, I caught her head and snapped her neck back, like so." I demonstrated. "I crawled in her den to hide, and there was little Daisy, barely old enough to have her eyes open. I couldn't leave her orphaned and alone."

"Wow. Independent, compassionate, hunter, dog trainer, and beautiful. How is it no one's snatched you up yet?" he asked.

"Well, there was someone a couple years ago, but he died. Climbing accident." The walls slammed down in my heart, and I stood abruptly. "You know, that wind is chilly. Did you feel that? I think I'm going to get a scarf before dinner. It was very nice to meet you, Iain."

"May I walk with you to your house?" His eyes were

hopeful.

"That's okay. I'll only be a minute."

"Shall I save a place for you at dinner?"

I couldn't help but smile. "Yes, thank you. I would like that."

This time, when Iain reached out to shake my hand, I offered mine as well. He took it gently and raised it to his lips. Blushing furiously, all too aware of Quinn's glare, I marched across the meadow to the house.

In truth, I wasn't cold at all, but I wanted a moment to compose myself. It disturbed me that I liked Iain, and I didn't know what to make of Quinn's reaction. Perhaps Granny was right. Perhaps he did love me, but whether he would ever act on it was anyone's guess. And she was certainly right about one thing. I wasn't getting any younger.

Lost in my thoughts, I entered the house. A strange smell snapped me back to the present—something akin to soap, or cleaning supplies. Then she stepped from the shadows.

I jumped back, slamming the door. "What the hell?"

A red-haired woman in traveling clothes dipped a curtsy. "God at your shoulder."

Suddenly a horn blared from the speaker in the corner of the room. The Josephites were here.

CHAPTER 5

I STARED, SHOCKED. THE long red hair. The pack. The traveling trousers and the sweater with bunnies dancing around a flaming Cross of Michael. It had to be her.

Another blare from the speaker in the corner made me run to the window. Soldiers were already piling out of a truck, and an armored car was pulling up behind them. "Holy shit."

"What is it?" Her eyes grew round with fear.

"It's your people. They're here looking for you. Dammit. What'd you have to come here for?"

She looked wildly around the room, as if seeking a place to flee. Then she threw herself to the ground at my feet. "Please, kill me. In the name of Christ, I beg you. Don't let them take me alive."

Kill her? Furious at her presence and all it meant to my people, I'd have been happy to. But it would have made a mess, and there was no way I could hide her body before the Joes found it.

If I turned her in, we might get seeds. We might not go hungry for the first winter of my life. Then I thought of Granny's stern look, reminding me this girl was her niece. My cousin. But if I hid her and the Joes found out, they would surely kill us.

Then, unbidden, Harmony's words came to mind. "A dead Joe, and we get seeds. Sounds like a good deal to me." The last thing I wanted was to be like Harmony.

I looked out the window again and saw three soldiers coming directly toward the house. *Think, Deena.*

I snatched the girl by her arm and dragged her toward the back door. To my amazement, she dug in her heels and fought back. "No. Kill me, please. If they take me alive they will—"

I slapped her. "I'm not turning you over, and I'm not messing up my house with your Joe blood. Now shut up and come on."

Her eyes flew open with surprise, and she touched her cheek, the red already rising, but she resisted no more.

Pulling her out the back door, I half drug her to the outhouse, careful to stay out of view from the meadow. I opened the door, and a terrible stench hit my nostrils. The board bridge groaned under the soldiers' boots. I shoved her in first and followed her. Then I pointed to the seat. "Down the hole."

She balked and grabbed her nose. "Oh, God, no."

"If they find you now, we're both dead. Get down the effing hole."

We heard voices. The Joes were at the back of the house. With a grimace, she jumped onto the edge of the seat and swung her legs over the reeking pit below. I grabbed her hands and lowered her down, backpack and all. A slight splash told me she had landed.

"What about the outhouse?" The man's voice was hard.

"I'll get it," came the answer. He sounded like a boy.

I jerked up my dress and sat down. When the young man opened the door, I shrieked with genuine fear. "Can't you let a lady do her business?"

He quickly shut it. "Uh. Sorry." His embarrassment, along with the peach fuzz on his chin and the single stripe on his shoulder, told me he was new to terrorizing Secs.

I waited a count of thirty and exited the outhouse with as much calm and dignity as I could muster, shutting the door behind me.

A grizzled vet strode up and grabbed me. Then he shoved me down the hill and scolded the youngster. "You don't wait around for Secs. Get her down there with the others. I'll finish up here."

"Yes, sir, Sergeant Jacobs."

I glanced over my shoulder, and the youngster timidly encouraged me with his rifle.

Jacobs opened the door to the latrine and glanced toward the hole. "Ugh." He shook his head. "You people are disgusting."

When he shut it and walked away, I released a breath I didn't know I was holding.

Approaching the fire pit, I saw their officer in charge had already singled out Granny as our leader. She stood two steps in front of our people, who were corralled nearby under the guns of a dozen soldiers.

Quinn, his face drawn with tension, stood toward the back of the group with the Middle Meadow people. He gave me a warning shake of his head, his reminder to me to not lose my temper.

The women, underneath scarves they had wrapped around their hair and faces, cowered close to the men. I did not move to cover my face. I wanted a clear line of sight.

Iain, standing behind Granny, caught my eye, and I joined him.

"Ah. Is this the last one?" the officer asked, glancing my way, his smile and cat's eyes calling to mind the lion whose claw I wore.

He snapped a riding crop against his tall, black leather boot, and I jumped at the sharp crack.

I felt a hand on my back, and though Iain still looked forward, I knew it was his. I barely knew him, but his calm touch was a comfort, and I appreciated his quiet strength.

The officer snapped his crop again. Granny didn't flinch. "Yes," she said, her voice steady. She stood her full height and stared him in the eye. It was bold of her, but I took her cue and straightened my back.

A quick survey showed me the captain of that morning was nowhere to be found. The officer in front of me wore an insignia on his collar that I didn't recognize, but what caught my eye was the series of tiny interlocking ceramic discs at his throat. I gasped quietly. Dragontech armor. I'd heard of the armor of the elite soldiers, but I'd never seen it.

The tattoo in the center of his pale forehead told me how he came by such a prize. Under his close-cropped blonde hair stood the ashen Cross of Michael, symbol for the sword of the angel that Joseph battled to learn the secret of the only seeds that grew after Ash Wednesday. This man was one of Joseph's own guards.

My knees felt weak, and I quickly looked down, afraid he would read in my face that I had what he wanted.

I could turn her in now, and this would be over. But this man. This man would never give us the seeds. This man would kill us all.

The officer focused his attention on the full table, spread and ready for our feast. "I see you were about to dine. Ah. A stew of some kind, a few little cakes, fresh mushrooms . . . Sergeant Jacobs, bring me my chair." His voice was calm and arrogant, not only conveying power, but pride in using it.

"Yes, sir, Major Norris." Jacobs hurried to do his bidding. He returned soon and unfolded a canvas chair beside the table.

The major strolled across the front of the group. "Now. I will need someone to serve me. Any of you men want to share your wives?" His eye glinted evil amusement as the men rustled closer to their women. Iain's hand dropped from my back, and he moved slightly in front of me.

Norris turned his wicked smile to Granny. "How about you, you old Sec whore? You've clearly spent your life on your knees serving men."

Without a thought, the spit was past my lips and in Norris's face. Quick as a viper, he slashed his crop across my chest, the tiny barbs on the shaft shredding my dress and my skin.

Iain jumped to grab the crop, but Norris was faster. His shot splattering Iain's blood into my eyes. I screamed and threw up my hands. With a swift kick from Sergeant Jacobs, my legs went out from under me, and my nose was in the dirt. Women screamed, and a boot slammed down on my back, knocking the wind out of me. I thought my ribs would break.

I turned my head and saw Iain's face beside me, already pale. He gasped rapidly for breath, his eyes wide and blinking as dark, frothy blood bubbled from his chest.

Granny's voice shook when she spoke. The blast from Norris's pistol still echoed in my ears, and I barely heard her say, "Please. Let me help him."

Norris laughed. "Stand over there, old woman," he ordered and then turned his attention back to me. "When I lift my foot, you will not move except to rise to your hands and knees. If you understand, say, 'Yes, Master'."

He ground his heel into my back, and fury burned through me. Involuntarily, I cried out in pain.

"Do it, Deena!"

I heard a slap, followed by gasps and smothered cries. Iain groaned, and his face screwed up in agony as he fought for the air that would not come.

"Yes, Master." My heart choked on the words.

"I'm sorry. I don't think all of the filthy, inbred bastards over there heard you."

His heel dug in again, and I hated the plea in my voice. "Yes, Master."

"Good Sec. Now I'm going to lift my foot, and we'll see if you really understood."

The pressure released, and I slowly rose to my hands and knees, wiping the dirt and blood from my eyes. The pain from my ribs reverberated through my body with every motion. Raising my head, I glared at Norris.

He laughed and strolled around me to where I couldn't see him. A deep, hearty belly laugh. "This one has fire."

His crop came down on my back, and I bit off my scream. "I did not give you permission to look at me."

Through the top of my vision, I saw his boots strut toward the canvas chair. He sat down and casually crossed his legs. "I believe I will start with one of those little biscuits. Serve me a biscuit, Sec dog."

I moved my foot to rise, and felt Jacobs' rifle at my head. "On your knees, Sec. You'll serve the major on your knees."

Anger burned through me as much as the pain. My long hair dragging through the dirt, I crawled on my hands and knees to the table where I reached over the edge for the biscuits. I picked up the plate. Then, using only one hand, like a three-legged dog, I hopped over to Norris and held it up, careful not to look directly at his face.

Norris plucked a biscuit from the tray. Studying it, he said to Granny, "Maerina . . . That is what you call yourself, isn't it? How such a noble lady as the Prophet's wife could be related to a shabby old heretic like you is beyond me. Tell me, Maerina. Where is Tamar?"

"I do not know Tamar." Granny's voice was already steady again.

"Oh, my. That was a bad choice." I could hear the delight in his tone. The crop came down on my back again, and my elbows crashed in the dirt, still holding up the platter.

"Please. I've never met the girl." Granny's voice cried my pain. "I know you're looking for her because two of our people met your patrol this morning, but the girl isn't here."

Sniffing the biscuit he held, Norris curled his nose. "What is this, a dog turd? Sergeant Jacobs, these Secs were about to eat dog turds. It's certainly a good thing we came along when we did. Dispose of these."

"Yes, sir, Major." Jacobs took the plate from my hand and threw the biscuits into the fire.

"You, slave." Norris lifted his crop, and I flinched involuntarily. He chuckled. Poking me with it, he said, "Serve me some mushrooms."

I hastened to do his bidding, cringing with each excruciating movement but determined I would not let him see my pain by faltering. I held the bowl as high as I was able, and my back screamed with the effort.

Norris picked off a mushroom and studied it, turning it this way and that in his hand. "Why, look at this. These mushrooms are overcooked. Indeed, you Secs should thank me. Sergeant, dispose of this burnt slime and build up that fire. We may need it."

The major stood abruptly and turned to the women. "Uncover your faces." Cold impatience rang in his voice, as if he'd suddenly grown tired of his game. The women, shuffling and murmuring, their eyes wide with terror, hesitantly removed their shawls.

Norris approached and took a flashlight from his belt. He was not satisfied until he had shined it in each woman's face.

He strode back and stood beside me, still on my hands and knees. "You will remain here while we search this meadow. If we find the girl, this one goes in the fire." He booted me down in the dirt. There was no mistaking who "this one" was.

What if they find her? If I turn her in now, would he spare me? No. This man would burn us all.

I lay still, afraid to move as the majority of the soldiers hurried to do the major's bidding. My eyes found Iain's and held them for a brief moment. Then, with a slight gurgling sound, his life passed on. Drowned in his own blood.

Granny wrapped me in a shawl while the four remaining soldiers sneered with disdain. Then she helped me sit on the log closest to where the women and children stirred restlessly.

Norris settled back into his chair, eying us like the hawk that knows the prey is his for the taking.

"Tell me. Who here sings? I know you Secs are always

frolicking about when you should be working. Surely one of you can sing? Yes?" he asked.

Arys' wife, Charlotte, started forward, but Arys took her arm.

Norris smiled. "Come now, don't be shy. Let your woman help us pass the time." He aimed his pistol at me.

Charlotte shared a glance with Arys. His fear for her was palpable, but he let her go. She stepped to the front, shaking so hard I thought she would fall over.

She cleared her throat and, her voice quavering, intoned *The Ballad of Our People*. It was a song I had always loved before that moment, but somehow it seemed dirty and violated for falling on Josephite ears.

At the end of the second verse, Norris cut her off. "No, no. Something lively. This is your celebration, after all."

Charlotte was at a loss, tears streaming down her face. Norris snapped his crop, and she jumped. Clearing her throat again, she began a ditty our old people enjoyed about love, clean winds, and beautiful skies on the top of the world.

She hadn't been singing long when Sergeant Jacobs returned and spoke into Norris's ear. The major's wicked smile grew. "Build up the fire, Sergeant. We're going to need it."

They found her.

CHAPTER 6

NORRIS STOOD AND WALKED toward us. I squirmed inside, and it was all I could do not to beg for my people's lives and to tell him that they didn't know. But I would not condemn myself before he accused me.

He flicked his crop at us as if he were wagging a long, black finger, his face as pleased as the cat that ate the canary. "It seems you Secs have been naughty, haven't you? Hmm? Can anyone tell me our bargain? You grow our hemp, and we allow you to live."

Hemp? I held my breath.

Norris spoke as if educating children. "You meet your quotas first, and then you take your allotment. All other hemp is to be reported to your field monitor and turned over. Yet here you are with a hidden tunnel full of hemp bales." He pointed toward Granny's kiln shed. "How many were there again, Sergeant? Twenty bales?"

"You." Norris pointed the crop toward Granny. "Explain this."

"They are our allotment. Two of our weavers died of the lung fever last winter, so we haven't used them as quickly as we usually would have. We've been very careful to save them and use them parsimoniously."

Norris laughed. "Did you hear that, Sergeant? The Sec said 'parsimoniously.' Have you ever heard of such a quarter word coming out of a two-bit Sec?"

The sergeant growled his reply. "No, sir. Never."

"If you have twenty unused bales this time of year, you have twenty too many bales. Sergeant, load those bales on the back of the truck."

Jacobs sent four men scurrying to do his bidding.

"As for the rest of you, it seems the Lord will spare you tonight. The girl is not here. But you have been most difficult and uncooperative. You will be punished."

Norris turned to the sergeant. "These Secs look a bit fat to me. I understand you found food ferreted away with the bales?"

"Yes, sir. Dried roots and meats."

Norris stared at us, and his evil smile turned into an ugly glare. "Throw it on the fire." He pointed toward our laden table. "And get rid of that trash too."

"Please," Granny said. "It's all we have."

Norris sneered. "Good. Michael grant that you die like the cursed scum you are." He spun on his heel. Jacobs opened the door of the armored car for him, and the vehicle sped from the meadow, leaving the sergeant in charge of destroying our lives.

Numb, I watched our bales of hemp come up, one by one, and go into the truck. And then, every bean, every hemp seed, every hard-earned scrap of dried venison, and even the baskets that held them—food for the whole meadow for a month—went into the flames, and we were helpless to stop it.

Then, as suddenly as they had come, they were gone.

CHAPTER 7

I WAS BARELY AWARE of the motion when Granny signaled two Iredale men to pick up Iain's body.

Quinn rushed to my side. "How bad is it? Let me help you to the house."

"No, I have to talk to Granny." I pushed him away, and the effort broke open my wounds. I gasped.

Granny's voice was brisk. In command. "Not now, Deena. Let Quinn help you." She turned away. "Flynx, if I were them, I'd double back and watch us. You follow and see what they do. Take Old Sally."

"Yes, ma'am." Flynx grabbed Sally's halter rope and jumped on her back, galloping out to reconnoiter the Josephites.

"Granny, I really need to talk with you." It was hard to be insistent without attracting too much attention.

"I'm sorry, but there's work to be done. Darryn, please have your people inventory their belongings and ask them to bring any food they are willing to share. We're obviously in a bad way."

Quinn tried to steer me toward the house, and I shook him off. "Granny, you really need to know this."

She ignored me as if I were a three-year-old tugging on her

skirt, so I tugged at her skirt while she spoke. "Tinker, Arys, Zander. Collect everything you have to trade, and bring it up to the house. We'll send Deena and Quinn for factory bars tomorrow—for God's sake, Deena. What is it?"

In a low voice only she and Quinn could hear, I said, "She's here."

"What?" Granny froze and stared at me, her mouth agape.

"She's here. Tamar is here. She showed up when the Joes did, so I dumped her down the outhouse."

Even in the firelight I could see her go ashen. She stared blankly for the briefest moment before regaining her composure. "Tell no one." She turned back to our people, who were already leaving to follow her orders. "Belay that order. Stay in your houses, and I'll be back down to collect your trade goods shortly. We'll get through this, people."

Harmony flew at Granny, Bane and Greagor at her side. "We'd better get through this. If it wasn't for Archer and her bad attitude, we wouldn't be in this mess."

Bane pointed at Iain's body, being carried away. "And that man. He wouldn't be dead if it wasn't for her."

Everyone froze and stared at Harmony and her son. I cringed. Were they right? The food, Iain's death. Were they my fault?

Granny's voice was ice. "They did it because they are Josephites. That is what they do. Blame serves nothing. If you don't have solutions right now, you have no need to talk."

Harmony put her hands on her hips and stuck out her chin. "I have a solution. I say we hunt down that girl and sell her to the Josephites for food."

I jumped in. "What part of 'stupid' do you not get? Norris shot Iain for the fun of it. He beat me on my hands and knees for the fun of it. You take him the girl, and he'll burn us all just to warm his toes at the fire."

"You got no more than you deserved, you little hellcat, spitting in his face like that." Harmony gesticulated wildly, her apron flapping around her. "You made us hungry. What are you going to do to fix it?"

"Enough." Granny's voice rang with authority. Harmony glared at her, challenging. Granny met her stare with steel. Finally Harmony looked away, crossed her arms across her chest, and huffed.

Granny turned and addressed our people. "There'll be no more talk of hunting Tamar. Deena is right. Norris would love the excuse to kill us all, so even if you come across her, I'd advise you to say nothing. I'll come around to pick up your trade goods shortly, and Deena and Quinn will leave for the Big Box at first light to buy enough factory bars to see us through the month. Now let's get moving."

The group broke apart, holding each other and whispering among themselves. We headed toward the house.

Granny stopped us at the board bridge. "They may have left a bug, so when we go inside, speak normally, but don't speak of the girl until I've cleared the house. Understand?"

Quinn and I nodded. Once inside, I was relieved to see that the Joes hadn't messed things up too badly. They were apparently aware of the fact that a young woman was too big to hide in Granny's pottery vases or the cook stove, so pretty much everything smaller than a breadbox was undisturbed. I already knew they hadn't discovered our books, the necklace, or Granny's tiny stash of first aid supplies. They would have killed us over those things.

Granny set straight to work scanning the house with a small electronic device she'd managed to keep from her army days.

I wanted to speak normally while she searched, but I found I couldn't speak at all. Instead I retrieved our first aid supplies from the hidden cupboard in her washroom. Quinn heated water and placed a couple of bowls and a water filter on the table.

Turning my back to him, I lowered my dress to my waist and covered my breasts with my shawl before sitting down. He handed me his own flask. I drank deeply and closed my eyes, relishing the slow burn that worked its way through my body and welcoming the numbness that came with it.

I felt the flask nicked from my hand and looked up.

"That's enough," Granny said. She pointed to my eyes and then indicated the room with her finger. I knew what she wanted.

Studying the room with my tracker's vision, the curtain rod caught my gaze. The end cap wasn't quite as flush as usual. I pointed to it.

Granny nodded, and Quinn set his chair underneath it. She moved the detector closer to the rod end, and it played a song from the War—a song of rebellion and victory that sounded absurd in the moment.

She turned off the device and pried open the end cap. Then she pried a tiny robot out, its legs wriggling, and pinched it between her thumb and forefinger. She set it on the floor and crushed it with the heel of her boot.

Granny nodded. "Okay. I think we're clear now. I'm going to take some of your clothes for her. Quinn, come with me and fish her out. Let's get her inside. I have a plan. And Deena, you be civil to this girl. She's no doubt been through enough."

I snorted. Civil? Civil was the last thing I wanted to be.

My stomach growled. I looked in the gruel pot. There was barely enough for breakfast.

I took the warm water from the stove and one of Granny's pottery cloths from her shelf and started cleaning the dirt from the bloody, filthy stripe across my chest.

I would be eating if it wasn't for her. Iain would be alive if it wasn't for her.

A few moments later, I smelled a terrible stench. A woman gasped, and I turned to see the Josephite staring at my bloody back.

I got my first good look at her. My anger rose, and I sneered my disdain. She was delicate, as if she'd been carried on a pillow all her life. Her long red hair, pinned loosely in an ornate gold clip, framed her perfect, porcelain face and neck, marred only by a small cross-cut behind her left ear where her microchip had been. She gave a womanly shape to my shirt that I never could, and worse, she looked better in my pants than I did. In her hand was her smelly sweater with its ridiculous dancing rabbits. When she saw me, she reached for the pendant she wore on a gold chain around her neck—a tiny, clear dome with a seed inside.

But her cerulean eyes were the most striking. Why did she have to have those eyes? When I looked into them, I couldn't see the bottom. They were the eyes of an old soul. They were Granny's eyes. What right did this Josephite woman have to my granny's eyes?

"What happened?" Her voice was timid.

I couldn't help myself. "What happened was you, Bunny." I spit the words with all the hate in my heart.

"That's enough. Tamar is here now, and it's our task to keep her safe. Tamar, come in and sit down."

"Thank you. God at your shoulder." Hesitantly, she moved to the chair across from me. I refused to look at her. "Pardon me, but would you please have some water and a bit of food?"

"No, we have no food, thank you very much." I glared at her.

"Deena. That will do," Granny said, her eyebrow crawling into her hairline. She took the sweater from the girl's hand and hung it on a peg on the wall by the stove. Then she brought more warm water from the stove and started cleaning my wounds. "Quinn, would you please fetch us all a bit of gruel? I think if we're careful, we can make it last another day or so." He moved to do her bidding.

Granny worked at the deep dirt, and I flinched.

"I'm sorry, sweetie. I know this hurts," she said.

Quinn served the three of us half of what was left in the pot and leaned back against the wall by our front window.

Granny turned her attention to the girl. "So tell us how you've come to be here."

The woman did not pick up her spoon, but instead reached for her seed pendant and studied Granny quietly before answering. In a matter-of-fact tone, as if she were detached from herself and reporting someone else's story, she said, "Joseph killed my mother. Now he wants to burn me. My grandmother, Ruth Dobbins, always told my mother and me that if we ever needed anything, we could come to her sister in the stone house above the city."

Quinn bowed his head and shook it, staring at the ground. Worry furrowed his brow.

The young woman lowered her eyes in silence for a moment and then lifted her spoonful of hemp gruel to her nose and sniffed it. I stared, shocked that she would appear so fussy about the only food we had to offer. She glanced at my face and then quickly put the bite in her mouth.

Her eyes brightened at the taste. "This is delicious. What is it?" she asked, her tone ringing with sincerity.

I couldn't believe it. "Seriously, Bunny? What must you Joes eat? Plastic bags and dog barf?"

Granny poured some moonshine from the flask over my wounds to clean them.

"Ouch. Holy crap, that hurts." I fought to hold still.

"Go on," Granny said, ignoring my writhing. "Why would he kill your mother, and why does he want you?"

Clinching the pendant in her fist, she looked down and took two more bites of gruel, appearing to not hear the question. I couldn't help but admire her control. She had to be starving, but she ate as if she were at an afternoon tea between two full meals. A lady.

When she spoke again, her voice was monotone and barely more than a whisper. "My mother was a scientist. I was her assistant. Joseph did not like the project we were working on, so he broke in and killed my mother and took her other assistant away. I escaped through the tunnels under the city. That was three days ago. I was supposed to meet a coyote in your ruined town at the base of the mountains, but he wasn't there." She looked up at us, apology in her eyes. "I'm sorry I've caused you trouble."

I glared at her and looked away. At least she knew she was a pain.

"Don't you worry about us. We've weathered worse," Granny said. "And I have a plan."

Just then the bridge boards announced a visitor. Quinn flicked the curtain aside to see out, and Bunny jumped up.

"It's okay," he said. "It's Flynx."

"Let him in." Granny motioned to Bunny to sit back down, but instead the woman edged toward the back room.

Her eyes wide as saucers, she asked, "Who is this person?"

"It's okay," Granny said. "He's a brave man and has no love for the Josephites."

Flynx entered and rubbed his shoes on the mat, and Quinn shut the door behind him. "You were right, Granny. They sent back a . . . What the hell?" He had just spotted Bunny.

"Flynx, this is my niece, Tamar. Tamar, this is one of our trusted friends from North Meadow, Flynx."

Bunny nodded her head at the horrified man. "God at your shoulder."

He looked back and forth from Bunny to Granny, opposition in his every fiber. "Oh no, the hell you don't. Flamin' Michael on a biscuit. We've got to get her out of here now."

CHAPTER 8

"FIRST, TELL ME WHAT you know," Granny said. Flynx gave Bunny another look and shook his head. "Those goat-bugging Josephites stopped at the fork in the road, and Norris ordered half of them back. They're camped at the split boulder on the north ridge."

"That certainly does make things a bit more difficult." Granny motioned for Bunny to sit back down. Staring warily at Flynx, who was summing her up with his eyes, Bunny edged her way back to her chair.

"You stink, girl," Flynx said.

"Deena dropped her in the outhouse," Granny said. "She was there the whole time."

Flynx looked at me with pleasant surprise on his face. "Good thinking."

"Thank you."

Granny sprayed my cleaned wounds with Stem Skin, a stem cell antibiotic that would help me heal in half the normal time.

"All right, then," she said. "This is what we'll do. I'll collect all of the trade goods. Before dawn, Deena, you and Quinn will leave for the Big Box to bargain for all of the factory bars you can get. Around five hundred should get us through until we have some fresh food growing."

"How does that solve this little poxy problem?" Flynx asked, pointing at Bunny as if she were an inanimate object.

"Please watch your language, Flynx, and show some respect for my niece. It's simple," Granny answered. "She will go with them."

"She'll what?" Quinn and I asked in unison. Bunny emphatically shook her head.

"Now calm down." Granny shook the can of Stem Skin and sprayed it once more across my back and chest. "Think about it a moment. She'll be with two Sec men, and her face will be covered like a Sec woman. There won't be anything unusual about that. She needs to stay away while that patrol is watching the meadow, and especially with Harmony wanting to hunt her down and sell her. While you're gone, Tinker and I will put around that my niece by marriage . . . What were you calling her, Deena? Bunny? Bunny is a good name . . . that Bunny is coming up from the Borders to stay for the summer."

I smacked my hand down on the table. "Right. You really think, after the Joes were here looking for her, that you can just change her name and say she's your niece?"

Granny gave me the Eyebrow of Impending Doom. "Smacking the table? Really? How old are you? I'll be up front with the Tinkers. I took them in when they were refugees, after all. The story is for the outside Secs and Harmony. She's not the brightest goat in the herd, but if we have to, we'll remind her who feeds her."

"That plan sucks." I looked around for support, but found only neutral eyes. My shawl had loosened a bit, and I re-secured it across my breasts, suddenly conscious of my nakedness. I hated arguing while feeling half naked, but I gave it my best shot. "Granny, she can't come with us. She'll slow us down. She'll wander off and get lost or get us caught. You can't be serious about this."

Bunny chimed in. "I've never been in the forest until

yesterday, and . . ." She turned to each of us, her eyes imploring. "I don't want to seem ungrateful, but it was terrifying. Isn't there some other way?"

"You'll be fine with Quinn and Deena. Deena knows the forest, and Quinn knows the Josephites. He could talk his way out of Atonement if he had to." Granny's voice held a confidence I did not feel. "Flynx, what do you think?"

He turned his sharp eye on Bunny. "Cut her hair and dye it. Put her in an old dress, and she could pass if she hides those lily hands of hers. Give her your old boots to wear . . . How are your feet holding up after being on the road?"

Bunny blushed and looked down, as if discussing her feet was a bit too personal. "My feet are well, thank you."

Granny leaned her head under the table where she could see Tamar's feet. "My boots should fit her."

Flynx nodded his approval. "I think it's a good plan, Granny. Kiln shed tunnel's blown, so she can't stay there. Quinn's is too risky. Even if the Joes didn't find her, it's likely that another Sec would. She has to be somewhere else with that troop patrolling our rim, so it might as well be with these two, and they'll never look for her under their own noses."

My anger erupted, and I stood abruptly, knocking my chair over. "We have enough to worry about scrounging up food for the meadow without taking along that . . . that . . ."

I tried to think of a word vile enough for her—the reason I was beaten, and my people starved. I glared, shaking with fury. The dancing bunnies on the sweater hanging on the wall behind her seemed to mock me. Weak little farcical things in unnatural clothing, laughing and dancing around a Cross of Michael. I wanted to skin her and them both. "That Bunny," I finished, and I hastened to my room to change out of my shredded dress and to try and reconcile myself to my new reality.

***

THE NEXT MORNING, I said my goodbyes to Granny and Daisy, and we set out on the two-day journey to the Big Box. The night was waning, and Pisces kissed the western mountaintops, but we did not yet have the benefit of daybreak.

To avoid the troops' night vision equipment, we skirted the long way west along the cliff side before veering back to the southeast to catch the main trail. It was no more than a deer track, and while it was quite plain to my and Quinn's eyes, we soon saw that Bunny would be lost if we let her out of arm's reach.

I found the thought of losing her in the forest to be a perfect solution, and thinking of ways to do that helped me pass the time. I seriously considered it for a while, but then I reminded myself that she was under Granny's protection and, therefore, mine, so I resisted temptation. Reluctantly.

Bunny was more of a pain than even I had anticipated. She jumped at the slightest noises, balked off the trail, and grabbed at the back of my pack to keep her balance over the rocks. I didn't know who was more scared, her or the chipmunks she startled. Only the birds didn't bother her. In fact, they seemed to be her comfort, and she adeptly imitated their calls, delighting in their replies. As far as I was concerned, though, this was just one more thing distracting her from getting ground between us and the Josephite patrol.

When the first rays of morning lightened the mountaintops and we were still less than a mile from the meadow, I'd had enough. I rounded on her. "Pull yourself together, Bunny. At this rate, our people will starve to death before we get back with that food."

Quinn seconded me, but his voice was much kinder and more patient than my own. "It's true, Bunny. You need to calm down and pick up the pace. We figured two days down and two days back. Our people have just enough to last that long. After that, they'll only have what we bring back and what we can hunt."

While he spoke, I climbed up on a large boulder to look around. What I saw sent shivers up my spine and compounded my sense of urgency. I backed down, grabbed Bunny's hand, and drug her up with me, dropping low and crawling on my belly near the top. I handed her my binoculars and said, "Stay down. Now look straight across at twelve o'clock. Just watch. You'll see a flash."

Sure enough, after a moment, a small sparkle of reflected light drew her eye to the ridge. "That's the Josephites camped above our meadow. That flash is off their binoculars. They're looking for you. They might have seen us and sent someone to find us already. Is that what you want? Because if it is, my life would be a lot easier if we cut you loose here in the forest."

A squirrel skittered to my left as if on cue, and Bunny jumped, searching wildly for the source of the disturbance. Satisfied it wasn't a lion or a bear, she took her seed pendant in her hand and closed her eyes.

"What are you doing? We need to get going."

She kept her eyes closed. "Shhh."

"Oh, now that just takes the gruel."

I glanced at Quinn, and he cautioned me to silence with a finger to his lips. Irritated with them both, I jumped off the rock, leaving her there.

A moment later, Bunny joined us. "I'll do my best. Perhaps it would help if I stay between the two of you."

"Fine. We can do that," I said. "Let's go."

Without asking Quinn if he preferred to lead or follow, I struck out up the trail at a brisk walk and left it to them to keep up. Whether it was the daylight, the sight of the Josephites, or her prayer ritual that gave her confidence, I soon saw that Bunny was more focused and stable. I kicked it up to a traveling jog, hoping the movement itself would help keep her on course.

It took until dawn-thirty, the time when the sun was halfway between breaking and noon, for Bunny to ask for a rest. I had to admit I was surprised she made it that far.

We stopped at a spot that had a view of Gap and the open plains below us. It was narrow, but I loved the sight of the expanse.

I shed the pack of trade goods, breathing a sigh of relief to have lightened my load by sixty pounds or so. The Stem Skin had done its work, but my wounds were still fresh and tender, and the pack had been rubbing in all the wrong places.

Taking out our canteens, Quinn and I took small sips while Bunny guzzled hers.

"Whoa, careful, there," Quinn said. "You need to make that last at least two days."

"Oh, sorry." She put the cap back on and stowed the canteen.

Irritated that she would be so ignorant, I allowed myself a dig. "I suppose in Joe Land you never have to worry about water, but you're in our neighborhood now, Bunny, and we can't waste things like that."

She looked down, flushed, as if embarrassed at breaking some social convention.

"Hey, Archer, don't be so hard on her. She has a lot to learn." Quinn gave me a dirty look, and I suddenly felt ashamed that I had been rude to someone in my care. Granny certainly would have given me the Eyebrow.

I offered her an olive branch. "You're doing much better now."

Quinn gave me a "good Archer" nod and joined in. "Really. You seem to be in great shape. I never expected you to handle that pace."

Bunny gave him a shy smile and glanced down, blushing. I remembered how she flinched at having to speak to Flynx about her feet, and I wondered if she'd ever spoken to men before at all.

"I worked out every day," she said. "Mostly I'm a dancer, but I also had gymnastics and the Praise Worship Drill Team."

"Seriously? You were on the PWDT? Were you part of the flag corps?" Quinn asked.

Bunny, encouraged, gave him a bright smile that started with her eyes. "You know us? How would a Sec know us?"

"Well, I haven't always been a Sec," he said, "But it's a lot better than the work camp was back when I was a kid."

"Really?" she asked. "Which one?"

"Camp Gabriel. Down southeast of the city."

"Oh," Her face went studiously blank, as if she were fighting a visible reaction. I didn't know one camp from another, and I wondered if there was something in particular about that camp to make her suddenly so guarded.

Quinn, caught up in his reminiscing, didn't seem to notice. "But I remember the Pagan Games and the Super Bowl. That was the one day they'd let us off. We'd all collect around the holoscreen in the middle of the camp for the game, and I loved watching the drill team. You girls were hot . . . I mean, um, you were really good."

Bunny laughed. "It's okay. I've only been there three years, so you wouldn't have seen me. But you would have liked us too. We sparkled. This year, we've got a routine worked up to *Joseph Fought the Battle of Jericho where* we all bring down our flags and go into a drop, like this, right when it gets to the walls tumbling down." She demonstrated, waving an imaginary flag and falling to a knee with her head bowed.

Quinn laughed. "Hey, you're pretty good. Too bad you'll miss it this year."

I had no idea what a Pagan Game was, but Quinn looked so excited that I wondered if he was going to start pretending to wave a flag himself. I studied Bunny a bit more closely, and I began to see what he saw—a beautiful woman. Suddenly I felt mannish and awkward in my hemp cargo pants and camouflage turtleneck, looking like some wild forest boy.

I had two choices. I could be mean to her and be the bad guy in Quinn's eyes, or I could fake a civility I did not feel to keep them from bonding without me. "Speak English here, please. None of that Joe talk."

"Football," Quinn said, as if that explained everything.

Bunny was a bit swifter on the uptake. "Football is a game played by two teams of men. The goal is to get a ball across a field while the other team tries to take it away from you and run back to their own side with it. It's actually a leftover from Old America.

"The drill team is kind of like a cheerleading squad. We don't do as many acrobatics as the cheerleaders, but our costumes are every bit as cute, and we have large flags that we wave in patterns to music during the half-time show."

"Cheerleaders?" I asked. The words she said were English, but they made exactly no sense to me.

"Oh, yeah, cheerleaders," Quinn said, smiling and nodding.

Bunny giggled and blushed again. Then to Quinn's delight, she began to demonstrate. "Cheerleaders make up chants and acrobatic routines. A cheer would go something like, 'Lift the Pagans. Sing their praise. Joseph loves them every day. Team for God and Team for Right, crush the other team tonight. Goooooooooooo, Pagans!'" She finished her display with a jump, her arms in the air.

I resisted the idea. Could she possibly be serious? "I don't understand. You think we Secs are all pagans and therefore bad, but you're cheering for us during your football games?"

Bunny and Quinn shared a look of confusion and then cracked up laughing. "No, no," Bunny said. "'Pagans' is the name of a football team. We cheer for the football team."

The bulb went on, and I was furious. "What the hell is that? And you." I poked the air toward Quinn. "You should know better."

Quinn jumped back, looking stunned.

I wheeled on Bunny. "You label all Secs pagans, and you do your best to kill us off in the name of Joseph. Then you name a ball team after us and say they're fighting for Joseph and your

God? What is that about?"

It was Bunny's turn to be confused. "I . . . It's an honor, really. We name our teams after fierce fighters. The Pagans are the best team in the Western Province League. Really, no one thinks of you when they talk about football. They only think of a great football team."

"Maybe they should think of us." Disgusted, I glared at both of them and considered booting Bunny off the side of the cliff. She was only a couple of feet away from the edge, after all. It wouldn't take more than a nudge.

An awkward silence enveloped us. I capped my canteen, shoved it in my pocket, and picked up my trade pack and my bow.

Bunny caught sight of my weapon. "So, um, your bow. Is that why they call you Archer?" she asked.

On some level, I knew she was trying to break the ice with me, but I liked the cold. I'd had enough of Bunny and her pompous world where my people were nothing but a symbol for savagery.

I set the pack back down and pointed at a rabbit, barely visible under a bush fifty yards upslope. In a single movement, I nocked my arrow and drew. It struck my target with a small puff of dust.

Turning to Bunny, I couldn't keep the hate from my voice. "They call me Archer same as I call you Bunny."

Quinn lifted his finger, and I knew he was about to go off on me, but before he could speak, the earth shook beneath us. The ground slipped, and he dropped to his knees. I toppled over, grabbing at a nearby tree root. A roar rose from the earth and filled the air, but even that couldn't drown out her scream. Grappling at the air as she slammed to the ground, both Bunny and the trade pack slid past me toward the lip of the cliff.

CHAPTER 9

W ITH ONLY ONE HAND free, I couldn't save them both. I didn't think. I grabbed Bunny and held fast to her arm. She scrabbled back up the hill toward me while the pack tumbled over the cliff with all our hopes for survival inside. Rocks crashed down, and a snake, awakened from its hibernation, slithered across my hand on the tree root. It was all I could do not to let go.

The ground beneath us slipped. Bunny screamed again. I sought Quinn for help, but he was doing all he could, holding our other packs with one hand and clinging to his own tree. Just when I thought my grip would fail, the shaking stopped. After one last low rumble, all was silent.

Bunny lay still, and I didn't know if she'd been hit in the head with a falling rock. I was afraid to let go of the tree to find out. Then Quinn's hand was on mine. He took Bunny from my grip and pulled her to her feet, helping me up next. Shaken, we moved as far away as we could from the cliff's edge.

Quinn kissed his hand and touched it to the ground, and Bunny fell to her knees and took hold of her pendant to pray. As for me, I took a deep breath. Watching the two of them, I found it a great irony that two such seemingly different belief systems could manifest in such similar ways, though it had always been my contention that there were only so many ways to be a decent person, regardless of which deity got the credit.

Finally Bunny looked up. "Deena—"

"That's 'Archer' to you," I said. "Only family calls me Deena, and then only Granny." I wiped some dust from my pants, irritated to find a hole in one of my pockets.

"Archer, thank you for saving my life," Bunny said. "You had every reason to grab the pack, but you didn't. You saved me instead. All my life, I've been told that Secs caught Josephites in the woods and skinned them alive, but just now you set my life above your own people. I don't understand, but thank you. You should have been born a Christian."

"Seriously? Did you really say that?" Her religious arrogance chaffed me, but I was also taken aback and somewhat confused by the rest of what she'd said. She was right. We needed that trade pack to buy food. I didn't like the idea that, in the moment, I'd chosen a Josephite over my own people. What would my people think? Had I betrayed them with my weakness?

I shrugged, uncomfortable with her gratitude, and a part of me regretted what I'd done. "Yeah, well, I don't understand, either. Tell you what. You can be my slave now until you save my life." I winked at her with a graciousness I did not feel. "Besides. 'Ain't no fat lady singin' here,' as Flynx would say. Let's see if there's any chance of getting that pack back. I'll take a look."

"Wait." Bunny glanced around, decidedly anxious. "Shouldn't we be moving on? I mean, what about aftershocks? We can't get caught on this narrow spot again."

"Bunny, you don't understand. We. Have. No. Food. We have to get that pack back."

"She's right," Quinn said. "Without that pack, there's no point in going any further. Now why don't you sit down over here with your back to this tree? That way, any aftershocks won't knock you off your feet." She did as she was told, and I was glad to have her parked out of the way.

I lay on my stomach and cautiously crawled toward the edge of the cliff. The ground was loose scree, and I realized we were lucky we hadn't all slid off along with the pack.

Peering over, I was delighted to see the pack had caught in a tree—we just had to rappel down and get it. Then I gulped. The tree was on an overhanging slope that dropped off into the void only a few feet below it. The strongest of us would need to hold the rope, and the lightest person would have to retrieve the goods. I was certain Bunny had never rappelled, so that meant me. I cringed at the thought. I hated climbing, and I really hated heights.

I wriggled back away from the edge and stood up. "We're in luck. Sort of. It's only about thirty feet down, stuck in a tree."

"Can you use your techthread to hook it so you don't have to go down there?" Quinn asked.

He was referring to the roll of fiber on a spool that snapped into my pocket knife. Thin as a thread, but strong as a hemp rope.

"No. It's barely balanced. If we tried to hook it with something, we might knock it off."

"Well, thirty feet's not too bad."

"Yeah, right." I tried not to think of all that open air beneath the pack, easily a thousand-foot drop. "Okay. Let's get 'er done."

Quinn pulled our rope out of his pack, and I made a seat harness of sorts for myself.

"I'm ready." I gave the rope one more tug to make sure the harness was secure.

"No, you're not," Quinn said. Without explanation, he pulled out Clarisse and used the machete to whack off a few feet of rope at the other end.

"What are you thinking? We might need that length." I was appalled at his waste.

Without answering me, he tied the ends together and twisted

it into a figure-8. Holding it out to me, he said, "Here, put this on. The last thing I want is you flipping over backward with that pack."

I looked at the rope, feeling stupid for not thinking of a chest harness. "I knew that." We both knew I was full of crap. I put my arms through the loops.

Quinn started to wrap the rope around the tree I'd been holding.

"Wait, Quinn. That tree was slipping. If there's an aftershock, it might come out altogether. You'll need to hold the rope."

"Well, that's pretty iffy too."

"Are you saying you're weak, or that I'm fat? Because I'm not fat."

Quinn laughed. "No, you're definitely not fat."

"Are you saying I'm too thin? Because that would be pretty cheeky of you."

Bunny stood abruptly. "How can you two joke at a time like this?"

Quinn and I shared a moment of amusement, and I said, "Bunny, all our times are times like this. When else are we going to joke?"

"We need to hurry." Her voice and eyes implored us to get a move on. Then she threw up her hands and shook her head, giving in to the reality. "Here," she said, striding toward us. "How can I help?"

"How about this? Do a half hitch on that tree to give you some friction, and Bunny, you get in front of Quinn and help him hold it. Does that work for you two?"

"Sounds good," Quinn said. "Get those gloves we gave you to hide your hands, Bunny. You'll need them if the rope slips."

"Yeah, don't talk like that," I said. The thought of the rope slipping made me break out in a cold sweat.

When all was ready, I lowered myself over the edge of the cliff, feeling my way down the nearly vertical face with my hands and feet. The pack hung from a branch by one strap. I glanced down to mark its location, and unfortunately, I saw the whole world stretched out beneath it. My head spun, and my stomach rose within me. I fought the illogical urge to dive toward the ground.

I called out to them. "Wait."

Quinn's voice drifted down. "You okay?"

Bile burned the back of my throat, and I swallowed it down. Taking a deep breath, I determined that I would do this thing. Our people needed it. "Yeah, no worries." Slowly, I once more felt my way down the side of the mountain toward the trade pack.

The spruce tree it was caught in grew almost perpendicular to the cliff wall. It seemed to take forever until I was level with it, only to find the bag was just beyond my reach. I was going to have to fly for it.

I called up to Quinn. "Tension." Then I launched myself off the side of the cliff and swung. Reaching out, I caught a strap on the first try and plucked it from the branches.

"Yes!" I swung back in toward the side of the cliff, triumph filling my heart.

Once braced, I turned slightly and picked up the end of the rope to tie the pack between my legs. Balanced precariously with one toe on the side of the cliff, I was glad to be in the home stretch.

Don't look down. Just don't look down.

Suddenly the ground shook. My feet slipped, and my heart stopped. I lurched uncontrollably toward the edge of the overhang and a thousand feet of open air.

CHAPTER 10

I THREW MY BODY against the pack and the mountainside and scrambled for some kind of a hold. A seedling tree came off in my hand. I repeatedly jolted toward the void. A bird's nest bounced past me. My toe hit a tiny shelf, and I paused. Then, with the next shake, my foot was over open air.

My fingers felt rock. I dug my hand into a niche, and the tension in the rope returned. Bringing my right knee up, I found a sliver of ledge, and I clung like a burr while the earth gave one more great heave before it stilled.

Trembling in terror at the empty space below me, I closed my eyes and forced myself to breathe, afraid of quivering right off the side of the mountain.

I had no idea what was going on up top, or if I could expect any help. I only knew that one knee and a few fingers were barely enough to stay put, much less enough to gain the upward momentum it would take to climb the side, especially with the pack. My mind wanted to panic, and I forced it to obey me and be still.

Then I felt a pull on the rope. Pushing with it, I got my left foot back onto something approximating ground.

"Archer. Archer, answer me."

Quinn sounded so far away. I was afraid the effort to answer him would cause me to lose my balance, so I kept forging upward.

"Arrrr—cheeeerrr."

A few feet up, I felt a tiny ledge with my toe. Taking a deep breath, I returned his call. "Here." It was the only word I would risk.

I willed myself to look no further than my toe while I turned out once more and this time got the pack tied on. With both hands at my disposal and the steady upward pressure on the rope, I couldn't climb that cliff face fast enough.

The only place I looked was up. Thirty feet. Twenty feet. Ten. And finally, the most welcome sound I'd ever heard.

"I'm here. Give me your hand," Quinn said. He pulled me onto firm ground. I crawled as far away from the edge as I could and then collapsed. I didn't trust myself to stand.

"Are you okay?" Bunny asked, hovering over me and holding out a canteen while Quinn untied the trade pack.

I was not. I was shaking and terrified that I'd almost died because my people had to have that trade pack. Because the Josephites were starving us once again. At the sight of her porcelain-smooth Josephite face, my terror sought out the more comfortable emotion of anger. "No, I'm not okay. I knew I couldn't trust you to hold the rope for me. You and your lily-white Josephite hands."

Her mouth fell open, and she stepped back in the face of my fury.

"You're out of line," Quinn said, his calm, quiet tones admonishing.

Furious with him for defending her, I rounded on him, but what I saw caught me up short. Behind him, the tree they had wrapped the rope around lay broken and almost completely uprooted. I looked back at Bunny and saw the blood on her shredded gloves. She quickly turned away.

I felt uncomfortable with the conflicting emotions rising up inside me. "Wow. You really didn't want to be my slave, did you?" I said.

Quinn, his face red with emotion, said, "I'm sorry, Archer. The ground went right out from under me with the first wave. She's the one who held. If it had only been me, you'd be dead."

I didn't know what to think or feel. Saved by a Josephite. A Josephite, of all things. It was too much to process except for one fact. I owed her an apology. Me. Apologize to a Josephite. A Josephite who had saved my life. *Damn.*

But my integrity demanded it.

I cleared my throat and paused before speaking the words. "I'm sorry, Bunny." It hurt my lips and my pride.

She shrugged. "No worries. It was the right thing to do."

I was tempted to let her brush it off, but I was not willing to be a smaller person than she was. "No, really. I'm sorry. I assumed you were the one who dropped the rope. I was wrong to think that of you."

She studied my face, as if assessing my sincerity, and I was uncomfortable with her gaze. "Thank you," she finally said. "Apology accepted."

In my heart, I was glad, but I couldn't stop myself from saying, "You should have been born a Sec. Now come on. Let's get to a safer spot, and I'll doctor your hands."

She gave me a small smile. "Okay."

After a silent quarter mile, we found a wide spot. The earthquake had uprooted a few trees, but it was a good place. I set down my pack and began to take off my bow, when I remembered the rabbit I'd killed right before the first quake.

"Oh, wait. I'll be right back. I'm not losing that food, and I'm sure not losing my arrow." Before Quinn could protest, I headed back up the trail.

The bush I had marked my place by when I took the shot was still there, and it only took a moment to find the arrow and my prey. I paused, staring at the dead animal in my hands, thinking of the threat I'd made when I killed it. The person who took that shot had wanted to kill the Josephite girl, and now, such a short time later, that same person owed that same Josephite her life. Shrugging off the surreal feeling, I gutted the rabbit, bagged it in plastic, and tied the bag on my belt. Then a stick snapped in the forest near the trail.

I nocked my arrow, feeling a gaze I could not see. Was it a coyote? A lion? A human? Or was it only my imagination? I sorely missed Daisy, who would have answered my questions with her demeanor.

The hair stood up on the back of my neck. I backed slowly away and up the trail until, hidden by the trees, I turned and ran. By the time I had returned to Quinn and Bunny, I felt silly.

"Here, I'll do that," I said, reaching for the first aid kit Quinn held. "It would be helpful if you sew up that tear on the trade pack, please. You're better at that than I am." He wasn't, actually, but my fingertips were raw and my hands scratched up from the climb. I thought it would be easier for him to sew at that moment.

"Thank you," Bunny said.

"Don't thank me yet," I said. I opened the small flask of moonshine. "This won't feel good, but it's the only antiseptic we have."

She nodded, and I could see in her face she had no idea what was coming. Best to get it done.

I poured the alcohol we made from fermented gassplant across her bloody palms, cringing on her behalf and bracing for her screams. But they never came. She bit her lip and bore with it.

"Good job," I said. Far be it from me to not give credit where it was due.

I applied a bit of Stem Skin and bandaged her palms before doing my best to wash the blood from her gloves with a bare touch of water. Giving them back to her, I grinned and said, "Tell the truth. You just didn't want to be my slave, right?"

She laughed. "Can you blame me? Really. A bit of skin was

a small price to remove that debt, praise Michael."

The sun was pushing past noon when we hit the trail once more. We should have been to Lookout Point by that time, but I made the conscious decision to hold my tongue about it. No point in complaining. This time, Quinn set the pace at a traveling jog, and I stayed behind, watching out for Bunny and reassuring her that the chipmunks and bugs weren't out to kill her.

At noon-thirty, the time when the sun was halfway between high noon and sunset, we reached Lookout, my favorite overlook. It was a place I often visited to dream of a different world. Rushing ahead, I climbed onto a wide, high rock and paced back and forth while I waited for the others.

When Bunny and Quinn joined me, Bunny gasped at the sight of the world laid out at her feet—the vast expanse of fields with their grid of windmills and the tiny bugs of the workers so far below us, weeding and separating the stands of gassplant. In the distance, Promise City towered above the plains, surrounded by Defender's Wall and capped by the Dome, the biosphere where Joseph lived. His own little kingdom within a kingdom.

Bunny clutched her seed pendant. "How great Thou art," she said.

"You know, Bunny," I said, "you really have to stop saying stuff like that if you're going to pass for a Sec. Those God and Joseph and Michael references. Even Christian Secs don't talk that way."

"Oh, I guess you're right," she said. "There are Christian Secs?"

I turned away and rolled my eyes. Quinn chuckled and answered her. "Lots of them. Granny's one."

"Oh." She sounded surprised. "And are you?" she asked him.

"Me? No. The God of Joseph is far too cruel for me." He kissed his amulet and tucked it into his shirt.

"What about you, Archer?" she asked.

I shrugged and said, "This is the best view in all of the foothills. Let's just enjoy it while we can." I pointed to the dark cloud I had seen in the south the day before, now reaching the southern limits of Promise City. "That ash will be here by nightfall."

Bunny looked south. "Capulin again. Joseph's volcano."

We all stood for a moment, watching the south wind turn the endless rows of windmill propellers as it blew the shadows of the high clouds across the fresh fields.

Bunny shook her head in wonder. "I think I understand now why you'd rather be Secs. You're completely free here, aren't you? No rules. No one watching you. No one telling you who you have to be."

Free? I was not free to be a woman. I was not free to read and write. I was not free to own property or plant what I chose. But I had to admit she had a point. When I was alone in my hills, I was completely me, and I was enough. If that was freedom, then I was free.

But what about freedom for my people? What about a freedom where we didn't have to isolate ourselves to be who we were? Where we were free to prosper as we were able? I would have to think on that.

I pointed out landmarks to Bunny. The road that led straight as my arrows through the plains to the airborne turbines far to the north, the work camp we would pass through the next day, and the Secs in the distance, plowing the fields of South to prepare them for the hemp, the staple of our society. And I found to my surprise that I rather enjoyed telling her about our world.

"And check out that rock over there." I handed her the binoculars again. "See how it's perched on that tiny little overhang? We call that Land Mine Rock because it marks Land Mine Canyon below it. I'm kind of surprised the earthquakes haven't knocked it loose by now. Anyway, you'll see it from the ground in the morning." "Uhmm . . . Why would I see it from the ground?" Bunny sounded wary.

"Oh. We'll need to go through the land mines. But don't worry, we have a good path. I haven't been killed out there yet that it took."

She practically squeaked when she spoke next. "Land mines? You have land mines?"

"We don't. That's one of the fields the Joes seeded during the war. They ambushed our army in that canyon down there. It was a slaughter, but Granny says we took a lot of the bastards with us. My father was there." I pointed out the canyon below us. "They never take them out, you know. They only put them in." I could not keep the bitterness from my voice.

Bunny knit her brow. "I'm sure the Temple would do something about that. Perhaps your Field Monitor could tell them for you?"

Quinn and I stared at her with disbelief, and, life saved or no life saved, my irritation began to rise. There was just no reply to something that ignorant.

"Let's get going," I said.

"Sounds like a plan," agreed Quinn. He jumped off the rock and reached up to help Bunny. I waited for him to give me a hand down, too, but once Bunny was firmly rooted, he turned away. "Come on, Archer. You can enjoy the view another time."

I hated pretending to be a man. It always got me treated like one. I acted like I didn't notice his oversight, but I couldn't deny to myself that it rankled me. *Be nice.* "We're too late to get through the field before dark, and we can't risk it once the sun goes down, but we can camp right above the canyon and be ready at first light."

Bunny shuddered. "You can't be serious."

"No worries, Bunny," Quinn said. "Like Archer said, there's a good path."

I could tell she wasn't convinced, but I didn't much care. It was what we had to do.

Smoke and ash clouded the sky while we traveled. We pulled up our scarves across our noses and slowed to a walk to save our lungs. It was annoying, but it was nothing like what Granny told of the dark years after Taupo blew.

"The Earth is atoning," Bunny said. "That's what the Josephites say when the volcanoes rumble and spew ash."

Earth atone? What nonsense. "Yeah, well, we Secs say the Earth is in mourning because Josephites infested it."

Quinn shot me a dirty look.

"Well, that's what we say, isn't it?" I shrugged. "Besides, why would the Earth need to atone? What do you think it's done?"

"Everything needs atoning. Nothing, and no one, is perfect."

"That's crazy. Let's say you Joes are right, and your god made everything. Why would your god create something and then require it to atone for not being perfect in his eyes? He could have made it something different in the first place. I mean, how twisted is that? Help me out here, Quinn." I hoped he would help me, anyway.

"I have to agree with Archer on this one, Bunny," he said. "Anything She creates is perfect, except in the eyes of her creation that is so vain as to judge itself. We are not ours to judge."

"We are not ours to judge," Bunny repeated. "I like that thought."

"Surprisingly un-Josephite of you. Don't you believe you have to burn women to pay for the sins of society?" Quinn said, flashing her a charming smile as he held out a hand to help her over a bit of deadfall across the path. Why did he suddenly look so handsome?

Bunny paused. Her face closed, and she glanced over her shoulder as if checking to make sure no one was listening. "No. I am not a Josephite."

"What do you mean you're not a Josephite?" I asked.

"You're Joseph's granddaughter. What else could you be?"

Her face clouded over, and her voice became agitated. "He does not claim me, nor I him. He abandoned my father and killed my mother. Even Grandmother says he's a liar, and that there was never any battle with the Archangel Michael for the seeds. He exploits people's love of God, and that makes him the worst sort of sinner."

Her words surprised me. Of course all Secs knew that Joseph was a fraud, but I was taken aback to hear one of his own say it.

"So if you're not a Josephite, what are you?" Quinn asked.

"Christian. My grandmother was a Christian. My mother was a Christian. My father is a Christian. I am a Christian." Her voice became wistful. "My father even leads a Christian group within the city. We are known simply as the Underground. This seed I wear, this is our symbol. It's how we know each other. There are a few thousand of us now, and they helped me escape the city."

"Wow," I said. I knew Quinn never believed in Joseph as the Prophet of God, even as a child living in the city, but I never thought of non-believers as being an organized group with a recognition system.

"Don't your people have a symbol?" she asked.

I stopped and picked up a small stick to draw in the dirt. "Every meadow has its own symbol. This is ours." I drew three arrows forming a triangle with a sprouting seed in the center. "The triangle of arrows shows we are from Middle Meadow, but the sprouting seed is common to all Secs. The Joes don't know this, but we use these symbols to mark safe passages for other Secs."

"Yes, I've noticed it on some of the trees we've passed."

"What does your seed mean?"

Bunny held up her pendant. "This is a mustard seed," she said. "'It is the smallest of all the seeds on earth; yet when it is sown, it grows up and becomes the greatest of all shrubs, and puts forth large branches, so that the birds of the air can make nests in its shade.' Mark four, verses thirty-one and thirty-two," she quoted. "Grandmother taught me that is how the Kingdom of God grows."

"Yes, well, no disrespect to your grandmother, but Granny taught me a thing or two about seeds too," I said. "It says in there somewhere that the Kingdom of God is like seeds. They get scattered, they sprout, and they grow, and no one knows how. Not your temple, not your grandmother, and certainly not you."

Quinn snorted. "What's this? You're suddenly the biblical scholar? I thought all you believed in was running and shooting and dressing like a dude."

I glared at him. How dare he insult me like that? "I am, Quinn. I believe in 'I am.' I'll leave it to you two to assume you know what God is and wants."

Bunny shifted her pack and spoke with confidence. "I would not presume to speak for God, but I know what I believe. I believe in the holy scripture as God's truth revealed to man, as my grandmother taught me."

I suddenly remembered that I didn't like her one bit. "*Belief?* *Belief* is not a thought, and nothing is true just because you decide it is. No. *Belief* is taking in a fugitive because it's the right thing to do, without knowing if you and all of your family and friends are going to burn alive because of it. *Belief* isn't written, and it doesn't have a name. It's what you do."

Enough. I jogged down the trail and left them to keep up or not.

Soon it was dusk. I was glad for the wind coming down off the mountain. It lifted the smoke a bit, so I took my scarf off my face. I found some flat ground near the path and collected firewood to cook the rabbit while Quinn showed Bunny how to make indentations in the ground and fill them with pine needles for our beds. The wood was crisp and brittle, the kind I could almost start a fire with using only warm breath. Placing dried pine needles and shavings at the center, I built a teepee of twigs with larger sticks arranged above for rapid incineration. I prided myself on one-spark fires, and I loved it when I could get the whole thing to burst into flames at once. This looked like it would be one of those.

I struck my flint, my spark landing perfectly on the tinder, and said, "Y'all watch this. Quick." I knew I was showing off.

With one strong, steady breath, the pile burst into flames. Bunny's primal scream shredded my ears. I jumped up. Bunny ran, and before Quinn or I could stop her, she disappeared into the night.

CHAPTER 11

"**W**HAT THE HELL?" I asked, stepping back from the roaring fire.

Quinn, his eyes wide and his mouth agape, shook his head, as confused as I was.

"Well, we'd best find her. She couldn't have gone too far." I wrapped some dried grass around the end of a stick to use as a torch, not wanting to waste my flashlight batteries if I could help it.

Quinn and I located her from the sound of her hyperventilating. She was cowering behind a tree a mere stone's throw from camp. I rushed toward her, careful not to set the forest on fire with my torch. She screamed again and scurried behind another tree.

"Put out the fire. Please, for God's sake, put out the fire!"

"Stop, Archer. She's scared of the fire," Quinn said, pushing past me to get to Bunny. She rushed into his arms and hid her face in his chest. "It's okay," he said, stroking her hair as if she were a child.

"I can't put the fire out," I said. "I have to cook dinner— unless you want to get worms. Just settle down and come on over."

Quinn spoke to her in a low voice, and she shook her head, still hiding her eyes against him. "Go on. I'll stay here with Bunny until you're finished cooking."

I felt my body tense up and became aware that I was grinding my teeth. Without a word I returned to my fire, the one I had been so proud of only moments before, and I cooked the rabbit in silence. Then I put out the fire, turned on a small, battery-powered lantern, and called them over.

I split the tiny rabbit three ways and got out three bear bars, the travelling food I carried made from bear grease, hemp seeds, and dried berries. The Josephites had found most of them and destroyed them, so we only had enough for two hungry days, and we were already half a day behind.

I handed Bunny her share of the rabbit. After holding her seed and praying briefly, she lifted the roasted leg to her nose and sniffed it.

"Is there a problem?" I asked.

"No. It's that I've never seen real meat. All of our meat is cloned in factories. It grows right in the packages," she said.

"Oh, I remember that," Quinn said. "This meat is much better."

"No, really," I said. "It's terrible. I think you should give me your share."

Bunny smiled, apparently thinking I was joking. "Thank you for my dinner, Archer." With no further ado, she ripped into the meat, her enthusiasm mirroring the zeal that I felt for my own meal. Then she turned to me. "And thank you for putting out the fire."

Her sincerity almost softened me toward her. Almost. I grunted and continued to eat as slowly as possible, trying to fool my stomach into thinking supper was more than it really was.

"So was it the Atonements that made you this way? You know. Afraid of the fire?" Quinn asked.

Bunny paused, and I could swear I saw her eyes glisten in

the lamplight. "They were right under my balcony in Prophet's Plaza. It was terrible. The screaming. The smell of burning flesh . . . My grandmother and parents took every chance to protect me from them, but Joseph noticed. He forced us to watch. That's one of the things that gave me the courage to run from the city."

She turned to me, her eyes penetrating. "That's why I begged you to kill me. I would be happy to die for my Lord if that is His command, but I can't bear the fire."

I shifted under her gaze. I had never watched a person burn alive, but I had seen charred animals that had been caught by forest fires, their twisted carcasses crying out their pain and terror. My heart began to open to her.

"I understand." Quinn said. "They killed my father and Atoned my mother."

Bunny delicately placed her rabbit bones on a flat piece of wood she was using as a plate. When she spoke again, her voice was quiet and low, soft with a thousand sorrows. "Joseph killed my mother, too. The last time I saw her was in her laboratory. Me and my mom and her assistant, Barbara. Joseph and his Swords of Michael had just burst in. My mother told me to run. Then she stabbed herself in the throat so that they wouldn't take her alive."

A profound and solemn silence spread outward from the pit of my stomach, taking me deeper into my awareness than I had been since Faebin died. I knew she was sharing a sacred pain with us, and I treated it as such, gifting her with my still tongue. When Quinn closed his eyes and squeezed her hand, I knew he felt it too.

Soon though, the intensity was more than I could take. I wanted a different direction. Something familiar and comfortable. "Damn Josephites. I say we butcher every one of the bastards and feed them to the lions. Better yet, let the lions have them fresh and warm."

Bunny startled like I'd slapped her.

Quinn glared at me with reproach. "Not the time."

I looked away, embarrassed that I'd said the wrong thing, but irritated by his disapproval. I tried again. "So why does Joseph want you, anyway? What were you doing?"

Bunny studied me a moment, as if peering into my soul. "It's not important," she finally said.

I shrugged. Whatever. I wasn't going to beg. "We'd better get some sleep. We've got a long way to go tomorrow. I'll take the first watch."

"You think that's necessary?" Quinn asked. He pulled his techcloth blanket from his pack.

"The Dixie bears are coming out of hibernation about now, and without a fire . . ." I felt a little silly, but I thought I'd better mention it. "And, well, I did feel like something was watching me earlier on the trail when I went back for the rabbit."

Quinn looked suddenly alert and nodded. "I'll take the first watch. I'm not tired, and you just yawned."

Bunny cut in. "Excuse me, but what are Dixie bears?"

Gathering the rabbit bones to boil the next morning for breakfast, I explained. "Don't worry. They're cute, furry little things. At least the babies are. You can cuddle them, and the mother won't mind."

"Arrrr—cheerrr." Quinn's voice held warning. "Dixie bears happened when polar bears came south after Ash Wednesday and bred with grizzlies. Granny named them Dixie bears because they're like the carpetbaggers who came down on Dixie after the American Civil War, going after the weak and vulnerable. They're the only animals here in the forest that will hunt you down, except for the occasional man-eating lion."

"Lions? You have lions too?" Her eyes grew wide, like a scared doe against a cliff face.

I couldn't help but feel a bit sorry for her, leaving everything she knew to be a babe in the woods. Literally.

"Tell you what," I said, "If you can stand it, Quinn and I will build a fire. That will keep them away."

Bunny looked at the fire pit where I'd cooked the rabbit and then back at the indentation with her techcloth blanket waiting for her. Mine was just beyond it. "Trade places with me, and I'll try. Please. Only stay between me and the fire."

I tried to sound gentle. "If that works for you. We'll settle in and let Quinn light it. Are you all right with that?"

We curled up in our ultra-light techcloth blankets and did the best we could to get whatever rest we were able find within ourselves, but my dreams were restless, filled with shaking ground, free falls through the air, and the sound of Bunny's screams.

Bunny's screams!

CHAPTER 12

I OPENED MY EYES. Bunny screamed again, fighting against a man who was dragging her up the trail. Quinn struggled with another. The glint of a knife, perilously close to Quinn's throat, flashed in the dying fire. Grabbing my bow, I rolled to kneeling and nocked an arrow. From where I was, any shot I took was likely to hit Quinn if it passed through his assailant.

I dropped my bow and grabbed my knife from my boot. The man smacked Quinn's hand down on a rock, breaking his hold. I took aim and threw, burying my knife in the man's back.

He arched up, crying in pain. Quinn grabbed Clarisse and sprang to his feet. The man wheeled around, and Quinn slashed the machete down on his neck. Blood sprayed, and Quinn jumped back. The man fell to the side, bleeding from his jugular.

Quinn turned to me. "Where's Bunny?"

"That way." I pointed up the trail. He snatched his rifle, and we made chase.

A man cried out. We came around a corner to find Bunny's abductor sprawled on the ground, his head on a large rock where he had fallen. Bunny was kneeling beside him, checking his neck for a pulse.

"Get back." I grabbed her arm and pulled her from the man's reach in case he was faking.

Quinn approached, his rifle ready. He needn't have worried, though. The man was out cold.

"What? He just stumbled?" I asked.

Bunny clutched at her seed pendant. "Well, no, not exactly. I saw the rock in the path and helped him fall into it." She moved her foot to indicate that she had tripped him.

"Wow," Quinn said. "How'd you manage that?"

Bunny shrugged. "I'm a dancer," she said, as if that explained everything. "Please tell me he isn't dead."

I took a good look at the man's face while Quinn checked once more to confirm a pulse. In the moonlight that sifted through the trees, I recognized him. "Wait a minute, Quinn. That's Bane, Harmony's brat. The other one must be Greagor."

Quinn hunkered down next to the inert man and rolled him onto his back to get a better look. "Damn . . . You know we should kill him."

I crossed my arms over my chest, uncomfortable at the thought of killing one of our own, even a food thief. That's what Josephites did. "I know, but I don't like it."

Bunny gasped. "No."

Quinn, his voice calm, tried to explain. "Bunny, he was hunting you. His friend tried to kill me. They were going to turn you in for seeds. I'm betting anything that's who was watching Archer yesterday, because if there's anything I know about Archer, it's that she doesn't spook for no reason. If we let him live, he will kill us."

Quinn was right. I knew he was right, but it didn't sit well. Bane was a cruel, twisted bastard, but he was still a Sec.

"How about this?" I said. "How about we tie him to a tree and pick him up in a couple of days on the way home?"

"And let a lion eat him?" Quinn asked. "How is that more humane?"

Bane began to stir.

"Let's take him with us," Bunny said.

I threw my hands up in the air. "Now there's a serious pain in the ass. Why couldn't you have dropped him on a bigger rock?"

Bunny shrugged. "Thou shalt not kill."

"So you leave it to us?"

Quinn ignored us, stroking his beard and thinking. "How about we take him with us past the mine field and leave him there? The mines will protect him from the bears and lions. We'll pick him up on the way back."

"Pick him up and do what with him?" I asked. "Keep him prisoner on our trip? And what about when we get back to the meadow?"

"We'll deal with that when the time comes. Granny will know what to do." Quinn kicked Bane in the ass, and the would-be kidnapper opened his eyes and groaned.

"Where's Greagor?" asked Bane.

"He's dead," Quinn said, "And you should be too. Don't forget that." Quinn tied Bane's wrists behind his back and pulled him to his feet. Pointing at Bunny, he said, "You owe that woman your life, and that can change at any moment."

Bane looked at Bunny and spit, hitting the ground by her feet. "Don't need no Joe bitch mercy, but you sure will when the Doman finds out you killed his son."

Bunny ignored Bane and absently clutched her seed. "Thank you," she said to Quinn. "You're a good man."

We headed back to camp. I felt a bit sick to my stomach. Bane had spoken the simple truth. The Doman of South was powerful, and he was in bed with the Josephites. If he found out Quinn had a hand in Greagor's death, he could cause all manner of trouble for us.

When we approached the area, a strong odor assaulted my nose. I put my hand up to stop the others and signaled them to be silent with a finger to my lips. Bane protested, but Quinn quickly muffled him with a hand over his mouth.

Creeping forward, glad to be downwind, I saw the massive hulk of the Dixie bear—a pale mountain of silver with dark circles around its eyes. The hell spawn of arctic tundra and savage wilderness. Absorbed with its task of dragging Greagor's body to its stash, it didn't even acknowledge my presence. Once it disappeared into the forest, I brought the others back to camp.

The last hours of the night were restless ones for all of us. Quinn and I took turns keeping watch while Bunny tossed on her burrow of pine needles and Bane fretted at his bonds. When the first sunshine lightened the sky, we all gave up on sleep.

While the rabbit bones from the night before boiled to make our breakfast broth, I dabbed a spot of water at my face and hands in an effort to freshen up. Then I did my best to clean the blood off Quinn's shirt. He had been lucky, and most of it had sprayed away from him.

The rabbit broth was thin and unsatisfying, but no one had the bad taste to complain except Bane. Somehow, we didn't have enough to share with him. That didn't stop Bunny from offering him hers, though.

"No way," I said. "If you don't want yours, give it to us. Bane can live a few days on water until we get back with the factory bars."

Bunny looked at Quinn for support, and Quinn shrugged his shoulders. "Hey, I was ready to kill the guy, so he's lucky to be getting air right now, much less our food."

Bunny squirmed a bit, staring at the collapsible bowl full of broth. When she next glanced up at me, I gave her what I hoped was a good imitation of Granny's Eyebrow of Impending Doom. Finally, clutching her pendant with one hand, she held the bowl to her lips and drank half. Then she handed the other half to Bane.

I rolled my eyes and shook my head but didn't bother to protest any further.

We covered our faces with our scarves and descended into the smoke and ash that had settled into Land Mine Canyon. Quinn led with Bane in tow, his hands tied in back of him and a rope around his neck to keep him from running.

Soon the volcano's discharge enveloped us, and I could taste the smoke in the air. Our visibility decreased to about a hundred feet before we reached the bottom.

Quinn put up his hand for us to halt. Handing me Bane's rope, he disappeared into the haze and returned a moment later to guide us to the sign at the entrance of the field—a drawing of a person being lifted in the air by an explosion.

When Bane saw it, he balked, only to be pulled backward by Quinn's hand on the leash.

"You can't make me go through there," said Bane. "No way."

"Can you tighten that enough to keep him from talking?" I asked.

Bunny clutched her seed. "Isn't there an alternative?"

Between lack of sleep, an empty stomach, my own fear of the minefield, and two too many extras on an emergency run for food, I was out of patience. "Bane, shut up. You don't get a vote. And Bunny, if you want an alternative, you can stay here and play with the animals until we come back. Any other route would leave my people hungry for days, and neither one of you counts as much as they do."

"But these are land mines." Bunny spoke as if to a child.

"Thank you, Captain Duh."

Quinn shot me a warning glance, and I toned it down.

"Look," I said. "We have a solid path if you just stick to it. I've been through here a hundred times and never had a problem." I put my hand on Bunny's shoulder to comfort her.

"But what if one goes off?" she asked.

Quinn stepped up beside me, ignoring Bane, who futilely fussed at the knots that bound his hands. "Then it goes off. But you either stay here and wait, or you take that chance with us.

We're leaving now."

Bunny took hold of her seed and prayed, a habit I was beginning to find annoying. But when she opened her eyes she seemed to be calmer. "I will go with you."

"Good," I said. "Let's get on with it."

I studied the field through the ashy haze, assessing what we were up against that morning. A light wind down off the mountain promised to push the murk ahead of us. Sparse vegetation populated the landscape, interspersed with a few rusty metal objects protruding from the ground—mines that the shifting of two decades had lifted and exposed. Others had sunk down just as far. Seemingly random posts scattered the field, but I knew they weren't random at all. They were our only indication of the safe path through.

Quinn pointed to the closest post and explained to Bunny. "This is where we start. The field is about a third of a mile wide and about one hundred yards deep. We'll go one at a time with plenty of room between so we don't all die if one goes off."

Bunny shuddered beside me, and I heard Bane's gulp.

Quinn continued. "I'll go first. Then Bane twenty feet behind me. Then Bunny, and Archer bringing up the rear."

With no further ado, he entered the field.

"Okay, Bane, your turn," I said when Quinn had reached the second post out. Bane hesitated, looking like he was about to barf. I added, "You know, I'll bet that Dixie is about finished with Greagor by now."

That did it. He entered the field, and when he reached the end of the leash, I dropped my end.

When he was about twenty feet in, I signaled Bunny to go.

"Please," she said, her hands pressed together. "Please let me stay with you."

I saw how she trembled, and it occurred to me that she might balk and run wild if I wasn't holding onto her. "All right. Hold onto the pack, but don't pull on it. That's really annoying."

"God and Michael bless you." She moved behind me, and,

true to her word, I could barely feel her hand on my pack. I sighted on the first post and entered the field before she could think about it any longer.

The smoke obscured Quinn, but Bane was all too visible. "Hurry up, Bane. I want you well in front of us in case you screw up and set something off."

His voice was near panic. "I can't find the next post . . . I can't . . . oh, wait. There it is."

He still didn't move. I took out my knife and aimed. "Bane, you walk, or you'll drop. I've had it with you."

Seeing I meant business, he started forward. Bunny and I sighted in the second post and turned forty-five degrees to meet it.

"Good job, Bunny," I said when we reached our goal. "You see that next post where Bane is turning? That's where we're aiming at now."

Her eyes big, she glanced about nervously. I thought a distraction might help. I took her hand and held it behind me, and I walked forward. "So, Bunny. Tell me about your world. What was your normal Josephite day like?"

She seemed glad for something to think about besides the mines. "I would get up at six o'clock for morning prayers and breakfast with my father, Joshua. Then I would roll him into our garden, and he would read to me from the Bible. That was always our special time together."

"Roll?" I asked. It made no sense to me.

"Father's legs were paralyzed in an accident. That's when Joseph cast him aside in favor of his brothers."

"Oh. I'm sorry to hear he's crippled. That must be hard."

"It's okay. He's not crippled. He just can't walk."

We turned at a post and sighted on the next one. I could still see Bane two stops ahead, but no sign of Quinn. I found that rather disturbing.

I asked the next question as much to distract myself as to distract Bunny. "What would you do after breakfast?"

"I would go down the tunnel to my mother's lab where I worked with her and with my neighbor, Barbara. She was in the Underground too. Anyway, around one o'clock, my mother and I would go back to the house for lunch and midday prayers with Father."

"Wait a moment, Bunny. See that one over there?" I pointed at the next post. "That's the next one we want. Okay. Go on. What did you eat for lunch?"

"Naomi, she's my nanny, she made me strawberry smoothies every day and brought them to me in my room. I had a beautiful stained glass window there. It was a lion and a lamb lying down together in a field of mountain daisies. You know, the flowers painted on your water table."

"Do you have mountain daisies in the city?"

"No. We don't have them there, either," she said.

Reaching our goal, I pointed straight ahead. "See Bane? That's where we're going next. And look." I pointed above us on the cliff to our right. A wind had kicked up and cleared enough smoke for us to see Land Mine Rock looming out of the haze. "We're almost halfway. So why was your mother's lab in a tunnel?"

Bunny paused a moment before she answered. "Mother was a bioengineer. She was working on developing new strains of seeds for the Underground. That's why Joseph wanted to shut us down. You see, he knew we made—"

Before Bunny could finish, a sickening lurch beneath my feet jolted my stomach. She bolted against my grip, and I threw her down on the trail beneath me, pinning her with my body while the aftershock rocked our world.

The ground shook for an eternity, rattling us like a squirrel in Daisy's teeth. Then, as soon as it began to subside, I heard it. A resounding crack that shattered my ears.

Above me, almost in slow motion, Land Mine Rock bounced off the cliffside and plummeted directly toward the minefield. And us.

CHAPTER 13

UNABLE TO RUN, I covered Bunny with my body and my own head with my arms. The boulder hit the field and bounced. A mine exploded, blowing chunks of the rock in every direction. Some stayed where they landed, and others rolled, setting off more mines in their wake.

Certain I would die any moment, I hunkered over Bunny, surprised by my own calm and acceptance. Would Quinn survive? Would he get enough food to save our people? And Granny. Would she survive without me?

A mine exploded fifteen feet away. Dirt rained down. Then the canyon filled with a deafening silence. Finally I hazarded a glance. The smoke had intensified ahead on the trail, obscuring any sight of Bane.

"Arr—cherr." My ears were still ringing, and Quinn's voice sounded like it was at the end of a long tunnel.

"Here. We're here. Me and Bunny. Bane, are you there?"

After a moment of silence, Bunny became frantic, pushing me up and away from her. "Dear Michael, he's dead. We have to go back."

Still on my knees above her, I gripped her shoulder firmly and looked her in the eye, trying to channel Granny. "Enough of that. The only way out is through, and that kind of nonsense will get us killed. Now. We will stand up, you will put your hand on my pack, and you will not let go. Do you understand?"

Quivering like an aspen leaf in a Chinook wind, she nodded her assent. I stood and turned toward the next post and gave Bunny a pack strap to hold onto, focusing on nothing but the tall steel bar reaching for the sky in front of me.

When we neared it, I saw Quinn standing in the path, staring toward a hole about twelve feet away. Bane's body lay flat out on the ground, just off the trail.

"Is he dead? Dear Michael, is he dead?" Bunny's voice was about three pitches higher than normal.

"I can't reach him to tell," Quinn said. "Bane? Bane?"

His leg, bent backward, quivered, and I couldn't tell from my position if he was trying to move it or if those were death rattles. His arms, still tied at the wrists, twisted in an unnatural angle that turned my stomach. Shrapnel protruded from his shoulder and legs, and blood oozed from a head wound.

Quinn shook his head and took a step toward us. "He's dead. Stay where you are. Archer, don't let Bunny see this."

Bane's pack had settled in the trail near the next post, which had been knocked into the path by a flying rock. Quinn picked up the pack and set the post back in place, propping it with rocks before coming back to us. "You two let me get ahead again before you follow. Hang tough, Bunny. We're almost out of here."

"I don't think he's dead," Bunny said. "His hand moved."

"Stop looking, Bunny. Just pick a spot on my pack and stare at it. Like Quinn said, you don't need to see him like this."

"We can't leave him. We should at least bury him if he's dead."

"Too much risk. These are two-step mines. They don't explode when you step on them; they explode when you take your foot off. He might be on top of one, and I'm not going to die for a dead guy. Now come on. Hold the pack strap, and don't let go."

My own nerves stretched to the limit, I faked a confidence I did not feel when I moved past Bane toward the next post. Soon we saw the hull of the burned-out army jeep that marked the edge of the minefield. The wind coming off the mountain had lifted the smoke a bit, and we were able to take down our scarves to breathe.

When we crossed through a newly sown hemp field planted by the Secs of South, we startled a couple of rabbits and a slow snake. I let the snake go, but the rabbits weren't so lucky. I did refrain from comparing them to Bunny though.

Reaching Old Highway 93, I took out the woven brown scarf I had packed, as well as a pair of old sunglasses and a small jar of pimple sap, a gooey, light brown concoction Makenzie made for her teen children. "Across that road is Joe Land. Sorry, Bunny. You have to put these on now."

She took the scarf from me and stared at it in her hands for a moment. "We were always told you wear these to keep yourselves apart from us. I never knew you had to do it for protection." With no further ado, she wrapped the scarf across her face the way Granny had shown her.

By dusk, we were halfway through the gassplant fields with their endless rows of windmills. They always reminded me of a picture of terracotta soldiers in one of Granny's books, ever attentive and in perfect order, perpetually ready to respond aggressively to the slightest breeze of fortune.

The young gassplant crop stood three feet high in rows of clumps—genetically engineered and cloned fuel, straight from the hand of the Archangel Michael to Joseph.

Clusters of Josephite widows and orphans busily weeded the young crop under the watchful eyes of their male guards. The women, their permanently bent frames clothed in identical brown hemp dresses, bobbed up and down with their hoes like feeding birds. Most of them barely glanced our way when we strode through in single file, though an occasional worker used us as a reason to pause and wipe the sweat and dirt from her brow with the edge of her apron. In contrast, the children stopped and openly stared, pointed, and whispered to each other until gruff voices ordered them back to work.

Ignoring those most unfortunate of Josephites, Quinn and I passed through the small, scattered groups of laborers as we would pass through the trees in the forest, neither staring, nor allowing ourselves to forget that the forest held dangers.

Bunny, however, gawked behind her veil and sunglasses, turning her head constantly, sometimes slowing until Quinn or I gave her a nudge. She seemed to be particularly interested in the compound itself with its supersized greenhouses sprawling across the plains.

We were almost past the bulk of them, a good half a mile from their camp, when a middle-aged woman dropped her hoe and reached for the hose of her water pack. So hot and red that she had quit sweating, she fell to her knees, struggling to suck the last drop.

Quick as a snake in July, Bunny took out her canteen and closed the gap between herself and the woman. Quinn and I leapt after her, but we were too late.

Seeing Bunny only feet away, the Josephite woman threw her fingers up in front of her in the Cross of Michael. "Get thee from me, Sec!"

Bunny, stopped cold by the woman's hostile command, staggered backward and tripped. I caught her arm to keep her from falling, and Quinn scooped her up and threw her over his shoulder.

Then a voice boomed over us. "What in the name of the Prophet is this?"

CHAPTER 14

I TURNED AROUND, AND my jaw dropped. Standing before me was the largest human I'd ever seen, and he was a Josephite camp guard. I had to tip my head back to look him in the eye. He had black hair, dark skin, and a ragged scar across his left cheek, and his muscles could have challenged a Dixie bear. And he had friends. Three friends.

The Josephite woman crawled toward the giant. Stepping to her, he lifted her up more gently than I could have imagined. Her accusation was barely audible. "That Sec. She attacked me."

I took mental inventory of my weapons. My bow was taken down and in my pack. No good to me. Two knives at hand. Maybe if I started with the big one . . . but I knew it was no good. Not only were there four of them, but more Josephites immediately collected in a circle around us.

Quinn set Bunny down and stepped between her and the guards. "Please. She was only trying to give this woman some water. You can see she's dehydrated."

The giant looked skeptical. "What filthy Sec would ever give water to a child of the Prophet?"

"She attacked me," the woman repeated. "She was going to

strike me with her canteen, but I stopped her with my Cross of Michael." She once more held up her hands in front of her with her fingers making the sign.

The giant took a step closer. "Sounds like we need to teach a few Secs a lesson."

My heart pounded. Bunny cowered close to me, and I hoped they wouldn't beat her, too. I searched the circle around us, looking for the weak link. Maybe we could run for it.

To my surprise, Quinn suddenly relaxed and smiled at mountainous man. "Go ahead and try, Luke. You never could beat me," he said.

The giant squinted and studied Quinn. Then he grinned. "Quinn? Is that really you? We all thought you died." Luke stepped forward and took Quinn up in some manly cross between a bear hug and a back slap.

"Nah," Quinn said. "It'd take more than a few jacked-up camp rats to get rid of me. Damn. You've grown up."

The giant turned to his henchmen. "Hey, guys. This wild Sec here used to be a big brother to me." He pointed to the scar on his face. "If it wasn't for him, this would have been through my heart. He taught me poker, too, back when I was just a kid."

The other guards still appeared skeptical, and a rough-looking blonde spit on the ground and said, "That's even more reason to beat the crap out of him."

Luke scowled at him. "Not on my watch." He looked around the group of workers and guards and raised his voice. "Get back to work, you lazy scabs. God made you so he could give the world enemas."

With a few murmurs and backward glances, the Josephites obeyed him.

Under his breath, Luke added to Quinn, "I have to say stuff like that to keep my job." Then he turned his attention to Bunny. "I see you went native. That your woman?"

"Her? No, no. She's his cousin." Quinn jerked a thumb toward me. "My good friend, Archer, and his cousin, Bunny.

She's never been out of the meadow before, and she's kind of slow. She didn't know she wasn't supposed to talk to the Prophet's children. She saw that woman over there needed a drink of water."

"Well, that was decent of her, in spite of her being a Sec, and all. No offense," said Luke. "Where you headed?"

Quinn stepped back with us and gently guided us in front of him in a clear gesture of departure, "Down to the Box. Sorry I can't stay and talk. We've got to get our seeds back to the meadow for spring planting."

"Well, then, Prophet's speed be with you," said Luke. "And keep your eyes open. The Swords are looking for a woman. The Prophet's own granddaughter, in fact. If you find her, they might give you an extra allotment."

"Hey, thanks. I'll be sure to keep a look out," Quinn answered. "Good to see you, Luke," he said with genuine warmth.

Luke gave him a light back slap. "You, too, Quinn. Stop back by one of these days, and I'll take your money."

Quinn laughed. "Right. You and who else? Take care, buddy."

Quinn calmly shepherded us down the rows of gassplant. We silently covered ground for the short time until it was dusk, when the camp horn wailed its call to the workers to end their day.

Once we were alone in the fields, I could hold my tongue no longer. "Seriously, Quinn? All the times we've been past that camp, and you never told me that was the one you ran from?"

Quinn shrugged. "Didn't seem important."

"Well, it was important today. I don't know what those Joes would have done . . . Well, actually, I do know." I rounded on Bunny. "And you. What were you thinking? We never talk to the Joes. We don't look at them. We don't think about them, and we sure as hell don't give them our water."

Bunny pulled off her veil and sunglasses. With her jaw set,

her voice was firm. "The woman was ill. She was going to pass out. I don't apologize."

I stopped and stared at her, aghast. "You don't apologize? I freakin' save your life, even putting you ahead of my own people, and you're ready to throw me away for one of yours?"

She glared at me straight in the eye. "I have no people. There is only right and wrong, and I did what was right."

"You bitch!" It was all I could do not to slap her. My people and I were laying it down for her, and she didn't value our lives as much as she valued the people who had betrayed her. I was ready to turn her in myself.

I felt Quinn's hand on my arm, and he spoke as if to children. "That's enough. Look, Bunny. I appreciate your compassion. I really do. But you have to act like a Sec. Secs only talk to Joes if Joes speak to them first. That was a good way to get us killed back there."

Bunny's brow knit, and she reached for her seed, thinking. When she finally spoke, there was no hint of anger or rebellion. "I'm sorry. I didn't know it was like that. That's not what I was taught."

"Hey, wait a minute. Why will you hear it from him and not from me?" I put my hands on my hips.

She met my eye, and her calm raised my ire even further. "Because he was polite."

"Oh, you've got some nerve—"

Quinn cut me off. "Enough. When are you going to learn, Archer? It's not what you say, it's how you say it. Now let's get going, and no more fighting. The last thing I need is you two acting like she-cats in a tote sack." He turned and started out at a traveling jog without checking to see if we followed.

Bunny didn't move. "Is it far?" she asked. Something about the exhaustion in her voice broke through my irritation. She started rubbing her temples, and, for the first time that day, I noticed how bedraggled she was. Her shoulders slumped in her filthy, rumpled dress, and her back bent as if the pack would break her. I was tired too, but not nearly as tired as she was.

"Here, Bunny, let me help you with your pack. It isn't far now—only a mile or so to an old well house where we can eat our rabbits and spend the night. It's safer than staying in the fields."

She took off her pack and sat down. I gave her my canteen. "You can do this, Bunny."

Sighing, she looked down. I lifted her head and gazed into her eyes, willing my energy into her. "You can do this thing."

She closed her eyes and rested her head on my hand. Then she nodded and stood. "Yes. Yes, I can. Thank you."

***

AFTER A QUIET NIGHT of exhausted sleep, we woke before dawn and slipped through the fields to the road that ran along Defender's Wall, the dividing line between the civilized and the savage. It was a matter of opinion as to which side was which.

Crouched low in the gassplant, I surveyed the area in the growing light of morning. In the northern distance, tall, cylindrical Vertical Farms surrounded the Big Box warehouse complex. To the south, one small group of Secs from South Meadow approached on the road. No Joes in sight. Our timing was perfect.

"Okay, Bunny," I said, checking her headscarf one last time to make sure it was firmly anchored. Only her sunglasses peeped out between the folds.

Quinn shouldered his pack. "Don't talk if you can avoid it, Bunny. It's about five miles to the Big Box. Walk with your head low and stay between me and Archer. Let's go."

"Wait." Bunny took her pendant in her hand and bowed her head.

"Bunny," Quinn said, his voice urgent, "we need to go."

"No. It's all right," I said. Bunny's hand shook as she held her pendant, the motion resonating with my own discomfort with what we were doing. "One more minute won't hurt," I told Quinn. I used the pause Bunny created to take a deep breath and center myself.

Bunny finished her prayer. "I can do this now," she said with more calm than I felt.

"Yes, I know you can." I knew nothing of the sort. "But you need to hide that necklace of yours, and don't take it out again. No Sec would have one. Ready?"

Bunny tucked her necklace inside her tunic. "God is with us," she said. "We will be okay."

"Watch the 'God' thing," I said, checking the road again. The small group of Southerns I'd seen earlier was now north of us, but another, larger group flocked toward us in the distance to the south. It was time. "Let's go."

Bunny tried gamely to keep up, but the days had worn her down with all of the travel and nothing to eat but a couple mouthfuls of scrawny rabbit and a few bear bars. We were running a full day behind schedule. Quinn and I exchanged worried glances more than once, but there was nothing we could do. It was clear from the way she dragged her feet that Bunny had no more to give than she was already giving.

Swifter travelers passed us throughout the early morning. Some were Southerns, mostly men, walking and bicycling with their packs of trade goods. Some were camp Joes, mostly women, packed by the dozens into the backs of creeping old farm trucks. Occasionally, a Josephite military or Temple vehicle buzzed by, parting the people on the road and coating us with dust.

Now and again, passing Southern acquaintances waved a greeting to Quinn. The Southerns were known to be Josephite sympathizers since the Joes put their textile factories in Southtown. The rest of us Secs saw them as Joe-sucking traitors like Bane and Greagor had been.

Unbidden, my mind flashed on my last sight of Greagor,

his broken body gripped in the massive jaws of the Dixie bear. South would not take kindly to the killing, no matter what he was trying to do to us.

And Bane. I didn't look forward to telling Harmony her son had died in the minefield. She was already out for my blood. As much as I despised her, I didn't like my own meadow being an emotional war zone.

Quinn's voice pulled me out of my thoughts. "Hang in there, Bunny. We'll find a place to rest a while once we get inside."

The Vertical Farms loomed large when we drew close to the Big Box. Two cylinders stood along each of the north and south fences, and four more lined up along Defender's Wall behind the large warehouse. Seven stories tall and completely enclosed, they contained the climate-controlled environments where the Josephites grew food for the work camps. Though I couldn't see them over the wall, I knew countless more of those cement cylinders fed the occupants of Promise City year round so that the entirety of the plains could be devoted to the gassplant the Joes needed for fuel.

The Big Box was turning a brisk business when we arrived just past dawn-thirty. Guards in tidy brown hemp uniforms of simple button shirts and pants kept watch on either side of the two security gates leading into the enormous trade warehouse where venders hocked their wares and Josephites bartered for Sec goods. But most importantly, the Big Box held the Seed Vault. It was the only place where Secs could obtain seeds beyond the hemp the field monitors issued each year.

Dozens of camp Joe women clustered about the Joe entrance, laughing and joking. Their line moved quickly, the Readers scanning the microchips embedded in their necks—chips like the one Bunny had cut out the day she ran. Children of all ages tumbled around them, fussing, playing, and clinging to their brown skirts.

We fell into the Sec line, which was a long, silent, single file made up mostly of men. An occasional veiled woman stood with a male family member, her eyes and head lowered, looking as small and inconspicuous as possible. There were no Sec children in our line.

Bunny stared about, her veil and sunglasses doing little to hide her frank curiosity. "Slouch and look at the ground," I whispered in her ear. Nodding, she gave it a shot, but soon her head was back up, and she gawked about, radiating her natural confidence and causing me to remind her once more to tone it down.

After we checked our weapons, we approached our first barrier, parcel search. I put the trade pack through the screener and walking under the detector arch, grateful for the delicate Josephite sensibilities that demanded they develop a way to detect weapons without rewarding the guards with a crotch shot that would reveal my deception.

Once inside the vendor area, I put my pack back on with practiced speed, watching Bunny from the corner of my eye. Her proud carriage made me cringe, and I lowered my head, as if my own act could lower hers. She was entirely too presumptuous, facing the guards while handing them her pack and passing proudly under the detector arch, her head high.

Clearly amused at what would have been forward behavior for a Sec woman, a parcel search guard left Quinn waiting on the far side of the arch while he picked up Bunny's pack and walked around the end of the counter with it. "Here, let me help you with this," he offered congenially, holding up the pack for her to put on. She turned her back on him and held out her arms in a natural gesture, as if he were helping her with her coat.

Sensing imminent disaster, I jumped to Bunny's side, even as the guard grabbed her ass, but I wasn't quick enough. She spun on him, and the slap on his face resounded through the courtyard.

CHAPTER 2

CRYING OUT, THE GUARD backhanded Bunny to the ground. I yanked her behind me like a sack of seeds and infused my voice with all the venom I could muster. "You act like a whore."

Quinn tried to get through security to us but was barred by a rifle.

We had the full attention of both Secs and Joes in the courtyard. I faced the Josephite guard, keeping Bunny behind me. Bunny's handprint lit up his face, and the other guards laughed at his expense.

He turned to his friends and roared like a wounded Dixie bear. "Did you see that? That skank slapped me." Rounding on us, he pulled his knife. I backed away, almost falling over Bunny, who was scrambling up from the ground behind me.

"Yeah, I saw what happened." Another guard stepped up, mirth making his features appear almost kind. "What have I told you about playing with the trash? You'd be better off grabbing a dog's ass than wasting seed on a Sec anyway. Now get back to work. And you . . ." He turned to me, and his face and voice became ugly. "Keep your bitch on a leash or leave her at home."

"Yes, sir. Thank you, sir," I said.

I hustled Bunny behind the man selling boots made of hemp and tire rubber and a woman laying out hemp lollipops. Quinn was with us by the time we reached a quiet corner. I was too angry and rattled to speak while he drew us close and shielded us from view.

"Bunny," he said, "you'll kill all of us. Everyone who has helped you. You *have* to be like a Sec woman."

Bunny sniffed, tears slipping out from under her sunglasses and down into the scarf across her face, but there was an edge to her voice when she spoke. "Are you saying that was my fault? How could you think that?"

Quinn implored me with his eyes, and I knew he was at a loss to explain woman matters to her.

I saw no benefit to pulling punches. "Yes, it was your fault. Was it right? No. It's just the way things are. Look around. Do you see any other Sec women holding their heads up and looking those guards in the eye? No. You're swimming with sharks now, and you'd best not bleed. Suck it up and keep your head down no matter how it hurts your pride because this just isn't about you any more."

Bunny took off her sunglasses and wiped away her tears, smearing the pimple sap that helped hide her features. "Okay. I'm sorry." Putting the glasses back on, she lowered her head with resignation, and when we walked again, she slouched her shoulders and shuffled her feet in a perfect imitation of the Sec women around us.

It tore at my heart. For some reason, it hurt me more to see her surrender her pride than it did to see the women of our people, who were never allowed pride in the first place. Disguised as a man, I never covered my face or kowtowed like other Sec women. Watching Bunny yield, knowing what it must have cost her, I felt I was the one who had surrendered instead, and everything in me wanted to cry out at the injustice.

Inside the building, we were overwhelmed with smells.

Cooking smells. Barbeque, cakes, breads, cookies . . . sample tables everywhere, manned by little old blue-haired ladies in white dresses with yellow-checked gingham aprons emblazoned with the logo "Esther Widows." Crowds of camp Joes crowded around them, scooping up the goodies before they could even hit the serving trays. There were no Secs there. Secs were not allowed the samples—not unless we converted.

A slick preacher with his high, white collar and his silver Cross of Michael on his chest stood nearby holding his Book of Joseph and his loaf of white, fluffy bread, ready to share the word and a meal with Secs who wanted to atone for their sins.

I'd seen it once. A mother with seven children, almost crawling with their hunger. She was from a "Sinning Meadow." One the Joes had punished with starvation for not meeting their hemp quotas the previous year. She offered the Preacher herself for Atonement if he would only save her children. The Preacher blessed her and gave her family the loaf of bread. Then he sent her to the fires and her children to a work camp, except for one, a pretty adolescent girl named Delilah. She was sold to Maverick's.

Quinn and Bunny stood behind me in the line at the trade window where I was to exchange our goods for credits to use in the store and the Seed Vault. At the pricing station, I placed my finger on the ancient print scanner for identification and heard a female computer voice. "Sprague, Archer. Male. Middle Meadow. Dark brown hair, gray eyes, five feet, eleven inches tall, one hundred forty-two pounds, twenty-one years of age." The evaluator, satisfied that I was Archer Sprague, pulled up my blinker account on his screen.

He peered at me over his reading glasses, his voice as cold and impersonal as the computer's. "Your balance is one hundred forty-seven credits. Do you have any trade goods?"

I emptied the contents of the trade pack onto the desk— bone and pottery jewelry, leather wallets, woven swaths of cloth, carved antler combs, and Makenzie's dancing animal sweaters that the high-class Joes like Bunny wore—quality goods that we had spent the winter making. We knew the Josephites would offer us a pittance for them and then turn around and sell them at a thousand times markup to upper-class Josephite society, who wanted to distinguish themselves with hand-crafted items.

The evaluator carefully sifted through the articles, keeping a tally on his calculator. I had no say in the process. There was no standard, and the price was up to each evaluator's discretion.

When Granny, Quinn, and I had tallied up the goods before we left, we calculated a minimum of two thousand credits. Enough to buy around five hundred factory bars and a few extra seeds beyond our allotment of beans, corn, and squash. I'd never dealt with this fellow before, though, so I had no idea what to expect. I waited quietly, not wanting to show weakness by talking too much.

Finally he spoke in a distracted tone. "One thousand five hundred for the lot of it."

My jaw dropped. It was all I could do not to fly across the counter at him. "You're clearly new at this because that can't be right. Didn't you see the quality?"

Quinn hushed me with a glare and stepped up to calm the situation. "Please, sir. Would you mind looking again? We bring these items here often, and we're wondering if there might have been a mistake."

A man with a red supervisor's beret stepped up and looked over the evaluator's shoulder. "What's going on here?"

"These Secs don't think my price is fair," said the evaluator.

The red beret glanced our way and said, "The price is the price. Take it or leave it."

I panicked. We had to have at least four hundred and fifty of the bars if our people were going to survive. I was about to plead our case when I felt a nudge at my arm and looked down. Bunny held out her hand, holding a pair of woven gold earrings. They were a match to Granny's Bucellati necklace that we kept under the floorboards, and I knew right away where she'd gotten them. They were her grandmother's.

I felt Quinn's hand move away, and I knew he had seen them too. Though it momentarily flashed through my mind that we might be jailed for having kept valuables during the Exile, I had to try. Taking them from her hand, I held them out to the supervisor. "These, too. How much for these?"

Red Beret peered at the earrings and then at Bunny. "Where did you get these?"

"They were—" I started, but he put his hand up to stop me. "I asked the girl," he said.

Bunny kept her head low, but her words were soft and clear. "They were my grandmother's. I'm newly arrived here from the Borders to marry. Those earrings are my dowry."

She took hold of my arm to indicate I was her fiancé. I patted her protectively on her hand.

Red Beret eyed us suspiciously. "So why are you parting with them?"

Bunny said, "My fiancé's people are hungry. The Swords of Michael came to their meadow and destroyed all of their food. They need the money to buy factory bars to feed their people until the crops come in."

The supervisor's eyes narrowed. He turned to the evaluator. "You may go on break. I will handle this."

He sat down in the evaluator's chair and examined our goods, running the cloth between his fingers and checking the weight and suppleness of the leather wallets. After close examination, he said, "Two thousand seven hundred twenty for the contents of the pack. Another three thousand for the earrings."

Over five thousand credits. That was more than we'd ever had before. But the earrings. They matched Granny's necklace. I knew Bunny was telling the truth when she said she got them from her grandmother and that they were meant to be her dowry some day. I had seen the contents of her travel pack, and she didn't have much. She would still have to pay a coyote to take her to Mexifornia and then set up a life there.

Before I could change my mind, I reached out for the earrings and handed them to Bunny. "Here, hon. You keep these for your dowry. We'll do fine now that we have a fair assessment."

I turned to Red Beret. "Thank you."

He ignored my gratitude, charged the credits to my blinker, and then looked past us to the line. "Next."

We didn't speak until we were well into the depths of the warehouse, walking down aisles of woven hemp dresses, hemp shoes, and kitchen utensils that lay between us and the factory bars. Finally I had to ask. "What happened back there, Bunny? Why was he nice to us?"

To my surprise, Quinn laughed and answered for her. "Didn't you see the chain on his neck going under his shirt? There was a seed on the end of it, like hers."

Bunny's whisper held the smile that was hidden by her veil. "Exactly. He's part of the Underground. The Swords of Michael hunt us down. I was hoping he would be sympathetic if I mentioned your persecution."

I put one arm around her and gave her a hug, a new appreciation blooming in my heart. "You know. You might be all right after all. Now if you two will go get the factory bars, I'll get the seeds. We can be back on the road home by noon."

Bunny's shoulders sagged, and her gaze dropped, reminding me how exhausted she was. "You know," I said, "If we hurry, we'll have time to rest a bit before we have to go."

We definitely had no such time. It would take us at least two days to get back, and even then I didn't know if the Josephite patrol that Norris left behind would be gone. I was already thinking of caves where we could install Bunny if we had to. But with both her feet and her traveling spirit dragging, I knew it would only take longer if we didn't let her rest a bit, and, truth be told, Quinn and I needed it too.

My stomach rumbled, and I did my best to ignore the delectable smells emanating from the sample tables while I passed through the warehouse toward the iron gates and armed guards of the Seed Ministry Auxiliary Station. I hated buying the seeds, but I knew Quinn was even more claustrophobic than I was, so I always volunteered for the job. Nevertheless, my hands started sweating when I approached the Vault.

Turning up the collar of my turtleneck to hide my pulse, I stepped to the first gate and gave my empty trade pack to the guard for inspection. I walked under the bio-detector arch, which registered my exact amount of organic material, both my body and anything I carried. It was accurate down to a single seed, even one as small as Bunny's mustard seed.

The guard lifted the bar on the entry gate, and I flinched at the metal-on-metal scrape. It clanked shut behind me, and, for a brief moment, I couldn't breathe. I was a prisoner inside the vault of seeds with my one exit locked until my enemies chose to open it and let me out. For a wild hill woman, it was like being buried alive.

As quickly as possible, I purchased okra, tomato, and yam seeds to supplement the allotment of corn, beans, and squash the field monitor would deliver. With the extra credits I had, thanks to Bunny's clever thinking back at the trade window, I added in a small packet of green chili seeds. Filling my trade pack and thinking of the bounty we would have this year made it easier to ignore the hollow in my stomach. I was ready to get to a factory bar.

I stepped from the vault and exhaled a breath I didn't realize I was holding. Then I hurried to meet up with Quinn and Bunny. They had the bars. Five hundred of them. I had no idea what five hundred looked like until I saw them stacked like cement bricks in the cart.

"Damn," I said. "I'll only say this once. I am not looking forward to carrying all that for two days to get home. Let's pay for this and then rest our feet a minute."

We paid for our factory bars and turned in the blinker. Then we bought three tickets for the holoscreen, a massive rectangle that generated 3-D images and played whatever the Josephites were broadcasting at that moment. Quinn and I had no particular interest in the goings-on of Joe Land, but for one credit each, we could enjoy cushioned seats with adjustable backs. The idea of getting in a good nap before another two-day journey was worth putting up with the Joes for a few minutes.

Two dozen camp Joes and a handful of Esther Widows and Big Box employees on their lunch break crowded into the choice Josephite section where they had the best view of *Kingdom Idol*, the show that was playing. I'd seen it once or twice before. It was a contest between preachers, and the Josephites voted for the best one. I found their nonsense comical, but only because if I didn't laugh at it, I would cry with despair.

We headed for the partitioned Sec area toward the front, a place where the 3-D always looked like a squashed oblong because of the angle. Unfortunately, the smattering of Secs blocked the remaining seats, and we had to crawl past them to reach our destination. I was glad to see they were from South, so we had no need to make up excuses for choosing the seats furthest away from them.

Bunny became quite animated when she saw that we would catch the last half of *Idol*, and her whisper was a bit too loud. "This is my favorite show. I hope Pastor Bob wins. I got to meet him once, you know."

"Shhh." I put my hand over her veil where I thought her mouth was and leaned close to her, glad for the darkness when a sour-looking Esther Widow three rows back turned her full attention our way. "Bunny, you can't say things like that. People are staring."

I glanced over my shoulder and saw the Widow pointing at us and talking to her friend. Suddenly I wasn't quite so tired. "Quinn, we should go. People are staring."

He took a look from the corner of his eye. "They're just gossiping old women. Look, we all need the rest. It's okay. They won't know what to think of what she said, but Bunny, you can't to that again."

Bunny nodded her assent, and we turned to the show. We each ate a factory bar, and then Quinn rocked back, put his hat over his eyes, and presumably went to sleep. Bunny sat in rapt attention, watching the show, and I kept an eye on the widows behind me.

Finally satisfied they were no harm, I closed my eyes and drifted off to haunted dreams of Dixie bears and land mines. Smoke filled my restless imaginings, and talk of fire.

Suddenly a scream shattered my sleep. Bunny grabbed my arm and wrenched it, and I opened my eyes to see a fireball shooting toward us across the room.

CHAPTER 16

I JUMPED OVER THE back of my seat, dragging Bunny with me. Then I realized the inferno was coming from the holoscreen. Quinn flew over his own seat and pulled Bunny up from where she huddled in the floor with her hands over her head, quivering and crying, a slave to her pyrophobia.

"Stupid Sec thought it was real." Laughter erupted around us, and a Josephite threw his drink on us. "That'll put your fire out."

I wiped the sticky beverage from my eyes in time to see the sour Esther Widow behind us curl her lip and start pushing past the others in the row.

"Let's go," I hissed, afraid the Widow was calling a guard. I grabbed my pack and shoved through the Southerns blocking my path in my effort to reach the door before the Widow did. Quinn picked up Bunny and carried her behind me. Fortunately, we were far more agile, even with our loads, and we rushed past her row, leaving her to shake her fist at us in vain.

Quinn put Bunny down at the door, and I hid her crying face against my chest while we exited into the main warehouse. She had lost her sunglasses, but there was no way we could go back for them.

"We have to get out of here," Quinn said.

I shook my head. "No. She can't go through the gate like this. Get our stuff and meet us over at the bathrooms. I'll send her in to wash her face, and I'll have her put on some pimple sap."

"Well, keep it short. That woman looked like she wasn't finished." Quinn gave me a manly back slap, and we split up.

Bunny trembled while I steered her across the warehouse to the ladies room. "Archer, back there, I—"

"Never mind. I know the fire scares you."

A Josephite man leered at her shapely hips, and I put my arm around her protectively. Bunny didn't notice, which was just as well.

"No, it's not that," she said. "That was the news. They were showing the news. That fire—"

"It's okay. I know you're scared of the fire." I wasn't sure why she was still talking about it, but I wanted her to shut up. We were navigating through camp Joe women looking at piles of brown hemp dresses, and I didn't want her saying anything that would attract their attention.

Bunny stopped and took my sleeve. "You have to listen."

"What is it?" I asked, pulling her over to a tower of canned beets that no one was coming within ten feet of.

Tears streamed into the scarf across her face. I took off my own Maui Jim sunglasses and gave them to her.

Shaking, Bunny whispered. "That was a house fire. My friend . . . my mother's assistant—Barbara Conway—they say she was killed in that fire, but I know they took her from the lab. She must be dead. Now there's no one left but me who knows." She stopped and sniffed loudly. I drew her closer to the beets, further away from any people.

"What? Knows what?" My voice was sharper than it should have been, and though I was compassionate that she lost her friend, we really didn't have time for therapy at that moment.

Bunny leaned in close. "The seeds. My mother's work. I'm

the only one left who knows about—"

"You!" The Esther Widow stood at the edge of the beets.

I should have known she'd like canned beets.

She jabbed her finger at us. "I know your kind. You're up to no good. You stay right here," she said. She waddled away toward a guard a few aisles down as fast as her arthritic hips could take her.

I grabbed Bunny and whisked her past the rest of the canned goods, through the hardware, and behind the farming implements. Peeking back, I saw the guard arguing with the adamantly gesticulating Esther Widow on the spot where she had seen us by the beets. This was definitely a time to hide in the bathroom.

Once we got to the ladies room, I pulled the pimple sap from my pack. Leaning in close, I said, "You're going to have to go in alone. Your face is a mess. Use cold water, and don't be shy with this stuff."

Bunny shook her head, her eyes wide with fear. "No. You can't leave me."

"Look at me, Bunny." I gestured toward my clothing. "I can't go in there. Now suck it up and do what you have to do."

Sniffing, she nodded, took the pimple sap from me, and went in.

I stood there waiting, tapping my toe and shifting from one foot to the next. Suddenly I realized that I had become uncomfortable.

A camp Joe woman opened the door, nearly smacking me with it. The men had segregated bathrooms for Secs and Joes, but there were never enough Sec women around to justify the expense. That, or the women weren't worth it to them. I didn't know, but either way, this Joe woman stood there glaring like I was some degenerate demon in her midst, holding the door wide as her children filed out like little ants.

Motioning briskly with her hand, she directed them as far away from me as possible. That was fine with me, but while she held the door, the sound of flushing toilets and running water overwhelmed me. I cringed and crossed my legs. There was no denying it. I needed to pee.

But where? I couldn't go in the ladies room while I was dressed like a man. Did I have time for the men's room before Bunny came out? I'd never looked in there, but why not?

A Southern was entering, so I walked behind him, thinking I could use a stall. Apparently, though, Sec men didn't have the luxury of stalls. I found, to my dismay, the only things available were urinals and two open toilets. With three men in there, I didn't stand a chance. I was going to have to wait. I went back to my post and stood, crossing and uncrossing my legs and shifting my weight back and forth.

Bunny finally opened the door. I grabbed her and hustled her away from all of those flowing water sounds and toward the front of the warehouse where I hoped to intercept Quinn on his way to join us.

He looked excited as he approached. "I have good news. Bumped into Spooge, and he'll take us all the way to Maverick's. I had some business there anyway."

Spooge? I loved Spooge, but he thought I was a dude. I was his one true friend, but only so long as he thought he could get some man love off me one day. Bottom line in that moment? I could pee as soon as we were away from the Big Box if we were in the fields, but there was no way I could pee around Spooge.

"No. We can't. What if he recognizes Bunny? You know how jealous he is of my friendship. He'd turn her in for sure."

Quinn cocked his head and gave me an incredulous stare. "Seriously? You want to turn down a ride that would cut a day and a half off our trip when we've got this load to carry? I'm willing to take the chance if Bunny is. Now come on. He's loaded up and waiting on us. I already picked up our weapons and stashed them in the truck."

Bunny tugged at my sleeve. "I prayed for this. It's a gift

from God. I'll keep my mouth shut. Please. I'm sorry, but my feet can't take much more."

A Southern nearby tipped his canteen and glugged loudly, spilling a few drops down his shirt. *Agh.*

"But what about the Joe patrol in the meadow? They might not be gone yet."

Quinn threw up his hands. "So we'll see them before they see us. If they aren't gone, we'll hide Bunny in a cave. She can't take much more, and our people are going to be getting pretty hungry by tomorrow."

He was right. Our people needed the food. But I really was worried about what Spooge would do.

"There they are." The old Widow pointed us out to the guard, her biting voice drifting across half the warehouse.

Quinn and I simultaneously pushed Bunny toward the door. Damn. I was just going to have to hold it.

Spooge leaned against the side of Maverick's dually pickup truck, which was loaded with coolers full of meat and fresh produce. Even I had to admit he was beautiful in his leather boots, tight jeans—real denim jeans, not hemp—and black t-shirt. His platinum blonde hair had a healthy shine and was slicked back in an avant-garde style. A rare smile lit up his young, effeminate face when he saw me, only to melt into a scowl when his eyes fell on Bunny.

Glancing behind me, I saw the guard with the Widow reach the exit gate and talk to one of his compatriots, pointing our way. I rushed Bunny to the truck and started getting in, planning to greet Spooge properly once we were on the road, but he would have none of it.

Spooge curled his lip and glared at me. "No way. Ditch the fish, or nobody rides."

CHAPTER 17

"SHE'S NOT A FISH, Spooge. She's my cousin up from the Borders for the summer. I don't even like her. Can we please go?" I threw myself on his mercy, knowing he liked to feel he was in charge.

"Yeah? Well, what do they want her for, then?" he asked, jerking his head toward the approaching guards.

"It's not her they want. It's me. Please. Could we go? We can ditch her halfway if you want." I folded my hands together in an imploring gesture.

He glanced at the guards and then back at me, Quinn, and Bunny. With a brusque nod, he gave his consent. Quinn picked up Bunny and fairly tossed her in the back, jumping up behind her while I bounded into the cab. Spooge pealed down the road, leaving the guards in a cloud of dirt.

I crossed my legs, not worrying that I didn't look manly. Spooge was the last person who would care about such a thing. "Thanks for the ride."

He gave me a sidelong glance. "I've always got a ride for you, sweetie."

I ignored his double entendre. I knew he only made them with me because he trusted me to never call his bluff. He loved me because I was the only person in his world who didn't want anything from him. Except, at that moment, a ride to the nearest outhouse.

I glanced in the side mirror on the truck and saw the guards receding in the background, still spitting and shaking their fists. "Check out those pricks. They're still mad."

Spooge shot a look to his own mirror and laughed. "What did you do to them, anyway?"

He hit a bump, and I squirmed. "Not a thing. Just pissed off some old blue-hair who likes canned beets. You know how sour those Esthers are. All they've got to do in a day is hunt down people looking at them funny."

"Yeah. I don't know why they don't burn those bitches. Probably don't want them smelling up the city." Spooge shifted gears with a jolt, and I forced myself not to groan. "And what's with the fish?" he asked.

"Don't call her a fish. I told you, she's my cousin come up from the Borders for the summer."

Spooge snorted. "I hear Borders tarts are juiciest. If she's still cherry, Maverick might have a use for her."

"Spooge, I'll get out right here if you don't keep a civil tongue in your head." I half hoped he would pull over and boot me out. At least then I could pee.

Silence filled the air, and when he spoke, I heard the edge of anxiety in his voice. "You're not replacing me, are you?"

In answer, I pulled a hemp lollipop from the pocket low on my leg where I always carried one just for him. "I didn't give her this, did I?"

He grinned, and the hard face of the sex worker beamed the innocence of the little boy I'd met so long ago, the day his father sold him to Maverick to settle a gambling debt. I didn't know then what was happening to him or why he was crying at the back door of a brothel, but I knew he needed comfort, so I had given him the treat from my pocket. Now it was our tradition. Makenzie made them for barter, so I always kept one with me, knowing I would run into him eventually.

He held it up, about to put it in his mouth, and then stopped, frowned and handed it back. "Wash that thing off, will you? Looks like you spit on it and drug it through the dirt."

"Wash it?" *No. Not water. Anything but water.* I squeezed my legs a bit tighter and tried to trick my brain that I didn't really need to go.

"What? You don't expect me to eat road dirt, do you? That may be okay for you Secs, but not for a classy ho boy like me."

"Screw you, Spooge. Give me your water. You don't expect me to use my own, do you?"

He laughed and handed me his travel coffee mug. I held it up to my lips to drink. No way was I using coffee to wash a freaking lollipop.

"Don't bother," he said. "It's only water today."

I took a drink anyway and then leaned out the window of the cab to wash the candy, practically wetting my pants as it flowed over my hand and dribbled into the wind. Then I noticed it. A transformer station. Big enough to hide behind and pee.

"Spooge, wait. Pull over." I slammed the coffee mug back in its holder and shoved the lollipop at him. "Please. Pull over now."

"What? Why?" He took the lollipop and stuck it in his cheek.

"That station. I saw . . . a marmot. I saw a marmot run behind it. I need to kill it."

"A marmot? There's no marmots around here."

"Oh, so now you're a hunter? You going to give me food? No, that's what I thought. So please just pull over. Now."

I was out of the truck and flying the few hundred feet to the transformer station before Spooge had fully stopped.

Quinn's voice reached me. "Archer, what are you doing?"

I waved him off, hoping he wouldn't follow me. Finally hidden from view, I hunkered down and got to business. *Ah.*

As I enjoyed the moment, giving myself a chance to air-dry, I became aware of a humming sound above me. Looking up, I saw the heavy wires that carried energy down from the airborne wind turbines far to the north. They connected to poles inside the chain-link fence that, in turn, lodged in large canisters where the massive jolts were broken down into bite-sized pieces the Josephites could use. Then the little bites of electricity were sent back out through the smaller wires heading east, into the city.

On that high spot in the plains, I could see them connecting to poles inside Defender's Wall, right next to the tall vertical farms that fed Promise City—farms reaching seven and eight stories into the sky, proudly sneering at all of the hungry people outside the walls.

My stomach growled with the hunger I'd been trying to ignore. *Sorry bastards. We go hungry while you have your year-round farms.* Five million people inside, and all of them eating from those vertical farms that were, in turn, eating from that little transformer station.

Then, as I hunkered there on the plains, cursing my oppressors, an inkling of an idea started to form.

"Archer."

Quinn trooped around the corner of the station, and I jumped and pulled up my pants.

"Oh," he said. "So that's what that was all about. Why didn't you say so?"

Right. Like I wanted to talk about peeing with him.

"Quinn, look. We can starve the Josephites."

"Are you freakin' crazy? Let's go before Spooge ditches us."

"No, look. He won't ditch us. These wires. See how they come into the transformers and back out again to the vertical farms?"

"Yes. That's why they're called transformers. Come on, Archer."

"No, listen. Those vertical farms, they run on electricity,

don't they?"

"Yes. Let's go."

"The Josephites don't store food since they have these vertical farms going all year, right?" I held up my hand to stop him from talking. I knew the answer. "So if we take out the electricity, the Joes go hungry, don't they?"

Quinn stopped a moment and studied the wires. "It won't work. If we cut the wires, they'll just fix them."

"Yeah, but what if we take out the transformers? That would kick their ass."

Quinn thought a moment. His brow puckered and then smoothed, and a smile broke across his face. "Yes . . . Yes, it would . . . Ha ha! . . . Yes, it would."

He swept me up in a bear hug and twirled me around as we laughed. What could be more perfect than starving the Josephites? Finally we had a way to fight back.

Quinn set me down with a kiss. It was a joyous kiss. A sweet kiss. A we're-finally-going-to-screw-the-Josephites kiss. It was a perfect kiss right up until he realized he'd kissed me.

He released me and stepped back, turning red. "Uh . . . Yeah, uh . . . That's a great idea. I don't know how we'd do it, but it's a great idea."

I touched my fingers to my lips to hide my grin, encouraged by his discomfort. Perhaps there was something there for me with him after all.

Spooge blasted the horn, and a large animal shot from the far side of the station, bounding across the plains toward the foothills.

"Quinn, there he is." I grabbed for my bow, only to realize I'd left it back in the truck. The majestic buck I'd tracked through the hills that Reunion morning, seemingly a lifetime ago, stopped and gazed my way, his head high, as if mocking me in my weaponless state.

Quinn shook his head, his mouth agape. "Wow. What's he doing here, and where's a rifle when you need one?"

The horn blared again, and I jumped. Wondering how I was going to explain hunting a marmot without my bow to Spooge, I rushed back to the truck.

CHAPTER 18

MAVERICK JOE'S REARED UP from the rolling plains before us, a singular monument to a time past. A three-story red brick mansion surrounded by several outbuildings and shadowed by towering cottonwood, birch, and conifer trees watered from Maverick's own well. I had never been inside the main house, but Spooge spoke of plush, smoke-filled chambers where Maverick lived along with his favorites.

Spooge pulled up to the back door, and two pretty young men bustled out. They began unloading under the direction of an old runaway Esther Widow who cooked for Maverick's household.

"Thanks for the ride, Spooge. It was good to see you," I said while Quinn helped Bunny from the truck.

He grinned. "Come back for a real ride some day."

I laughed. "Trust me, Spooge. I'm not the man you think I am."

He winked and pointed at me with the stick from his lollipop. "Give me three hours, you will be." Then he sighed and looked at me with longing. "Gots to go. Virgin sacrifice at The Retreat tonight."

Quinn stepped between us. "Take care, Spooge." Spooge turned away and gave Quinn a wave with the back of his hand before disappearing into the house.

"You two wait here," Quinn said. "I need to talk to Maverick about some Debbie."

I put my arm around Bunny so no one would mistake her for incoming goods. "Be careful, Quinn, and please be quick about it."

"No worries. Should only be a few." He strolled toward Maverick's office, a building behind the mansion.

Bunny and I moved to an isolated corner of the backyard lawn. I loved the thick, soft grass. It was a rare treat for me to get to feel its cool, moist freshness beneath me.

Bunny pulled a spare scarf from her pack and laid it out beside me, turning in a couple of circles before sitting down, as if she were looking for the exactly perfect place to rest.

"Who's Debbie?" she asked when she was finally settled. "Quinn doesn't have a . . . well, he's not the sort of guy who . . ."

And why did this matter to her? "You mean does he do the hoes? Maybe. I don't know what Quinn does with women when he's away from the meadow." My voice was sharper than I had intended. I didn't like thinking of Quinn with other women.

Bunny leaned away from me. "Sorry. I thought that since he mentioned someone named Debbie . . ."

I laughed. "Debbie isn't a person, it's an aphrodisiac. Distilled THC. Supposedly turns up sex about ten notches. Quinn named it after some girl in a magazine he found in the dump and kept under his bed back when he was a teen."

"I didn't know you could do that with hemp."

"Not hemp. Marijuana. Quinn has the only fertile seeds left on the planet. Anyway, Debbie's one of the staples he trades to Maverick in exchange for clothes and fuel and blinkers, and pretty much anything else we might need except food. Brings in Maverick's best customers."

Bunny's eyes opened wide. "How did he get fertile seeds? And for marijuana?"

"Some Joes he used to work with down at that camp we passed. Doesn't matter now, though. Not like they had any seeds for food."

Bunny looked over her shoulder as if making sure we were alone. She leaned in close to me and seemed about to speak when some sex workers came in with their lunch and settled near us on the grass.

Bunny sat back and stared at them in their short shorts and midriff tops until they noticed her and flipped her off.

Blushing, she turned back to me.

"But I don't understand," she said. "Why did we go to the Big Box? If Quinn has this 'Debbie,' why didn't we just trade with Maverick for food?"

A darkness shrouded my heart, and I spoke softly. The words were hard to say. "The last Joe who traded food to a Sec was a minster's son. He was tortured to death along with the Sec he'd traded it to. The Joes brought them to our Fall Gathering in South. Made us all watch. I was five. Sliced them open and burned their guts while they were still alive." The memory made me shudder, and my mind balked. "No. Even Maverick won't trade us food."

When Quinn returned, he carried a package the size of a large marmot. It was so tightly bundled in hemp wrappings that I wondered if he'd have to blow it open with gunpowder.

"What's in there?" I asked.

"Nunya."

"Nunya?"

His eyes crinkled with mischief. "Nunya business."

With no further ado, he tied the package onto his already overburdened pack, and we set out toward the parking lot for the walk back to the meadow.

We rounded the building and saw men in hemp cargo pants and cotton Josephite jackets joking while they sauntered from their government jeep into the converted rodeo arena, the place where middle-class Joes congregated to indulge in alcohol, drugs, cards, sex shows, prostitutes, music, and dancing. One of them nodded Quinn's way.

"Ha. What luck," Quinn said. He immediately peeled off toward the Arena. "Come on, you two."

"Quinn, wait, what are you doing?" Fatigue was starting to set in, and I wanted to get home.

He turned and grinned, walking backward toward the building as we reluctantly followed. "I'm playing poker. But don't worry. I'm playing for all of us."

With no more explanation than that, he held open the door, and we entered Maverick's den of iniquity.

CHAPTER 19

"WHAT'S HE DOING?" BUNNY asked, grabbing at my sleeve like she wanted to crawl in my pocket and hide.

"I have no flaming idea, but keep your scarf tight and stick to me so there's no way they'll think you're a prostitute.

I pulled Bunny close and directed her with purpose through the crowd of lewd men who leered at beautiful, naked people performing obscene acts with poles and with each other on a stage. A holoscreen across the south wall broadcast the action live for anyone in the room who might be missing the show. I knew that somewhere Maverick had a transmitting station where he connected that same show to select private homes in Promise City. For a price, of course.

Two whores at the nearby bar, a pale blonde and a dark-skinned redhead, turned their attention to us. Specifically, to Quinn. He was a favorite at Maverick's. More than that, he was generous with the workers, and they, in their turn, were quick to do his bidding. With a shared whisper, they sauntered over.

Bunny and I split away from Quinn when the whores joined us, though I nodded politely in passing. I knew they thought of me as an oddity—a young man who was good friends with

Spooge and who wanted no woman or boy. But Quinn had a special status with the staff, and as his companion, they conferred it to me as well and kept their curiosity to themselves.

Blondie and Red kissed Quinn on the cheeks, and each took him by an arm.

"Hello, ladies. How are my favorite girls today?"

They giggled. I gagged.

Bunny and I moved quickly, locked together, looking anywhere but the stage or the holoscreen, aiming at the far end of the room where six of the fifteen card tables had games going.

Suddenly Joseph's voice pounded through the room, and his face filled the holoscreen. The Josephites in the room, including the whores and the performers on the stage, immediately stopped what they were doing and knelt, bowing their heads to the floor. Bunny started to drop down, too, but I dug my hand into her armpit to keep her upright and to remind her she wasn't one of them any more.

The balding Prophet looked older than dirt, and the wattle under his chin shook when he spoke, though the rest of his body was surprisingly fit and toned, or at least it appeared to be from the muscular shoulder and arm revealed by his spotless, white toga. "For the Archangel Michael placed in my hand the Seeds of Heaven when I defeated him on that first Ash Wednesday."

In unison, the Josephites sat back on their heels, touched their fingers to their hearts, their lips, and their foreheads before returning to their prostrate homage, chanting, "God bless his Holy Prophet. God bless the Holy Seed of Heaven."

Joseph continued. "Sprung from the Godfire of that day, the Seeds of Heaven shall feed and comfort the Atoned."

Again, the Josephites genuflected and said, "All praise, oh Holy Prophet, Shepherd of the Atonement."

"Go forth and sin against me no more, and you shall have life."

"Oh, Holy Prophet. We give you praise. You give us life."

Bunny and I, along with Quinn and a handful of Secs from South, stayed standing through this daily noon ritual while Joseph intoned a prayer.

Quinn waited quietly near the bar that separated the poker tables from the carnal pleasures, a whore kneeling on each side of him, until Joseph finished. Then the Josephites stood and resumed their frolics as if nothing had happened.

Quinn approached a table where one of the men from the parking lot was settling in with several men in suits bearing Ministry of Virtue badges on their collars. Releasing the whores with pats on their hands, he stood behind a chair with Blondie and Red flanking him like his honor guard and said, "Deal me in."

The Virtue Suits physically recoiled, the nearest ones moving their chairs away from him. One sneered and said, "This game's for credits, Sec, not hemp seeds." The rest of them laughed except for the man from the parking lot, who leaned back and crossed his arms, a slight smile on his lips.

Quinn took a blinker from his pocket and ran it through the scanner at the edge of the table, displaying a substantial number. The men quit laughing. The man from the parking lot grinned, and his eyes twinkled behind his round spectacles.

"Deal me in," Quinn repeated.

"Hey, you're not supposed to have that," said a Virtue Suit, pointing to the blinker.

I put my hand to the knife in my sleeve, my full attention on the table.

"And you're not supposed to be here," Quinn replied with a smile that didn't reach his eyes. The whores behind him giggled.

The Virtue Suits stared at each other in uncertain silence until the man from the parking lot broke out in laughter and said, "Good to see you, Quinn. Have a seat. Game's Jericho Hold 'Em."

"Thanks, Dave. Don't mind if I do."

The Virtue Suits shrugged, and one of them started dealing the cards.

I relaxed and steered Bunny toward the far end of the bar. Marty, my favorite bartender, was on duty that day. "Yo, Archer. What can I do you for? Free the Cuban?"

Marty's cheerful voice held genuine good will. A tall, sturdy, reliable fellow, he always had a smile and a kind word on his lips . . . and a loaded twelve gauge under his counter. I had no idea what such a nice guy was doing in a place like that. I assumed he was crazy or seriously perverted on some level. I never knew him well enough to find out which.

Slipping a blinker from a hidden pocket in the high neck of my shirt, I passed it to him and returned his greeting. "Hey, Marty. Yes to the Cuban and some well water for both my cousin and me. And take a credit for yourself." I liked Quinn's brew well enough, but now and again, I wanted Maverick's rum, and it had been a long day. My stomach rumbled, and I tried to ignore the irony of the fact that I could purchase rum, but not food.

"You got it," Marty said, pouring up our drinks and crowning each with a twist of fresh mint.

Bunny tugged at my sleeve. "Get me out of here." I noticed her hands shook, and her breathing was rapid. I wondered if she was going to faint.

I gave her a quick hug. "Hang tough. You'll like the next part." Her quivering rattled my arm, almost spilling my drinks while I guided her to the unmarked door in the shadows of the room. After exchanging a nod with Quinn to let him know where we were, I punched in the security code I was privy to because of his special relationship with Maverick.

Immediately, the trashy underbelly of life transformed into an intense wave of cleansing beauty. Rare tulips, daffodils, hyacinths, and other spring flowers burst rainbows around us. A mesmerizing kaleidoscope shifted by the gentle, misted breeze from concealed humidifiers, balming us with the scent of life's essence. Three walled-off acres of heaven. Maverick's pride.

I paused and closed my eyes, savoring the splendor and letting it permeate my soul. How odd to me that such a ruthless bastard as Maverick should posses such a treasure. That the same calloused hands that beat his sex slaves could care so gently for each blossom.

Bunny cautiously crept from under my arm. When she took off the sunglasses, I could see her eyes were as big as saucers. "How could so much of God's beauty exist in such a terrible place?"

"Just wondering that myself. Sort of."

"Does he have mountain daisies? Like the ones on your cabinet?"

"No, even Maverick doesn't have those. Come on. You can tell me what you know about these plants."

Bunny read to me from the bronze plaques mounted in front of each grouping while we strolled along the paths, filling in her own tidbits and anecdotes as she did. I was surprised at how much she knew, and I was glad to see that the exercise seemed to help her regain her center.

In time, we reached the far wall near the silos. Small, artistically embedded lattices enhanced the garden's intricate beauty. They also served as peep holes onto the driveway in front of the Retreat.

The Retreat consisted of three converted silos at the end of the garden where the elite of Josephite society indulged in their hedonistic pursuit of heavenly visions. Many an intrigue was born at those picturesque lattices at the expense of the unsuspecting customers. Functional art, as Granny would say.

Bunny settled on my favorite stone bench in a corner where we had a good twenty-mile view out of a woven ocean scene. We sipped our drinks, soaking in the healing calm.

Bunny rubbed the side of her face, and I remembered the guard's backhand. "Here, let me see that," I said.

I unhitched her veil, accidentally smearing off some pimple sap to reveal irritated skin underneath. "Oh, wow. Looks like this concoction is burning your skin a bit. Sorry about that. We'll get back to the meadow this evening, and you can take it off. If the patrol is gone, that is."

Even underneath the rest of the brownish-yellow pimple sap, I could see her cheek was black and blue. "That guard really clobbered you. Too bad we don't have any cold meat to put on it."

"God be praised, I shall never have cold meat on my face. That sounds disgusting."

"Shhh. Secs don't talk like that. And don't be so prissy. Prissy Secs don't live long. Here, hold still." I reapplied the sap I'd smudged and then surveyed my work. The bruise was still visible through the icky smear, but at least it helped serve to mask her features a bit.

I felt sorry I couldn't help her with the pain of her cheek or her raw skin, but there was something I could help. "Let me see your feet."

Bunny curled her knees and tucked her feet up under the bench. "No, really. They're fine."

"Don't be so proud. I know you were limping back there. I could tell by the way you leaned on me. Now let me see your feet."

She shrugged and unlaced her boots while I pulled a plastic baggie of salve from my pack.

"Wow." I'd gotten blisters that bad when I broke in new boots. Once. I saw the raw, bloody patches on the backs of her heels, and my stomach tilted. I was impressed that she was handling it so well. "Hold still. This will numb it for you."

I tenderly cleaned the wounds and rubbed the salve on them before covering them with patches of hemp. She reached for her socks, and I stopped her. "No, it's okay. You just relax."

Gently, I bunched each of her socks up with my thumbs and settled them over the sores before retying her boots for her.

"Sorry you can't let them air for a while, but it's always best to keep your boots on when you're around Josephites."

"Thank you, Archer." Bunny smiled. "You know, we're taught from birth that Secs are unwashed demons who eat their own children, but I'm starting to think that might not be true. I think you're a beautiful person." Her blue eyes filled with mischief. "You should have been born a Christian."

I snorted a laugh. "You should have been born a Sec. Then you wouldn't be in this mess. Besides, maybe we still want a plump adult for dinner. I mean, children are only the gateway meat, you know. Now put your veil back on before we're all cooked."

Her smile widened, and she said nothing. She covered her face with the cloth, but her eyes crinkled at the edges as if she knew something about me I didn't. Granny did the same thing with the same eyes. Irritating as hell.

I glanced out the lattice and saw a row of three black bugs on the horizon. Stepping only on the garden stones, I closed in on the wall where I had a good view through the peephole. "Limos. Hey, Bunny, maybe you can tell me who these Joes are."

She joined me, standing tiptoe to see. "They're from inside the Dome for sure, or they wouldn't be in limos. Why would anyone from the Dome come here?"

I raised my eyebrow. "Really? You have brothels like this in Joseph's house?"

Bunny's eyes were suddenly glued to a blue hyacinth next to her feet. "Well, no. I didn't think of that."

I tried to hide my amusement.

When the caravan approached, Maverick himself strode out in front of the Retreat to greet his guests. He sported traditional Old American West attire which accented his strong, ruggedly handsome features. His short, brown beard was immaculately groomed, and he looked like the picture of a wealthy rancher we had in a book at home. When he took his cowboy hat off his head to dust a grasshopper from the brim, the sun shone strong on his shoulder-length brown hair and flashed off the plethora of heavy gold chains he wore around his neck—chains like Granny's necklace. Maverick loved gold like he loved his garden.

A polished, thirty-something woman stood slightly behind Maverick and to his left. Her strappy high heels and clingy red dress displayed her remarkably enduring charms to perfection. She was apparently the cruise director for the event, having a staff of two dozen beautiful men and women dressed in provocative maid and butler outfits standing behind her near the door of the silos. It was her job to make certain the men were thoroughly fulfilled in their "heavenly quest" before sending them home to their proper Joe wives.

The first limo pulled into the driveway, and the uniformed driver leapt out to hold the door for four men. When they got out, I saw their immaculate white suits. Their faces shone with anticipation. "Do you know them?"

"God's fire. That tall man is the Minister of Distribution. He's one of Joseph's closest henchmen. He has the final say in who gets what seeds. I don't know the others."

I was impressed. I had watched this routine before, but I'd never known who these people were. I knew they were fancy, but I had no idea they were quite that fancy.

Maverick greeted the minister and executives and introduced them to the madam. She escorted them to the door of the silo and turned each over to a maid and butler pair before returning to Maverick's side.

When the second limo emptied of four more men, Bunny pointed to a stocky, balding fellow and said, "Oh. That's the Pagan's head coach, and that fellow next to him is the Sports Minister. I forget his name. Hmmm. I don't know the other two." Like before, Maverick greeted them and turned them over to the capable hands of the madam.

The third limo was already in the driveway. A driver opened

the door, and three men stepped out. "Oh, my. That's Jimmy Roberts, the Evangelism Minister, and Wayne Jenkins. He's in charge of the War Department. And the old guy is George Baker, the Health Minister. Yuck. He'll need a health minister if he's here for these girls."

I laughed, glad she was able to joke about it. "Nah. Spooge tells me they only take virgins to the silos for the likes of these. That's what he meant earlier when he called it the virgin sacrifice. Hey, there's one I was wondering about. He's always here after Atonement Sunday . . . Ugh. What a pig. I wouldn't touch him with someone else's . . . well, you know." I indicated an obscenely obese middle-aged man whose five black hairs were greased and combed over the top of his balding head.

Bunny squeaked and turned away from the lattice, flattening her back against the wall and squashing a hyacinth at her feet.

"No!" I fairly lifted her and dropped her behind me onto a garden stone. Squatting, I quickly buried the one bloom she'd knocked off the flower and tidied the scattered mulch, keeping an eye out for anyone who might have seen.

By the time I finished, she was at the path. I hurried to her side, forcing myself to remember that she didn't know, but I couldn't keep my fear out of my voice. "Maverick would kill us if he knew you did that."

She fussed with her veil, and I thought she was making sure it was firm across her face, as if whomever she'd seen would appear behind us. "I'm sorry. I'm sorry. It's just that . . . that was the Minister of Justice. He chooses the women for Atonement."

"I don't care if it was Joseph himself, you don't mess with the freakin' flowers."

She reached again toward the veil and then seemed to force her hand back down.

I was about to ask her what she was doing when we heard voices. The Esther Widow from the main house came into view across the garden, followed by a dozen beautiful young women, fresh-looking boys, and girls as young as ten or so. My heart sank to see them, meticulously groomed and perfectly turned out in costumes as varied as dancing dresses and leather and slave chains to evening gowns. Several moved like they had been drugged. The rest simply looked terrified.

A tall young woman dressed as a Josephite schoolgirl in a plaid skirt and knee socks caught my eye, and I caught my breath. She was striking for two reasons. First, she clutched at an Underground pendant in a gesture reminiscent of Bunny's, and second, she looked eerily like a slightly younger, plumper version of me.

But something was wrong about her. Something about the way she drug her left foot when she walked, and the way the right side of her face seemed a bit frozen. Then, when she glanced my way, and I saw her vacant eyes and the fresh line of an incision near her hairline, I knew. Chills crept up my spine. The Josephites had mapped her brain and cut her.

Beside me, Bunny gasped. "Barbara. Barbara's alive." Her voice brimmed with joy at seeing her mother's assistant intact. Then she saw what I saw. "Sweet Jesus, no. They must know now. She had to have told them."

I clamped my hand over Bunny's mouth and pulled her to a small path through the foliage. The Widow's head came up, seeking out the voices she'd heard. Our voices. And now was not the time for her to come asking questions.

Dammit, Quinn, hurry up.

As if in answer, Quinn appeared. "Archer. Over the wall. That patrol from the meadow is inside asking Marty about you."

Oh, crap! I released my hand on Bunny's mouth and spun on my heel. Then a voice called, "Freeze."

CHAPTER 20

"HANDS IN THE AIR and turn slowly." I was relieved to identify the voice of the blonde captain and not Major Norris.

Bunny and I did as we were told, and I wondered if my hands were shaking as much as hers were. Two soldiers had Quinn by the arms. The captain came forward, recognition showing in his face.

Another guard grabbed my hands out of the air, held them behind my back, and moved me away from Bunny. Even before I saw him from the corner of my eye, I felt Spooge approach behind me.

The captain looked Bunny up and down. "Show me your face." His voice was calm and even, as it had been on our first encounter. I forced myself to stare down at Bunny's feet, scared that if I looked up at Quinn, the Josephites would see the terror in my eyes. But I could see her movements through my peripheral vision.

Bunny removed the sunglasses with deliberation, folding them carefully. Then came the moment of truth. My stomach clenched when she reached up with her right hand and unpinned her veil, pulling it back carefully from her face, revealing her visage smeared with pimple sap.

Will they kill us here? Will they kill our meadow? Granny, Flynx, and the Tinkers?

"Hair, too, and wipe that off," said the captain. Bunny straightened her back and lifted her chin. Then she pulled off the scarf. Her newly-dyed brown hair fell out of it, just brushing her shoulders in the Sec style.

Will they burn us or only shoot us?

Through my eyelashes, I saw Bunny use a corner of her headscarf to wipe off the brown pimple sap. Her hand trembled, and her work was slow.

The captain snatched the cloth from her and wiped her cheeks clean in two swipes. Then he tipped her face up where he could see her clearly.

My knees almost collapsed. *The Godfire. No doubt. The Godfire.*

The guard holding me gasped. "Sweet Michael."

"Damn," Spooge said. "That has to hurt."

Startled to hear sympathy in his voice, I glanced up at Bunny's face and squelched a whoop of joy. She was covered in hives. Between that, her dark hair, and the large bruise on her cheek, her own mother wouldn't have recognized her.

Bunny clasped and unclasped her hands at her sides. It was clear to me that she was fighting not to scratch her own face off in that moment.

The captain studied her swollen features and asked, "What is your meadow?"

Bunny lowered her eyes. "I'm from the Borders, sir." She kept her eyes down and her body still, and I was surprised to hear a Southwestern drawl in her voice.

"Do you have any proof?"

"Only my word, sir, and my fiancé here to vouch for me." Her tones were demure, her eyes down, and her body still.

Spooge glared at me, and I realized what he thought. My eyes opened wide, and I deliberately turned them toward

Quinn, hoping Spooge would believe that Bunny meant she was his fiancé, not mine. There was no telling what he would do if he thought Bunny was actually marrying me.

Quinn got it and stepped in. "Yes. This is my bride. I met her at the Big Box this morning."

Spooge's eyes narrowed. He knew a line of crap when he heard one. Nevertheless, he rose to the occasion. "It's true," he said. "I picked them up this morning from the Big Box. They'd been on the South road."

The captain turned to me. "Are you the archer from the Middle Meadow?"

"Yes, sir. I'm her escort. I left for South after your patrol stopped us the other day."

The captain studied my face, and I willed it to innocence, hoping he could not hear my pounding heart. Then he turned back to Bunny and returned her scarf. "You may go."

He pointed to the garden door where the line of virgins was entering the Retreat. "Search those silos."

"Sir." Spooge stepped in front of the captain, blocking his way. "The Guidance Retreat is already in progress. If you go in there, the Josephites you find won't allow you to leave."

The captain lifted his chin and clasped his hands behind his back, considering the situation. He glanced over at the virgins entering the silos to his right and back at Spooge. With a nod, he turned on his heel and strode toward the Arena. "Come, men. There's nothing for us here."

The rest of the patrol followed.

Bunny's knees collapsed, and Quinn caught her. He sat her on a nearby bench, and she reached for the seed under her dress.

Spooge rounded on me, his face red with fury. "I don't know what you're up to, and I don't want to know, but get this fish out of here. Now." He stalked away toward the silos.

"Thank you, Spooge," I said to his receding back.

I could barely hear his "Whatever" before he passed through

the door.

CHAPTER 21

"FLAMING MICHAEL ON A biscuit!" Flynx slammed his fist down on our table. "Why didn't we see this before? Take out the power grid . . . Ha, haaa . . . I love it."

Bunny paused halfway through a bite of her factory bar. Her eyes were wide in her still-puffy face, and she stared at us as though she'd never seen us before. "But if you shut off the power, the Josephites will starve. They don't store food like Secs do. They have to have their vertical farms and cloning factories to survive. It will be chaos."

Daisy plopped down with her bone in a sunbeam at my feet and gnawed it loudly. I casually brushed a bit of her hair off my skirt, which Granny had made from the scraps of my dress while we were gone. Then, with steel in my heart, I looked up and met Bunny's eyes deliberately. "Are you there yet?"

Bunny drew in a quick breath, shocked as if I'd slapped her. I wasn't surprised. I also didn't care. I may have decided she was okay, but that didn't change how I felt about her people.

Granny sat ramrod straight and glared at us. "You're a damn lot of fools, and you'll bring down the Godfire. Don't you remember the Loveland Massacre and what happened with their little rebellion?" Her voice was heated, but I noticed she kept her anger from her hands while she doctored Bunny's feet, still raw from the many days of travel.

I fetched a pottery cloth and began cleaning the table. "Loveland was different. They were in open rebellion. The Josephites will never know this was us."

"Of course they'll know," Granny said. "They always find out sooner or later. Then they'll come kill us all."

Quinn set his empty tea mug on the table where I had just wiped and then leaned back against the wall and crossed one ankle over the other. His voice low and calm, he said, "I don't think so, Granny. The Josephites have lots of enemies. They think we're bugs. They would never suspect this was from us when they have the Eastern Rebels and the Underground to blame. Granny, this can work."

Granny lifted the Eyebrow of Impending Doom. "I expected more sense from you, Quinn. The Josephites will find out, and they will kill us all. What good is there in that? Even if you could find some miracle to take down Joseph, it's not like we'd be in charge with him out. Some man like Norris will take his place, and that could be even worse for us."

I put Quinn's cup in the sand barrel and wiped off the tea ring it left behind on the table. "You have to understand. You may be resolved to this life, but we want something better. We have to try."

Sitting, I took a ball from my pocket and began bouncing it on the surface in front of me.

Granny grabbed it midair. "Practice sitting still, child, you make me tired just watching you . . . I'm old, but I'm not dead. I understand you want something better, but this isn't the way to do it. We fought the Josephites with everything we had. I lost two sons to the fight. What do you think you have that we didn't?"

Daisy's teeth crunched loudly on her bone. I rose and took it away, giving her a hemp rag toy instead. She looked up at me, her eyes sad, and I handed the bone back to her. She resumed her chomping. I sat back down.

Flynx cut in. "I was there for the war too. No disrespect, but this is a chance worth taking. That engineer down at Maverick's told Quinn that if two stations go down, the whole grid shuts off. Joseph's whole gig is rigged around feeding people. If they go hungry, think what a blow that will be."

Bunny shook her head, her eyes shining with tears. "B-but you won't just starve people. Think of the ones on special diets who won't get their food. And the people in the hospitals. They won't get medical care if the power goes out. Worse, think of all of the people on oxygen and dialysis. You'll be killing the sickest and the weakest."

I stood abruptly, causing Daisy to jump up. "How many Secs do you see on oxygen? How many Secs get special diets or medical treatment? More Secs get shot in the face by Joes than ever get penicillin. We have been starved and butchered at the will of the Josephites for over twenty years, and enough is enough. It's time for them to taste their own medicine."

Bunny cringed, my brittle words breaking across her.

Granny glared. "Deena Sprague, sit back down right now."

"No, ma'am, I won't. I'm done talking. I'm done listening. You always tell me we have to make our own fair, and now I've got the chance to do it. I'm taking it."

I grabbed my bow and stormed from the house, Daisy at my heels with her bone, but I was barely out the door when I was caught up short. Across the bridge stood Harmony, tears streaming down her face, and her eyes glowing pure hatred.

CHAPTER 22

GRANNY HAD TAUGHT ME well. I never lied to my own, and I owed no truth to my enemies. We had told Harmony when we got back the night before that Greagor was eaten by a Dixie bear, that Bane came with us to bring my cousin up from the Big Box, and that he died in the minefield. We hadn't told her Bunny was with us all along, and we hadn't told her they had tried to kill us.

Seeing her standing there, wretched in her grief, I couldn't help but be moved. I remembered losing my father and Faebin. How much worse to lose a son, even a food thief like Bane? But there was nothing I could do for her.

Arys, his face grim, gave me a polite nod. Then he took her by the shoulders and steered her back toward the meadow. Though she went with him complacently, her eyes left me haunted.

I climbed up to my favorite glade to put my thoughts in order. One after another, I drummed my arrows into an aspen tree thirty yards downhill, Daisy sprawling near me with her bone.

What if Granny was right? What if the Josephites found out and came after us with the Godfire? I'd heard tell of the

Loveland Meadow Massacre. The Josephites did nothing but burn people for days until every man, woman, and child they found had been tortured in the flames. Granny had raised me on the story of it since I was a small girl.

No. Loveland was open rebellion. They won't find out about us. We'll be too careful for them.

And what of Bunny's objection? We would kill a lot of innocent people . . .

No. This is war. A war we didn't start.

Still . . . to what end?

Wind snaked across the far slope of the canyon while I fired my meditations, the dancing treetops the only testament to the gusts. Was there some other, parallel plane of existence where the energy of our actions, intentions, and emotions snaked in the same way across some unseen landscape, only visible to that plane's inhabitants by the rustlings they made as they passed? In that other plane of existence, was Norris still destroying our food? Was I still helpless to stop it? A smiling face and a catchy beat flashed through my memory, and my breath caught in my throat. In that other plane, was Iain still alive?

No. I would be helpless no more. This was war, and we finally had a weapon worthy of our adversary.

Daisy and I hiked to Quinn's house to work out a plan. The one-room stone cottage sat in a narrow canyon, half a mile above the meadow where his marijuana plants and moonshine still were unlikely to be found by the forest-fearing Josephites. He had moved there around the time I turned fifteen.

I entered to find Tinker's son, Freefall, sprawled across the top of the rolled-up mattress that was pushed against the plastered wall. His brother-in-law, Zander, sat on the floor underneath what I jokingly called the Shrine of Clarisse. It was an expanse of pegs where Quinn hung everything from his backpacks to his cooking utensils, with a special spotlight position for the prized machete right in the center. The rest of the room held a potbellied stove, a cooking platform, a table with two chairs, and a small chest of drawers. I noticed the mysterious package from Maverick's now sat on top of that chest.

I liked the Spartan nature of the room, but Quinn was still a bachelor. It was all I could do to not grab a broom and start sweeping out the dirt that had fallen from so many boots going through the room.

Flynx offered me his chair at the table. Daisy, wagging her tail, dropped her bone, and pressed a cold nose against each of the men, taking inventory of her "dog pack." Freefall scratched her behind the ears with one hand, swigging from his flask with the other. Daisy settled beside him to enjoy the pampering. I took a Jacob's Ladder toy from my pocket and clicked it back and forth.

"Okay, boys. Let's make a plan," I said, ready to go down and start shooting Josephites at Defender's Wall if need be.

"Flynx is already on it," Quinn said.

"Tell me."

Flynx smiled like he knew a great secret. "Simple. We shoot the Michael-pegging transformer canisters. Their fluid leaks out, the electricity arcs inside, and the windings are destroyed. Like Quinn's engineer friend said, we take out two stations, and we take out the whole grid."

It sounded too easy to me, but Flynx had been a combat engineer for the Josephites before the final battles—before he defected and became a hero of the Western Resistance. I had no reason to think he didn't know his stuff and every reason to think he did.

Quinn looked up at the ceiling, stroking his beard and tipping his chair back on two legs. "But won't they just fix them? I mean, why take that kind of risk if they're going to be up and working the next day?"

Flynx jabbed a finger toward Quinn. "Good question. When I was in the army, the Josephites kept their supply of spare transformers at the truck yard. We pour rust remover powder down the ports of the spares. Then the Joes install them and fill them with fluid. The acid eats out the insides. Shouldn't take more than three days before those transformers go bad too."

A light bulb came on for me, and the Jacob's Ladder clicked erratically in my hands. "Wow. That's twice the blow. We shut them down, and as soon as the Joes think they have them fixed, the power goes out for good. I love it. How long until they make new transformers?"

Flynx grinned. "Could take months."

I returned his smile. "And how will Joseph possibly explain that one? I mean, he's got that whole schtick going with the Atonements and the food supply. Hot damn, Flynx. That's effing brilliant."

Flynx gave me a nod and then looked at me like he was noticing me for the first time. "By the way, you clean up real nice, girl. You should do that more often." He looked at the other men. "Holy Mary on a virgin. What's wrong with you boys leavin' this smart, pretty thing untapped?"

I blushed to my roots and stared at the floor, pleased by the intention of his compliment while being embarrassed by his crudity.

Quinn grew red in the face and popped his knuckles. "Flynx, you will not speak about Archer that way. What's wrong with you? Now you apologize to her and stick to business before I kick your ass all the way back to North."

Flynx looked askance at Quinn. "Oh, so *that's* how it is . . . Sorry, Archer. No offence intended." He sounded most unrepentant.

Eager to be talking about anything else, I stared him in the eye and asked, "How do we get there?"

With one last wary glance at Quinn, Flynx shrugged and said, "Easy. We break into the truck yard and use their own trucks for the job. Each of two teams will take a truck to their assigned station. We do the transformers simultaneously and then hustle back to the truck yard and scoot on home. By the time the lights fade and go out, we should be a long way away."

Zander shifted, his broad shoulders filling the wall he leaned against. "No way. How do we get to the truck yard? And how can we get away on foot once we're back? We could never get that far that fast. They're sure to be on us."

"I'm still working on that one," Flynx said.

We all paused and thought a moment, and then I smiled, an idea coming to mind. "We get there in a limousine."

The guys looked at me like I was crazy.

"Okay, maybe not a limo, but we could borrow one of the Joe cars from Maverick's while they're inside doing the Debbie. We take the Joe car to the truck yard and back. Whole mission shouldn't take more than a couple of hours, right? And even if someone sees it, the Joe it belongs to is sure to want to hush it up. You know the old saying, 'Rebels don't recognize Secs, Secs don't recognize Joes, and Joes don't recognize each other at Maverick's.'"

"Could work," Quinn said, "But be sure that Maverick would do serious damage if he suspected we took a john's car. The Joes are his business as much as my goods are."

"One problem," Freefall said, rolling over and sitting up on the mattress. "Won't there be a lot of Joes around?"

We thought a moment, and then I remembered Bunny and Quinn's conversation on the way to the Big Box. I sat forward and grinned, feeling like the Cheshire Cat of my Granny's stories. "Two words. Super Bowl."

"Yes!" Flynx fist pumped.

Quinn looked up, a touch of sadness in his eyes, and he nodded his agreement.

"The what?" asked Freefall.

Quinn explained about the one time in the year when all of Josephite society stood still for a football game.

Freefall whistled low. "That's perfect. If we could be in place during the game, we could shoot the transformers while the stadium's still full. That would kick them in the balls."

Quinn nodded his agreement. "It would certainly hit them where they live."

Anticipation lit Flynx's features. "We only have a couple of months. We'll need to case the stations and set up replicas here in the woods for practice. Archer, can you get south this week and map the station there for us?"

I frowned, thinking. My meadow desperately needed me to hunt, but my heart wanted to focus on fighting Josephites.

Quinn saw the same issue. "I'll go. We need Archer's hunting skills here with our food gone."

"Good man," Flynx said. "I'll take care of the north station and the truck yard. We'll meet back here in a week."

Flynx, never one to dawdle, collected his pack and bedroll from the corner of Quinn's cabin where he always kept them ready when he came to visit. Then he bid his adieus and patted Daisy on the head. She stood in the door, her tail drooping, and watched him trek down the dry creek bed to the meadow.

Zander and Freefall also stood to go. "You coming, Archer?"

"No," Quinn said before I could answer. He offered no further explanation.

My heart pounded in my throat. *He wants to be alone with me.*

"Okay," said Zander. "Bring Bunny on down this afternoon, and we'll put her to work with the babies. Makenzie and Mariah will be glad for the company." He waved, and they left.

Somehow, the sound of my Jacob's Ladder was silly in the silence. I put it away, and for the first time in my life, I willed my hands to stillness.

Feeling Quinn's gaze upon me, I glanced up at him and quickly looked away, finding Daisy with my eyes and pretending to be absorbed in watching her settle in a sunbeam with her bone.

Quinn reached for the mysterious bundle he had carried back from Maverick's and put it in front of me on the table.

"Open it."

I looked up and was surprised by the twinkle in his eye, like he knew a great secret. I returned his smile, glad for the tension to pass. "A present? For me? I love presents." I picked up the package and shook it, trying to guess its contents. It was heavier than it appeared, with some dense material inside.

He laughed. "What makes you so sure it's a present for you? Maybe I'm just too lazy to open it. Did you think of that?"

I put it down and gave him my best fake pout. "Now you're teasing me. Shame on you. You can open your own packages if you're going to be that way."

"Okay," he said, reaching for the bundle.

I snatched it back. "Don't you dare."

With a smile and a sidelong glance at him, I slowly tugged at the outermost hemp wrapping. Very, very slowly. I untied one side of the package, smoothing out each wrinkle of the material and tidying it in every way I could imagine before moving on. I had the second side half unwrapped when I stopped and started bundling it up again. "I don't know. Maybe I should take it home and open it there."

Quinn laughed. "Dear God, girl, you're a worse tease than those strippers down at Maverick's."

"Worse? No, sweetie, I'm better." I winked at him playfully.

He reached out to grab the package from me, but I swept it from his grasp. "Okay, okay."

When I set it back down, I untied the remaining knot as fast as I could and threw open the layers of hemp. Gasping, I froze, unable to peel my eyes away from the garment that had been hidden within.

Slowly, I reached out and touched it, loving the cool feel of its interwoven ceramic disc construction. Taking it in both hands, I held it up. It was shaped like a tunic. Heavier than a shirt, but lighter than my winter parka. I turned it in my hands, and the garment flowed like water. It had half-sleeves, a high, turtleneck-type collar, and openings at the left shoulder and neck and down the left side. Cords and alloy clasps secured it in such a way that it could be adjusted to an extent for size.

I remembered the only time I'd see this material up close—at Norris's neck—and I blinked back a tear. I breathed one word. "Dragontech." The exclusive armor of the Josephite military elite—the most flexible, bulletproof armor in existence—and here it was in my hands.

Quinn, unable to hold back any longer, laughed with childlike delight at my reaction.

"How did you get this? Will they come looking for it?" I knew he was a wizard at getting anything but food, but this?

"Nope," he said. "It's legit. Turned a few trades—okay, a lot of trades—called in some chips, and caught a Joe at the right place at the right time. You know how it goes."

No. I didn't know how it went to obtain something like that—something so valuable it would have bought the meadow's seeds for a lifetime if the Joes would have permitted it. It was another Bucellati necklace. Something so valuable that it could get us killed if the wrong Josephites found it. But this was a necklace we could use.

I held it out to him. "Here," I said. "Please put it on. I'd like to see you in it."

Taking the dragontech, Quinn tried to put his muscular right arm through the sleeve, but it squeezed so tight above his elbow that it almost stuck. We laughed. "You'll need to get that fixed," I said.

"No," he grinned. I have a better idea. "Stand up and lift your arms." This time, I did as I was told. To my amazement, he slid the armor sleeve onto my right arm and fitted the shoulder. "Never go through a minefield again without it, okay? Hold this," he said, handing me the front of the open garment.

I took it in my right hand and held it to my left shoulder while he took the back of it behind me. Reaching for my long hair to gather it up over the armor, his hand brushed against the back of my neck.

An involuntary gasp escaped my lips. Pausing, his face near me, his hot breath quickened on the bare skin below my ear. Heat flooded my body, and I froze, not knowing what to think or what to do. I only knew that something had changed, and I liked it.

Slowly, he pulled my long hair over the back of the dragontech, his hand gently smoothing it down to my waist. My heart pounded in my throat, and my knees began to quiver. Gentle as a caress, Quinn settled the back of the armor to my neck and shoulder. Reaching around me, his body close, his breath still searing my neck, his hand touched mine and lingered. An electric shock jolted through me.

"Relax," he whispered in my ear, taking the front of the dragontech from my grasp. I shuddered and closed my eyes, molten lava burning through my veins, melting at the touch of his strong hands while he fastened the armor at my arm . . . at my shoulder . . . at my neck . . . beside my breast . . . at my waist . . . Standing behind me, he reached around and down the front of the armor to lift my lion claw necklace out and lay it gently between my breasts. His fingers burned my skin.

He leaned his face close to my ear, his rapid breath coaxing the heat from my loins. Desire consumed me. I turned in his arms, and my mouth found his. Closing my eyes, I melted into him, awakened in ways I thought I would never know again, ready to give myself to him in every way.

Suddenly I felt a slight push on my shoulders, and I found myself groping at air. My eyes flew open, hurt and confusion a midwinter blast on my psyche. My jaw dropped, and I stared at him, waiting for an explanation.

Quinn backed away, looking at the floor. Looking at the stove. Looking at the table. Looking anywhere but at me. He cleared his throat. "I'm sorry. You need to go."

"No, Quinn. It's okay. I want this." I hated the note of pleading in my voice.

He stared at me. His face hardened, and his voice cut

through me. "Go home to your Granny. Now."

It took me a moment to understand what was happening. Here I was ready to open up and trust again after these long years alone . . . ready to give myself to him with no reservations, . . . and the son of a bitch didn't want me. He'd give me a gift worth Joseph's ransom, but he wouldn't take me for his own.

Rage poured through my veins. I tore open the clasps on the armor. "Who do you think I am that you think you can screw with me like that? Some stupid whore to be used and thrown down? Some Josephite trash to be burned at will?"

He took a step back in the face of my fury. "No. It's not like that."

I struggled out of the armor and threw it to the ground. "Keep your damn trinkets. You were born an effing Josephite, and you'll always be one."

I ran from the house, Daisy at my heels. The path was a blur, and I didn't stop until I reached a clearing. Unbidden, my feet had sought my favorite glade above the meadow. The week flooded in on me. Iain's death, the burning of our food, the killing of Greagor, and the death of Bane . . . Secs. We'd killed a Sec. And Bunny. What were we thinking to take her in? *I should have tossed her off the cliff myself.* Granny's disapproval, and now Quinn's rejection.

Falling to the ground, I found my arms full of fur. Daisy nuzzled me gently. My Daisy. The one I could always count on. The one who never left me. I hugged her close, burying my face in her warmth, and I cried out my sorrows.

CHAPTER 23

"**N**O. HE DID WHAT?" Bunny gaped at me and leaned back. I twirled a knife between my fingers. Granny, Bunny, and I sat at the kitchen table having a cup of tea for our dinner, pretending it filled the empty spaces in our bellies that the shared squirrel had left behind. Daisy curled at my feet with her bone, and her stomach rumbled in spite of the bites we'd given her. Granny brushed my hair to sooth me while I told them about Quinn's gift and sudden rejection. I didn't mention our plan to kill Josephites.

"You heard right. Jumped back like I'd stung him and started talking like I was a little kid. 'Go home to your Granny,' he said." I stabbed my knife into the board planks of the tabletop.

"Stop that. Stab Quinn if you must, but leave our table out of it." She pulled the knife from the table and moved it out of my reach.

"I hate him," I said, taking a small ball from my pocket and rolling it around on the table with the palm of my hand.

"No, you don't." Granny resumed her brushing.

"I do. As I live and breathe, I will find a way to hunt, guard the hemp, find a husband, have a family, grow old, and die without ever speaking to that patronizing assclown again. I swear I will."

Bunny snorted, and I glared at her. "What do you know about men, anyway?"

She smiled gently. "Not much. But I have loved, and I know a man in love when I see one. He loves you. Be patient. He'll come around."

"She's right, Deena," Granny said. "He could have gotten that armor for himself, you know. He's just lost a lot of people that he's loved. He may not even be able to open himself that way anymore. Surely you can understand and forgive him."

"I don't care about understanding. I haven't married him, and I didn't give birth to him, so I don't give a damn why he did it. It only matters that he did. I don't know where I'll find a man, but I'm not waiting for Quinn."

Granny chuckled. "I know it feels like the end of the world right now, child, but give it time. These things have a way of sorting themselves out."

It was a nice idea, but as tired and hurt as I was, I didn't quite buy it.

The next morning when I woke, the dragontech was folded on the kitchen table.

Granny, standing at the stove in her ragged robe and boots, saw me and put on water for tea to go with my daily allotment of one factory bar. "Quinn said he'd be gone a few days. He asked me to see that you got that."

"Humph," I said. I took down my hunting pack, and Daisy danced around me in anticipation. Seeing the layer of dust the pack had collected when Granny sanded her pots the day before, I shook it outside the door before sitting at the table to check my gear.

The dragontech dominated the space.

I set my hands to work. "Did he say anything?" An apology? An explanation? An insult, even?

"No. He only said he was going to be gone a while. No message."

I wanted to not care, but I couldn't help myself. I picked up the armor and searched through it, looking for a note, a symbol, some sign that he acknowledged what had passed between us. But there was nothing.

With Granny's back turned, I hugged the armor to my chest and closed my eyes, burning again at the caress of his hands and hearing his voice once more whispering in my ear. "Relax." And his kiss. I touched my fingers to my lips, and my world began to spin. A single tear slipped down my cheek before my fury overtook it. *No. No crying.*

Bunny joined us with a yawn. Seeing my pack on the table, she asked, "Going somewhere?"

"Hunting. Factory bars won't replace real meat. Will you be okay while I'm gone?"

"No worries for me. I'm held in the hand of Jesus," she smiled and kissed her seed necklace.

"Yeah, well, just in case Jesus is too busy fighting the Eastern Rebels this week, stay near Granny and Flynx. Absolutely no proselytizing, and watch the God and Jesus talk. I don't want to die as a matchstick. Avoid Harmony at all costs. She had murder in her eye yesterday. I don't know how she could know who you are for sure, but you need to stay away from her, especially now that your hives are getting better and that bruise is fading.

"Keep a scarf with you at all times in case the field monitor drops by. The other women cover up when he's here, too, and his main interest is the hemp crop. He won't notice one woman more or less, but it's best not to tempt fate. Any questions, you two?" I asked, caressing my bow and arrows and setting them beside my pack.

Granny laughed a great belly laugh. I realized how I had spoken to her, and I felt a bit sheepish. "Deena," she said, "I can't imagine how I lived all of these years without you telling me what to do."

"Yeah. Sorry about that." Standing, I took the armor and

headed to my room.

"You're not going to wear it?" Granny asked.

"No, I'm not going to wear it."

I stowed the dragontech in my drawer, and I went on about the business of my day. That business was to hunt. Until the seedlings went into the ground and drew in the game, the only food my people had was the factory bars, catch from small traps, and what I brought in. Meager fare at best, but if I did my job, it would be enough to keep us alive.

For the next five days, Daisy and I hunted. The moon was dark, and the deer were cagey. We began by searching near the glade where I had seen the majestic buck, hoping he would make my job easy by showing up and falling down before my arrow. But it was not to be.

From my rumbling stomach to my rumbling thoughts, I had never been so distracted on a hunt. We were going to starve the Josephites. Finally a weapon worthy of our enemies. But when Granny found out we were serious, she was going to be seriously mad. And what about Bunny? A cold fear swept through me when I thought of her and the task of hiding her from the Josephites. She was a Godfire time bomb if there ever was one, but the most troubling thought was Quinn.

I dreamed of him at night during what little sleep I got while keeping the fire fed to ward off the lions and the Dixie bears. Some nights I reveled in his hot kiss and the caress of his hands, only to wake to my own emptiness and a fire gone cold. Other nights I searched through a misty forest for him, calling out, feeling the panic of loss, only to find him and hear his harsh voice once more. "Go home."

With all that churning in my mind and heart, it was no wonder it took me four days to bring down a scrawny buck. My father had always told me a hunter's heart must be at peace to draw the game. On that trip, it seemed my purpose was to prove him true. When I finally got home, I passed the meat off to Makenzie, minus a haunch for us, and collapsed into bed for a day and a half.

Granny was clearly displeased when I finally came out of my room, her eyebrow perched high on her forehead. "Flynx stopped by to say that he and Quinn are back. He asked me to tell you that you'll be needed in three days. Deena, I know what you're doing, and I forbid it."

CHAPTER 24

B UNNY, CARDING MOHAIR AT the table, pursed her
lips and seconded Granny with a judgmental glance at
me. I almost wilted under their scathing disapproval,
but something inside me stood firm. Win, lose, or draw, this
was a tree I had to climb. I lifted my chin and surprised myself
with the calm in my voice. "I'm sorry, Granny, but you've
always taught me to follow my heart, and this is what my heart
is telling me to do."

"Nonsense, you silly girl. It's your pride talking, and you'll
get us all killed."

"I'm going to get us killed? You keep Joseph's Most Wanted
here under our roof, and you're worried about *me* getting us
killed? That's a hell of a nerve."

Bunny's hands stopped. Her visage softened to pensiveness,
and she turned red. "You're correct, Archer. The Josephites
might kill you and all of your people because of me, but killing
more innocents does not make it right."

Granny nodded in agreement. "Hiding an innocent girl is
very different from setting out to kill thousands."

"You can't be serious. They're Josephites. They're the
enemy. And besides, you heard Bunny. The sick and the weak.

How many sick or weak Secs do you see? And I'm not killing the Josephites. I'm just killing their power grid. Let their God decide which of them dies."

Granny rounded on me. "Dammit, Deena, do not make me bury another child." She turned away quickly, but not before I saw the tears glistening in her eyes. I hadn't seen her so afraid since the night they took my father away. I thought of him and the two uncles I'd never met—the ones with the oldest headstones in our graveyard.

My heart softened toward her, but my resolve did not. "I'm sorry, Granny, but as you say, we are each born to our own destiny."

Bunny softly intervened. "I understand wanting to fight Joseph, but there are other ways. You cannot imagine the might of Joseph's army."

"There may be other ways, but this one is mine."

I reached for Granny and hugged her close, surprised to feel her quivering with emotion. "I promise I'll be careful if that helps."

She sniffed and let go of me. "No, it doesn't. But thank you for your promise. I do love you, child."

"I love you, too, Granny." I kissed the top of her head. "Soooo . . . Quinn didn't stop by himself?"

Bunny glanced up with annoying sympathy, and Granny shook her head. "No."

Confused emotions roiled inside me. Was he avoiding me because he couldn't deal with his feelings for me? Was he trying to pretend nothing happened? Perhaps he wasn't thinking of me at all. Perhaps to him, nothing did happen.

I shook my head and took down my pack. Daisy raised her head from where she lay and gave me a look as if to say, "Seriously?" But with only three days until the start of training, I had to try for another deer. It would only be marmots, rabbits, and squirrels after that until the seedlings went in.

Truth be told, I was glad for the time. Thinking of Quinn

made me want to run away into the forest. Someplace where I knew where I stood, and there was only one rule—kill or be killed. I got lucky that time and found a yearling doe a day away from the meadow. Between her and the buck, we would survive.

I awoke the next morning with a confusion of excitement and trepidation. It was still dark when I raised the window over my bunk to let Daisy out, careful not to whack the sill against the top bed where Bunny slept. I slipped into my clothes and followed my dog, avoiding the kitchen. The last thing I wanted was Granny pinning me down, asking my whereabouts. Unfortunately, with training upon us, Quinn was not as easy to avoid.

Along with facsimiles of the transformer stations, Flynx had designed an obstacle course at the base of the cliff above Quinn's house. While I climbed toward it through the forest, I realized that Quinn was a short distance behind me, occasionally flashing his light on my back.

Painfully aware of his presence, I wondered if he liked what he saw. Then the anger bloomed inside me as I remembered the tone of his voice and his harsh words. I mentally kicked myself for caring what he thought at all.

That's when he finally spoke. "Archer, about the other day. I'm sorry."

I spun on him, my eyes and voice hard. "Why, Quinn? What are you sorry for?" Hurt and proud, I wanted him to acknowledge either that he loved me or that he'd led me on. Whichever it was, I needed to hear him say it.

He stepped back in the face of my vile temper and his shield went up. His eyes and voice turned to steel. "Never mind. Let's just see to the job."

"Fine. To the job." Spinning back around, I resumed the climb, fighting off tears. I hated him for being so cruel, and I wished I had been kinder when I had the chance.

When I reached the cliff, Flynx, Zander, and Freefall were

already waiting beside timber bridges, a large rope net, and lines hanging from the top of the precipice. I had a physical memory of falling while retrieving the trade pack, and my stomach dropped. "Flynx, we're just blowing up transformer stations. Why would we need to climb any cliffs?"

Flynx ignored my question and started us out with some calisthenics and a run. It wasn't until we returned, Zander and Freefall panting as if they had been at it all day, that he finally addressed us with a stern voice. "We are here for one purpose and one purpose only. To take down the Josephites. To do this, we have to work as a team. We have to know each other's strengths and weaknesses, and we have to know how each of us will react when the shit hits the fan. That's why we're going to start with this obstacle course. Now up the ropes with you. Last one to the top pegs St. Peter tonight."

Looking up the cliff, I gulped. My eyes sought Quinn without my permission, but he looked away. My temper flared. *So that's how it's gonna be.*

I ran to the rope and pulled myself up, my feet walking up the cliff. As if I'd called him out, Quinn was one step behind me on the next rope over. Straining with every muscle, there was no way I was letting him beat me to the top. But being a man in his prime, he had the advantage in the muscle department. He was gaining.

Anger pushed me on. I scrambled and clawed every way I knew how, digging my toes into the most precarious places as long as it was enough to keep me ahead of him.

In my haste, I didn't notice an old hawk's nest. When I put my foot down, I realized something was wrong and quickly kicked out my leg, accidentally shooting the whole nest off the rock and directly into Quinn's face.

"Aaaghh!" He stopped where he was until he could brush the mess off enough to see again. When he finally looked up at me, there was a glint of anger in his eye that I'd never seen before. It cut me to the core, and I blinked back tears, unable to speak. As a way of apology, I slowed my climb and let him overtake me. He did so without a glance in my direction.

Soon I noticed an inordinate amount of dirt falling on my head. Looking up, I saw him kick out in my direction with each step as he climbed. He was doing it on purpose!

That was it.

I renewed my sprint to the top, but I had given too much leeway. He beat me. Nursing my wounded pride, I rappelled back down the cliff, on some level glad my anger was stronger than my fear of heights that day.

Flynx pointed to the rope net next. As before, I jumped on first to get ahead of Quinn, ready for him this time. When he was a foot off the ground, I got my chance. With all of the hurt feelings and anger I'd nursed for the past few days, I stepped on his hand below me. Not a stomp. I didn't want to do permanent damage. Just enough to let him know who he was messing with.

The next thing I knew, his strong grip was on my ankle. He jumped down, taking me with him. We hit the ground, my breath rushed out of me, and before I knew it, he flipped me over his knee. His hand came down hard on my backside.

"If you're going to act like a petulant child, I'm going to treat you like one." He swatted me three more times and then tossed me off to land on my butt in the dirt.

Flynx was on us both in a heartbeat. "Paul's pocked pecker! Go fuck, fight, or run a footrace, but get the hell off of my course!"

Quinn and I shared a glance, angry and abashed.

Flynx balled up his fists, shaking with anger and disgust. "You heard me. Get the hell out of here, and don't come back until you're ready to work."

I called Daisy to me. Furious with myself and hating Quinn even more, I threaded my way downhill through the trees. First day of training to kill Josephites and I had gotten eighty-sixed from the field. What was I thinking, letting Quinn get to me that way?

About halfway back to the meadow, I heard a crack of a twig several yards behind me. *Is he following me? Will he apologize?*

Without looking back, I aimed toward a large juniper tree, casually placing it between me and my follower. Rather than continue forward, I used its cover to double back and wait. There was no way he was getting out of this one.

CHAPTER 25

MOMENTS LATER, Harmony minced her way past the tree. Disappointment flowed through me, and I mentally shifted gears. She stopped and searched the forest.

"I'm right here," I said, coming up behind her.

She jumped, spun around, and took a step back. Then, visibly mustering herself, she regained that step and stood firm.

"Why are you following me?" I held my voice even, and I waited.

The red worked its way from her neck into her cheeks. Her growl was almost inhuman. "You think you're getting away with it, don't you? But you're not. You'll pay for this, Archer Sprague. I'll see that you do."

With that, she turned and ran, ignoring the branches tearing at her arms and hair.

The urge was strong to call out my innocence. That Bane had attacked us first. That Greagor had tried to kill Quinn. That Bunny deserved our mercy as much as she did. But I kept my peace, knowing that nothing I could say would reach her.

Her eyes haunted me through my day, along with the uncomfortable feeling that something was at work here that I didn't understand. Over and over, I reviewed the events with Bane and Greagor in my mind, and each time I came to the same conclusion. It wasn't our fault.

But that night I dreamed. People. Masses of people. More people than I thought were possible. And the flames of the Godfire chased at my heels, overtook me, and burned into my soul.

The next morning, it took more than a splash of water to clear my head of the night, but I was determined to make up for my rough start at training. Flynx allowed me back, and I helped my teammates every way I could think of. Even Quinn. And he did the same.

Before long, we learned things about ourselves and each other that we had never suspected. I wasn't as strong as any of the men, but I could outrun them all. Quinn was the most efficient, finding exactly where to place his foot, how to angle his body, how high to jump, and how low to stoop. Zander was the strongest among us, and Freefall was as smooth, lithe, and graceful as a lion. But for all of our youthful skill, Flynx put us to shame, running the course faster and more capably than any of us. I had to admit, I found all of the men most impressive.

We only had a couple of weeks to devote to training before the planting began, and Flynx didn't waste a minute of it. In fact, he was a dragon awakened. We did the same course two days in a row, and then he said, "This morning, ladies and gentleman, we're starting from the top and working it the other direction."

"You mean run the course backwards?" asked Freefall, rubbing sleep from his eyes.

"Hell, no. Yesterday was backwards. Today is forwards, but since you want to run it backwards, turn around and run backwards."

We also practiced martial arts, learning to pin and throw each other.

"Don't lie there humping the Gabriel-screwed ground. Get

up and go at him again."

We made human-shaped targets and practiced with firearms.

"Why are you aiming at his knee? You want him to dance? You shoot his knee, and he can still hop. You shoot his hip, and he won't get up. Shoot his hip."

Quinn obtained grenades, and we practiced throwing rocks of similar size and shape.

Flynx ran us through the obstacle course until we dropped, all the while encouraging us with irreverent epithets. "Paul's pocked pecker, that's pathetic!" "Get your limp angel-ass up that wall!" or "Joseph in a vice grip! If you can't walk, crawl!"

Just as challenging for me as the physical drills was a more cerebral endeavor. I had to learn to tell time.

Our mission depended on a synchronized effort, and only Flynx and Quinn had grown up with watches and clocks. Freefall, Zander, and I had work to do. The idea that numbers had anything to do with the sun's course through the sky was a completely foreign concept to us.

After several days of flunking at basic watch reading, I questioned Bunny about her watch under the guise of curiosity. She explained things much differently than Flynx did, and with her help, I got the hang of it.

On the mornings we weren't running the obstacle course, we practiced our mission. We learned every building, wire, and transformer in each of the stations and the truck yard by working through the areas Flynx had reproduced in the forest using piles of rocks, chunks of wood, ropes, and weighted plastic jugs. We tried different pairings and learned all three layouts to find how we worked best. Ultimately, we decided that Flynx, Zander, and Freefall would take the large station to the north, and Quinn and I would take the smaller one to the south.

Soon we developed a routine. After mornings of physical exertion at the course and the "stations," we ate our factory bars and practiced martial arts and weapons. Then we parted ways to take care of our duties for the meadow. I hunted marmots, rabbits, and squirrels for the stew pots while Zander, Flynx, and Freefall joined in the plowing, and Quinn saw to his own horticultural endeavors. I couldn't remember a time I'd ever been so tired.

Even more oppressive than the work was Granny's constant Eyebrow of Impending Doom that she flashed at me every time I came in from training.

"Archer, you're going to get us all killed."

"Yeah, well, you've got Bunny, and I've got this. Let's see who gets us fried first."

With so much time spent training, there was no way to avoid Quinn. However, we no longer spoke to each other about anything that didn't involve the mission, the planting, or some other business of the meadow. But every morning, I woke and saw the drawer that held the dragontech. If Bunny was already gone for the day, I took it out, held it to my breast, and closed my eyes, remembering his caress. Touching my fingers to my own lips, I recalled how it felt to be close to him, feeling his breath and his kiss, and my body burned. Then, with a sigh of overwhelming emptiness, I put the dragontech back in the drawer and reached for my men's clothing to go about the business of my day.

The new moon came, and with it the marathon of planting season. The entire meadow, Flynx included, worked to exhaustion getting the hemp seedlings from the greenhouse into the ground under Zander's expert direction. Once the plants were out, we had to nurture and protect them, and it was all done on top of mission practice.

Guarding the seedlings in the field was my job. Deer and rabbits, hungry from the lean winter, stalked our hemp, our lifeblood, waiting at the edge of the meadow for nightfall so that they could slip in and steal a few bites. A small herd of hungry deer and a few ravenous rabbits could wipe out half our crop before sunup. As a result, the start of my day shifted to sundown. But the silver lining was that the game came to me. Hunting was only a matter of staying awake.

The poor, hungry deer couldn't help themselves. They were scrawny and lean, but they were abundant, and I bagged five in two weeks without leaving my post. Of course, that made more work with skinning, butchering, and stretching the meat on the drying racks inside the fenced kiln yard.

With so much work bringing the meadow together, I got the chance to watch Bunny grow into her new Sec life. She played with the meadow children and showed them tricks like shadow puppets and folded cloth designs. She always had kind words and corny jokes on her lips and an infant in her arms. She listened to everyone who spoke as if nothing were more important than what they were saying, even if they were being stupid. She even wrestled with the goats and held them for Charlotte to doctor, winning over that timid heart. I saw my people looking for reasons to be near her. She had them all eating out of her hand.

All except Harmony, that is. Each time she saw Bunny, she gave her a look that chilled my blood, and she refused to speak to the girl. Bunny, in her turn, had only smiles and kind words for the old shrew, but I noticed she found ways to keep her distance from the constant hostility.

In this manner, our exhausting planting season evolved into growing season, mixed in with constant mission practice. The mohair was washed, and the Tinkers and Weavers, with Bunny's help, were busy with the carding and the spinning when they weren't weeding in the field. Granny worked at her pottery wheel at all hours, preparing for her big end-of-season trading trip to the city. The seedlings thrived, and they soon grew big enough to survive a bite or two from the hungry deer. Venison filled the drying racks, and the garden crops in the greenhouse began to produce. The factory bars were just enough to carry us through. We would survive the season.

Before we knew it, the moon had waxed and waned twice,

and the Super Bowl was upon us. We were ready for anything.

CHAPTER 26

"HOLY CRAP. WE WEREN'T ready for this," Freefall said, staring at Maverick's driveway. It stood empty in the dusky light except for a lonely little jeep that was sure to be missed.

Flynx put a steadying hand on him and calmly said, "We steal one of Maverick's."

"No," Quinn said. "There has to be another way."

Zander searched the horizon. "It's only dusk. They'll show in time."

Flynx shook his head, the tail on his coonskin hat mirroring his negative gesture. "If there were any orgies tonight, they'd be happening by now. If we don't get to those stations by nine p.m., we're screwed. Everything we've worked for will be done."

"Look, guys," I said. "Leave it to me. I'll get Spooge to loan us his truck."

"No way," they said in unison. It was the first time I'd ever heard them agree on anything.

Quinn scowled. "Spooge is a slime, but he isn't stupid. He'd figure it out and sell us to the Joes in a heartbeat. We have to find another way."

"He covered our ass with Bunny, remember? He may not like it, but if we give him enough blinkers, he'll do it. Besides, I don't hear any better ideas happening here."

"She's right," Flynx said. "That little snake will do anything for money."

I put out my hand. "Come on, guys. Cough up your credits, and let me get us a ride."

Reluctantly, Quinn pulled a blinker from the hem of his shirt, two from false pockets in his pants, and another from his collar. He held them out to me and then pulled them back, removing the one he'd had in his collar. "This should be enough. Those reds are five hundred each, and the blue is two fifty. Bring back a red if you can."

"Really?" Flynx asked, his voice incredulous. "What were you going to do? Pay the damn transformers to shut down?"

"Hey," Quinn said. "You never know when you'll need a little money. Like now."

Flynx shook his head. "All right. Archer, you score the ride. Quinn, you go play poker like normal. The rest of us will wait in the bar. I want to be out of here by seven-thirty p.m. sharp."

I hid Quinn's blinkers in various places on my body, and we walked to the Arena. The place was as dead inside as out, almost empty of Sec and Joe alike. We stood just inside the door and let our eyes adjust to the light. No stage show, no crowd of lascivious men, and almost no employees.

Blondie and Red leaned on the bar where Marty ignored them and watched the holoscreen of pre-game activities. The whores' perpetual "rode hard and put away wet" look expressed itself that day in the form of red, white, and blue lingerie. Since the women ignored the Joes camped out at the poker table behind them, I knew the men had already done whatever Debbie they were going to do that day. The two whores turned their attention to us. Specifically, to Quinn. With a whisper and a giggle, they sauntered over.

I took three deliberate steps away from Quinn and turned to

the holoscreen to avoid seeing his reaction to his "friends," but what was on the screen was far more disturbing than anything that was happening behind me. Rows of dancing young women, forty or so in all, occupied the stadium field. They wore tiny, blue skirts with white trim topped by red, sleeveless midriffs that showed cleavage in the deep V of the neckline. Prancing in white boots and waving large blue and white Kingdom flags in time with the music, their skirts flipped with each beat to flash the sequined Western Province flags on their shiny, white panties. In such scanty clothing, waving their flags in a peek-a-boo game across their half-naked bodies, they looked like nothing more to me than a horde of Maverick's fan dancers, Joe style.

The girls abruptly halted their flags in the shape of a Cross of Michael on the field. The Joes cheered from their poker table, and the cameras panned around the stadium to show the roaring crowd. My mouth dropped open. So many people. Thousands and thousands of them, all in one place—more than all of the Secs put together.

I knew five million people lived behind the walls of Promise City, but that was only a number until I saw the stadium packed to capacity. No wonder us few thousand Secs left in the hills to grow their hemp meant nothing to them. Rebellion rose within me, and I vowed that we would mean something before the day was out.

Above the roar of the crowd, the announcer's voice called, "Let's give it up for the Praise Worship Drill Team. Thank you, ladies. I was most moved by that brilliant performance. Joseph's blessings on you. And now, our own holovangelist celebrity, Pastor Bob, will lead us in prayer."

It took me a moment to compute what I heard. So that was Bunny's Praise Worship Drill Team? Somehow I couldn't reconcile the sight of those trashy outfits with the shy, virginal geek making folded cloth animals for the children back in the meadow.

"Catchin' flies." Quinn's voice startled me, and I snapped my mouth shut. He passed me to get to the poker table, Red and Blondie on his arms. The Joes at the table were Dave the Engineer and his crew, so Quinn had no trouble getting into the game.

Flynx, Freefall, and Zander headed for the corner table, and I went straight to the bar.

"Free the Cuban?" asked a friendly voice.

"Thanks, Marty, but not today. Only water." I handed him a five-credit blinker and a piece of paper that had a picture of a bow and arrow on it. "Please get this to Spooge and take a credit for yourself."

I downed the water in one gulp and then fidgeted with the glass, running through the mission in my mind in an effort to control my nerves. Spooge had to loan us his car, or we would have to do what Flynx said and steal one of Maverick's.

Leaving the glass on the counter, I slipped out to Maverick's garden, knowing Spooge would look for me there. Except for a few of Maverick's favorites at leisure, it was just me and the foliage. I gravitated to a secluded bench in the far corner under an apple tree, which was now full of half-ripe fruit.

The dragontech hidden under my turtleneck was hot, and it itched. I scratched at my neck. I had considered leaving the armor at home, but decided that I would have only been cutting off my nose to spite my face.

Honeysuckle bloomed along the fence behind me, and hummingbirds fussed among themselves in the late afternoon, defending their territories. A flowerbed across the path from me embraced a new rose garden, the mulch still fresh on top.

Ordinarily, the beauty would have lulled me into relaxation, but today I was strung tighter than my bow. What if we couldn't find the spares? What if the transformers didn't actually shut down? What if we were caught? I tried staring at the roses in front of me and appreciating their beauty, but instead, I found myself visualizing our mission one more time. Lost in my thoughts when Spooge appeared in front of me, I jumped.

"Easy now. I see you ditched the fish," Spooge said with a smile in his eye.

I drew in my breath. I had never seen him like this. His blonde hair gleamed a shade of gold that only came from water washing, and he stood at least an inch taller than when I'd seen him at the Big Box at the end of spring. A white silk shirt, unbuttoned two buttons too far for decency, perfectly displayed his strong, tan body. His tight white linen slacks accentuated the reasons he was a favorite at Maverick's. His clothes were the finest I had ever seen, and they brought out a maturity in him I had not noticed before.

"You clean up," I said. "Stop with the rude comments, and I'll let you sit with me." I reached in my pocket and pulled out the hemp lollipop that he knew I had for him.

Reaching for it eagerly, he popped it in his mouth and grinned, once more the sweet, innocent child. He sucked on the lollipop with gusto, the stick protruding from the corner of his mouth.

"What's with the makeover?" I couldn't help but stare.

"I'm a Greeter now. Highest price in the house," he said. His pride reminded me of how I felt when I brought in my first buck. "Still free to you, though," he added with a wink.

"Congratulations," I said, not knowing what else to say to that accomplishment. "The look suits you."

"So you like this, do you?" he asked, reaching toward me. His expression changed from an innocent child to a fox with a rabbit in sight.

I snatched his approaching hand and turned my face to his, only a few inches away. "Back off, Spooge, or I will bitch-slap your balls."

"Oww. You do hurt a girl." He took his hand from me, shaking it dramatically as if it were burning.

Ordinarily, I would have laughed, but I was far too worried about securing a vehicle in time. As if for emphasis, the lights came on along the footpath. I hated to rush him, but I had no choice. "I won't BS you. I need a favor."

"Everybody does. What makes yours different?"

I pulled a blinker from the pocket in the back of my turtleneck. "I come bearing blinkers. The guys and I need to borrow your truck for a few hours. Five hundred. No questions."

He snorted. "My truck? You mean Maverick's truck that he let's me drive? Yeah, right. What? You going to the Super Bowl?"

"No questions," I repeated.

I turned the blinker back and forth in my hand. He studied it, his face growing serious. "No questions? Sounds risky. Make it fifteen, and we'll talk."

"A thousand," I countered, taking the second red blinker from a pants pocket and putting it with the first.

"Holy shit. You are serious. No way. Not the truck. If Maverick saw it gone without me in it, he'd have me flogged."

"We only need it for a few hours. I promise we'll bring it back in perfect condition. Twelve fifty, and that's my final offer."

He stood, and his face hardened. "No, Archer. Not for any price."

CHAPTER 27

"**S**POOGE, COME ON. YOU have to." I hoped I
sounded insistent rather than pathetic.
"You'll get me killed, and yourselves as well. I
can't believe you even asked me that. Good to see you, but
I've got work to do."

"No. Please, wait. Sit with me a bit." I knew if he walked
away now, I didn't stand a chance.

His brow furrowed, but he shrugged and joined me on
the bench. I sighed in relief, and he cleared his throat. We
sat silently a moment. I studied the flowers in front of me,
wondering what approach to take next. For some reason, their
arrangement reminded me of a picture I once saw of Vitruvian
Man. "Tell me about these new flowers. Roses?"

"Real roses. Flown here all the way from the Southeast
Province. We call this the Virgin Garden." He put the sucker
stick back in his mouth to chew on.

A sense of dread washed over me. "Why do you call it that?"

"Remember when you came through with the fish? There
was a girl that day. Looked a lot like you, in fact. Could have
been your little sister. Anyway, the Minister of Justice beat
her to death. I guess she chomped him good when he shoved

his pecker down her throat. It was bad. Didn't even screw her first. Just killed her. Probably couldn't have done her anyway, after that bite." Spooge snorted. "I've never seen Maverick so mad at a customer. That piece cost him a fortune. The minister flew in these roses to placate him, so now they're all here—the virgin and the roses. See? The yellow ones are her arms, the pink ones her legs, the red are her head, and that pretty white one, that's right over her—"

"Stop. That is too much information." Shaking, I fought to not vomit, thinking what those bastards would have done to Bunny if they'd caught her.

Seeing how upset I was, Spooge put a calming hand on my arm. "Sorry. I thought you knew. It's the secret to Maverick's garden. Whenever there's an accident or some john gets carried away, well, it's not such a bad end to be cut up and turned into something as fine as flowers, is it?"

Yes. It sounded bad to me, and I was out of time. I stood up, determined in my course. "Then I'll just have to steal a car. Don't rat me out." I walked away.

Within three steps, he jumped up and grabbed my arm. "You can't do that. He'll kill you. He keeps all kinds of eyes in his garage. You won't get out of the driveway."

"I have to try."

"Dammit, Archer, what's so important?"

"It's really best you don't know. But I would rather die than not do this thing, so I'll take my chances. If I don't come back, well, just know you're very special to me, Spooge."

"Does this have something to do with that woman you had through here the other day? And don't give me some bullshit about her being your cousin or your fiancé."

I smiled. "She really is my cousin, and she's pretty cool. But I promise you, there is no way she's my fiancé."

He twizzled the lollipop twig between his teeth. "Damn you. Take the truck, but have it back in three hours. And it had better be spotless."

I grinned and jumped toward him with a hug, catching myself at the last moment and switching to a manly backslap. "Thank you."

I turned away and fairly danced up the path. "Keys in it?"

His voice stopped me. "Ahem."

I turned, and he held up his fingers, rubbing them together. "Twelve fifty."

"Oh, yeah." I took the blinkers from where I'd stashed them. "Thanks. We won't let you down."

"Damn right. And if you do, I'll kill you myself."

I knew he meant it.

The blinkers vanished into his slacks. "It's parked behind the house. I'll send Delilah with the keys in about forty-five minutes. Will you know when that is?"

I held up my arm with the watch and smiled.

"Oh, hey," he said. "Welcome to the modern world." His eyes and voice hardened. "Okay. Wait here until I'm well gone. Three hours max on the truck, and don't you screw me."

"I would never screw a friend, and you know I'm your friend." I smiled.

Again, the little boy in him filled his eyes, and his face became as open and trusting as a child's. "I think you're my only real friend," he said. He turned, took a step down the path, and then turned back. Taking the stick from his mouth, he asked, "Why do you always bring me the candy?"

I knew he wanted some declaration, some reassurance, something to build a dream on. I thought of how I could never be the man he thought I was, the lover he wanted . . . all of the things I could never give him. I gave him the truth. "Because I can."

He returned my smile, stuck the stick back in his mouth, and sauntered toward the garden door.

***

W ITHIN THE HOUR, FLYNX was ignoring me while I played with all of the buttons and levers in Spooge's truck that I never got to play with when Spooge was driving. I pushed a lever low on my right, and my seat moved. I startled. Then I propelled the seat backward, forward, up, and down and inflated it in different sections. Strung taut, I appreciated the distraction of exploring the vehicle, finding a multitude of buttons, lights, and special compartments. I turned a knob. Water sprayed down the windshield, and two blades shot up from nowhere.

Swerving slightly, Flynx barked, "Michael's poxy pecker, girl, cut that out!"

Soon we parked Spooge's truck on a well house road, deep in the gassplant field and only a stone's throw from the truck yard. We crept up on the truck yard, hidden by the seven-foot vegetation across the road from it, and we waited. Before long, two patrol dogs, the ones Flynx had noted when he cased the place, trotted along the fence in front of us. He dropped them with two muffled cracks from his silenced .380. Quinn ran forward with one of Flynx's lockpickers, and we bolted across the road and through the gates.

From left to right, Freefall and I searched the outbuildings for the spare transformers while the others wired two trucks. One by one, we used the lockpickers on the doors, only to find rolls of wire, spare tires, administrative offices, windmill propellers, or tools. When there were only two buildings left, I looked up. The ash from Capulin wasn't too heavy, and I could see the fireworks over Promise City. The game had started. If we didn't get to those transformer stations well before it ended, we wouldn't catch the Josephites in the stadium. The impact would suffer, and even worse, the roads would once more fill with Josephite traffic. We had to hurry.

"Let's split up," I said, heading for the farthest building.

Freefall grabbed me by the arm. "No. We need to stay together. What if you run into trouble?"

"If there was going to be trouble, we would have found it by now. We killed the dogs, and Flynx didn't see any people the day he was here. Now you take that building, and I'll take this one. Meet me back here."

I moved out before he could protest. Once inside the warehouse, I pulled out my penlight, and bingo. There they were. In short order, I opened up each portal and poured in the powdered acid that would kill the replacement transformers within three days of being filled with liquid. Seeing the plan coming together, my adrenaline raced. I slipped out of the building and locked it behind me.

Before I'd taken three steps, an arm squeezed my neck in a vice from behind, and the cold steel of a gun barrel chilled my temple.

A wicked voice growled in my ear. "Hee hee. The Prophet knew I wanted to kill a Sec tonight."

CHAPTER 28

HIS BREATH REEKED OF liquor.

"Hey!" Freefall's voice rang out from in front of the next building.

Still pinching my neck in his left arm, the guard pointed h' pistol toward the sound.

With the weapon redirected, I stomped on his instep w' all my might. He shifted his weight, imbalanced. I grabb his outstretched wrist with one hand and brought my weight down on the crook of his elbow with my own bent a twisting him around my body and down. He slammed to ground beneath me, landing full on his bent neck.

I heard the snap, but it didn't compute. Flipping him o stomach, I pinned him beneath me, his hand twisted up b his back, just as I'd practiced under Flynx's supervision gun was out of my immediate reach, so I pulled my ow held it to his head.

Freefall ran up beside me. "Damn, that was sweet. job." I nodded to acknowledge the compliment. Then I the man with my gun, and he made a strange gurgling "Cover me."

I checked the man's pulse. It was faint, but it wa

Then I noticed a twitch in his right leg that niggled a m
Faebin had twitched like that when he lay on the ledg
back broken. I pulled my knife and jabbed the man in the l
of his thigh. No response.

"I'm going to flip him over." His body was completel
limp, but he definitely had a pulse. Nausea began to rise in
me. I took a deep breath and forced it down. "He's paralyzed.
I broke his neck."

"Good. We don't have to kill him. Let's roll him over there
and leave him."

A witness. That didn't sit well with me. "I don't know. That
sounds like—"

A shot cut me off, and the man's blood and brain matter
splattered the dirt.

Freefall jumped back. "Oh, shit. Oh, shit."

Flynx holstered his pistol. I hadn't even heard him come
up. "Saints pugging Peter. Get in your trucks and quit screwing
around." He turned and strode away, shaking his head. "Noobs."

Freefall stared at the body, his eyes wide with horror.

I grabbed his arm and pulled him with me as I jumped to
Flynx's heels. I was glad to have a veteran to show me how it
was done. Of course we couldn't leave a witness, and the man
had tried to kill me, after all. I would think on it no more.

I jumped into the passenger seat of the waiting truck next
to Quinn. Zander opened the gates, and we were off. We blew
down the south road toward our assigned station, Clarisse
between us on the bench seat. "Only forty minutes to get in
place. What took you two so long?" he asked.

I tried to sound nonchalant. "A guy tried to kill me."

Rubbing my left knee, I shifted uncomfortably in my seat.
The adrenaline was wearing off, and a dull pain told me I'd
pulled something when I twisted the guy to the ground.

"What do you mean a guy tried to kill you?" Quinn asked.
"Are you all right?"

I explained what happened and was oddly comforted by his

lack of reaction. He said, "You locked up the building so they won't know you got in there. Don't worry about it. It's nice if they never know we used their own trucks for this, but it's not critical. You did what you had to do."

I shrugged. "Yeah, I know. Freefall's a mess, though. Killing Joes isn't quite what he thought it would be."

"And him the talker." Quinn paused. "You wearing your dragontech?"

I noticed he didn't look at me when he asked. "Yes. Under my shirt."

"Good."

We didn't speak while we sped up the empty road. Soon the gassplant fields changed from grasses that towered over my head to rows of cuttings laid out to dry before harvest, their bud-like crowns ripe with petroleum that would be gleaned by the Josephites to keep their war machines running.

In the middle of nowhere, Quinn slowed and turned on a dirt road through a field.

"What are you doing?" Honestly. Didn't he know we were pressed for time?

"Taking a shortcut. Takes ten minutes off the main route. Don't worry, I know where I am."

"Dammit, Quinn. You need to stick to the plan." "You know, sometimes you should just trust me."

I crossed my arms and glared out the window, not trusting anyone or anything in that moment. We bumped over the rutted, rocky side road far too fast for safety, but we soon turned back onto the main road, and the transformer station was in our headlights.

"See?" he said. "You should trust me."

"Okay, you were right. We've got twelve minutes, and we might not have made it in time the other way."

"Thank you." He grinned smugly.

Suddenly the truck lurched hard to the left, and my head slammed against the door. An open can of tools rolled out from under my seat. Quinn stomped on the brakes and wrestled the wheel with all his strength, barely saving us from tipping the unwieldy vehicle. A tire had blown.

My nerves snapped. "Dammit. Son of a bitch! We picked up an effing nail on your shortcut."

Quinn's jaw dropped. He'd never heard me talk like that, except the day he had given me the armor. "To the job, Archer. We know the way home," he said, his calm voice a salve.

We limped the last hundred yards up to the gate on three tires and a front rim, only ten minutes before kickoff.

Pulling myself together, I jumped out to pick the lock on the double-sided gate. I studied the transformers, trying to find a way to turn our bad luck into an advantage, and I noticed two large metal pods full of later model transformers, side by side and thirty feet in from the gate. Flynx said we couldn't take them out with bullets like the earlier models, but it occurred to me that a tank of biodiesel could do the job.

I jumped back in and grinned at Quinn. "Park it over there by the metal pods."

"Why?"

I grinned. "Now it's your turn. You just have to trust me."

He rolled his eyes and shook his head. "You're the one with trust issues, not me."

"Right." I produced my pocketknife and popped out the spool of techthread. "Will this lead the Joes back to us?"

"No. Joes and Rebels have that too. It's made in China," he said.

"Okay, thanks." I grabbed the can under my feet and dumped the rest of the tools, taking the screwdriver. Then I jumped out and rolled under the truck.

"What are you doing? We have to do this thing in three minutes."

I didn't take the time to answer him because I didn't want to argue. Taking a grenade from my belt with one hand, I turned on my pen light with the other and searched the underside for just the right nooks and crannies. Careful of the hot spots, I found a place I liked right next to the fuel tank.

I wedged the grenade in and then placed my other grenade beside it. I popped the spool of techthread out of my pocketknife, and I let out several feet of it. Then I connected it to the two grenades, leaving no slack between them. Double-checking to make sure the safety levers were securely in place and would not pop up, I held my breath and carefully—so very carefully—pulled out the pins. Then I stabbed a hole above the midline of the fuel tank with the screwdriver and filled the empty tool can with biodiesel.

Scooting out from under the truck, I set the can of biodiesel between the two pods of transformers to create vapor, and I left the cable spool on the ground where I could find it quickly to attach it to the gate on our way out.

Joining Quinn in the shadows, I told him what I had done. "Are you frigging crazy?" he exclaimed.

"Maybe," I replied. "How much longer?"

Quinn's gloved fingers counted down the final five seconds, and we shot into action, knowing Flynx, Zander, and Freefall were doing the same.

Quinn ran left, and I ran right. The transformers, around eighty of them, clustered in small groups throughout the station where they had been added on in sections over the years. Trained beyond the need to think, our feet ran their patterns, and we put two bullets into each canister. Within minutes, they all leaked fluid in a slow bleed that would shut down the Josephite world.

We met back at the parked truck by the metal pod. "Done," we said simultaneously.

Not stopping to catch my breath, I snatched up the cable spool beside the truck. "Okay. I need to get this over to the gate without pulling out the grenades." Keeping the barest amount of slack, we backed away, unrolling the cable as we went. We stepped outside and closed the double gates, relocking them behind us. Gently tightening the cable, I secured it to the gate panel that, when opened, would increase the tension on the lines and dislodge the grenades.

Time to get away. "Now what?" I asked Quinn.

"We run like hell." Urgency tightened his voice.

"We can't go through the fields. Even the Joes could trace our footprints back to the hills," I said.

"If Flynx is right, we have about twenty-five more minutes before their lights go out." Quinn gazed across the plains. "The work camp I was at is about two miles south from here up this road. It's paved all the way, so let's save these." He walked to the road and began removing the deer hide covers from his boots.

"What? Why would we run toward a work camp? And don't tell me to just trust you."

Quinn sighed. "You should just trust me. There's a tunnel there that will get us a half-mile out into the fields. No footprints. No followers. Home late tomorrow. But we have to get inside the camp to get to it."

"So we're breaking into a Josephite camp to get away from the Josephites?"

"Yes," he said.

With no further ado, he turned and ran up the road. I quickly pulled off my own boot covers, thinking it would be nothing to catch up to him on the smooth, paved surface. I was wrong.

Within a mile, I was limping slightly, my knee rebelling at the strain. "Quinn, slow down."

"Can't. We've got to get through the camp before the lights go down, or the eyes inside will see us before we see them."

"I'm sorry, but I'm doing my best. That Joe bastard back there got my knee."

Without stopping, Quinn pulled a plastic envelope from his pack. Inside was a cooling patch. "I got this from Maverick a while back. Put it on your knee. It'll help."

I did as I was told. Soon I could feel the cold creep into my muscles, numbing them. The pain subsided enough that I was able to keep up.

Relief vied with trepidation when we spotted the dim lights of the work camp with its barns and living quarters. True to Quinn's prediction, everyone appeared to be gathered around a holoscreen in the courtyard, watching the game. Three-story building walls formed part of the camp's perimeter, the rest being completed by a large fence with rows of concertina wire at the top, which was angled to keep people in rather than to keep them out.

"Follow me," Quinn whispered, clutching at his side, breathless from the run. Leading me to a corner window well at the end of a long dormitory, he jumped inside, and, using Clarisse, he flipped up the manual lock. Then he slid the window open. With a beckoning gesture to me, he disappeared into the basement of the structure. Gulping, I dropped down the window well behind him.

My skin crawled. I'd never been in such consummate Josephite territory, and it reminded me of being locked in the seed vault at the Big Box. Surrounded by Josephites with no easy exit.

Quinn locked the window behind me, took out his penlight, and flashed it around the room while we drank deeply from our water packs. Orderly boxes lined the walls, bearing such labels as "Dresses, Size 4," and "Boots, Size 12 youth."

He tiptoed over to the door, peeked out, and nodded his head in satisfaction. "Okay. We slip down the hall and out the side door. We'll have to cross the compound and get into the tool shed. The entrance is under the boards in the back of the shed, or at least it should be."

"What do you mean 'should be'?"

"Well, it was there twelve years ago."

"You mean we're in a Josephite camp, and you don't even know if there's a way out?"

"Hush. Follow me." Quinn slipped into the dark hallway

and made a silent run to the end. I had no choice but to follow. Soon we were down the hall, up the steps, and peeking through the outer door. From where we stood, I could tell Quinn was right. Hundreds gathered around the holoscreen, watching the game. For now.

Then the lights flickered. I caught my breath and grinned at Quinn. It was working. He held his fingers to his lips and pointed to a building across an open stretch with a sign that said "Clinic." So soft I could barely hear him, he said, "I'll go when they start cheering. Wait until I'm in the shadows before you follow. Only move when they are cheering." Before I could question, the Josephites whooped with glee, and Quinn ran across the bare patch to the clinic shadows.

At the next cheer, I joined him, and we dashed around back, placing the building between the Josephites and ourselves. The lights flickered again, and this time, they dimmed. The Holoscreen flashed off and back on again, and the crowd booed their dismay in unison.

Quinn leaned close to me. "See that shed between us and those huge greenhouses? That's where we're heading."

Two guards walked out from the other side of the clinic and stood in front of the shed, looking back at the holoscreen and talking. I recognized one of them as Luke, Quinn's friend who we had run into on the way to the Big Box.

The other guy took out a small flask and glanced around before taking a quick swig. "I can't believe that idiot fumbled on the five yard line." He passed the flask to Luke, who waved it away.

"Ah. What do you expect?" said Luke. "Bunch of Gabriel-bugging Patriots. The Pagans should tip that team, or at least send them flowers for the piece of ass they're giving up tonight."

Move, move, move! I must have actually whispered the thought because Quinn turned to me with a finger over his lips.

The lights dimmed a bit more.

"Yo, Luke, what's happening?"

"I don't know, man . . . Whoa. There goes the screen." The lights faded fast and went out. "What the hell?"

Suddenly the night was pitch black, and I couldn't see my own hand in front of me. Before I could wonder what to do next, I felt Quinn's hand on my wrist, pulling me forward. People cried out in the dark, and Luke's flashlight beam snapped on, not fifteen feet away.

"Who's there?" he asked. My toes flew, my aching knee forgotten in the rush of adrenaline. The guard's beam swept the ground, and Quinn fairly lifted me up the steps of the tool shed. Mercifully, the door was unlocked, and we were through it in seconds.

We stood with our backs to the wall while the flashlight beam came in through the window, illuminating the tool shed and showing us that things had, indeed, changed in twelve years. Quinn's wood floor was gone, linoleum in its place. There was no tunnel. We were trapped.

CHAPTER 29

T HE LIGHT MOVED ON and left us in inky darkness, surrounded by hoes, rakes, and boxes of gloves. "Now what?" I asked. "Do we fight our way out the front gate with farming implements?"

"Let me think."

His hand, still gripping my wrist, tightened. Then he was pulling me toward the back of the shed. "This linoleum isn't that new, and it's marked off in nice, big squares. That would make it easy to hide a trap door. The tunnel might still be here."

We pushed our way through the tools until we reached the back of the shed. Quinn knelt down and began testing tiles. Then I heard a sound at the door. I grabbed his arm in fear, and he brushed me off, continuing his search. I started checking the tiles, too, my fingers seeking the edges of the squares to try to lift them.

Luke's voice reached me. "I could swear I saw someone coming in here. Suppose they sabotaged the lights?"

"I don't know. Looks like all of Promise City is out. Not just us," said the other guy.

"Well, we'll give a look." The beam drew closer. On my last desperate attempt, a tile budged. Tugging Quinn's sleeve to get his attention, I flipped it up and reached underneath, ecstatic to find a rope.

I didn't wait. Grabbing it, I quickly lowered myself hand over hand, Quinn's boots in my face as I did. My penlight went on as soon as my feet touched ground, and I jumped out from under him to give him room.

Glancing up, I saw Luke's face above Quinn's, framed by the opening. I gasped and pointed, not knowing if I should fight or flee as he shone his light down in our faces.

Luke's companion called out. "You find something over there?"

Luke's brow furrowed, indecision in his eyes. Quinn looked up and Luke smiled a greeting. "Nah, nothing." He gave Quinn a thumbs-up sign and replaced the tile. Two stomps came from above us, and the tile snugly settled into place. Luke's voice receded as he said, "Let's get those generators going."

Quinn jumped down beside me.

"Damn, Quinn. What kind of hold do you have on that guy?" I shook my head, awed by my companion.

"He's just grateful. I scored some medicine for his baby sister once. I guess it saved her life. He's the kind that's loyal to his own, and the Joes aren't his friends. They aren't his family. They're only who's in charge."

I turned my flashlight on and shone it at Quinn, who grinned like a boy who'd just tricked his way out of field work. I couldn't help but smile back, and we savored the delicious relief of the moment.

Then I flicked my light around. The beam illuminated dozens of broken planters, overturned, half-charred shelves, and shreds of hoses, lights, and wires.

"This was the old growing operation," Quinn said. "I guess I made kind of a mess when I left. But they did try to sell me, after all."

"Is this how you got your marijuana seeds?"

Quinn nodded. "Yep."

"Wow. Impressive. Now let's get out of here."

Quinn laughed. "This way."

Shining his light on the ceiling to create a larger field of illumination, we set out at an easy traveling jog toward the well house a half mile away.

We exited the tiny building to find the gassplant fields in that section laid out in mountainous rows to dry, a good twelve feet wide and four feet tall. Fortunately for us, the rows ran the direction we were going, so we didn't have to cross them horizontally. We didn't look back until we'd covered another two miles.

When we were three miles from Highway 93 and the safety of the full-grown hemp field beyond, I tried to tell myself my knee wasn't hurting, but I failed. "Quinn, I need to rest."

"You do?" The surprise in his voice flattered me. "Damn. That son of a bitch must have gotten you good."

I felt sheepish about being injured. "Yeah, well. He was pretty fat." I looked toward the transformer station, unable to make it out in the darkness, even though a wind had come up and cleared out much of the smoke that had been hanging over the plains for the past few months. "Do you suppose the grenades didn't work?"

"Could be. But the rest of it sure did."

We grinned again. I looked up into the night. "Have you ever seen so many stars? I'm so glad it's a clear night. Your goddess must have arranged that."

Quinn and I stared at the holes in the sky. Without the lights of Promise City to obscure them, they had multiplied like mice in a silo, obscuring the constellations I knew so well until picking them out was an achievement of my memory and not my eyes. There was nothing in that moment but earth and an endless sky, and I was awash in awe. How tiny we were in the face of Creation.

"She moves in mysterious ways," Quinn said. He took out his amulet, kissed it, and replaced it under his shirt.

We stood quietly a moment longer, when Quinn cleared his throat. "You know, Archer, about that day, I just . . . well, you've been my sister for so long."

Anger leapt within me. "Stop. Just stop. I don't want to talk about it again. At least give me that."

"No. You're going to listen to me—"

He never got the chance to finish. A brief series of explosions ripped the night, and flames shot high in the air. I whipped out my binoculars in time to see subsequent explosions across the station. The grenades, fueled by the gas and vapors from the truck, had blasted the transformer station into oblivion.

"Did you see that, Quinn? We did it." Laughing, I jumped into his arms, and he swung me around. Suddenly all of the barriers between us were gone, and we were completely blended in our joy. He set me down and leaned toward me, but I'll never know if he was going to kiss me because what I saw over his shoulder sucked all of the triumph from me in a heartbeat.

Fire. The dried gassplant surrounding the station—dead plant matter filled with petroleum—was a horizontal bomb, and we'd thrown down the match. Flames roared across the plains, and the wind was blowing them straight toward us.

CHAPTER 30

SIRENS BLARED FROM THE work camp. We ran like hell away from the flames that already bore down on the camp's gates.

"Holy shit. To the road," Quinn said. He grabbed my hand and pulled me up the row through the drying piles of petroleum matter. We raced to get across the natural barrier of the road that lay between the inferno and the hills beyond.

I shook loose of his grip, adrenaline erasing the pain in my knee and allowing me to match his pace, but when I glanced over my shoulder, it was clear that the fire was outstripping us by far. My world condensed to a pinpoint of terror. Though we were less than a mile away from the road, we were already winded. I didn't know how we would make it.

My knee gave way, and I stumbled. Quinn caught my arm and kept me from falling. "Archer, look. We're almost there. We can do this."

My gaze followed his, and I saw the slight reflection where the moonlight glanced off of pavement, less than a half a mile away. But the fire, too, was less than a half a mile behind us and gaining ground. Strengthened by the sight of safety, I willed my knee to hold out just a bit longer, and I fairly flew across the field.

But it was no good. Heat engulfed us. Flames roared twenty feet in the air, not three hundred yards behind us and closing in. There was no way we would make it to the road, and I faltered. Confusion gripped me. *No. I'm not supposed to die this way.*

Quinn stopped and reached for his gun. "If you can't do this, I will."

No! It isn't time! Then a sound edged over the thunder of the raging beast behind us.

"Archer, just know that . . ."

I pointed toward the sky. "Listen."

It was the drone of planes. The Fire Planes that blanketed the fields with chemicals, forming a fence around the flames to contain them. "Quinn, we don't have to make the road. We only have to be alive when the plane stops the fire."

He cocked his head and listened. "Hell, yeah." He holstered his pistol, and we ran once more. As the flames bore down on us, I hoped our suicidal delay was not, indeed, suicidal. But the plane was near enough that I could see the fire parked hard at the line it drew, a fifty-foot spread of salvation stopping the fiery death cold in its path. If only we could stay in front of the blaze long enough for the plane to drop its protection over us. I drove on in anticipation of being wrapped in that saving blanket from the sky, ignoring the heat that seemed it would cook me even without the flames. Only a few more seconds to safety.

"One problem," Quinn said, puffing out the words while we ran. His voice was all but lost in the drone of the plane and the roar of the fire bearing down on us. "The chemicals. They're toxic. On skin."

"What?"

Quinn grabbed my hand, and we dove head first into the mountainous row of gassplant. Scrabbling under grassy layers to the ground, I didn't know if the fire would consume us first or if the noise would. Then the plane was over us, and I could only hope the petroleum grass would be enough to keep us from taking in the fumes.

Huddling in our burrow of hay, I moved like I was at the bottom of a pot of gruel. With great struggle, I tied my scarf over my nose to protect me from the thick layers of dust. Opening my eyes was out of the question.

Terrified, I reached for Quinn's hand. I didn't know if the hot hay would burst into fire and consume us any second, or if the toxins that coated it would succeed in stopping the flames. I didn't want to wait to find out. Tugging at Quinn, I tentatively tunneled under the gassplant in the direction I hoped would take us to the road.

The hay was heavy on our backs, and my lungs strained to find enough air. I always thought being in the seed vault was being buried alive. Now, I knew differently.

The going was slow. I fought my way forward under the weight of the grass, the stalks of the cuttings scratching off my skin. Anxious, I reached out to find Quinn every few moments. He did the same with me, and in that manner, we struggled forward inches at a time.

Soon I realized the fire would have killed me already if it hadn't been stopped, and my fear subsided. But how far did we have to go to get out from under the chemicals? I wanted to ask Quinn, but there was no way he would have heard me, and I didn't have the air to waste on shouting.

Writhing on, I found it harder and harder to breathe. I felt something bite my hand, and had no idea if it was a rat, a snake, or a spider. Would it kill me? No. It wouldn't have the chance. The hay would do that. I struggled on.

Just when I thought I didn't have the strength to fight through one more inch of hay, the heat abated, and the weight on my back lightened. Quinn's touch found my arm, and with renewed hope, I pushed on. Soon I scrambled to my hands and knees and burst through to the top, not knowing or caring if we were out from under the chemical blanket. I took a deep breath.

The air tasted of smoke, but at least it didn't taste of hay.

Quinn popped up beside me and gasped. "Look at that, will you?"

His hand was on my head, brushing debris from my hair and face. I opened my eyes and cried out in joy. We were at the road. The smoke billowed thick behind us, and the flames burned low inside their chemical barrier. The sheltering hemp field lay just across the black ribbon, and with it, safety.

"Holy Mother," Quinn said, kissing his amulet and bowing his head.

I took my own moment to breathe deeply into my center. I exhaled slowly and coughed, my lungs still burning. Then Quinn took my hand and we walked across the road into Sec country.

When we entered the rows of hemp, a foot taller than ourselves, the wind shifted, directing the smoke away from the mountains and back toward the field. Before long, the air cleared a bit, and the pain in my lungs subsided.

I pulled one of my two canteens from my belt and wet my scarf to wash myself, unable to bear one more moment of the disgusting filth I'd just crawled through.

"Quinn, you go three rows over and don't peek. I'm taking a bath. You could stand one too.

He laughed. "Only you would think of that now."

"Granny would too. Something she learned in the Army. No matter where you are or what you're doing, you'll do it better if you're clean. Now go on."

I quickly stripped down to my underwear, glad to find the dragontech was as effective at protecting me from the hay as it was supposed to be at protecting me from bullets. "No peeking," I called again.

I heard his voice, muffled by the plants. "Not an issue."

I refused to admit to myself that I wished it actually *were* an issue. I shook out my clothing and washed. The night air rustled the hemp around me and brushed leaves against my bare skin. I took a moment to enjoy it while I walked, only putting on my tank top and traveling shorts when I neared the edge of the field.

Any other time, it would have been hubris to leave my breasts unbound, but that night, I knew the Josephites had better things to worry about than a Sec woman traveling with a Sec man. I thought of the explosion and smiled. Two for one. Their electrical grid and their petroleum fields all in one pop.

We exited the hemp field, and I stumbled. A sharp pain shot through my knee.

"Are you okay?" Quinn was already waiting for me, which called my attention to how slowly I was moving. It was usually me waiting on him.

"Not really, but I'll make it. I'll just be glad when we get through the minefield and on up to Lookout."

Quinn's brow furrowed. "We'd better go the long way along the foothills, then. You shouldn't be climbing with that. The slopes will be easier."

"No, I can make it. The up isn't so bad with knee stuff. It's the down that's the killer."

He shrugged. "Don't be too proud to ask for my help if you need it."

"I won't. I promise."

We started forward, and I tried to hide my limping and the fact that I still quivered inside from the ordeal of the inferno and the twenty-ton, grassy bug palace. "Helluva match we lit, huh?"

Quinn laughed. "Damn, Archer. Blowing up that station—you don't do things halfway, do you?"

His humor was contagious, and my spirits lifted. "Nope. You know me."

"Here. I see you limping. Quit trying to hide it and hand me your pack."

"All right. But I'm only doing it because it makes you feel manly."

"Yeah, right. Now be a good girl and say thank you because we both know I'm doing you a favor."

"I might sort of maybe appreciate it. Will that do?" I gave him my sweetest smile. He rolled his eyes.

Soon the shell of the army jeep loomed in the distance. I stopped. We were at the edge of the minefield.

"Quinn, can you see the signpost?" I was having trouble locating the first path marker in the dark.

"Over here," he said. "I know we usually spread out, but in the dark, I think we should stay together."

"No, Quinn. There's no need for both of us to die if one of us screws up." I shuddered, remembering the last trip through the field. "You've done this more often, so you go first."

"But can you see me in the dark? Tell you what. I'll go first, but I'll wait at each marker."

"Okay. I can live with that." I actually did prefer to stay with him, but I knew it wasn't safe.

About halfway through the field, I noticed Quinn had stopped ahead of me and was searching the ground around him. "Hey, Archer. Check this out. Isn't this where we left Bane?"

I caught up and verified the landmarks. Sure enough, it was the spot. But he was gone. No trace of him at all. "Okay. I thought it would be sort of creepy to see his body here, but not seeing him is creepy as hell. Suppose he walked out of here?"

"Maybe. He could be at South right now. But you'd think they'd have come for Bunny, wouldn't you?"

"You'd think so." I pondered the situation a moment. "Maybe a lion drug him off and got lucky through the mine field."

"I don't know. It'd have to be one damn lucky lion."

"Could be it stepped on a mine while it was dragging him off and it vaporized them both."

"I suppose anything is possible, but I don't like the looks of this."

I didn't want to say it, but I agreed with him. There was

definitely something unsettling about the absence of Bane.

Quinn shrugged his shoulders and headed for the next landmark. After pondering the empty ground a moment, I decided I had enough to worry about without borrowing trouble that might not exist.

In fifteen more five-year minutes, Quinn announced he was at the edge of the field. I only had one more short stretch to cross. I followed him to the rim of the field, and I finally started to relax inside, almost feeling giddy. Only a few more feet and we would be home safe. My pace picked up in spite of my limp. In fact, I fairly skipped with joy those last few yards.

"Watch out," Quinn said, but I had no interest in caution.

"Quinn, we did it! We kicked some ass on the Jo—" My knee gave out, and I stumbled sideways. I felt the click as much as heard it. My blood froze. I started sucking in air in fast, shallow breaths while I consciously made myself stand still. I was on a land mine.

CHAPTER 31

QUINN KEPT WALKING. "COME on, let's get out of here."

I felt the sweat break out on my brow, and I forced myself to take one deep breath and exhale slowly in spite of my pounding heart.

Quinn turned and started back my way.

I held up a hand, careful not to move my lower body, and I kept my voice as soft and even as I could. "No. Stay back."

"What is it?" I could hear fear that told me he knew, but he didn't want to know.

"I'm sorry, Quinn. My knee gave out. I'm afraid you'll have to go on without me." A sob caught in my throat, and I once more turned to my breathing to gain control.

"What are you talking about?" He shone his flashlight on me and then focused the beam at my feet, just off the path. He hunkered down next to me and put his hand to his head, as if the undeniable reality would split his skull wide open. "Oh, Archer."

We were still for a moment, and then I took one more deep breath, remembering my mantra from my favorite book. "What is, is what must be." A calm washed over me.

"It's okay, Quinn. Tell Granny I love her. Tell Bunny I love her too. And please take care of Daisy for me. Kick Harmony when you get the chance . . . and Quinn . . . I—"

"Would you shut up? I'm trying to think. I know your dad told me how to do this once."

I blinked at him, aghast. Here I was about to vaporize in a red mist, and he was telling me to shut up? But he looked like he had an idea, swinging the flashlight around me and surveying the immediate area, so I did as I was told.

Soon he pulled out Clarisse and started digging around my foot.

"What are you doing? You're going to get us both blown up."

"Calm down. I remember your dad telling me how Flynx got him off of one of these when they were mapping the field. First, we have to burrow around it and find where the detonator is under your foot."

My knees felt weak, and I began shaking. I needed to do something and not just stand there waiting to die. "Here, let me help." I started to hunker down to dig with my hands.

"No!" Quinn held up his hand to stop me. "Don't shift your weight. You could set it off. Here." He handed me his flashlight. "Hold it right where I'm working."

"All right. I can do that." Holding the light, I noticed the beam quivering on the ground. Consciously, with the same effort I used to slow my heart before a shot, I gradually forced my body to stillness. The ground was hard, but Quinn was strong and diligent. By the time the beam steadied in my hands, he had burrowed around the mine.

"Looks like it's under the ball of your foot. Okay. Next we need to get something between your foot and the detonator that can hold it down. Any ideas?"

I thought of the small knife I had in my pocket and pulled it out. "Will this work?"

He shook his head. "No. It has to be big enough that we

can keep pressure across the detonator while we replace your weight." He stroked his beard a moment. I mentally inventoried my belongings and came up dry. Then he did something that touched my heart. He wiped off Clarisse and held her up.

I laughed, a bit punchy. "If you get me out of here in one piece with that thing, I'll never make fun of her again. But Quinn, you realize you'll never get her back if you do this?"

"Yeah, well, I wouldn't encourage me to think about that if I were you." He forced a smile.

"Quinn, it would make more sense if you leave."

"Stop breaking my concentration." He reached down and gingerly slid the machete under the edge of my foot. My foot slid ever-so-slightly with it. He stopped.

"This isn't working. We need some water to help it slide. Do you have any?"

"I'll do you one better," I said. "I've got grease. Look in the outside right pocket of my pack." Bunny had made me some lotion out of plant oils she'd gotten from Makenzie during the summer.

After carefully extracting the lotion, Quinn sniffed it and rubbed a bit between his fingers. Then he smeared it on the machete. When it was thoroughly slathered, he tried once more to slip it between my foot and the detonator. This time, it slid right in and kept going until half of the blade stuck out the other side.

"Okay. Stand right here. I'm going to go find a rock we can use to replace your weight on the detonator."

"No, Quinn, that's too risky."

He tweaked me on the chin as he would a child. "No more of that talk."

Quinn disappeared into the dark. Every now and then I could hear a rock dropping or a "damn" or some other such expletive. While he worked, I looked up at the stars—so very many stars—and I wondered if this would be the last time I would see them.

A nobler woman would have picked up her foot. Died. Prevented Quinn from dying with her in his folly. But I was not that noble woman. He had given me hope, and I didn't want to miss out on anything.

Finally he came back into the glow of the flashlight, rolling a rock the size of a large child in front of him.

"What? How fat do you think I am? That's a rock for a Josephite girl."

He laughed and almost rolled the rock off the path. "Leave it to you to make a joke at a time like this."

"Yeah, well, what other time is there?"

He stopped rolling the rock and sat down on it. "You know, speaking of time, I've been trying to talk to you, and this seems as good a time as any."

"You can't be serious. I'm standing on an effing land mine, and you want to talk?" "It's because you're standing on a land mine. At least this way, you can't walk away from me."

I looked at him askance, suddenly more afraid of him than of the explosives under my foot. "Quinn, why are you doing this?"

Quinn took a deep breath and then looked up and locked eyes with me. "Because I didn't want us to die without you knowing that I love you."

"Right, I know. I'm your little sister, and you love me. Now roll that rock over here and let's get going." He was going to give me the "you're a great sister but I don't want you for a lover" speech. And I knew that, once he spoke it, he would kill my hope, and I couldn't bear that.

His face grew somber. "No, Archer. I mean I love you. As a woman."

He blushed so furiously I could even see it in the flashlight beam. I waited, afraid to breathe.

"I know you're my foster sister, so I hope it's not too creepy. But you're not a little girl anymore, and you're not really my sister. And I love you. So there. Now let's get you off that landmine."

I wanted to wrap myself inside his words, but I didn't trust him. "Why?"

He looked baffled. "What do you mean, why?"

"I mean why now? What happened? What's different? We both know you could have had me back at your cabin, but you pushed me away. Why should I believe you're not going to do that again?"

"Because I've had time to think since then. I'm sorry. Look. I was confused. I just . . . I didn't want to violate you. How do you go from being siblings to lovers?"

My heart melted, but it was too much to digest in an instant, so I deflected. "Siblings to lovers? Southerns do it every day."

His face went blank. Then he cracked up. "You got me there. Now let's get you off that landmine." He stood up and rolled the rock in front of me. "Here's the tricky part. You need to crouch down and press on both sides of Clarisse as hard as you can. Then you'll move your foot, and I'll lift this rock onto it."

"Okay. But do one thing for me. Stand over there while I move my foot in case I'm not pushing down hard enough."

"No. I'm not leaving here without you."

"I'm touched. Really, I am. But I can't let you be that selfish. Granny needs you. Bunny needs you. The whole meadow needs you, and we just hit the Josephites where they live. You need to stick around to finish them off."

He said nothing for a moment, considering my words. Then he reached out and took a strand of straw from my hair. Stepping forward, he took me in his arms and kissed me. First with reservation and then with hard passion that deepened to tenderness. Then he turned away from me down the path.

Dizzy, I touched my lips and savored the feel of him. When I thought he was far enough away, I didn't wait for him to turn around. I crouched, pressed the ends of Clarisse as hard as I could, and moved my foot.

It didn't explode.

Joy burst through me. It was working. "Quinn, get back here. Quick. Come get the rock. It worked."

He was already there, heaving the rock onto the machete.

With a deep breath, I released my pressure on Clarisse and stood up.

With all pretense of calm abandoned, Quinn swept me up in his arms and carried me from the minefield, and when he finally set me down, he held me like he would never be complete without me again.

CHAPTER 32

IT WAS HARD GOING with my bum knee the next day. Hot and swollen, it forced me to rest it often. Quinn practically carried me the last few hundred yards of steep path down into the meadow while Daisy danced her greeting in front of us.

Granny jumped up from her pottery wheel, bumping and ruining the tall column she was throwing in her haste to wrap me in her embrace. "Oh, Deena. I was so worried. When Freefall and Zander came in and told me they'd left you in the middle of a fire on the plains . . ." She paused and let go of me to wipe a tear from her eye. "Well, you're here."

Bunny left off clutching her seed and jumped in with a hug. "We were so worried. And the fire. Freefall and Zander said they could see it all the way across the horizon. We thought you'd become Atonements."

Granny stepped back. "Look at you," she said. "Your skin's half flayed, and your knee's half as big as your head. Sit down right now. Have you eaten?"

She turned to Quinn and pulled down his head to give him a kiss. "Your skin too. What happened to you two? I'd think you'd been keelhauled through dried hemp stubble to look at you."

I laughed. "Practically." I took the bowl of gruel Bunny offered. "Thank you. It's good to be home." I took a big bite and savored the flavor of the late summer stew—venison and fresh vegetables, and even some fat from goat butter. I was touched by their warm greeting, but Granny asked her next question, and the fuzzy feelings slammed into a wall.

"Now that I see you're in one piece, just what were you thinking? Going down and blowing up Josephite transformer stations? Taking out their power grid?" Obviously satisfied we weren't dead, she gave us the Eyebrow along with a pointed finger. "Quinton. Deena. You have no idea what kind of hell you have wrought upon us. Now you two go wash up . . . Quinn, use my room. You're not leaving here until I know exactly what you've done so I can decide how we need to handle the Josephites when they come looking for the terrorists."

Soon we were clean, and I had on my skirt and spare shirt. Quinn began the story, and Granny interrupted periodically with questions. We didn't mention that Spooge knew we had taken his truck, but I did tell Granny about the guard I encountered at the truck yard.

"You snapped his neck? Show me the move," she said, her military past getting the best of her. I demonstrated gently on Quinn. "Handy. Were there any bullet casings left behind?"

"No. We used revolvers and kept the brass. No footprints, either. We covered our boots with deer hides."

"Good. Go on."

Bunny remained still and silent, growing ever paler, clutching her seed while we told about sabotaging the spare transformers and stealing the trucks. But to my surprise, she spoke up when we told about the Josephite compound.

"Were the greenhouses still there?" she asked, her voice barely audible. It carried a fear, the source of which I could not ascertain.

I thought about it. "Yes. Why?"

She ignored my question. "Were there plants growing in them?"

I found her question exceedingly odd. "I suppose." I pictured the greenhouses in my memory and realized I'd seen a shadow of corn against the side before the lights went out. "Yes. There were plants. Why?"

Again, she didn't answer. She said. "This is most important. Did the fire destroy the camp?"

Quinn intervened. "No. I remember hearing the sirens. They had their emergency generators up to pump water, and they have their own fire trucks. There was a fire there once when I was a kid. They're fast about getting a buffer of chemicals around the camp."

Bunny kissed her seed and bowed her head.

"Why all this interest in the camp, Bunny?" I asked. I could see by the way Granny leaned toward Bunny that she, too, was interested in the answer.

"No reason, really. The grower there was a friend of my mother's. That's all."

Her answer sounded lame to me, but Granny jumped back in, and I had no chance to pursue it.

"Go on," Granny said. "After you set the world on fire, then what did you do?"

I knew she would freak if she knew how close we had come to baking, to smothering, and to blowing up, so I gave her the abbreviated version.

"Sounds like you did a good job for what you were doing, but I still say you shouldn't have. They're sure to find out. They always do. And then the Godfire will come in their wake. Oh, child. What have you done?"

"I've destroyed the Josephite power grid, and I'm proud of it. Without food, we'll see how long they last before they start tearing each other apart. Who knows? Maybe Bunny's dad can step in and take over if they get crazy enough."

Bunny looked up from where her hands were folded quietly

in her lap. In a clear, certain voice she said, "No. A religious movement must be countered with another religious movement. Joseph rules by the force of starvation. My father has no such force, nor does he have the force of a martyr for his cause. Simply throwing Promise City into chaos will not be enough to rid us of Joseph or to bring the Underground to power. Joseph must be revealed for the fraud he is, and the Underground must have a rallying point ready to replace him—a sign from God that the Underground will prevail."

I thought about that a moment. I had never considered the religious and political vacuum that would be left by the absence of Joseph. "Maybe this alone won't be enough," I said. "But you watch, Bunny. This is the beginning of their end."

"Or ours," Granny said. She shook her head and put water on the stove to make a poultice for my knee.

***

WE WAITED TEN DAYS without news. Freefall and Zander had returned that same night to report a smooth mission, but Flynx had stayed close to Promise City, gleaning information. During that time, we cleared and stocked a nearby cave with emergency supplies in case we had to run quickly. We practiced escape routes through the forest with the children, and we set up a watch line down the jeep trail.

When that was done, we waited. I carded wool with Granny, Bunny, and Makenzie's girls. I killed two more deer that were irresistibly drawn by our ripening hemp. They were fatter than the ones at the beginning of the season, and we enjoyed them with fresh corn and squash from the greenhouse. I watched the road each day, eager for some news, wondering if we had succeeded, and if the Josephites were in chaos. And more than anything, I made love with Quinn.

We made love at his house. We made love in the forest. We

made love in the barn. We even made love in the middle of the hemp field, laughing when Harmony almost caught us in flagrante delicto. Her hateful glares didn't move me. She was nothing to me.

I had forgotten the deep and abiding pleasure of a man's touch, and Quinn's touch felt like coming home. I opened my heart to him and embraced the fact that I needed him—that I was in it win, lose, or draw. And when he held my hand, and we laid flowers together on Faebin's grave, I felt a release and a renewal that I'd never thought was possible. For the first time since Faebin died, all was right with my world.

Granny and Bunny caught on quickly, and Granny could not hide her smiles. Bunny, however, was deeply concerned for our souls.

"Archer," she said one morning when Daisy and I climbed in the window after spending the night at Quinn's house. "I may be innocent, but I'm not stupid, and I know you and Quinn are keeping company outside of marriage. I am concerned for the state of your soul."

I laughed and handed Daisy her favorite bone. She curled up on her pile of rags at the end of my bed, and I picked up my carved bone comb to sort out my hair. "My soul is more complete than it's been in years," I answered, deflecting her negativity with my happiness shield. "Besides, aren't all us Secs going to Hell anyway?"

Bunny propped herself on her elbow and met my gaze in the reflection of the mirror. "I believe that if you accept Jesus as your savior and become a Christian, you will be saved."

"You think I need saving?" I asked, not sure if I was being insulted, but deciding not to get bent out of shape. After all, Bunny was always saying insulting things with the best of intentions. I had learned over the summer to listen to her heart rather than to her mouth.

Bunny leaned her head down from the top bunk and explained as if to a child. "Every one of us needs saving. Jesus says that only through Him can we be saved. He says, 'I am the way, and the truth, and the life. No one comes to the Father except through me,' John fourteen, six. You have to believe in Jesus to be saved. It's not personal. It's just the truth. Right now, you are living in sin."

Since she was so serious, I fought to suppress a smile. "I appreciate your concern, but my soul is fine. Checked it just this morning. It was quite content." I cleaned my face with a washcloth.

She was not to be deterred. "But it's quite plain. I'd be happy to read it to you from my Bible sometime."

I squeezed my washcloth into my basin filter and sat back down to braid my hair. Then, remembering the feel of Quinn's hands wrapped in my long locks, I decided to leave it down.

"I've read it. Perhaps we should just agree to disagree. That's the beauty of being a Secular. We get to disagree. But I'll admit, a wedding would be nice, and don't you dare tell Quinn I said that. He hinted at it the other day, but I wouldn't want him to feel pressured."

"Archer, that's wonderful!" She sat up and clapped her hands. "We'll have Charlotte weave an especially beautiful cloth to make you a dress. And perhaps we'll even find some mountain daisies to lace through your hair. I could do that for you. You have long hair like a Josephite girl, you know."

I looked at the daisies painted on my dresser. She was right. The white flowers would be perfect for my hair. "Too bad there aren't any."

"You know, I don't believe they're really extinct. And if there's not a mountain daisy out there somewhere, maybe I could make one for you. I helped my mother make seeds."

"Do you have the equipment for that?" I asked, forming the kernel of an idea.

Her face clouded. "No. No one does, now that there's no electricity. Don't you feel at all bad about sabotaging the transformer stations? Surely innocent people have died."

I thought about her question. I remembered the guard at the station with the gun to my head, delighted at the chance to kill me. He would have, too, if I hadn't taken him down. I thought of Iain. Such a beautiful, loving spirit, but Norris shot him and left him to drown in his own blood. I knew my answer.

"I regret having to hurt people like you, if there actually are any other people like you. But we are at war with the Josephites, and it's a war they brought to our doorstep. I get that you're caught in the middle, but you're going to have to choose sides."

"It's easy for you to say that, but I wonder how you would feel about that if you saw the fruits of your labors."

I thought about the guard lying there twitching, his neck broken, and I shook it from my memory. "I guess we won't know, will we? Now come on and get up. There's wool to be carded. And what do you think? Blue or green for a dress?"

Bunny laughed. "Green. It's the color of jealousy, and you'll be the envy of every Sec woman with a catch like Quinn."

"He's a good one, isn't he?" The glow of contentment filled my soul.

But chaos to order, and order to chaos. Flynx returned.

CHAPTER 33

THE FOUR OF US were at our evening work, Granny throwing a tall column at her wheel, Bunny carding a never-ending pile of mohair, Quinn cleaning his rifle, and me fletching arrows beside him when Daisy jumped up and barked, wagging her tail. The bridge boards announced a friend, and Flynx burst through the door.

He threw his arms open wide. "Success!"

"Good to see you, Flynx," Granny said. "We were starting to wonder if you'd ever come home. Now get back outside and take those filthy boots off."

Flynx did as he was told. Thanking Granny, he helped himself to the gruel she pointed to. Then he pulled up a chair next to Bunny.

Bunny shifted uncomfortably, and I noticed Flynx had a strong smell of the road about him.

He settled in and glanced at Quinn and me. "Glad you made it back. That was one hell of a fire you two started. Michael's bum on a pike pole. Wish I'd thought of that myself."

Quinn leaned over and gave me a quick kiss. "That was all Archer."

I blushed with pride. "Serendipity, really."

Bunny looked askance at us and returned to her work.

"Ah, what's this with you two all cozy?" Flynx asked. "You get tired of fightin' and runnin' foot races?"

A slight smile touched Quinn's lips. "You might say that."

"Quiet," Granny said, her voice full of alarm. We all froze and glanced at each other, our eyes questioning.

She got up from her wheel and stepped outside to look around. "Did you hear that?" she asked over her shoulder. "Did anyone follow you, Flynx?"

"You know me better than that, Granny. Nobody catches old Flynx in the dark. It's my gift."

Granny shrugged and came back inside.

Flynx rubbed his hands together. "I've got good news and good news. Which should I start with first?"

I bit at the game. "Oh, I don't know. How about you start with the good news?"

Flynx grinned from ear to ear. "Joseph. Is. Screwed."

Bunny's hands stopped in her work. Quinn and I leaned forward, my fletching and his gun completely forgotten. Even Daisy raised her head and pricked her ears at the intense tone of his voice. Granny was the only one who appeared to be unmoved, smoothly shaping a large bowl on her wheel. She said, "Flynx, watch your language in my house."

"Sorry, Granny." Flynx continued. "It was just like we planned. After the first couple of days without electricity, people started to run out of food. Right? So then they fixed the stations with those spare transformers. Power came up about eighty percent, just enough for them to think they were going to be fine."

Flynx laughed. "Then three days, and *pow*." He slammed his fist against the table. "Grid started bleeding out like a gut-shot buck. Within the day, there wasn't one light bulb working in all of Promise City."

"Woohoo!" I jumped to my feet, almost knocking over our table, and turned to Quinn. We shared a grin and a double high five. "Then what?"

"The army took all the food. Cleaned out every vertical farm in the city. Joseph is rationing some back, but it's mostly for his own men. And without any way to store it, what isn't getting eaten is going bad. Fights broke out through the city. Folks are killing each other and stealing food."

"Have they booted Joseph?"

"No. It's going to take more than that to get rid of him. He's telling them it's a sign that there's sin hidden in the City. That it's some heretical group spreading the work of the devil and they have to root them out. He's stepping up Atonements, but some say that's not enough. Some are lighting women on fire in the streets, to pay for the unaccounted sin. Hahaaaa!" Flynx fairly crowed.

Bunny's voice was almost inaudible. "You have been in the city to see this?"

"Me? No. Dave, the engineer that hangs out at Maverick's, told me. Says they have to make new transformers, and they can't do that without electricity. They're going to have to get them all the way from New Jerusalem. They won't be fixed for at least another week or ten days."

"Have many died?" Bunny asked. I noticed she was pale, and I wondered if she was about to faint.

Flynx shook his spoon once in her direction. "What do you think? It's not only the women they're setting on fire in the streets. Hospitals are all but shut down, and the sick and the old are dropping like flies in a deep freeze. But most of them are killing each other for food. Joseph closed off the Dome and put people under martial law. Says God's testing them to weed out the unbelievers."

"Yes," I said, taking down our medicinal moonshine from the shelf. "This calls for a toast."

"Deena, put that back," Granny said. "There'll be no drinking over this."

Bunny choked back a sob. "How can you be happy about

this? You're killing innocent women and children."

"I'm not. They're killing their own. I just turned off the lights."

"I can't stand this," she said, the tears flowing freely down her cheeks.

"Well, you won't have to," Flynx said. "You're heading to Mexifornia. That's my other good news. There's a coyote going over the glacier. A guy named Mo down at Maverick's. Seems some Joes don't want to stick around for the fun. He's staging at North, and he'll be leaving in three days. Says you can come along for the ride."

"You told him who I am?" Her eyes grew wide with fear.

"Course not. I told him you ran from a work camp. He don't give a sh . . . he doesn't care as long as you can pay. You can pay, right?"

"Yes."

"Then it's not a problem."

Surprised and dismayed by the sudden turn, I glanced at Bunny. Closing her eyes, she reached for her seed. No matter what we told her, it was the one Joe thing she would not give up.

I didn't realize how I had grown accustomed to her presence until that moment, and the thought of her leaving brought an emptiness to my heart that I was not willing to accept. "No," I said. "There has to be another way. It would be safer to go over the glaciers in the fall. And besides, the Josephites are busy with other matters. Even Norris wouldn't notice her right now."

Quinn put his hand on my shoulder. "Archer, the Josephites are distracted. That means it's the perfect time to get Bunny out of here. Besides, who knows who Harmony will tell when she gets the chance?"

Bunny opened her eyes. "None of you are safe while I'm here, and I'm not safe either. The truth is that Joseph's men could come in here any day and find me. God has provided this opportunity, and I must take it."

My anger flared. "It's not right. This is why we fight them, Bunny. If you stay, we'll hit them again and again, and we'll keep them so busy they'll forget about you."

"I don't want that. They're my people too."

"Granny, help me out here," I said.

She was putting the final touches on the rim of her bowl when she looked up at me. "We'll all miss her, Deena, but to everything there is a season."

Flynx shook his head. "What the f—? . . . Sorry, Granny . . . What the hell, Archer? Of course she has to go. But let Zander take her to North. We've got somewhere else to be. We've got a mission."

"You have a plan?" Quinn asked.

"Damn straight. We're cutting the head off the snake. Their security's down. Now's the time to go after Joseph. Let's get in there and kill the bastard before they bring the lights back up. We'll never have another chance like this."

I blinked and glanced to Quinn for his reaction. He gave the slightest shake of his head, confirming my gut reaction. Granny said it out loud. "Flynx, you're crazy."

"No, I'm not. Listen. Didn't you hear me? Their security's down. No readers. If we can get over the wall, I know those tunnels under the city like I know my own pecker. Joseph's head is ripe for a silver platter."

Bunny sniffed and sounded grave. "You'll never make it. He has his own generator for the Dome. You may have shut down the grid, but Joseph will still have the readers inside. You'll never get close to him."

"She's right," I said. "We can go for their water supply, or we can burn down more of their gassplant, but Bunny knows what she's talking about. If she says the readers are up, then the readers are up, and there's no way we can get in and out."

"You're going to listen to her? Didn't you hear her just now? She's still nothing but a Joe puppet whining about our victory. They're the enemy, and so is she, and now's the time to take them out. Can't you see?"

Bunny looked like she'd been slapped and Granny's eyebrow shot up.

Quinn moved between Bunny and Flynx. "Flynx, you've been on the road a long time. Why don't you head on up to my place? You can stay there for the night. We'll talk again tomorrow."

"Who do you think you are, talking to me like I'm some little kid? Granny, surely you can see what's happening?"

Granny calmly crossed the room and opened the door. There was steel in her eyes and in her voice. "You've lost your senses and your manners. Leave my home now, and don't come back until you've found them."

Flynx stood with his mouth hanging open, looking aghast, turning from one of us to the next, seeking support. When he didn't find any, he slammed his fist on the table again and pointed his finger at us. "You watch. You'll be thanking me." He stormed from the house.

I felt ill. I didn't mind conflict with the Josephites, and even killing Greagor and leaving Bane was only something I had to do, but fighting with Flynx? My commander and friend?

I was heartsick. I turned to Quinn, and he took me in his arms for a hug, but it was all too brief. Releasing me, he said, "Get down your pack. Bunny, you too. We'll leave in the morning for North."

Bunny took hold of her seed. "Yes," she said, looking away from us. "It seems it's time for me to go."

Granny cut the bowl from the batt and stood up from her wheel. "Quinn, you go on and get ready. Archer, empty this slip bucket out in the kiln shed for me. I'll help Bunny get what she needs for the journey."

Quinn carried the bucket of thick, muddy sludge for me, and we walked out to the kiln shed where Granny had her tools to recycle clay. Then he kissed me. "Don't let Flynx bother you. He's only road weary. You know how it can make you crazy. He'll calm down and see sense."

He gave me a smile and tweaked my chin. "Cheer up. The goddess has her reasons for everything."

I returned his smile, though I didn't feel it in my heart. I wasn't so sure his goddess had her reasons, but I saw nothing else to do for it in the moment except go on with the business of the day.

I emptied the slip bucket and backed out of the kiln shed, shutting the door behind me. When I turned around, Harmony was right across the dry creek bed from me, arguing with Arys. He pulled her away toward the meadow, but not before she gave me a look that made my blood run cold. It wasn't anger, pain, or even the hatred I'd seen since we returned from our fateful journey back in the spring. No. It was a look of pure triumph.

CHAPTER 34

"WHAT DO YOU SUPPOSE it meant, Quinn?" I was still troubled about Harmony while the three of us hiked through the forest with Daisy, the noon sun above us. I scratched under the collar of the dragontech. It was hot, but I hadn't seen Ernesto and Cecilia since Reunion, and there was no way I was going to miss the chance to show it off.

"Will you stop worrying about it? Maybe it meant she had gas. There's no way she could be sure of anything, and it doesn't matter. Bane was dead when we left him, and Bunny's taking off, so she won't have that either. She can't hurt us."

"You didn't see her. She looked like the lion that made off with the goat." I waved Daisy back to us so she wouldn't get too far away and draw in a Dixie bear.

"Calm down. Even if she did steal a goat, she's got no teeth. She can't exactly gum it to death."

"I suppose you're right. Still . . ." I couldn't beat back my unease each time I thought of her face.

Bunny had been quiet through the morning. She'd shared tearful goodbyes with the Tinkers, Zander's family, Arys, Charlotte, and their baby the night before, and she seemed to be a bit stunned while she walked along.

My knee was doing much better after a week and a half spent mostly horizontal with Quinn, but it was starting to trouble me a bit. I looked forward to putting it up for a few days at Cecelia's house. It was always easier to rest in someone else's house where there were none of my own chores to be done.

Quinn and I tried to draw Bunny into conversation a few times, but she was withdrawn and reticent. She clutched her pendant often and bowed her head to pray as best she could while we moved up the trail. Finally I could take it no longer.

"What are you praying for, Bunny?" I expected her to say she was praying for her people.

"I'm thanking God for you."

It was simple. It was matter of fact. I was touched. I glanced toward her, and she stopped.

Gazing intently at us, she said, "Quinn, Archer, thank you. I've never properly thanked you and your people for what you've done. You saved me from my most heartfelt terror. I can face anything God asks, but I can't face what humans do. I can't face death in the Godfire." Bunny shuddered. "As I journey on down this unknown road, I will never forget your courage and your kindness."

For some reason I couldn't explain, a deep foreboding clenched my heart. I told myself it was only a feeling, and I shook it off. I hugged her close and kissed her on the top of her head. "Good thing we're not child-eating demons, huh?"

We laughed, and I gently wiped a tear from her cheek.

"I know what Atonements are," Quinn said. "I never could have turned you in."

I gave her one last squeeze and let her go. "Bunny, I was so sad after our fight last night. Can't you understand that the Josephites gave us no choice? After a lifetime of starving us, denying us education and property, they came in, shot one of us on a whim, and destroyed all of our food. This isn't getting better. This isn't changing. We had to do something."

"I know you are suffering. I've lived among you now all summer. I felt what it was like to be hungry with you, but I don't believe in killing innocents for any reason."

"I don't want to kill the ones like you—the ones who follow your father in the Underground. But look at it this way. Anything that hurts Joseph will help them."

"Perhaps there's another way. Something that would keep your people from starving, even if you can't defeat the Josephites. Would it be enough for you if you at least didn't go hungry?"

At that moment, Daisy, fifty feet ahead of us on the trail, pricked her ears and barked a warning. A little Josephite girl ran from the forest toward the shepherd, a wide smile lighting her face and her arms open wide. "Fluffy."

CHAPTER 35

BUNNY AND QUINN RUSHED forward, and I followed them as best I could, urgency deadening the pain in my knee. While Daisy loved the children she knew, I had no idea what she would do with a strange child in the middle of nowhere. I needn't have worried. The dog immediately recognized the tot as a puppy and started licking her face. The child chortled and grabbed great handfuls of Daisy's fur.

I knelt down beside her to ask her name, and a man's voice carried through the woods, answering my question. "Ruuu-thieee." The sound was followed by a woman's voice, calling the same name. Quinn chambered his rifle and turned toward the sound of the incoming people.

The child smiled at me and pointed to herself. "Ruth. That's me."

As surreal as the situation was, it was impossible to suppress my laughter. She was simply too cute.

"Over here," called Quinn. "She's over here."

Bunny knelt beside me, brushing pine needles from the grubby child's wispy, blonde locks. "How old are you, Ruth?"

"I'm this many." Ruth held up three fingers, then four,

and then three again. Her hand, like the rest of her, looked like someone had spit on it and rolled it in the dirt. I took out my scarf, wet it, and offered the child some water before I started cleaning her hands. She took it greedily, and I cringed when she spilled a few drops down her simple Josephite dress, which was decorated with squirrels dancing around a Sword of Michael.

As I scrubbed her hands, she looked up at Bunny and me with wide eyes and asked, "Do you have food?"

I didn't think twice. I reached for a factory bar in my pocket and was unwrapping it for her when her father came into view. "No, Ruth. Get away from those people."

Daisy leapt between Ruth and her father and growled at him. The man stopped about fifteen feet away. "Ruth, come over here now."

Confusion clouded Ruth's face. I signaled Daisy down, and she reluctantly dropped to the ground, still rumbling.

"Now, Ruth," her father said, motioning urgently that she should obey.

The child pouted. "No. I want Fluffy."

Putting the factory bar in Ruth's hand, I said, "Here, honey. Take this. Go to your father."

"But I want Fluffy," she said.

I smiled. "It's okay. Fluffy will be here. I promise."

Ruth gave "Fluffy" one more pat on the head and walked toward her father. As soon as she was closer to him than to Daisy, the man snatched her up and backed away from us. That's when I noticed the dark circles under his eyes and his gaunt look. He was dehydrated.

Nevertheless, I was furious at the accusations in his stare, and I made no effort to keep the venom from my tongue. "How dare you? We were only—" Quinn stopped me with a hand to my arm, and Bunny shot me a "shut up" glare.

Quinn stepped between us. "Ruth came up. We gave her food and water, that's all."

The mother joined them, and to my surprise, Bunny pushed forward and spoke directly to the woman, ignoring her husband. "God at your shoulder, ma'am. I'm Bunny, and these are my friends, Quinn and Archer. We mean you no harm."

The woman, a scrawny carbon copy of her daughter, aged twenty years or so, stared at Bunny's seed pendant and grew wild-eyed. I saw she wore one of her own on her sack of a dress that was covered in frolicking puppies. They were Underground.

The woman threw herself at Bunny's feet and grabbed the hem of her dress. "You're the Angel. You're the Angel, aren't you? You've come to save us."

Bunny jumped back and looked to us for some explanation, as if we had one. Clearly, we didn't. She turned to the kneeling woman. "Ma'am, I assure you, I'm no angel. I'm just a woman."

The man put his hand on the woman's shoulder. "Suzanna, please." His voice oozed weariness, and he turned back to us. "Please forgive her. You wouldn't believe what we've seen these past two weeks. It's chaos. And when the Atoners came after Suzanna . . ." The man's voice faltered. "I beat them away. We barely got away with what we could carry."

"Atoners?" Bunny asked.

"They're the men who say the power is gone because we haven't Atoned enough. They set random women on fire in the streets. They tried to burn my Suzanna."

Bunny gasped.

The woman clutched at Bunny's skirt. "But the Angel's here now. She shall come from the forest, a seed upon her breast, and her arrow of truth shall light the way to our bounty. Look, Mahli, she has the seed. Only the Angel would have the seed in the forest."

I leaned down to whisper in Bunny's ear. "What's she talking about?"

Bunny shrugged and gave no answer, but the man heard us.

"Last week, our preacher prophesied again that an angel from the forest would save us from the Josephites with her arrow of truth. Please forgive her. She's quite shaken after what she's been through."

A thought occurred to me. "If things are so awful in the city, why aren't more people leaving?"

The man dropped his head and shook it as if trying to rid himself of a memory. When he looked up, his eyes were haunted. "They're trying to, but Joseph has the city under martial law. He's closed the gates, and no one is allowed to leave. Still, there are tunnels that a few of us know. And the others who came with us . . . they were shot at the edge of the wall right after we emerged. We were the last to get through."

A tear slipped down Bunny's cheek. Then she took the woman's hands in hers and looked her in the eye. Her voice was firm. "Suzanna, I am not an angel. I am a woman. I am not leaving this forest. I am going to Mexifornia, but you can come with me."

The man cut in. "Please. We haven't eaten in two days. We gave it all to Ruth. Can you spare any food?"

"Of course," Bunny said, taking off her pack.

"No," I countered, and Quinn and I pulled Bunny off to the side, leaving Daisy at her post.

"Bunny, you need that food to get over the glacier," I said. "We didn't share it with you to give away. You can't give it to them."

Quinn nodded. "Archer's right. You keep what we gave you."

Bunny frowned and bit her lip. "But you heard them. They haven't eaten in two days."

"Tell you what," Quinn said. "I'll let them share my factory bar. That should get them up the road, and they can eat at North. Then they can go with you to Mexifornia. Will that work for you?"

Bunny looked back and forth between us. "I don't like it,

but I understand. Thank you for sharing your food with them."

Quinn took out his factory bar. "Here, you two can split this. That should get you to the next town."

"Thank you." The man set Ruth down, ripped open the bar, and broke it in half to share with his wife. Ruth was just finishing the one I gave her.

Once the man and his wife had taken a few bites, Quinn continued. "When we get to North, we'll hook you up with a man who's taking some Joes over the glaciers. If you can pay, he might take you, too."

The man looked up at us. "What if we can't pay? We were lucky to get away with the clothes on our backs."

"Can you do anything in trade?" Quinn asked, his brow furrowing. I knew he was trying to find a way for the man to earn his keep.

"Yes, I'm an accountant. And Suzanna can sew."

I looked at her dress and hoped they had something more to offer.

"I can pay their way," Bunny said. "I still have those Bucellati earrings. Surely it will not cost more than those."

I hated the thought of the earrings that matched Granny's necklace going to a coyote. "You'll need those to start your new life. There has to be another way."

"No, Archer. I acquiesced on the food, but I will not leave these people to die." She turned to them. "It's settled. I'll pay your way. You are sure to find work when we get there. You can pay me back then."

I shook my head. Though I thought Bunny was foolish, I did admire her devotion to her principles. I noticed Ruth looking longingly at Daisy.

Kneeling beside the girl, I said, "I'm Archer." I pointed to Daisy. "This is Daisy." I looked up at her father. "Daisy takes a while to get used to adults, but she loves Ruth. Do you mind if they play?"

The man gave me a skeptical look and then nodded. I pulled

Daisy's ball from my pocket and took the little girl by the hand. We moved away from the group, and I gave Ruth the toy.

Ruth threw overhand. The ball flew about five feet and rolled another three. Daisy waited until it came to a complete stop before leaping in the air to pounce on it, as if it were a mole. Ruth laughed and clapped her hands. "Fluffy, Fluffy."

"Her name is Daisy," I said, laughing with the child.

Ruth smiled and shook her head. "No. She's my Fluffy."

"Oh, okay. Fluffy it is." Who can argue with a toddler?

While I sat and watched the two of them play, I became aware that I was rubbing my knee. It needed a rest.

"Archer, we should leave if we're going to set these folks up by nightfall," Quinn said, shouldering his pack.

I looked at him with Bunny and the Josephite family and suddenly felt overwhelmed. My party of three had doubled in size, and half were strangers to boot. Though Ruth was adorable, I preferred the quiet of the forest to the group hike, and my knee needed a break.

"I need to baby my knee, but these folks need to eat. Why don't you take them on down to town, and I'll catch up in a bit?"

He bent down where he could speak without being overheard. "I know you. You don't want the noise of all these traveling companions."

I smiled and kissed him. "Thank you."

He playfully nibbled my ear and whispered, "I'll be expecting a lot of gratitude from you tonight."

I giggled, stretched my arms, and faked a yawn. "I don't know. I'm pretty tired. I'm definitely going to need my sleep."

He tickled my exposed ribs, and I yelped, which drew Daisy over to lick us, wanting to join in the play.

Quinn laughed, pushed her away, and stood. "Be careful," he said. "If you're not at Ernesto's by dusk, I'm coming looking for you." He kissed me on the lips and then called, "Heading out. Let's move."

Bunny came to me. "Archer, will you be okay?"

It made me smile. "No worries, Bunny. Just keep an eye on Ruth for me. She won't want to leave Fluffy."

After a small fuss from Ruth and her slobbery goodbyes with "Fluffy," the group wound its way down the trail.

I went a short distance up to where a path cut off for the pass. It was the path Bunny would take on her journey to Mexifornia. A large rock with a comfortable hollow sat off the trail underneath a tree with the outermost symbol of North carved into it—a sprouting seed set inside a sun. I settled into the depression to take a nap and welcomed the rock's familiar feel.

Waking a short time later, I meandered through the forest with Daisy at my side, enjoying the peace and quiet. Keeping a slow but steady pace, I arrived at the top of the cliff overlooking North just after noon-thirty. Below me, majestic hemp plants filled the meadow, rippling in the breeze and waving green, palmy leaves in welcome. I closed my eyes and breathed deeply of their delicious aroma.

From where I stood, I could see the road that circumnavigated the broad field and led to the town on my left. I searched through my binoculars and found Quinn among the townsfolk. I smiled. He was shaking a man's hand outside of a house near the fields, and he and Bunny were saying their goodbyes to the little Josephite family. I watched them all the way to Ernesto's and thought about Cecilia's good cooking that awaited me. My stomach rumbled.

About twenty feet below me was a small hidden shelf protected by a low overhang. It led onto a deer trail that would take me to my dinner in half the time, but the way was steep, and my knee was fragile, so I told my stomach it would have to wait. I turned right to the path and the road that would lead me the long way into the town.

While I traveled, I thought about the summer. Bunny's smile flashed in my mind, and my heart clinched. I would miss her. I recalled the triumphant explosion of the transformer station and the terror of the ensuing fire. For five nights after that, all I saw was flames each time I closed my eyes to sleep. Shuddering at that thought, a notion came into my mind. The Josephites were hungry. There was meat in the forest for those who could catch it. I wondered how much they would pay for my venison, or, better yet, perhaps we could catch a Dixie bear and sell it to them. We could get coats and blankets and new boots for the winter.

A movement in the hemp field below me caught my eye. My heart stopped. I couldn't believe my luck. The majestic buck I had seen the day of Reunion and again by the transformer station was below me, strolling out from the field, grazing leisurely on the mature plants along the road at the eastern edge of the meadow. I marveled to see his rack, nearly fully grown and sixteen points. I'd never seen anything like it. There was no way I was going to miss him again.

Practically sliding down the hill in my haste, I dropped my pack in the trees by the road. Taking a carbon-shafted arrow from my quiver, I signaled Daisy that we were stalking. We slunk through the foliage, the hemp hiding our scent, until I judged we were level with the buck.

Consciously quelling my excitement, I peeked around the end of the row. Yes! He still grazed, upwind and only fifteen yards away. With his back to me, I didn't have a clear shot, but it was only a matter of getting level with him in the hemp field and shooting up the row. I took a step back into the field, my soul singing. What a prize I would bring in!

Then, like a scene from my memory, the buck sprang up and shot away. Two Josephite soldiers exited the forest across the road in front of me.

The one in the lead spoke into his radio. "Aye, major. All cleared for the Godfire."

CHAPTER 36

I GASPED. DAISY BARKED. Both of their guns came up, and I released my arrow.

My broadhead pierced the man in front, passing cleanly through his heart and between his ribs. It lodged in the gut of the man behind him. Both men dropped. Daisy flew with my arrow and went for the throat of the injured man, cutting short his cry. Another arrow nocked, I aimed for the eye of a third soldier peeking out from behind a tree. I released, even as a sledgehammer-force blow knocked me backwards off my feet into the hemp field.

My ears rang, and I fought for breath. The force of his bullet in my solar plexus knocked my wind out, but the dragontech had done its job. Fighting my way to my hands and knees, certain he would kill me any second, I dragged myself through the field, hiding from the shot that was sure to come. I forced myself to breathe deeply and slowly, opening up my lungs.

When the bullet didn't come, and there was no sign of pursuit, I belly crawled to the edge of the field and peeked out. Three bodies lay next to the road. Daisy stood over her prey, her jowls covered in blood. I didn't know if the third man was truly dead or luring me in. Pulling myself into a low crouch, I took out my pistol and crept forward.

My arrow had found the soldier's eye. I quickly searched for more soldiers but saw none. Remembering what Flynx had taught, I drew my pistol and put a bullet through each of their heads, just to seal the deal. Then I retrieved my arrows and pulled their bodies back into the forest, Daisy close at my heels.

Kneeling in the trees, I scratched Daisy behind the ears to calm both her and myself. Shaking inside, my heart racing, I forced myself to think.

The Godfire. He'd said they were cleared for the Godfire. It must have been Flynx. He must have tried to go in alone, and they caught him and traced him back to North. "Oh, crap, Daisy. Oh, crap. They'll kill us all." Dammit. *Okay. I can't lose it now. Think, Deena. You have to warn the town.*

But how long did I have? Searching the sky for drones, I listened above and around me . . . Only silence. Perhaps there was time.

I stripped the soldiers of their rifles and ammo and ran back to where I'd left my pack by the road. Quickly, I took down my bow and packed it, along with two of the ammo belts, strapping the third across my shoulder for my own use, should I need it. And then I ran.

The ammo and rifles were heavy, and my knee protested at every step, but none of that mattered if I didn't get to the town before the Godfire.

Glancing over my shoulder, I was encouraged to see and hear nothing out of order. My strength was giving out, and I was tempted to slow down. Tempted to tell myself it wasn't happening—that I had made a mistake.

And then I heard it. The roar of a biodiesel engine behind me.

I looked back over my shoulder and saw a troop truck emerging from the forest. It was the same kind Norris had brought into Middle that terrible night. But this time, there were more trucks behind it.

I redoubled my efforts, adrenaline obliterating the pain. A man at the edge of town saw me. I knew him but couldn't think of his name. Waving, I cried, "Run! The Josephites are coming!"

He didn't move. I grabbed his arm, panting, and his eyes grew wide with surprise.

"You have to run," I said. "Get everyone out. The Josephites are bringing the Godfire. I heard them. They'll kill us all."

He stepped back, confusion clouding his face, "You're the archer from Middle, aren't you? What are you talking about? We have no quarrel with the Josephites."

I glanced back. The trucks were nearing.

"Just run," I said, but I could see it was no good.

Winding my way through the loose web of structures toward Cecelia and Ernesto's, I grabbed everyone I saw and told them to run. Most ignored me, but a small few could see my urgency and turned to do as I said.

Daisy and I burst through the door at Ernesto's. "They're coming. They're bringing the Godfire. We have to run."

Cecilia and Ernesto, along with Thomas, the twins, and their other two children, were in the front room with Bunny and Quinn.

Ernesto laughed. "Good to see you, too, Archer. Now what's this about the Godfire? We've had no trouble with the Josephites."

Cecelia smiled. "Yes, come in, Archer. I made a stew."

"No. We have to run now." My voice cracked in panic. Why couldn't people understand?

"What's happening?" asked Thomas, standing up from the table where he'd been eating his dinner.

Quinn reached out for the extra rifles, and I shoved two of them in his hands, along with the ammo. "Flynx went into the city to kill Joseph while the power's down. They must have caught him. There were soldiers in the hemp field. They radioed for the Godfire. Now the trucks are almost here. We have to go."

Bunny jumped up from the table, still holding little Benito, and she ran to the window. A sound of anguish escaped her. "Dear God. It's too late. It's too late."

CHAPTER 37

ICLIMBED INTO THE sleeping loft to get a better view from the window there. The Josephite soldiers lined up across the front of the town, pinning the townspeople against the curve of the cliff. People milled about, confused. Some came out of their houses to see what was happening.

Mahli and Suzanna slunk back against the corner of a house. Ruth was nowhere in sight. They didn't seek cover, but a few Secs did, collecting their children and rushing inside. I knew there were tunnels and safe holes under a few of those houses. I hoped people would have the sense to use them.

Soldiers removed a canvas from the truck in the center. In the back was a machine that looked like pictures I'd seen of early cameras—large and boxy with a long glass tube protruding like a cannon. Suddenly the box of the machine lit up in neon white, and the light spiraled to the end of the tube.

A man stepped out of the lead truck, and my blood froze. His face was tattooed with the Cross of Michael, and when he flicked a crop against his leg, I knew. It was Norris.

My breathing grew rapid. We had to get out, but there was nowhere to go.

The Doman of North stepped forward, his hand out in

greeting. Norris pulled his gun and shot the man between the eyes. All hell broke loose, and people ran for cover.

A blue light spiraled to the end of the tube on the machine. Mahli and Suzanna dodged toward the door of a house and then burst into flames, spontaneously combusting from the inside out. Then another fire consumed the family beside them.

I scrambled backward in my shock and almost fell from the loft. Bunny screamed and bolted. I jumped down just in time to grab her and stop her from running out the back door. "Grab water. We'll run along the cliff to the right and head up the deer trail."

Ernesto took the rifle Quinn offered and said, "Thomas, get your gun. Cecilia, Bunny, take the twins. Marta, Runner, stay between your mother and Thomas. We'll stay behind the houses and shoot our way out."

"I'll go first," I said. I slunk out the back door and peeked around the edge of the house, my pistol in hand. Daisy quivered, tail between her legs, sticking to me like Velcro.

The soldiers pressed forward, shooting all who ran while the Godfire trolled to the north side of the village. A small boy rushed by, and a bullet shattered his skull in a spray of red mist. I dropped the soldier who had shot him as a flaming man beyond him cried out and staggered toward a house.

Quinn and the others joined me.

"Clear to the next one," I said.

"You run, we'll cover," said Ernesto.

We ran. A soldier dropped to Quinn's shot, and we ducked behind the next house. Almost tripping over Daisy, I turned and fired at the Josephites while Quinn and Ernesto joined us. Out of ammo, I holstered my pistol and switched to the Josephite rifle.

A woman exploded in flames behind us, and the smell of burnt flesh filled my nostrils. Bunny fell to her knees, trembling in terror. I pulled her back up.

In this way, we leap-frogged behind three more houses,

but we were stopped at the fourth. Ernesto peeked out and quickly pulled his head back. "Wait here," he said. "I'll make an opening in the line."

Ernesto dove through the back door of the house. I saw children huddling inside and motioned to them to join us, but they would not. Hearing two shots, I peeked around the wall to see a Josephite fall. There were two more behind him. Then an explosion rocked me, and the front half of the house burst into flames.

I ran out firing and dropped the two Josephites. We dodged behind the next house in our line, the last cover that lay between us and the open dash for the forest. Josephite soldiers went down, and the side of their line opened up. I raised my hand to signal a run. Thomas moved to go, but Quinn grabbed him back. A man and his son rushed past us and, ten feet out, burst into flames. The Godfire lay between us and the forest.

CHAPTER 38

"**D**EAR GOD, WHAT DO we do?" Cecilia cried. She shook so hard I thought she would drop little Maria. Marta and Runner stood beside her, clinging to her skirt.

I peeked around the corner and pulled my head back quickly. A bullet whizzed by. Then we heard a voice that sent chills up my spine.

"Now, Secs. I know you're there," Norris said through a megaphone. "Come out and let's get this finished, shall we? I have a dinner engagement with Joseph this evening to tell him how you died."

Quinn put his hand on my arm. "What did you see?"

"Norris is standing on the Godfire platform with two soldiers," I said.

"What do we do?" repeated Cecelia.

I didn't know, but Bunny did. She handed Benito to Thomas and said, "Norris wants me alive. I am the only person here he won't kill. I'll show myself to distract him and give you the chance to run. Then I'll make for the northern road by the hemp field."

"They're sure to have an ambush there," Quinn said. "You'd

never get out that way."

I flashed on an idea. "There's a trail on the northwest side before you get to the field. I'll go with Bunny and show her the way. We'll meet up with you guys at the fork to the pass."

Norris's voice cut through us once more. "Come now. Don't make me destroy another house. My solders will need them when they come to harvest your hemp." I could hear the smirk in his words.

"Let's do this," I said.

"No, Archer, I'll go with her. You stay with the kids," Quinn said.

"But I run faster, and you can carry the children up the cliff."

"But you don't run faster now with your knee messed up."

I knew he was right, and it was no time to argue. Bunny didn't give us a choice. She walked out from behind the house into clear view, taking off her headscarf so Norris could see her. The window above me gave me a clear view through the rooms of the house to the poised Godfire.

A soldier aimed the Godfire at Bunny. "No, you fool," Norris said, knocking him back.

"I know you know me," Bunny said, shaking and clutching her seed. "I'll surrender if you'll let the others live."

Norris grinned and laughed. Jumping from the truck, he took one step toward her before she ran. Quinn dodged out from behind the house, shooting. The soldier trained the Godfire on him, and Quinn's dropped him. Norris pushed his body off the truck.

Daisy dashed ahead, and I ran, pushing Thomas with the other three children in front of me into the forest. Only Cecelia trailed behind. When I reached the edge, I turned to look, just in time to see a movement from the corner of my eye. The Godfire swung her way and she fell to the ground burning with baby Maria flaming in her arms.

I turned back up the hill, fighting off my panic.

"Where's Mommy?" asked Marta when I caught up.

"Shhh. She wants you to climb to the cave," I said. I didn't want to lie to the child, but it wasn't the time to tell her that her mother and sister were dead.

Thomas caught my eye, and the pain on his face told me he knew what my answer meant. "Come on, Marta. We have to hurry. Mom wants us to hurry."

When we were halfway up, I could see above the trees. I frantically searched for some sign of Quinn and Bunny but found none.

Those who had survived the initial onslaught were crushed up against the cliff behind the town. I searched their faces for Quinn and Bunny while the Godfire slowly rolled their direction, stopping to obliterate an occasional straggler. I fought not to retch.

Then I searched the dead. My gaze moved from face to face until I found a face I recognized between the forest and the town—a friend of mine I had traded hides with. I caught a sob in my throat.

Then a slight motion caught my eye. Was that a twitch? A child, pinned by the weight of the adult on top of her, peeked out from under the shoulder of my friend's body. It was Ruth.

I passed Benito to Thomas and checked my rifle. Damn. Out of ammo. I set it down to pick up on my return.

"Take the kids up to the hidden shelf. I have to get that girl. I'll be right back."

Thomas took a step back. "Hell, no. We need you here."

I looked at Marta and Runner and knew it was going to be a hard climb for them. My hands were full, but I couldn't bring myself to leave Ruth behind. "Thomas, I have to do this. Look, the line is past her. No one will even see me slip up from behind. I'll be in and back before you know it. Please. Get the kids up to the shelf."

He set his jaw. "Then I'm coming with you."

"No. Your brother and sisters can't stay here, and they need your help to get up the slope. I'll be right back."

The vein in his neck pulsed. "Dammit, Archer. If you get yourself killed, I will curse you forever."

"Fair enough." I turned and almost tripped over Daisy, who was panting and slinking low to the ground. I motioned her to stay and took off down the hill without making a big deal of the command, hoping my nonchalance would convince her to disregard her instincts and obey me.

Once I reached the edge of the forest, I slipped behind the line of trucks and made sure no one was in them. So far, so good.

I found the shortest distance between Ruth and myself and ran forward, scooping her up in my arms. I turned and found the black steel barrel of a pistol staring straight into my face. I gasped. It was Norris.

CHAPTER 39

H IS CRUEL LAUGHTER RIPPED through my brain above the shooting and screams behind me. "Why do you look familiar, Sec? Ah, yes. You were on your knees the last time I saw you. What a day. Tamar caught, and you dead. You knew she was here all along, didn't you? No, don't answer. I'd rather just kill you."

I refused to close my eyes. He pulled the trigger. The impotent "click" surprised us both. He was out of ammo. Quick as a snake, he flipped the pistol in his hand and tried to club me. With only one hand free and the other full of Ruth, I couldn't properly block, but I could duck.

He grazed my hair with the butt of his gun. I pulled my knife from my boot and stabbed upward into his groin. My blade caught him in the thigh.

Screaming, he brought his hand down in an automatic defense. I gored upward, slicing through his pinkie with my follow through. I saw the other gun in his belt, and I ran, Ruth under my arm.

Expecting the bullet any moment, I made for the forest. His first shot missed. A brown blur flew past me, and I heard nothing but a savage growl. I made the tree line. Then another pop of a gun and a yelp.

Thomas stepped from behind a tree and fired as I passed him. Glancing back, I faltered. A soldier was down, holding what was left of his hip after Thomas's shot. Norris dodged behind a truck, and Daisy lay in the dirt, a large remnant of Norris's black uniform blowing away from her on the wind.

"Thomas, take her," I said, pushing Ruth his direction. "I have to get Daisy."

"Your dog's dead. Just go." He shoved me toward the trail.

I turned back. "No, I can't leave her."

He grabbed my arm. "Yes, you can. I left my parents; you can leave your dog. Now go so they all didn't die for nothing."

He was right. Even from where I stood, I could see she was dead.

A bullet slammed into the tree beside me. I ran, Thomas at my side. When we reached the children, I grabbed the Josephite rifle and Benito and scrambled up the slope, Thomas and I pushing the children in front of us.

We made it to the shelf. I hustled them to the back and lay down at the edge with my binoculars, trying to see something through the trees and the blanket of smoke that crept across the valley. The stench of burned flesh reached my nose, and I gagged.

Norris said he caught Tamar. Oh, God. What had happened to Quinn? I saw no sight of them.

A small band of Secs broke out of the far side of the hemp field. I couldn't hear the rifle's report but I saw them go down. Each of them. Quinn was right. They had an ambush set up. Did that ambush get him and Bunny?

In the town, a few of the structures burned bright orange, black smoke pouring out of them. I could hardly see through the haze to where the people clung together against the cliff, but I could see the Godfire. It burned a bright white, and the neon blue slowly spiraled down the coil. A dozen people ignited. Human candles. I had to look away.

When I turned back, Norris came into view, leaning out the window of his car. His driver was taking him to the far corner where the ambush lay. The soldiers emerged from the hemp field, and they spoke. Norris began smacking his crop repeatedly against the side of the car.

Then I saw a movement on the mountain across from me. It was Quinn. He was running through a bald patch on the deer trail with no Bunny in sight. My heart skipped a beat. Norris really did capture Bunny, but Quinn made it. At least Quinn was safe.

Then Quinn's arms flew into the air. He crashed forward and lay still. Behind him, a Josephite soldier hurried from the forest and removed the rifle from his grip, and then the smoke obliterated them from my line of sight.

CHAPTER 40

I WAS OVERWHELMED. MY ears rang, and darkness threatened to close in. *No, Deena. Not now.* I consciously fought to squelch my panic, but all I could think was that Quinn was dead, and Bunny was captured. I frantically worked the focus on my binoculars, desperate for any glimpse through the smoke.

I don't know how much time passed before Thomas's urgency broke through. "Archer." I looked where he pointed to see Norris being carried toward a truck below us on a litter. He was gesturing to three soldiers, indicating the cliff where we hid. They promptly peeled off and started up the slope in our direction.

Jumping up, I grabbed Ruth. "Runner, give Benito to Thomas. Marta, quick. Follow me."

Thomas hadn't moved. Instead he fired toward the soldiers.

A return bullet ricocheted off the cave wall above Marta's head. She screamed.

"Dammit, Thomas! You'll get these kids killed. Now come on."

"I'm tired of running. We can take them."

"Then you'll stay and fight alone. I'm getting these babies

out of here."

With one more parting shot at the soldiers and a glare at me, he took his screaming brother from Runner and shoved a pacifier in the infant's mouth. I scrambled the twenty feet up the slope with Ruth in my arms, pushing Marta and Runner in front of me. At the last tree, we paused. I looked back. The soldiers behind us had a clear vision of the thirty-yard expanse between us and the trees.

"Stop." I pointed, and even Thomas didn't argue this time. If the soldiers went back down or drew a bit closer, their vision would be blocked, but until then, we were stuck.

Ben let out another howl, and Thomas clamped the pacifier into his mouth again, but it was too late. One soldier pointed in our general direction, and they all three moved up the slope.

The temptation to bolt was almost impossible to withstand while we let the soldiers get ever closer, waiting for their blind spot only fifty feet below us.

Almost there. Runner, his eyes wide and nostrils flared, looked wildly from me to Thomas. *Almost there.* Thomas put his hand on his brother's shoulder. Marta squirmed. *Almost there.*

Suddenly Runner cut and ran. A branch broke off above my head, and a rifle resounded. Runner skidded in the dirt. Thomas returned fire. I grabbed Marta's hand and made a break for it. To my relief, Runner jumped up and joined our frantic race to the forest.

Thomas fired again before following us, and then all went silent for the space of ten seconds. The soldiers were in the blind spot. I ran ever harder, weighed down by the child in my arms and the one I half-dragged by the hand.

"To the trail," I called. Runner made it to the trees, heading for the path. I hoped we could get a bit of a lead before the Josephites came through the forest and found the trail.

When I reached the trees, I looked back to see the soldiers topping the slope. One pointed at us, and all three followed. We dodged into the forest. I made a beeline for the path, jumping deadfall and dodging branches, dragging a screaming Marta behind me.

I tapped her on the cheek, still holding her hand. "Shhh. Your parents are dead. You want to get your brothers killed too?" It was a lot to put on her, but better a traumatized child than a dead one. She got the point.

We reached the path, and I paused, releasing Marta to run ahead to her brothers. Surprised I didn't hear any sound of the Josephites, I slipped behind a tree, set Ruth down, and peeked out.

At first, nothing. Then I saw it. A slight movement a hundred feet away at the edge of the forest where the Josephites slowly picked their way into the trees and deadfall. They were sure to find the path in only another thirty feet.

I turned to run, but they stopped and drew together. I crouched down with Ruth and put my finger to my lips to emphasize the need for silence. She nodded.

One Josephite signaled with a nod, indicating the forest toward the path. Another shook his head no. They both turned to the third, waiting for an answer. The third looked into the forest and back at the open slope. After a moment's deliberation, he waved toward the slope, and they left as silently as they had come.

When there was no chance of them seeing my movement, I picked up Ruth and hurried down the path. By the time we caught up to the others, my knee screamed with every step. Night was falling fast, but we pressed on under the rising moon. Finally I saw the rock I had curled up on to take a nap earlier that afternoon. It appeared surreal to me. A landmark from another life. The one that had Bunny in it. The one that had Quinn and Daisy. I choked back a sob, and Ruth squirmed on my shoulders. I set her down.

"Come on," Thomas said. "We can get a bit further tonight."

"No. We camp at the pass." I didn't give him time to argue.

I turned up the path, Ruth and Marta in hand.

"Dammit, Archer. He won't be there. Let's keep moving."

An unfathomable fatigue washed over me. I sighed. "You'd argue with a sign post if you put it up yourself, wouldn't you?"

"What are you talking about?"

"Never mind. Look. We can't go any further. These kids are exhausted, and my knee has had enough. Let's get off the trail and camp here."

In my heart of hearts, I told myself that I didn't know for sure. I'd only seen Quinn fall. He may have tripped, like Runner had. Maybe Bunny wasn't captured at all. Maybe they were waiting for us a few yards up the trail. I didn't believe that, but I was too tired to open my heart and mind to the true implications of what I'd seen . . . of what Norris had said.

I pointed to a clearing off the trail, a small dirt patch with plenty of deadfall around for firewood. "Here. We'll camp here."

I put down my pack and rifle and pulled out my canteen. Passing around the water, I admonished the children to pace themselves. It was all we had to get home on. Then I broke my last factory bar into pieces and distributed it.

Ben was crying again. I cleaned him as best I could and used my headscarf as a diaper. Then I soaked a corner of cloth from my tunic for him to suck on and pre-chewed a bit of my own piece of factory bar to feed to him.

Runner had collapsed in a heap and curled into a fetal position where he lay. Thomas did everything he could, but he was not able to get the child to eat. Marta, on the other hand, gobbled hers down and wanted to eat her brother's as well. Ruth took a bite, said she didn't feel well, and gave her second bite to Marta.

"Thomas, please build a fire. I don't want some lion or Dixie bear coming in here and picking off a kid tonight."

"No way. What if the Josephites see it?" He was busy filling a large hollow with pine needles for Runner to bed down in for the night.

"They're scared of the forest. They didn't even follow us in here. Right now, the Dixie bears are more of a threat. Please just build a fire like I asked you to."

He said nothing to indicate acquiescence, but once he had his brother settled, he started gathering wood.

Opening my first aid kit, I took out my flashlight and looked the kids over. Aside from a cut on the side of Thomas's forehead and a few burns, he was fine. I rubbed a bit of salve on the burns. Runner had skinned knees from his fall, but his psychological wounds were what damaged him most. I kissed his forehead and left him curled up on the bed his brother had made for him. Marta was sound, but terrified and exhausted. She snuggled in next to Runner, but complained about seeing fire every time she closed her eyes. And Ruth. She had a small wound where a bullet had grazed her calf, and it seemed to have been a dirt magnet during our flight.

"It stung me, and I fell." Ruth looked up at me with wide eyes. I was grateful the wound was relatively small and only flesh. Probably a stray .22 from a Sec pistol.

I pulled out a flask of Quinn's top shelf shine from my first aid kit. "Okay, sweetie. I'm going to give you this stick to bite. This is going to hurt, but you can handle it. I've done it many times and survived. Are you ready?"

Without waiting for her answer, I poured the last of our moonshine into her wound to clean it. Forget biting the stick. She screamed bloody murder. Thomas rushed over and clamped his hand over her mouth.

"You can't do that . . . Archer, she can't do that. She sounds like a wounded animal. She'll draw the Dixies." I knew he was not trying to be unkind. It was the simple truth.

"Ruth, honey, I'm not trying to scare you, but there are big bears here in the forest. They like to scare little girls, and we don't want them to do that. It's very important that you be quiet while I'm cleaning your wound. Okay?"

Tears poured down the little girl's face. She nodded and picked up the stick. "I try." She put the stick in her mouth of her own accord, and I began again. This time, Thomas held her, too, and she buried her face in his chest and cried. I tried to be gentle and quick.

When I was finished, I took the child in my arms and rocked her. The motion was as comforting to me as it was to her, and my mind wandered, the day catching up to me. The majestic buck. Ernesto dead. Cecilia and Maria, bursting into flames. I saw the Godfire in my mind and heard the screams, and the stench filled my nostrils once more. The fact that I was holding Ruth was the only thing that kept me from vomiting.

Quinn and Daisy. Two thirds of my family. How could I ever live without them? And why would I?

My soul hollow and devoid of hope, I wanted to dissolve into the earth. For a brief moment, I imagined myself rushing down into the town and taking out as many Joes as I could before they killed me. But then Ruth stirred in my arms, and I knew I did not have the luxury of revenge.

Then I heard it. A soft grunting and a crack of a twig. My blood froze. There was something in the forest, and it was coming our way.

CHAPTER 41

I WONDERED WHY DAISY hadn't given us warning, and
then the realization flooded in. *She's gone. Dear God, she's
gone.*

I set Ruth near the fire. Thomas picked up his .22, but I
knew it would be no good against a Dixie bear. I guessed a
bear, because a lion would not have made such noise, and
Josephite soldiers would have made even more.

I held my finger to my lips, signaling the children to silence,
and I nocked an arrow in my bow. I didn't know what good it
would be except to be able to say I died fighting, but that was
something to me.

Another twig snapped, and Thomas and I simultaneously
aimed in the direction of the noise.

Then we heard a man's squeaky voice. "D–d–don't shoot.
Please don't shoot."

One Josephite soldier stepped into the edge of the firelight,
his hands up in a gesture of peace. Thomas took aim, but I
reached out and lowered his rifle. There was something familiar
about this skinny man with close-shaved hair. While keeping
his arms up and his fingers splayed, he slowly moved his left
hand in front of his face and pushed his round spectacles up

his nose.

"Talk fast," I said. I took my hand from Thomas's gun, and he lifted it again, keeping the man in his sights.

The man gulped. "Please. Your friends are with me. Quinn sent me to find you."

I knew his face, but I couldn't place it right off, and his words made no sense to me. "How do you know Quinn?" I asked.

"He—he—here. The girl said to draw this." His hands shaking, he knelt, picked up a stick, and drew Middle Meadow's triangle of arrows with the sprouting seed in the middle. "Quinn and I. We p–p–play p–p–poker. We play poker."

Then I knew. I gave Thomas an affirmative nod. "Dave, is it?" I waved him closer to the fire, my heart pounding. I was afraid to hope. "What do you know of Quinn?"

The man closed his eyes and breathed a moment, visibly melting with relief. "He's been shot. He and your friend, Bunny, they're over there." He pointed into the forest from the way he came. "We heard the scream and saw your fire."

"Quinn's alive?" My skin began to tingle. "Quinn's alive? And Bunny?" I was afraid to believe him. "But I saw him get shot. And a Josephite . . . wait. That was you that took his gun, wasn't it?"

He nodded.

With my bow in one hand, I grabbed a piece of burning wood from the fire. "Take me to them now."

A million questions beat against the back of my teeth, but first things first. Dave couldn't figure out exactly where he had come from through the forest, but to my eyes, it was as plain as if he'd driven a bulldozer through a hemp field. Soon my light found Quinn sitting with his back against a tree. His eyes closed, Bunny hovered beside him. When she saw me she rushed to me, her arms open wide.

"Oh, Archer. I knew you'd make it. I knew you'd find us."

I could feel her quivering. She was filthy and ragged and

scratched up from branches like she'd been in a catfight, but she was alive, and it was all I could do not to cry.

"Shhh. I'm here now." I'd never been so happy to see two people in my life. "Tell me about Quinn."

"We were almost to the forest when he was shot. The bullet is near his collarbone. We wanted to stop and take it out, but he wouldn't let us. Said we had to meet you no matter what."

I took a deep breath and bent down to examine Quinn, doing my best not to disturb him. My stomach dropped when I saw his shirt was crusted in blood. But that wasn't all. Fresh blood seeped out from under a makeshift patch at his collarbone.

Bunny followed my gaze. "Sometimes it slows but we can't get it to stop bleeding."

I nodded, unable to speak.

"Archer?" Quinn's voice was barely audible.

"I'm here, baby." In the spirit of first things first, I resisted the urge to kiss him and offered him my water instead.

He took my hand, a shadow of a smile on his lips. "I told you I'd get her out."

I hid my face from him, wiping a tear from my cheek, but I kept my voice light. "You're such a guy. Do you think you can walk a bit? We need to get you over by the fire. It's not far."

"Where's Daisy?" he asked.

It took me a moment to answer. "She's not with us."

Quinn's eyes filled with sadness. He took my hand and kissed it.

Dave and I helped him up, and we struggled through the forest. Bunny cleared our path as much as possible, and we settled Quinn by the fire where I could take a look at his wound. He flinched and ground his teeth, but made no sound when I lifted off the blood-soaked shirt.

The red seeping made it difficult to inspect the site, but it wasn't hard to feel the bullet lodged beside his collarbone. It could have been a much worse spot, but if we couldn't stop the bleeding, he would never make it home.

"What do you think?" Bunny asked, worry and exhaustion etched across her face.

I swallowed the bile that rose in my throat. "It has to come out. Thomas, please hand me my pack. Bunny, boil some water." My voice was low, slow, and strange to my own ear. It was the same voice Granny used when she told me that Makenzie had lost a child or that we would not have enough food for the winter.

Bunny wrung her hands, shifting her weight from side to side, hovering at the far edge of the firelight. "I can't," she said.

I sighed, impatient with her phobia. "We need boiling water now. Pour it in your tin, and I'll set it on the fire. You can stay over there."

"No, it's not that," she said. "We don't have any water. We were hoping you would."

"What? You mean . . ." I wanted to snap, but I stopped myself. Of course they didn't have any water. Who planned for this?

I thought about the little water I had left. I could wash Quinn's wound, or I could save it for the children. I looked over at them. The dark circles under Ruth's eyes told me she was dehydrated already. The others, huddled on the bed of pine needles, restless in their sleep, were sure to be no better off. It would be a long day ahead for them to get to Middle.

Fighting off desperation, I pressed as gently as I could across the hard knot of the bullet, hoping to persuade it back out the way it had gone in.

Quinn howled and blood oozed from the wound. "Damn, Archer. Don't do that."

"Sorry, sorry." It turned my stomach to see him suffering. At least the blood would push out some of the dirt.

I thought things through. We needed something to clean the wound. I'd used the last of the moonshine on Ruth. If it weren't for the children, I'd have used the last of my water without hesitation. And I'd brought a trade pack, not my hunting pack, which meant I didn't have my forceps to retrieve the bullet. I could cut it out, but it was deep, and my knives were not made for such fine work. How could I get the bullet out? I didn't know, so I focused on what I *could* do.

My motions deliberate, I took inventory of my first aid kit. There were no clean cloths left after bandaging Ruth, but I had some herbs. I took out the ganga joint I kept for emergencies, lit it, and held it for Quinn to take a drag. I knew the marijuana would relax his muscles and help alleviate some of the pain. But how to get the bullet out?

Quinn, using his off-hand, fumbled and dropped the cigarette. I quickly snatched it up and patted out the sparks on the ground. Thinking it would be less awkward for him, I reached for his smoking pouch on his belt to take out his cigarette clip. When I clamped it down on a tiny swatch of paper at the end of the joint, I got an idea. I unclamped the device and examined it in the firelight. It was a thin pair of pliers with metal teeth on the handle to hold it shut. It would work. I gave Quinn back the joint and cleaned the tool as best I could with my tunic.

"What is it, Archer?" Quinn groaned, shifted his weight, and took another awkward drag off the joint.

"Well, I've got the tool. If we can find some way to clean the site, I might be able to get that bullet out of there."

Putting the clamp over the fire to sterilize it, I looked again at the children and thought of the tiny bit of water left in my pack. Would it even be enough to clean Quinn's wound? Or would I waste it that way and then have nothing for the children? Even if I could get the bullet out, there was so much dirt in and around the wound that I might make it worse by mucking around with it. But the bleeding wouldn't stop until we got the bullet out.

Frustration overwhelmed me. I heard my own teeth grinding and realized I had clenched my jaw. Where I should have forced myself to relax, I only ground harder, on some level enjoying the pain in my teeth that reflected the pain in my soul.

I noticed Dave, holding the light for me, staring at the marijuana and looking hopeful. I couldn't believe it. Here was Quinn suffering, and this Joe outta nowhere wanted the only medicine I had to give him?

Quinn saw Dave's face, too, and held out his hand to pass the joint. I stopped him and rounded on Dave, glad for the excuse to attack. "Seriously? Can't you see he needs this?"

Dave shrugged, sheepish. "It's been a long day."

I snapped. "No shit. Thanks to you Josephites. And what are you doing here anyway? Why aren't you back there killing my people instead of mooching your friend's only medicine?"

Thomas stepped forward, rifle in hand. "Yeah. Why did you follow them?"

Thomas chambered a bullet and aimed the rifle at Dave. This time, I didn't stop him.

CHAPTER 42

D AVE LOOKED BACK AND and forth between us, his eyes wide. "Look, I'm an engineer." He held his hands out. "These hands build stuff. They don't kill people. There's so much chaos in the city that they had to pull us sparkies off the transformers to come kill . . ." He caught his breath. We waited silently for him to finish. "I'd been thinking about leaving anyway, and when I saw Quinn run past, I didn't think. I just did it. So here I am."

Bunny moved between Dave and the rifle. "And a good thing, too." Her sharp tone relayed her disapproval. "I never could have gotten Quinn here without Dave."

A wave of exhaustion washed over me. I gestured at Thomas to put the gun down. He reluctantly complied, but he kept it near to hand.

"Here," Dave said, taking a flask from a pocket in his pants and holding it out to me. "You look like you could use this."

I gasped and snatched it from his hand. With intensity of hope, I leaned in toward his face. "What is this?"

Dave rocked back on his heels away from me, fear in his eyes. "We told you we didn't have any water. That's moonshine."

My high-pitched laughter of relief almost brought me to

tears. "Okay. You can stay. But you can't have this back," I said, handing the flask to Quinn.

I waved everyone away except Thomas. Catching the handle of the clamp with a stick, I pulled it from the fire, careful to keep the tip from touching anything. Quinn closed his eyes and leaned back against the tree, letting the moonshine burn through his veins while the instrument cooled enough for me to touch. Then I handed him my knife. He braced the antler handle between his teeth and nodded. I didn't hesitate.

I slowly coaxed the clamp into the wound and tightened it down on the bullet. Quinn growled low in his throat, and his face grew red. Sweat broke out on his brow, but he didn't move. I gently guided the lump of lead away from his collarbone and out of his shoulder. Blood gushed out the reopened wound and dripped to the ground. Breathing heavily, he opened his eyes and looked at the bullet in my hand.

"Keep it?" I asked, and he replied with a slight nod. I wiped it off and put it in a pocket. I suspected it would end up in his amulet, but I would never ask him something so private.

I held up the flask where he could see it. He closed his eyes and nodded again. I poured the moonshine into his wound. He screwed his face into a grimace and arched his back, but no sound escaped. After shaking the flask upside down to get every drop out, I dried the area with a clean corner of Bunny's undershirt and tenderly fashioned a bandage with it as best I could. Then I used the cloth that bound my breasts to make a sling for him that would stabilize his arm.

"Deena," he whispered. A rush of affection shot through me. I had never heard my name on his lips before. Tenderly, I smoothed his hair and kissed him.

With his good arm, he reached up and drew me to him, and I returned his quiet embrace. Listening to his breathing, ragged with pain, I breathed with him until he steadied.

I wanted to crawl inside him and hide from the world, living or dying with his breath. We could go over the pass to

Mexifornia. We could run north to the savage lands. We could set out to find the Eastern Rebels and join in their fight against the Josephites. But then Ruth's voice asking for water pulled me back, reminding me that my life, at least at that moment, was not about me.

After checking the children, I told Thomas to feed the fire and then go to sleep. I would take first watch. He piled on the wood and then lay down, but he kept his rifle at hand and his face toward Dave.

Bunny, still at the edge of the firelight, reached out and squeezed my hand. I glanced her way and was touched by the tears in her eyes. She had come to love Quinn, too.

Time passed, and the fire burned low. I listened to the wind in the trees, starting at the top of the mountain and snaking its way down, roaring loudest right before the breeze brushed our skins. Was it bringing the Mother's healing spirits that Quinn believed in? Or was it only a phenomenon of science as Bunny would say? Either way, Quinn's bleeding slowly stopped. I breathed.

Ben cried, and Bunny took him from Thomas, who leaned back against a tree beside the other children, his rifle still at hand, and his eye still on Dave.

Dave, on the other hand, had propped himself against a tree across the fire from us. His eyes were closed, but he tossed about as if he couldn't get comfortable. He'd clearly never slept on the ground before.

I automatically sought Daisy and remembered.

Daisy. I didn't even bother fighting the tears that streamed down my face.

"I miss her," Bunny said, reading my mind. She took a factory bar from her pack. I said nothing when she handed me one and then broke off a piece of another and chewed it for little Ben.

Bunny comforted the infant, and I studied the fire. My voice sounded husky to my own ears. "Daisy saved me. Me and

Ruth." Again I heard Norris's evil laugh and saw his gun in my face. "I thought he had you. He said he did."

"No. I'm not sure why he didn't follow me," Bunny said." Ben swallowed the factory bar, and Bunny wet his cloth for him to suck on.

Dave snuffled and opened his eyes. "I can answer that. There was an ambush set up at the far side of the field." He waved his hand in the air. "That was my job. Norris was certain we'd pick you up. Instead when I saw you two running up the mountain, I told them I saw you go the other way. Said you were trapped in a house. That's when I ran too."

"God bless you, Dave. I'm sure you saved us," Bunny said. She was barely audible, and her eyes were closed. She took hold of her seed in one hand and lay down, curling up around the infant.

My eyelids became heavy, and I noticed that Thomas was still wide awake. "Thomas, tell you what. You take the first watch. Wake me when you need to sleep."

He responded with a nod, watching the dozing Dave, who was talking low and unintelligibly in his sleep.

Curling up beside Quinn, I listened to his heart, steady and strong. His spirit seeped into me, and mine answered in kind, drinking deeply from his soul, even as I offered him my own. Soon I released myself into him, and into sleep.

CHAPTER 43

BEN'S CRIES WOKE ME at the break of dawn. I slipped from under Quinn's arm and took the child from Bunny before giving her a hand up. Then Bunny and I picked our way along the path, hoping to remove the fussing child before he disturbed the others.

Bunny got him to swallow some water while I chewed a bit of factory bar for him, but she wasn't able to quiet him.

"Let me try," I said. She handed him back to me, and I automatically began bouncing and swaying as I did with the babies in the meadow. When that wasn't enough, I softly sang a song that Granny used to sing to quiet me as a child—a little ditty about raindrops and girls in white dresses. It was also about many things I had never seen, but they all sounded peaceful and good, and I wanted peaceful, good things for that boy. Eventually he settled, but I kept on bouncing and swaying because it felt good.

Bunny gazed at the child in my arms. "Ben," she said. "The tribe of Benjamin was destroyed." Taking hold of her seed pendant, she bowed her head. I did not disturb her.

When she finally looked up and spoke in her tired, even voice, her words shocked me. "You know, Archer, this was all your fault. You and Quinn and Flynx and the rest. Will you admit that to Ben when he asks how his parents died?"

I froze. "What are you saying? You were there. You saw how they came in and slaughtered us. It was probably because of you."

"Norris couldn't have been more surprised when he saw me. They were there because they caught Flynx. What else could it be? He went out to kill Joseph, and they caught him and slaughtered his town. It's that simple. If you hadn't shut down the grid, none of this would have happened."

My jaw clenched, and I quivered. Suddenly she was no longer my beloved cousin. She was one of *them*. "How dare you, you pompous, self-righteous Joe Bitch. You people starve us and kill us at will. You just saw your worst nightmare happen to a whole town of my people. Innocent people. We have every right to destroy you."

"Granny told you not to do it. She told you they'd find out and come to kill you all. What if they killed her too? What if Middle isn't even there anymore?"

The terror that thought brought with it served to fuel my anger. "We save your miserable ass from getting torched, just like you people would have torched this baby, and you dare judge us?"

Ben started crying. "Here," I said, shoving him into her arms. "You tell this baby that your people are better than his. You tell him he deserves to be burned alive, and you don't."

Sick with rage, I trekked back to camp, not caring if Bunny was following or not. Snatching up my bow, I stalked past the sleeping children and into the forest.

I chose a target, an old aspen tree, and shot arrow after arrow while the sky brightened. The solid thud of my strikes reverberated through my body, comforting me on a level too deep for me to understand. I knew it was time to go back and check on Quinn. I knew it was time to get everyone moving. I would do that after one more, I told myself, still shooting arrow after arrow, just trying to make it to the next reverberation, hoping that would be the one that would somehow bring me some peace.

I heard a branch crack, and I startled. Bunny was pushing her way through the forest toward me. Ben slept soundly in her arms. I turned my back on her and went to retrieve my arrows. Returning, I drew up to my full height and stared her down, boring through her with my fury.

Her eyes, on the other hand, were firm, calm, and clear, and her voice was serene and confident. "What if you had fertile seeds? Would that be enough?"

"What do you mean?" I asked. I spit on the ground. "There are no fertile seeds. You clone them all in your factories."

"Work with me," she said. "If you had seeds that grew fertile crops, would that be enough? You could grow them and get more seeds from the crops from year to year. They might not produce as much, but before long, you wouldn't have to depend on Josephites to eat any more. Would that be enough for you to stop fighting? To stop the killing?"

I was taken aback at the idea. Fertile crops? How could that be? "Just tell me what you're getting at." I turned and started shooting at the tree again. It helped me think.

"My mother made seeds. I helped her. That's why Joseph wants me. We made seeds without him, and they are seeds that make more seeds. They don't have to be cloned."

I stopped shooting. "Seeds that make more seeds?" She had my attention. "How could you do that?"

She pulled a holowafer from her pocket and turned it on. After tapping it a few times, she held it out to me. A dark-haired woman in dirty overalls appeared. She was slim and gangly and looked like an unmade bed, but the pure joy that emanated from her features made her absolutely adorable. I almost never liked anyone instantly, but I immediately wanted to take this woman home.

"Here, wait," Bunny said, her voice thick. She tapped the

device once more, and I heard the woman's excited tones.

"We have it. We've done it." She spread her arms, presenting the low stand of seedlings in tubs in front of her, filling several tables between herself and the photographer. "Crops that bear fertile seeds. Here's the gassplant. We also have hemp, corn, beans, squash, and strawberries. These are my daughter's favorite. Hi, sweetie." The woman winked at the camera.

Behind her, another woman watered plants of various sizes that filled the room under lights like the ones I'd seen broken in the tunnel beneath the Josephite compound. She turned and smiled to the camera, waving, clearly as excited as her compatriot in the overalls. My blood chilled. I knew her. Barbara Conway. The woman I'd seen at Maverick's. The one who now fed the Virgin Garden.

I glanced at Bunny. She held her seed, hugging herself, tears streaming down her cheeks.

"Mary," she said, sniffing loudly. "My mother's name was Mary."

I reached out and pulled her in, and she rested her head on my shoulder while we watched.

For the next five minutes, Mary explained that all of Joseph's seeds carried the exact same genetic sequence for resistance to the cold ashy climate, and how any disease attacking that sequence could obliterate every growing crop in the Kingdom. But she had developed seeds without the sequence that were able to survive drought, heat, and cold, something Joseph said could not be done. And she had done it without Joseph or prophetic visions.

Mary held up a hemp seedling in its little pot. "This is my prize. Say hello to Audrey."

Bunny's laughter came through the machine, and I smiled. Then the picture rocked. Joseph himself burst through the door, Norris two steps behind him. "You bitch," said Joseph. "I'll burn you on my own altar for this."

Joseph was quick, but Mary was quicker. "Run, Tamar,"

she cried. She snatched her shears from the table and stabbed herself in the jugular. Blood sprayed across the old man. Two soldiers pinned a screaming Barbara, and Norris turned toward the camera. The picture went black.

CHAPTER 44

I STOOD IN STUNNED silence, my stomach churning. Bunny took out her scarf and blew her nose.

"That was you holding the camera, wasn't it?"

Bunny nodded but didn't look up. Her voice was thin and strained when she spoke. "I was near our safe room. Mother had it built into the lab in case we should need to escape quickly. It had a solid steel door and led into the tunnels. We kept a bag ready there."

A crow cawed above me in the growing light, and chipmunks fussed up a nearby tree.

I was moved and saddened, but I was also baffled. "So why are you telling me this now?"

"Because that's not all. My mother killed herself so they would not map her brain and find the rest of her work. She had seeds. A stash of seeds and a greenhouse full of her experimental crops. And from what you say, they might still be there."

It had been a long night, and I struggled to make sense of what she was telling me. "You have seeds?"

Bunny nodded. "Yes. They're at a Josephite work camp—the one we passed on our way to the Big Box."

The implications began to sink in. Bunny knew of seeds. Seeds that provided fertile crops. Seeds that would feed our people for generations to come and the proof that Joseph was a fraud.

I sat down, stunned. "Bunny, why didn't you tell us this before?"

She sighed. "I tried a few times when we went to the Big Box, but once you saw that transformer station, your only focus was on destroying my people."

I shook my head, struggling to make sense of her reason. "*We're* your people. *We're* the ones who gave you refuge when they would have put you to the Godfire. *We're* the ones who risked being in that town down there because of you. Why did you hold out on us?"

"What would you have done if you had known? You were all about fighting and killing as many Josephites as you could. How could I trust you with this? And even if I could, what if you were caught blowing something up and they mapped your brain? What if Flynx had known? They probably caught him, you know."

I took a deep breath. She was right. I would not have trusted me with that either. "So why are you trusting me now?"

Bunny studied me a moment before answering. "Because now your illusions are gone. Now you've been baptized by the Godfire, and you finally know your enemy."

She took my hand in hers. "So I'll ask you one last time. Will fertile seeds be enough to stop the fighting? You'll need my biometrics to open the safe. We can go get them as soon as you say the word."

I leaned my head into my hands, and I considered. It wasn't freedom, but it was hope. It was a chance. A way to make our world more fair. It was something to cling to until the day the Josephites rotted from the inside, as Granny said they must, and our people came into our own once again.

I looked through the trees toward the camp where the

children stirred. If we could give them fertile crops, maybe it would be enough to get them to the day when they could win their freedom too.

A movement caught my eye, and I spied a young hawk spiraling its ascent, searching the ground for its breakfast. Food. The first requirement for life.

But then I closed my eyes, and the visions of North assaulted me—my friends, my people, dashing frantically, only to explode into human flames. Their screams echoed in my mind, and the smell of their burning flesh once more permeated my nostrils. I shuddered at the power of the Josephites. It was nothing to them to wipe an entire town of our people from the planet. To destroy our seed for all eternity. How could we face that? I knew my answer.

"No, Bunny, it's not enough."

She cocked her head. "You would still fight them? After what they just did? You still think your way is better?"

Exhaustion seeped through my bones. "No. I know I can't fight them. That's why I won't steal your seeds. We can't risk it. Don't you understand? We're beaten. We can't fight them."

Bunny looked baffled. "That's your reason? You're the woman who wears a lion's claw around her neck. You're the woman who scales cliffs and blows up transformer stations and saves children from burning alive. Now I give you a plan to save your people, and you forget who you are?"

"Enough," I snapped. She pursed her lips and gave me the Eyebrow I knew so well on that other face I loved.

"Look," I said. "It's the wrong time. We don't even know if there's a meadow left uncharred between here and South. Maybe some day your Underground will have its martyr and enough steam to take charge, but until then, we just have to be patient and make the best of it."

"That's it, then? You're quitting?"

"Yes. That's it. They win."

CHAPTER 45

JUST THEN TWO SEC men with a half a dozen bedraggled companions straggling behind them rounded a bend in the trail. I stood. I didn't know them, and they were armed to the teeth.

The man in front saw me put my hand to my pistol and held his own two empty hands up in a friendly gesture. "Ho there, friend. We mean no harm. I'm Mo from Lower Creek, and this is my boy, Monte. We're travellers."

"You're the coyote," I said, putting my hand out. "I'm Archer from Middle. This is Bunny."

"Yes, I remember you, Bunny. We met yesterday. Before . . ." He swallowed hard and turned to look at the stragglers. "Bring it up back there. Lions pick off the ends." He put his hands on his hips and spit, waiting for a woman and child to catch up. He turned back to Bunny and said, "We're still heading to Mexifornia. If you've still got your food with you, you can join us. Can't take the baby, though."

Bunny looked to me, hope lighting her features. I knew what she wanted me to say, but I couldn't say it. Instead I reached for the sleeping baby in her arms and said, "Yes, she has her food."

Her eyes begged me to change my mind, their profound pools of sadness drawing me in, but I held silent. Finally she shrugged her shoulders and said, "I have no reason to stay, sir. I will welcome your guidance."

When we got back to camp, we found that Thomas had his siblings and Ruth ready to travel. Quinn was pale, and his face was lined with pain, but he had the fire out and our gear packed up. There was nothing left to do but say goodbye.

I took Bunny up into a hug. "Please," she whispered. "Please reconsider."

I closed my eyes and saw the flames once more. The sweet, sickening smell of burning flesh and hair filled my nostrils, and I shuddered. "No. We can't risk it."

She bit her lower lip and nodded. Then she held out the holowafer. "But keep this. Maybe some day you'll be able to use it against Joseph. For your people."

"No. You come back some day and use it yourself. Some day when your Underground has its hero. This could help you nail the bastard. You'll want to be here for that."

She smiled. "I hope you're right. Thank you, Archer." She threw her arms around my neck like a child, and she held me. "I'll never forget you, dear sister. You would make a good Christian."

I laughed, holding her close. "Says my Sec sister."

We waved to them, and they disappeared down the trail, now with Dave and Bunny in tow. Dave didn't have food for the trip, but Mo and the rest thought an engineer would prove useful along the way, so they agreed to share what they had with him for as long as he proved his worth.

Even the children were silent when we set out toward Middle. Quinn insisted on carrying little Ben in his good arm. Thomas and I took turns carrying Ruth and helping the others. Runner seemed no better off for the night of rest, and he stumbled along, his eyes glazed over. Marta whined that she was hungry the few times that she spoke at all. And me? My knee was unhappy, but the hours of rest had done it good. We held a slow but steady pace.

A million questions worried at my mind while we traveled. Had the Josephites brought the Godfire to Middle? Had they destroyed our stores for winter? Had they captured Flynx and mapped his brain to know what we'd done? And Granny. Would she blame me like Bunny had?

And what if Bunny was right? Was that town burned because of me? Did Daisy die because of me?

I wiggled that in my mind like a sore tooth that demands the irritating attention of a tongue. But in the end, I always came back to the same devastating conclusion. It was war. There was no pretty way to go about it, and we had lost.

Quinn stumbled, and Ben cried, jolting me back to the present.

I noticed how pale Quinn was. "Here. I'll take the baby."

Rather than argue that he was doing fine, he handed me the child without a word.

"You know, maybe it's best if we rest a bit," I said. I turned to the group of children walking behind me. "Thomas, we're going to pull up here for a while. The children need some rest."

"No way," he said. "We've got to keep going."

I resisted the urge to smack him. Then Quinn practically collapsed where he stood, closing the matter.

I signaled a stop to Daisy and then caught my breath. It was going to take me a long time to learn to live without her.

Marta grabbed my tunic and pulled on it. "Archer, I'm thirsty."

"Me too," said Ruth, wriggling in Thomas's arms.

I gave them the last of the water, only a sip each, and they said together, "I'm still thirsty, Archer."

Runner lay down in a fetal position next to Quinn, and Ben started to wail. It was all I could do not to sit down and cry, too, but it was only noon, and at our pace, we would be lucky to get home before dark—if there was even a home to get to.

Then a voice boomed through the forest, rousing a nearby squirrel to flight. "Hey, hey!"

Freefall rode out of the forest on Old Sally. I never in a million years thought that he could be the most beautiful sight of my life, but he was, and behind him walked Zander and Arys.

CHAPTER 46

MY KNEES WENT WEAK with relief. They were alive, but were they on the run too?

I hurried to Zander, and he caught me up in a bear hug. "Is the Meadow still there? Is everyone safe?" I asked.

"Yes," he said. "The Meadow's fine."

Thomas ran up beside us, looking as relieved as I felt. "The bastards killed them. They killed them all," he said.

Zander's eyes grew wide in horror.

"The Godfire," I said.

Freefall stepped back and drew in a sharp breath. Arys sank down and dropped his head in his hands. "Oh, God. I'm so sorry."

It took a moment for his reaction to register with me. "Why would you be sorry?"

He looked up at me, his face haggard. "It was my mother. She knew you were going to North, and she's wanted you dead ever since I told her you left Bane to die in the minefield."

I was confused. "Bane was already dead when we left. There was nothing we could do. And how could you know that?"

"I looked for him and Greagor when they didn't come home. He was barely alive. He told me how the mine exploded. It was the last thing he said. I buried him in the forest. Mother blamed you and Quinn." He dropped his head back into his hands.

I shook my head, confused. "But what does that have to do with North?"

I could hardly hear Arys, his voice wretched with sorrow. "Mother was listening under your window the other night. She thought if she told the Joes that Flynx was going to kill Joseph, they would punish *his* meadow—North—and kill you two in the process."

Arys looked up at me. "She dressed as a man and went to find a patrol. She thought they would give her seeds, or even let her move into the city, but they didn't. When I got there, they were taking her away. There was nothing I could do."

Harmony. Her look of cold triumph finally made sense.

"We were on our way to warn you," said Zander. Then he glanced behind me and stiffened. "Where's Bunny?" His voice held an edge of fear.

I knew what he was asking. "We got her out. She left with the coyote. They're on their way to the pass by now."

Zander nodded. "I'm glad." He saw the road-weary group behind me. "You must be starving."

I caught his arm. "That's not all." I told him about Daisy and Quinn.

"Ah, sister," said Zander. He hugged me again and kissed the top of my head. "Let's get him home."

***

IT WAS EVENING WHEN we arrived. Granny waited with gruel at the ready to feed us. She held her questions, fashioning poultices for Quinn's and Ruth's wounds and my knee. The children ate, and then she sent them and Thomas to settle in with Zander for the night. All except for Ruth. Ruth stuck to me like a burr, and I rocked her in my arms until she slept, not knowing if I was comforting her or myself. Then

I left Quinn to fill in Granny on what had happened while I settled the child into my own bed.

I couldn't help but notice how empty Bunny's bed appeared. No pack beside her pillow. No clothes neatly folded at the end. I wondered how far they had gotten, and if her companions were being kind to her. More than anything, I missed her smile.

Returning to the kitchen, I heard Quinn ask, "Did Flynx ever come back?"

Granny shook her head. "No. The damn fool." She sniffed and took a kerchief from her pocket to wipe her nose. "I'm fine," she said, as if talking to herself. "I'm fine." She straightened and put the kerchief back in her pocket.

"It was our fault," Quinn said. With a glance, I could see he struggled with the same doubts I'd carried that morning. I wondered if Bunny had accused him, as well, and I braced myself for Granny's agreement. But she surprised me.

"It's never wise for mice to torment Dixie bears, but you did not make the Josephites slaughter a town. You don't have that kind of power." She sighed. "You see now that you cannot win against them as things stand. Something will have to change first."

I nodded. "That's what I told Bunny, but she wanted us to go against them again."

Granny cocked her head, her face incredulous. "Bunny did? What on earth did she want you to do?"

"She wanted us to steal seeds from a Josephite compound."

Quinn was as baffled as Granny. "Why would Bunny want you to risk that?"

"It's her work. The work she did with her mother. These seeds grow fertile crops."

Quinn's jaw dropped. "What? Fertile crops?"

I recounted the recording and what Bunny had told me.

Granny sat back in her chair, wide-eyed. "Good God. Do you have any idea what that would be worth to our people?"

Was she serious? "Yes. I do. Do you have any idea what

we've been through? We can't fight them." I spat out each word. "You said so yourself." I quaked at the memory of the flames, the screams, and the smell of burning flesh.

Granny poured me some tea. Once my cup quit shaking, she continued. "No. We can't fight them. But we can endure them. Fertile crops that didn't come from Joseph and his visions—that wouldn't only be food for our people, that would be a tool for his destruction. Ten, twenty years from now, we'd have enough seeds that we'd never need the Josephites again. It's not freedom, but it's a start."

"Granny, they burned everyone. They'd do that to Middle too. Don't ask me to do this."

"When you two took out their power grid, you were starting something you couldn't finish. But this . . ." she paused. "To have those seeds. That would be an end in itself." Quinn sighed and shook his head. "I know what they can do. I was there. But she's right. We have to get those seeds."

"We can't. They're in a safe only Bunny can open, and she's gone now."

"Deena," Granny said. She pointed toward Old Sally, who grazed her way across the meadow in the dusk. "That's why God made horses. If you leave first thing in the morning, you'll still catch her before they get to the pass. I can't make you do this, but think of those children you brought back. Think of that little girl in there. Think of your own future children and what it would mean to them. This is a risk worth taking."

I looked to Daisy's corner, her bone lying unattended beside her blanket and toy. Her final yelp rang in my ears, and once more I saw the Godfire. My friends. My family. My people. Gone. We could not fight the Josephites, and if they caught us . . . if they discovered we had the seeds, they would do the same to us. For all I knew, Flynx was taken alive, and the Godfire would be in our meadow tomorrow.

But if it wasn't, and if we had the seeds . . . we'd never starve again. What a chance that would be.

I finished my tea and put down my cup. "I'll think about it."

***

GRANNY GAVE QUINN HER own bed, and I insisted on staying beside him. Tossing restlessly on the floor, I ran from Norris and his soldiers in my dreams, seeing fire everywhere I turned. Flames burst up around me, scorching my flesh, until an arrow flew out of the dark. I heard a cry just before the arrow struck my throat, and I knew the cry was my own. Then Daisy, curled at my side, licked my hand and brought me back to myself, only for me to wake and find she was gone.

Quinn stirred and groaned. Angry, red streaks shot across his back and shoulder, radiating out from the wound. Trembling, I kissed his forehead, confirming the worst. His fever had begun.

I grabbed my bow and ran into the forest, finding my favorite glade by the light of the moon. Arrow after arrow, I shot, desperately searching for some corner of my mind to hide in where I could fool myself into thinking that Quinn would be fine. That North was not slaughtered. That Daisy was still beside me.

And while I shot, a refuge from the pain opened itself to me. A choice. Check out. Shoot Quinn, and then shoot myself. A kinder death for him; oblivion for me. The idea whispered through my heart like a warm breeze, and I felt the empty reed of my soul sway with its whims, weighing the pros and cons with no more concern than whether I would hunt for deer or for marmots. Live or die?

The thought of death mesmerized me. My struggles would be over. No more groveling before the cruel Josephites. No more grief, or loss, or killing. No more vicious winters or relentless, exhausting summers. And no more hunger.

Then I thought of Granny, and my cheeks burned with the shame of my own selfishness. It would devastate her. And what about Ruth? What would she do without her people if she didn't have me? It was one thing to take Quinn with me—he was going to die anyway—but it was another to abandon them.

Then what could I do to make things better? My mind turned back to Bunny's seeds—a hope for a future without depending on the Josephites to survive.

I envisioned the work camp, calculating how far away it was, how long it would take us to get there and back, and who I could take along. I pictured myself climbing from the tunnel into the shed. In my mind's eye, I stood at the door, seeing the greenhouses and seed office to my left, and the Clinic to my right.

Wait. The Clinic. It was sure to have a store of antibiotics. Excitement raced through me. If I did this thing, I could steal antibiotics for Quinn.

But the risk. Could we take such a chance?

Retrieving my arrows, I returned to the house while dawn lit the sky around me. If I was going to catch Bunny, I had to choose soon.

I sat once more on the floor beside Quinn's bed and rested my head on his thigh where the blanket would keep me from feeling his fever. Closing my eyes, I forced myself to breathe. Then Quinn's hand closed on mine. I looked up to see him caressing my face with his gaze. He lifted my palm to his cheek and kissed my wrist.

"Go, Archer. Goddess be with you."

A single tear slipped from my eye. He caught it on his finger, kissed it, and then held it to my lips. "Go."

CHAPTER 47

TWO NIGHTS LATER, I crouched in the burned gassplant stubble on a slight rise in the field, studying the Josephite camp below me. Though I couldn't see him, I knew Freefall was opposite me on the south side, surveying that part of the compound. Night blanketed the fields, and the new moon worked in our favor. The only hitch so far had been the pain in my knee, but it was still functioning, so I ignored it.

The camp teemed with life. Group after group of women and children marched in step, two by two, from the dorms to the chapel to the cafeteria under the watchful eyes of their male guards. The sound of singing periodically drifted up to my hiding place, sending chills down my spine and raising the hair on the back of my neck. With its high fences, concertina wire, and lock-step discipline, the camp looked like Hell on Earth to me.

About the time I began to despair that they would ever settle in for the night, the last lines of workers emptied the chapel and the cafeteria and entered the dormitories. Soon all of the buildings were dark, and only the patrolling guards remained outside. I counted two of them, but I couldn't see several places on the grounds. From all appearances, though, security was minimal. I marveled that the greatest prize in the Kingdom lay beneath me in those greenhouses, the key to ending Josephite domination, and the Joes didn't even know its worth to protect it from us.

I returned to find Freefall, Zander, Thomas, and Bunny waiting inside the tunnel at the well house. Zander seemed calm and solid as always. Freefall took a swig from his flask, and it was all I could do to not grab it from his hands. Thomas had braided his hair like a man's for the first time that morning. No one said anything. He'd earned it. And Bunny. She shivered, wide-eyed, as if she were going to bolt.

Clutching her seed, she said, "Archer, I'm scared. If they catch me, they'll burn me."

The last thing I needed was for her to fall apart. She was the most essential piece of the mission.

I took out my pistol and handed it to her. "Here. Take this, and if any Joes get close to you, shoot yourself. And don't worry, I'll kill you if they don't. That's why I call you Bunny, you know."

I'd been hoping to get a laugh out of her with that, but instead she stared grimly at the gun in her hand for a moment before putting it into the waist of her pants. "So what do I do? Two shots to my temple, and then you finish me off?"

I laughed. "Well, if you do your first shot right, you won't get two shots. But I was joking. You use the gun to shoot them, and I'll get you out of it. You seriously thought I would have killed you?"

My humor was lost on her. She clutched her seed and stared at me intently. "I'm not brave. Tell me you'll kill me if you have to."

"Stop talking like that."

Thomas shifted his weight impatiently. "Can we go?"

I held up a hand to him. "Just wait . . . Bunny, there's no need for anyone to die tonight. We're here as thieves. We'll be in and out, and they'll never know."

She grabbed my arm. "Tell me. I won't move unless you do."

Thomas threw up his hands. "Geez. I'll kill you now and take your damn hand. Come on."

In our own world, Bunny and I ignored him. Touched by her childlike trust, I took her pinkie, held up my own, and wrapped them together. "I pinkie swear. I will not let you die in the fire."

Her face relaxed, and she smiled. "You shouldn't swear, but I believe you. Thank you."

"Women," Freefall said, shaking his head.

"Okay," I said. "I saw two guards—one in a shack by the front gate, and one by the front door of the greenhouses. What did you see, Freefall?"

"Same thing, but there's one more stationed at the front of the dorm. You wouldn't have seen him from your side, but he doesn't have a view of the shed door unless he moves."

"Then that's the weak spot. We'll have to be extra careful for that twelve feet or so until we can get into the shadows at the back of the building."

"Why not crawl out a shed window on the shadowed side?" asked Zander.

"They're too small. Even I can't get through one," I said.

"Could I?" asked Thomas.

"Possibly, but it doesn't matter. Your only job here is to carry a pack home. You're to stay in the tunnel, ready to run. We'll just have to be careful." The five of us hustled down the tunnel toward the shed, following the beam from my flashlight.

"One last time," I said. "If any of us gets caught, the rest get back to the meadow any way we can. Protect the seeds with your lives, and evacuate the meadow to Iredale. Zander and Freefall, fill packs with the ripe food in the greenhouse. Corn first. It'll be easiest to spot. Then the beans and squash. Take fruit from the inside, and not more than one for every ten on a plant. Bunny and I will get the seeds out of the safe in the office. As soon as you're back to the tunnel, leave." I hadn't mentioned my plan to go back for the antibiotics, and I wanted them to be well away to make sure the seeds were safe before I took that risk.

Stopping underneath the trapdoor, I shined the light at the top of the tunnel to make an even glow around us. "Any questions?"

"Yeah. Shouldn't you have me stand lookout in the shed?" asked Thomas. "I could signal you through the window if a guard moves."

"No. You stay in the tunnel with Arys." What he suggested wasn't a bad idea. In fact, I'd thought about it myself, but I didn't want to risk the kid any more than I had to. "Anything else?" I asked. The four of them shook their heads.

I unslung my bow and set it at the bottom of the ladder to pick up on my return. Though I felt naked without it, we'd be in close quarters. I would have to rely on my knives and the pistol in Bunny's possession.

We tied back our long braids to keep them out of our way and checked each other's gear to make sure it was secure. "You know your armor shows at the neck?" Bunny pointed out.

"Thanks," I replied, pulling up the collar of my turtleneck. I thought again of how it saved me at North, grateful once more to Quinn. Quinn. I forced myself to put him out of my mind.

"Ready?" I asked. "Let's go make some fair."

Thomas jutted out his chin and Bunny shuddered. Then, my heart pounding, I jumped up the rope ladder.

CHAPTER 48

I LIFTED THE TILE, and adrenaline flooded my veins. With it came the heat—that tense, exhilarating mixture of fear and confidence that I could do anything if I only kept my head. One at a time, we climbed into the shed. Then we turned the tile over to Thomas, who remained at the top of the rope ladder to open it for us at our return.

Keeping a penlight low, we picked our way through the tools to the front door. I peeked out the window and mentally charted our course to the greenhouses and their office. Taking a moment to see my way to the Clinic, as well, I was gratified to see a window in the shadows toward the back of the building. I made a mental note for later.

One by one, we slipped out the door, jumped off the steps, and dashed to the shadows beside the greenhouses. By the time Freefall brought up the end, our lockpicker had us inside.

I froze. The sight that met my eyes in the dim light etched itself into my memory forever. Food. Acres of lush, green, abundant food. Not like our small gardens with their weak, withered plants growing barely enough to sustain our meager existence, but row after row of leafy greens and trees, copious in their fertility.

Freefall stepped forward and reached toward a ripe apple. I grabbed his arm and whispered. "We're not here to eat. Stay focused, will you?"

"You don't seriously expect me not to take an apple, do you?"

I looked at the ripe fruit I'd only ever seen in Maverick's garden, and my mouth watered. "Okay. One for each of us, and get them from different trees. But that's it. Got it?"

"This way," Bunny whispered. She pointed up a row of onions toward a door. I gave Freefall and Zander a nod, and they made their way to the corn while I followed Bunny to the office.

Once inside, I wondered if it was an office or a trash bin. Papers overflowed every surface, little shiny wrappers littered the desk, and the chair could barely roll for the stacks of folders on the floor.

I wouldn't have found the safe if Bunny didn't recognize it. About the size of Old Sally's hay bin, it crouched large, black, and heavy in the corner of the room by a pair of filing cabinets. I searched it for a handle, but found none.

Bunny took off her seed, kissed it, and placed it in an almost imperceptible notch on the side. A holographic display with a screen and a keyboard appeared in front of us with the question, "How many apples are in one seed?"

I snorted. "However many Joseph says, right?"

Bunny, didn't even glance up. "That would be the Josephite answer. We're the Christian Underground."

She put her fingers on the image of the keyboard and typed, *Only God knows.*

A green dot appeared underneath her words on the keyboard, and the display disappeared. I held my breath, waiting for Bunny to open the safe, but she didn't. Instead she held up her watch and turned on a timer, setting it to zero.

"Well?" I was impatient to clean out the seeds and get back to the tunnel.

"Well, what?" She looked up at me in wide-eyed innocence. "Well, what now?"

"Oh. Now we wait fifteen minutes." She said it like it was the most obvious thing in the world.

"Fifteen minutes? We have to hang out here fifteen minutes? You never mentioned that."

"I'm sorry. It didn't occur to me that you wouldn't know."

How in the hell would I know that? I bit my tongue. "So what happens after fifteen minutes?" My voice must have reflected my irritation because she took a step backward.

"Archer, I'm sorry. I thought you knew how these worked. After fifteen minutes, I have a three-minute window to place my finger on a laser scanner that will appear on the corner here. Then the door will open." "Three minutes? What happens if we miss that window? We have to wait another fifteen? Should I have brought my sleeping bag?"

Bunny's face grew very still. "No. If we miss that three minute window, we will never be able to open the safe."

I blinked. "Why not?"

"Because only my mother and I had key pendants." She held up her pendant. "Each key is single use until reset, and we have no way to reset it now that the lab is gone."

I consciously slowed my racing heart. This was not part of the plan. I looked at her watch. Twelve more minutes. Okay. Make the best of it.

The chair had been pulled out from the desk, so I sat down to rest my sore knee. Shiny wrappers covered the floor along with a few stray pieces of old popcorn. It was all I could do to not to clean the place.

Instead I opened the long, center desk drawer. Inside, I found the source of the shiny wrappers. A large paper pack with little foil sticks in it and the words "Joseph Chew" on the outside. It was gum.

"What are you doing?" Bunny asked. I pulled out a stick and put it in my mouth, replacing the pack in the drawer. It was too much for me to throw the wrapper on the floor with the others, so I took out my tin can and stuck it inside with the other bits of trash.

"I've always heard of this stuff," I said. "I only wanted to try it. This guy's a pig. He'll never know."

"Archer, you can't—"

A light came through the window. We dove under the desk, the beam barely tipping my foot. I could only hope that it was not conspicuous among the trash. Then the light passed on. I let out my breath.

Bunny quaked, her hand on the pistol I'd given her. "I can't do it. I can't kill anyone. If he comes in here, I can't kill him."

"Shhh. It's okay. I can."

I looked at her watch. Eight more minutes.

Another sixty seconds, and she began to breathe again. "Thank God, he didn't see us," she said.

Footsteps at the door caught our attention, and we both turned and froze. Then the doorknob turned, and the deadbolt rattled.

CHAPTER 49

I GRABBED BUNNY'S ARM and pulled her over the piles of folders to the window. With a cursory glance to make sure all was clear, I opened it and dropped her out. Jumping out behind her, I jammed the gum from my mouth across the latch and lowered the window until it was just shy of closed.

Bunny quivered, her eyes wide with fear. "We should run," she hissed. I put my hand on her arm to still her. Peeking into the room, I saw one man in the dim light. He glanced out the door before he carefully pulled it shut, and he did not turn on the light.

Crouching back down in the shadows under the window, I looked at Bunny's watch. Five more minutes.

Bunny started. A movement caught my eye. It was Freefall and Zander. They'd been in the greenhouse when the man came in and were now making their escape.

Freefall signaled to me, asking if we were okay. Bunny shook her head, "No," but I gave him a thumbs up. There was no way I was giving up. I'd kill the guy if I had to.

Three minutes. I peeked over the sill again to see the man sitting at the desk and searching through the drawers—the same thing I had done. Then, just like me, he pulled out a piece of gum and replaced the pack. I flinched when he tossed the wrapper on the floor.

Two minutes. I thought about ways to kill the man, who at that point had his feet up on the desk. He was very large. There was no way I could break his neck without getting the jump on him. I could stab him, but that would be a lot of blood. A shot would be bloody, too, and it would be loud.

Desperation crept into my mind. We had to get those seeds.

Then the man turned toward the window, and I got a clear view of his face. It was Luke. I gasped and dropped down, accidentally bumping the wall. Bunny jumped to run, and I grabbed her, holding my finger to my lips. I took out my knife.

What to do? How could I kill the man who had saved me? Would he save me again? But we had to have those seeds. Ninety seconds.

The window jerked open above me, and Luke leaned out. I had a clear shot at his throat, and I could have easily sliced it open. But I couldn't. Not Luke. He wasn't like the rest.

Before he could glance down, a voice called out from the front of the greenhouses. "Luke. Dude, where'd you go?"

The window slammed, and a hasty shuffle told me Luke was leaving the office. I jumped up, and the second he closed the door, I lifted the window, the gum having kept it from closing completely. I pushed Bunny through ahead of me and crawled in, promising myself I'd find a way to make gum a regular part of my life. We had the window closed before Luke exited the back door of the greenhouse and walked past.

A red glow appeared at the top of the safe. The biometric scanner.

My heart raced. Bunny gave me a nod and placed her finger on the rectangle. I heard a click, and the safe swung open.

I'm not sure what I expected. Perhaps a glowing light and the heavens breaking open with a chorus of angels. It was hard to believe that those small brown packages, all neatly labeled in rows, held the key to our freedom. I paused only the briefest moment before I joined Bunny in emptying the safe into our packs.

Soon we had every last seed, and the safe was sealed shut again, to be opened no more. We locked the office door behind us and slipped out the back of the greenhouse and into the shed.

Triumph shone on Bunny's face. I lifted the tile and helped her into the hole. "I knew we could do it." Her whisper rang with excitement, and I could tell that in another life, under different circumstances, she might have been a hunter like me.

I smiled and took a wad of plastic bags from my pack before dropping it down to Bunny. "You go on," I said. I've got one more thing to do before I join you."

"What are you talking about?" Her glow of victory turned to fear.

"That's a clinic on the other side of the shed. I'm going to get medicine to save Quinn. Now go." I closed the tile over her protests and slipped into the shadows.

I used my knife to pry open the clinic window, and I jumped inside, closing it behind me. I was in an exam room. Several cabinets and a sink lined the walls, and a padded table with what looked like stirrups sticking out of one end filled the center. I searched the room as quickly as I could, hoping it would be that easy to find Amephilexin. That was the antibiotic Granny said Quinn needed. I had pried that information from her without her knowing why. I discovered several first aid medicines and some odd metal tools but no antibiotics. I would have to find the storeroom.

In case there were eyes, I cracked open the exam room door barely enough to fit the tiny mirror on my pocket knife through the opening. The dim light illuminating the hallway showed that it was empty and that there were no eyes.

I peeked out and, using my penlight, saw a large number *four* beside the doorway I stood in. To my left, I located one, two, and three with my beam. I guessed those numbers marked other exam rooms, and that the storeroom had to be to my right.

Adrenaline racing, I tiptoed up the hall until the left side ended to form a *T* shape at a reception area while the right wall continued on. There was only one more door. It was behind the reception desk in the center of the *T*, and, sure enough, it was marked "Storage."

My back to the wall across from it, I edged my mirror out, only to jerk it back. There was an eye above the front door of the clinic, and it was pointing my way.

So close. What was I going to do? I could rush up under it and put duct tape over the lens, but someone was sure to notice. I could shoot it out, but, again, that would be a dead giveaway that someone was in the clinic. I needed another look at it.

I counted to ten and edged my mirror out again. I was in luck. The Josephites were too cheap to get proper security. The eye was rotating back and forth across the front waiting room like the old one that used to be behind Maverick's bar.

I counted and waited, checking every ten beats until I was sure of the cycle's pace. Then, when it was turned away, I checked the door. Locked. I whipped out my lockpicker, snapped it on the keypad, and jumped back behind the wall.

Standing there, I closed my eyes and took a deep breath, counting the cycle. A tiny light on the device showed me that the door was unlocked. I could only hope the five more beats it took for the eye to pass would not be enough for anyone to spot it.

When I'd counted to ten, I slipped my mirror out to confirm and then jumped to the door. Once inside, I had a similar reaction to the one I'd had in the greenhouse. So many drugs. Powders, pills, and liquids for everything from asthma to typhoid crowded shelves from floor to ceiling. Standing there in awe, I knew I was looking at a once in a lifetime opportunity.

I realized my mouth was hanging open and snapped it shut. *Quinn first.* It didn't take me long to find the antibiotics next to the first aid supplies. They were alphabetized in small hemp-paper boxes with the count "5000" marked on the side, along with the name of the drug and the dosage. Amephilexin was one of the first. I loaded a whole sack with the boxes, careful to take them from the back so they wouldn't be missed right away. Then I filled two more sacks with Stem Skin cans, morphine tablets, and Zithromillin, the only other antibiotic whose name I recognized.

I had three more sacks with me, but I knew I would be unwieldy if I filled any more, and the last thing I wanted was to be the raccoon caught with its hand in the jar, unwilling to let go of its prize to save its life. Then I spotted Fluditam—the antiviral that would save us from the winter lung fevers. Suddenly I knew how that raccoon felt. But I was no raccoon.

Using my mirror, I scuttled back to room four, out the window, and into the shed. I lifted the tile and saw Thomas's face at the top of the rope ladder. Startled, I jumped back. He had ignored my order to leave, so I decided to put him to good use and get angry later.

"Take these," I said, shoving the bags at him and almost knocking him off the rope. "Get out. I'll get one more load and join you."

"You're taking too long." Good sense mixed with the worry in his whisper.

"They've got Fluditam. Now go." As with Bunny, I lowered the tile on his protests.

I was quicker getting into the storage room the second time and had my last three bags filled to bursting with the Fluditam in nothing flat. My hands full, I made my way between the shelves to the door, awkwardly pulling out my mirror to check the cycle of the eye.

Triumph coursed through my veins. We had it all. We had fertile seeds, enough medicine to protect us for years, and Quinn would live. We had everything we needed to begin building our freedom.

I opened the door the barest crack for my mirror. A kick slammed it into me, knocking me back against the shelves.

Crying out, I threw my hands in front of my face. The Josephite crashed the butt of his rifle down on my head, and my world went black.

CHAPTER 50

T HE JOE GUARD THREW me to the floor, and the rug scorched my cheek, bringing me from my stupor but not my confusion.

"We caught the thief, Commander." I recognized the harsh tones of the fellow who had wanted to fight Quinn back when we were heading to the Big Box with Bunny.

Slowly, I opened my eyes and found myself in a dark office. A lamp with a single bulb lit the desk, and I could not see the man behind it. With a quick glance, I realized I was the only Sec in the room. Did they know about the others? I lay inert on the floor, waiting to see what would happen next.

"Pull him up." The deep voice filled the air around me. "I want a good look at him."

Large hands gently lifted me and helped me stand. I turned my head up to see Luke, who turned his face away.

The commander shined his desk lamp on me. I blinked. My head throbbed, and the darkness threatened to close in again. "So you're the one who has been stealing our medical supplies? Answer me."

Medical supplies? Did the others get away? They could map my brain. Should I kill myself now? How? My mind went to the knife on my leg, but I could feel by flinching my muscles the Joes had found it and stripped me of it. *Buy time.*

"Answer me, Sec." My ears rang with the power of his command. The mean guard to my right jabbed me in the kidney

"Yes. Yes, it was me."

"Hmmm. An honest thief." The commander sounded surprised. "Are there any more of you?"

"No. I'm alone." I didn't have to try to sound frightened.

The shadowy figure behind the lamp pointed a finger toward Luke, who nodded his confirmation of what I had said.

The mean guard studied my face. "Wait, sir. I recognize this one. He came through here causing trouble with some others back in the spring.

"No. No. This time I'm alone."

"How did you get in?" the commander asked.

Think fast, Deena. I noticed a window at the side of the office was cracked open to let in the air, and I remembered the night that Quinn and I blew up the transformer station. "The dormitory basement window. You'll find it open. That's how I got in."

Dear God, whatever you are, make them believe me.

Luke stepped forward and placed my lockpicker on the desk. "We found this on his belt."

"Good. Now go and check the dormitory window," ordered the commander.

In the ensuing silence, I thought through the night Quinn and I broke into the compound, once again picturing our movements. In the window, and . . . oh, crap! Quinn had locked the window before we left the room. I felt sweat break out on my forehead and hands. Did Luke remember me? Would he cover for me yet again?

My stomach churned, and my head swam. I wanted to melt into the floor. The mean one jabbed me with his gun and brought me to myself when Luke entered the room.

"Yes, sir. The storeroom window was open, just like he said.

I locked it up." Luke was careful not to look at me, so I kept my eyes forward as well.

"Hmmmm. And no clothing or supplies were taken?"

"No, sir. Nothing disturbed."

"I only came for the medicine. I don't want to be a thief. It's just that my brother is dying, and he needs this," I said. I'm wasn't sure why I dared appeal to his mercy.

The commander studied me. "Most peculiar. An honest Sec thief. There might be hope for you."

He turned the bulb away from my eyes and continued in a softened voice, as if speaking to a child. "God does not want you to have medicines, Sec. I'm sorry your brother will be going to Hell, but it is God's will that those who refuse Him and live outside of His Kingdom shall be punished with disease. However, I am a compassionate man. You don't seem a bad sort. Though stealing is a grave sin, I will not send you to the Ministry of Discipline. Instead I will send you to the Ministry of Reform where you may learn the ways of God and become one of His people. Take him." The commander sat down in his chair and picked up a file, indicating we were dismissed.

My blood ran cold. I had no idea what the Ministry of Reform was, and I had no desire to find out. Luke and the mean one dragged me toward the door. Giving in to panic, I screamed and fought.

"Wait." The commander's voice boomed. Hope sparked in me. The guards stopped and turned me around. Perhaps the commander had changed his mind?

Stepping from behind his desk, the commander turned up his lamp so that the entire room was illuminated, revealing him as a short, thin, balding man with round spectacles wearing a thin, hemp robe and slippers. "Bring him here." His voice had taken on a perilous edge, and I could not discern why.

My knees were weak, and Luke practically carried me back to the desk. Then the commander reached out his hand and ran his fingers underneath the collar of my turtleneck. Heartsick, I knew. The dragontech. He had seen it during my struggles. With one smooth swipe and a power I would not have suspected, he ripped through my shirt to reveal the armor I wore underneath.

"How did you get this?" All compassion was gone.

"It was a gift," I said, not knowing what else to say.

"Lies." He slapped me hard across the mouth. My vision blurred, and I tasted blood. "One last time, how did you get this?"

Think. "I was at North Meadow two days ago. I took it off a dead soldier that someone had shot in the eye." *Believe me. Please, believe me.*

The commander stared at me, searching my eyes for any signs of deception. "Take it off. Such gifts from God must never be defiled by his enemies."

"No." I panicked. If I took it off, they would discover I was a woman.

I thought I heard Luke whisper, "I'm sorry." I struggled futilely against his grip while the other guard unfastened the armor. Tearing it from my body, he took part of my breast binding with it.

"Whoa," said the mean one. "He's a she."

Luke said nothing, but his eyes filled with concern.

The commander looked me up and down with curiosity. "It's a sideways," he said.

"No, I'm not sideways. I like men. I have a boyfriend. I'm a hunter. Men's clothes are better for the forest. Please. He's dying. Let me go."

"A woman hunter in men's clothing? What could possibly be more sideways?" said the commander.

"We could convert her," suggested the mean one, leering at my bare breasts.

Luke glared at him, and the commander eyed the little man with disdain. "Are we Secs to behave like animals? No. Take her to the Program, and may God save her soul."

CHAPTER 51

T HE COLD WATER SHOCKED my naked body, and I cried out. Screeching burst from the embedded speakers—horrible rattles, squealing guitars, and repetitive accordions that shredded my sanity. Lights flashed, pulsing arhythmically, forcing themselves past my eyelids. Burying my face in my arms, I futilely fought to block out the raging forces permeating me with discord.

Wet and shivering, I curled in the corner of the tiny cement cell, so small I could not stretch out in any direction. The room was empty except for a water drip I could lick from, a food pellet dispenser on the wall, and a refuse bucket.

Time blurred. I only knew I was cold and so tired I could not think. Tightening my arms closer over my head, trying desperately to shut out the cacophony, my mind searched for other, calmer voices, but what I found in my head were only Josephite voices.

It had all started as darkness. I never knew what black was before—an absence of light so profound I couldn't tell if I was asleep or awake. And the silence. My head became so very loud. I didn't know how long it had lasted. Minutes? Hours? Days? Then came the penetrating blast of cold water from the ceiling and the blaring cacophony from the speakers. Then, just when I thought it would succeed in breaking my mind, it all stopped, and I was once again plunged into blackness and silence. Outer space. Only the voices in my head and the cold, wet cement floor under my naked body.

I put my hands to my eyes to make sure they were closed, and I saw once more the vision of Harmony, drooling while she pushed a mop toward me, the scar fresh across her forehead. Harmony in the Program. Her blank stare bore no recognition when Luke and the mean one dragged me past her down the hallway. Had they mapped her brain? Did they know Bunny was with us? Was Norris at Middle with the Godfire right now? Flames filled my sight, and the stench of burning flesh once more assaulted my nostrils. For a moment, I didn't know if it was real or imagined.

Desperate, I searched my brain for any tool to retain my sanity. I remembered a book of Granny's about a POW in a war long ago. A place called Vietnam. *What did he do? Math. He did math. I'll do math. One times zero is zero. One times one is one. How can that be? Just do it. One times two is two . . .*

Then, when I thought I might be okay in the crushing silence, the voice started—the voice barely loud enough to penetrate my skull. "You are an abomination. You defile yourself with women. A fiery hell awaits you where your flesh will melt, your eyes will be plucked by ravens, and you will burn in the Godfire for all eternity . . ."

Three times three is nine. Three times four is twelve. Three times five is thirteen. No. Not thirteen. Fifteen. Focus. Three times five is fifteen. Three times six . . .

Finally I fell into inner oblivion, only to be wakened by cold water on my naked body, the shattering noise, and the glaring lights—the cycle repeating once more.

Six times seven is forty-two. Six times eight is forty-eight. Six times nine . . .

Then came the exam room. "We'll need to break her down

to map her out for surgery. Let's see where she's at," said the man in the white coat. Panicked, I struggled against him while he strapped me to a table and attached electrodes to my head.

The doughy nurse's sweet smile chilled my blood with a colder fear than I had ever known. "This is for your own good, dear. Don't be afraid. We're doing God's work here."

Nurses in white forced my eyelids apart and inserted plastic brackets to hold them open. Pictures flashed. Anything and everything—Josephite children, food, violent sex acts—over and over while they tried to plot the most intimate anatomy of my thoughts. How long would it be before they stumbled across my real secrets and destroyed my people?

"Hmmm. This one's quite resistant to mapping. Let's try a bit of therapy," said the man.

"No. No." My voice sounded weak to my own ears. I struggled against the bonds.

The smiling nurse rolled over a new machine. Humming cheerily to herself, she peeled papers from adhesive dots on wires and stuck them to my temples and down my body. "Don't be alarmed, dear. We will be doing Association Therapy. It's a bit uncomfortable, but it's most effective. I'm sure you'll be pleased with the results."

Again the brackets that held open my eyes. The table tipped up, and a holoscreen lowered in front of me. Two naked women appeared and began kissing and touching each other. Then I heard screaming. My own. Pain devoured me, and time stopped. A fourth dimension. A pain so intense I could not even beg to die.

Over and over, the cycle went on. The consuming darkness, the cacophony of noise and light, the whispered voice condemning me to Hell, and the Association Therapy. My mind reached further and further to escape, and at times, the only thing I knew for sure was that I was quickly going mad.

Demon dreams attacked me. My father came in and held me close. "Quiet, Deena. Daddy's here. It's going to be all right now." Ecstatic to be in his arms once more, I looked up to see his face, only to find Norris leering at me. I screamed.

Then Granny was beside me. "No, child. It's over now."

"You're with me." I cried, and my tears burned my eyes.

Smiling, she turned and reached for a cup from mid-air behind her and said, "Won't you have some tea with me?" And then I saw it—the charred flesh peeling from the back of her head, exposing her skull. Panicked, I tried to back away, but there was nowhere to go. The cold, wet corner of the cement squeezed against me, and I couldn't breathe.

Then Granny was gone, and Bunny was in her place. "Come, Deena. The Atoned fly to Heaven in the arms of Jesus." The flames shot up between us, and I screamed, waking myself to another day in hell.

"Not yet," said the man in white. Every day he said it. "This one's stubborn. We can't operate until we have an accurate map, and we can't map while she's still fighting. Maybe tomorrow. Let's try a bit more Association Therapy."

Shivering in the corner, wet to the bone, I opened my eyes, only to snap them shut at the sight of the blinding white walls. I would say the noise lasted longer that time, but I really didn't know. I only knew they were winning, and I couldn't fight any more. How long before they discovered Bunny? How long before they found out about the seeds? Had I told them already?

That was it. I had to die. But how? I had fingernails. I could do it with my fingernails, and then they would never find out. I desperately raked my nails across my wrists and cried out in despair. The Joes had cut them to the quick. But I still had teeth. I put my right wrist to my mouth and bit as hard as I could, tearing the flesh, not even feeling the pain.

Suddenly the music and flashing stopped, and the lights were dimmed by half. I froze, my wrist in my teeth, wary for what they might do next. The door opened. The guard threw something at me, and I screamed. Some part of me saw it was clothing, but once I'd started screaming, I couldn't stop. It wasn't even coming from me anymore, and I didn't know how to make it stop.

"Damn, girl." He grabbed me by the hair, pulled my head back, and slapped my face. "Get dressed. Somebody saved your sorry pagan ass." He left, and I sobbed uncontrollably, hysterical both with joy and with the fear that he was lying—that it was just another trick to break me.

Slowly, I calmed myself and looked at what he had thrown at me. It was a Josephite dress. An ugly, shapeless, brown dress like the camp women wore. Unsteady, I sat on the floor and pulled it over my head. Then I curled up again as tight as I could, and I waited, the memory of cacophony still pounding in my head, and the lights still blinding behind my closed eyes. *Thirteen times two is twenty-six. Thirteen times three is thirty-nine . . .*

In time, the door opened. "Get up." A different guard prodded me with his rifle. Seeing I couldn't stand, he half dragged me through the door of the tiny cell and pulled me to my feet, handcuffing my hands behind my back.

Another guard joined us, along with a man in a dark gray suit, and they pulled me down the sterile maze of hallways. I searched for Harmony and her mop while we took one turn after another, every hallway the same. I was completely lost. *Will I get a piece of cheese at the end?* I giggled. *Stop it. Fifteen times four is sixty. Fifteen times five is seventy-five. Fifteen times six . . .*

A door. They were taking me toward a door. My heart pounded in my ears. Would they really let me out?

The guard opened it, and I blinked my sore, dry eyes in the blinding sun. A hot day. A large armored van was backed up to the opening, waiting. Perhaps it was real. Perhaps I really had been saved.

Then a man stepped from the passenger side, and terror gripped me. It was Norris.

CHAPTER 52

I SEARCHED DESPERATELY FOR somewhere to run, but there was nowhere. The Program behind me, and Norris in front of me. Perhaps he would kill me in a rage, and then at least my people would be safe. I closed my eyes. *Fifteen times ten . . . Fifteen times ten . . .*

Norris studied me curiously, and recognition dawned in his eyes. "You." In spite of his limp, he charged forward, his crop raised in his bandaged hand.

To my surprise, the man in the suit beside me stepped forward and stopped him. "Undamaged. That's the deal."

Furious, Norris smacked the crop down on the side of his boot, spun on his heel, and climbed into the front of the van.

I didn't know what was happening, but I felt some relief that Norris was not in charge.

The two guards lifted me and climbed into the back, dropping me on the floor between them. What did the man in the suit mean? Was he taking me somewhere else to toy with me, or could it be I had somehow been saved?

The man in the suit closed the doors, and the locks clicked. Soon the vehicle jerked away from the building. There were no windows in the sides, but ventilation screens in the roof let in light and air. Noises and smells filtered through. They would have ordinarily been frightening, but in my state, they washed over me. Hammering and voices and odors. Some of them made me cringe, and some of them made my mouth water. None of them were familiar.

Then came a more ominous sound—a dull roar of voices that grew louder as we approached. We drove slower and slower. A clear call came through. "Atone the whore!"

A woman screamed, and a man cried out, "No. She's pure. She's pure."

The first voice again. "She stole our food. Atone her!" More voices joined in, and soon a mob roared around us. The armored van crawled more slowly, and no amount of honking seemed to help.

Then came a scream I knew, followed by that terrible smell. I bent over with the dry heaves.

A sharp crack on the outside of the van caught my attention. Then there was another and another. Rocks hitting the vehicle.

A voice came over a speaker in the corner of the compartment. "Brace yourselves. We're going through."

The vehicle took a sudden turn right and sped up. A bump jostled me across the van. More bumps. Men and women squealed and shouted out all around us. Soon though, the road smoothed out once more, and the crowd and the smell were left behind.

It seemed like we traveled forever. Gradually, I could tell by the silence and the dust in the air that we were out of the city. Were they really going to set me free? Why would they do that? Was it a terrible trick? *It must be.*

Perhaps they were taking me to a work camp. I could escape from a work camp. But I'd never heard of them taking a Sec to a work camp. No. It had to be a trick. Norris was playing a cruel trick on me. I fought to keep my panic at bay.

Sixteen times two is thirty-two. Sixteen time three . . .

I was at multiples of twenty-six when the van lurched to

a stop and the engine shut off. The locks clicked, and the doors opened. The man in the dark gray suit stood waiting, Norris behind him. The guards pulled me to my feet. Keeping me between them, they helped me down and removed my handcuffs.

Squinting my dry, ravaged eyes, I saw we were on a dirt road off the main track between Maverick's and Promise City. My legs barely functioning, the Joes walked me around to the front of the van.

Gazing up the road, I had to stop myself from crying out with joy. It was Quinn. He was alive. His arm in a sling, he waited like a statue with Spooge by Maverick's dually truck about a hundred feet up the road. Zander, Freefall, and Thomas stood in the back, their hands open, showing they were unarmed. The seeds were safe. They were safe. Quinn was alive, and I was going free with my secrets intact. But at what price? How could Quinn have managed this?

And then I knew. Quinn stepped aside, and Bunny walked forward.

CHAPTER 53

S HE LOOKED AS SMALL and as scared as her namesake in her clean Sec dress and boots. Her hair, grown longer again during the summer, was down on her shoulders like a Josephite girl's. She moved her hand in a familiar gesture toward her seed pendant, but it seemed she couldn't find it. Instead she clasped her hands together and bowed her head in prayer.

Norris snapped his crop, and he and the man in the gray suit advanced, the guards shepherding me three paces behind.

Quinn bent to speak into Bunny's ear. After the briefest hesitation, she nodded and lifted her head, and they strode forward with Spooge. We met them halfway, about ten feet apart.

Tears stung my sore eyes. Bunny, quivering, glanced up at me and then bowed her head. It was all I could do not to retch. There had to be another way.

The man in the suit stepped forward, as did Spooge. Spooge passed the man something I could not see, and the man closed his hand on it. "Wait," he said, and walked back to the van.

Norris snapped his crop and smiled. "Tamar, you naughty little girl. I can't wait to see you Atone for what you have wrought."

Bunny shuddered, but she continued her prayers and did not acknowledge him.

Quinn, still weak from his ordeal, gazed at me, concern etched across his features, but he held his silence. Spooge, on the other hand, glared at me briefly and looked away, love and anger fighting for dominance on his expression. I hated it that he found out I was a girl this way, but I couldn't think about him right then. I was focused on Bunny. I wondered if the meadow had forced her to trade herself for me or if she had given herself up of her own accord.

While she prayed, her body stilled, and she seemed to take on a glow from within. Then she opened her eyes. Her gaze shifted from my bare feet to my legs, bruised deeply from fighting the bindings on the exam table, and then to my face. She paled, her fear palpable. Then in a clear, strong voice, she said, "I am truly sorry for the pain I have caused you and your people."

"Do not speak." Norris snapped his crop.

I jumped in fear, but Bunny sniffed with disdain. "Until I am dead, I am the granddaughter of Joseph. You will not speak me thus again."

Norris folded his arms across his chest in frustration. "It will be a pleasure to purge your demons," he said. Then I understood. He couldn't touch her any more than he could touch me. Whatever our fate, it was beyond his control.

I looked back to her and hoped she could see the love in my heart. "There's no reason to be sorry."

She studied me a moment and gave me a nod of understanding. Then her eyes shifted from my face to what was happening behind me, and she gasped. I glanced over my shoulder, and the sight of the suit returning with an orange-robed priest slapped me into awareness. They were going to burn her. I couldn't let that happen. I didn't know how I would do it, but I determined in that second that I would find a way to save her.

"Bunny, look at me," I said. "Remember my pinkie swear."

She appeared to be confused for a moment, and then her eyes opened wide with amazement. "You can't. I didn't do this to have you keep any promises."

"And I didn't make any promises to break them. I love you, sister."

"And I love you, Deena. My dear sister." She gave me a brave smile. "You would be a good Christian."

I did my best to return her smile. "Maybe so."

Then her voice grew firm. "But no promises. I forbid it."

I reached out to hug her, but the guard pulled me back. The man in the gray suit was there. Before I knew it, they pushed me toward Quinn, and Bunny was gone.

Supporting me with his good arm, Quinn rushed me toward the truck and jumped in the cab with me in his lap. Then Spooge sped up the road, leaving Promise City and the Program behind us.

CHAPTER 54

S AFE IN QUINN'S ARMS, I sobbed into his chest. What had Bunny done? How could I save her? The pain in my soul racked my body with spasms, and I cried out.

"Deep breaths, baby. You're hyperventilating." Quinn stroked my hair and kissed me on the head.

Quinn. He was alive. We had the seeds, and Quinn was alive. I was going home to Granny. Granny would know what to do. She always had a plan. Get to Granny.

Slowly I quieted, but a whirlwind of questions pummeled my befuddled brain. Why had Bunny traded herself? How did Quinn make it happen? Why wasn't he afraid for our Meadow? My thoughts flew like wood chips in a tempest, keeping me from catching them and organizing them into cogent questions. So I pushed out the only two words that would come. "What happened?"

Quinn stroked my hair, and his voice, low and comforting, was a sharp contrast to the disturbance his words created in my soul. "Bunny offered herself in your place. Spooge and I arranged the transfer through Maverick."

I lifted my head from Quinn's shoulder so I could see Spooge. His lips pursed, he stared at the road ahead. I could only imagine what he must have been feeling toward me in that moment. His only friend. The only person he trusted. The "man" he loved and who betrayed that trust so deeply.

I said the only thing I could say. "I'm sorry, Spooge. Thank you."

"I did it for the money." His tone could have cut granite.

I cringed inside, and my heart cried out at the wrongness of it all. But I knew there was nothing else to be said. Nothing I could do to make things right. He would come to understand and forgive me, or he wouldn't.

I lay my head back on Quinn's shoulder. "But the Joes will know we've been hiding her. They'll come kill everyone."

"Shhh." Quinn stroked my hair and rocked me like I had done for Ruth.

Spooge burst out, "I can see why you think we're that stupid, after the way you fooled me all those years."

"That's enough, Spooge," Quinn said, his voice as calm and low as if he was trying to tame a wild bear. Spooge tossed a glare our way and shrugged.

Quinn continued. "Spooge took care of that. He had the Minister of Justice on an eye, beating some high class Joe girl to death a few months back. That's what he gave to the suit. That was the price to save the Meadow."

"Maverick let you do that for me?" I knew blackmailing one of his powerful customers was going to be bad for his business.

"Now who's stupid?" Spooge asked, his voice dripping with contempt.

I felt Quinn's body tense. "I'm not going to tell you again. This isn't the time."

Spooge snorted, but said no more.

Quinn stroked my hair again. "You know Maverick. He can be bought."

I kissed his forehead and was relieved to find it cool. "How's your shoulder?"

"Better, thanks to you."

"How did you know I was in the Program? How did you find me?"

"The kid told us. Thomas. When you didn't come back, he crawled out the window. He saw you being taken to the commander's office and listened outside."

Thomas. It figured he'd disobey. But how could I be angry with him after he risked his own life for me?

"How long has it been?" I asked, not knowing what day it was.

"Four days," he said.

Four days. How could it have only been four days? Exhaustion washed over me. Still shaking inside, I didn't want to talk any more.

But it was harder to turn off my brain. How could I possibly find Bunny and save her in time? Granny would know. I felt like I was holding my breath until I could get to Granny and have her sort things out for me.

I felt the angle when the road began climbing into the foothills, but I was too tired to open my eyes. It seemed that Spooge was going to take us all the way up in spite of his anger. Snuggling in tighter, I released myself into Quinn's strength, and my soul embraced the comfort he offered.

CHAPTER 55

THE TRUCK DOOR STARTLED me, and someone lifted me from Quinn's lap. Terrified, I cried out and swung blindly, but strong arms pinned me to stillness. "Shhh, child. It's me. It's Granny."

I opened my eyes to find Zander holding me, Quinn and Granny at my side, and the whole meadow gathered around, staring silently.

Granny placed her calming hand on my shoulder and then leaned her head toward the pickup cab next to her and spoke in a voice everyone could hear. "Thank you, Spooge. You are as good a man as Deena always said, and you shall forever be counted a friend in our meadow, and family in my heart."

Spooge tossed her a blank look and then revved the truck, threw it into reverse, and roared out of the meadow without a backward glance.

Makenzie stepped forward hesitantly, her brow wrinkled in concern. "Are you okay?"

Her simple question opened the floodgate, and the others rushed toward me.

"What did they do to you?" Arys gasped, noticing my torn wrist and the bruises on my arms and legs.

"Have you eaten?" asked Charlotte. She held a loaf of bread in her hands.

"We'll kill the bastards." That from Thomas, of course, the fire burning in his eyes.

Dave, who had returned with Bunny, offered me his flask. I refused, and he drank from it himself and passed it to Freefall.

Freefall said, "I saved your apple for you."

Arys took my hand. "Please. Did you see my mother? Any sign of her?"

The hope in his eyes shredded my heart. I thought of the drooling, mindless shell mopping the floors at the Program. I briefly considered saying no, but I didn't want to lie to one of my own. So I told him the truth as I knew it. "Your mother is dead. I saw her body. I'm sorry."

Pain radiated from Arys' eyes. He nodded and hung his head. Charlotte put a hand on his arm, and they turned away.

The group parted to let them through, and I saw faces I thought I'd never see again. I wondered if I was hallucinating. "Kim? Shane? Lee?"

Quinn leaned in. "They were away visiting in Iredale when the Josephites came to North. They're all here with their families."

I closed my eyes and let the tears flow, and I found it felt very good to have my eyes closed. Somehow, it wasn't worth the effort to open them again.

Granny's firm voice seemed to be coming down a tunnel. "Deena needs rest. When she wakes, you may all come visit her one or two at a time."

My next awareness was the sound of the hay bailer out in the field. Then I felt coldness around my legs, and that cold felt good. I opened my eyes and found myself in my own bed with snow packed around my limbs. *Is this real?*

Little arms encircled my neck and a sweet, and a tiny voice cried out, "Archer. I thought you died like Mommy."

What?

Then it all came flooding in. "Ruth," I said. "Hi, sweetie. How are you?"

Quinn stirred beside me where he lay on the floor. His kiss was on my forehead, my cheek, and my lips. "Welcome back, baby."

Granny came in. Her joyful smile lit the room. "Let's get these cold packs off of you."

"How did you get snow?" I asked.

"There's caps on the mountaintops. Came a few days ago, so I sent Tinker's boys for some. I knew you'd at least be sore."

"Granny, is there anything you don't know?" She smiled sadly and shook her head. "Oh, child. I know less every day."

Quinn took the snow to the kiln shed tunnel, and Granny brought me some broth. She insisted on feeding me while Ruth settled in on the end of the bed.

"Where's Bunny?" asked Ruth.

It all flooded back. "What day is this? I have to save Bunny."

Granny's face turned grim, and her spoon paused midair before she put it back into the broth. "It's Wednesday, and you can't save Bunny. I'm sorry, Deena. You have to let it go."

I felt as if she had slapped me. I reached for Daisy and then remembered that too.

Throwing off my covers, I swung my legs out of bed and flinched with the pain. I couldn't recall ever being so stiff. "Atonement is Sunday. I still have time."

"Don't be silly. Now hold still. Let me rub some liniment on your bruises."

"Look. I promised her I wouldn't let her die in the flames. I have to save her."

Quinn came in. "She knew what she was doing. Sweetie, you have to calm down."

"Calm down? And what about that holowafer of hers? Did she leave it? If I can get in there and save her, maybe Dave can help us broadcast it. Then no one will want to kill her anymore. It might even help her Underground take over. I heard those mobs in the city. They're ready to blow."

Granny put her hands on her hips. "Yes, she left it, and no, you're not going anywhere. That's final." She turned away as if the discussion were closed.

I stood to follow her and almost fell over. Quinn caught my arm, but I shook him off. "Why won't you help me? If it was me, would you let them burn me?"

Granny spun on her heel to face me. "I will not bury my last child!"

I froze, caught by the tears streaming down her cheeks. So absorbed in what I wanted, what I promised, what I was going to do, I hadn't thought about what this meant for her. She loved Bunny too. And she loved me. Bunny needed me, but Granny needed me too.

I took her in my arms. "I'm sorry." She was right to be afraid.

Quinn took my hand and caressed it. "I'll talk to Dave. He said the power should have been up two days ago. Maybe we can somehow broadcast the holowafer and show the Josephites that Joseph is no prophet after all. But please go back to bed and rest."

The love in his eyes warmed my soul. "Yes. Talk to Dave. Maybe he can be some use. But I've been in this bed too long. I need out."

"Okay. We can do that."

Granny and Ruth left, and Quinn helped me into my skirt and blouse. Then we took a short walk around the meadow. Ruth, unwilling to leave me, stayed with us every step of the way. I was stiff, and it was difficult at first, but I found that the one silver lining of my captivity was that it gave my knee a chance to rest and heal a bit.

Once I got started, my muscles loosened up, and I enjoyed the sheer feel of the motion and the presence of home. I couldn't get enough. The warm hugs from my people. The sight of sky and trees. The feel of the air on my skin. In spite of everything weighing on my mind, it had never felt so good to be alive.

It also gave me time to think. If we could somehow broadcast that recording before Atonement, the Josephites would see that Bunny was innocent. That Joseph was the one who had some atoning to do.

That night at dinner, Dave bounced through the door, excitement glowing on his face. "I know how we could do it."

Ruth, sitting on my lap, waved to him. "Hi, Dave."

Dave waved back and gave her a smile. Granny sniffed the air around him. Then she patted him down, took the flask from his pocket, and gave him the Eyebrow. "Quinn makes this by boiling down plastic bags from the dump in acid and then distilling it. Did you know that? This is what he sells to the Joes. The stuff we use for medicine and our celebrations is the only shine we have that comes from the gassplant."

"Oh," said Dave. He cleared his throat and glanced back and forth between us in embarrassment.

Quinn and I exchanged a look of amusement, but Granny wasn't finished. "Not bad enough that you took it without asking Quinn first, you actually drank it. There'll be no more of this if you're going to live among us. Even our drunks produce something, or they starve. Do you understand?"

Dave reddened and looked a bit sheepish. "Uh, sorry. I'll keep that in mind."

"Now step back outside and wipe off your shoes. Then get in here and start earning your keep."

"Yes, ma'am," he said, and he did as he was told while Granny scooped him up a bite to eat.

I was eager to hear his news. "How can we do it?"

Dave's eyes lit up. "Well, the transformer stations should be operating by now, right?"

"If you say so," I said. "There was certainly power on at the Program."

Dave shook his head. "They have their own generators, so you can't tell by that. I just know the new transformers were coming in, and it all should have been running shortly after you were taken."

Quinn leaned forward in his chair. "So how can we broadcast the holowafer?"

Dave grinned. "It's simple, really. You know how Maverick transmits his floor shows? We take over his station and use it to hack into the Promise City holoscreen feed."

"Maverick?" Quinn said, putting down his spoon. "What do you think, Granny?"

"It can work. It may not be enough to save Bunny, but it can work. You know they'll want to hang whoever releases that holowafer, though. Maverick may not want to cross that line."

"Could we just storm the place and take it over?" I asked.

Dave choked a bit on his gruel. "That porn station's in a basement that doubles as a bomb shelter. There's no sneaking in there."

Quinn shrugged his shoulders. "But Maverick has one virtue. He can be bought. You want integrity, that costs extra."

"Then it's settled," I said. "We'll leave first thing in the morning. If we can broadcast this holowafer, we can save Bunny."

Granny gave me the Eyebrow. "You're not going anywhere. You still need rest, young lady."

"Archer, you're not strong enough to travel yet," Quinn said. "You're going to have to trust me. I got you out. I'll handle this too. We'll leave at first light, and we'll be back before supper."

I thought about getting mad and throwing a fit, but I didn't want to go there. For the first time in my life, I stayed calm in the face of opposition. "Granny, Quinn, I love you. Thank you for your concern. But I've got a promise to keep." I lifted Ruth down and stood up. "Please wake me at dawn."

I turned away and went to my room without waiting for their reactions.

***

NOON THE NEXT DAY found Dave, Quinn, and me watching Bunny's holowafer in Maverick's office. The room was as orderly as his garden. Elegantly arranged summer flowers graced vases on the wall of bookshelves behind him—shelves that held volumes as illegal as his business. I envied him that, wondering if time alone with his books cost as much as time alone with his whores. His large desktop was empty except for a cigar box, an ashtray, and his stockinged feet. We'd all had to take off our shoes upon entering his inner sanctum. His love of beauty and cleanliness was the only thing I could appreciate about him. That, and the fact that he could be bought.

When Bunny's mother got to the part about seeds, Maverick practically jettisoned to his feet. The gold chains at his neck jingled their richness. "Holy shit. You mean there are seeds out there? You have these seeds? What's your price, Quinn?"

I bristled, surprise and fear competing within me. With his garden, I should have known he would want the seeds, but that was the one thing we couldn't afford to give him at any price. I answered. "No. We don't have any seeds."

He sat back down and lit his cigar with a match. "Then what do you want from me?"

Quinn held out his hand for Bunny's holowafer, and once it was safely tucked away, he sat in the chair across from Maverick. "We want to use your porn station to broadcast this recording into the city."

"Ha." Maverick put his feet back on his desk and glanced at me where I stood behind Quinn's chair. "You seem to want a lot lately. But that's one you can't have."

"I have blinkers, shine, Debbie, whatever you want," Quinn said.

"Not the point. Grid's still down."

Dave stepped up next to Quinn. "That can't be. It was almost repaired when I left—brand new transformers. Everything tested out. It should have been up on Monday."

"Shoulda, woulda, coulda, bullshit. It's what Joseph says it is, and he says it's down. Says he's Abraham now, offering up his own seed for sacrifice. Says God won't turn on the power until his own granddaughter is Atoned."

Dave looked stunned. "That can't be." He sunk down into the chair beside Quinn.

Maverick wrinkled his brow and shooed Dave with his cigar hand. "No. You don't sit in my office. Quinn sits. You stand over by . . ." He stopped, looked at me, and shook his head. "Her."

Dave stood and moved beside me.

Quinn settled back, mirroring Maverick's body language in everything but the feet on the desk. "Why would he do that?"

I cut in. "I know why. That mob in there has lost its faith. He needs a big prophetic display to get them back on his side."

Maverick smiled and opened the box in front of him. "Want a cigar?"

The smell was pleasant, but I didn't trust him enough to accept his gifts. "No, thank you."

Maverick slammed the box shut. "Good. Wasn't gonna give you one anyway, but you're not as dumb as I thought you were."

Quinn shifted uncomfortably at that, and I put my hand on his shoulder to let him know I wanted him to ignore the insult.

"So that's the plan?" Quinn said. "Joseph is holding back the power until he burns Bunny so he can make it look like God is affirming him as the Prophet?"

"How very Joseph, don't you think?" Maverick stamped out his cigar and stood to indicate our time was done.

"Wait," I said. "Can't we force the engineers to turn on the grid? If we did that, we could play the holowafer in time to save her."

I thought I saw a slight smile on Maverick's lips. He sat back down. "We could. For a price."

"I have blinkers," repeated Quinn.

Maverick's smile gave me chills. "I don't want your blinkers. I want the seeds."

Fear gripped my heart. The seeds or Bunny? That was our choice? Those seeds were her life's work. Our salvation. But to let her die in the flames? I couldn't keep the edge from my voice. "There are no seeds."

Maverick's voice grew sharp, all hint of cordiality gone. "You think I'm some kind of Joe-screwed idiot? Get out. Get her out of here, Quinn. I know damn well you wouldn't keep that girl for the summer if she didn't give you something big, and now I know what it is. The seeds or no deal."

Quinn worked his calming charm. "Maverick, Bunny is Granny's niece. That's why we kept her. That's the only reason. If there are any seeds, they're still in that lab."

Maverick stared Quinn down, but Quinn remained relaxed. Finally Maverick said, "Then you don't have my price. We're done here."

My heart sank. There had to be something else he wanted. Anything but the seeds.

Maverick's bodyguard opened the door and held it for us. When we walked out, I saw Spooge at the top of a red-carpeted stairway, studying me from over the gold banister. I smiled and waved his way, but he only turned and continued his ascent. Would he ever forgive me?

CHAPTER 56

W E ARRIVED AT THE meadow as the sun dipped behind the mountains, leaving a warm glow in the sky. Needing to think, I made an excuse to Granny and Quinn and went straight to my glade.

Shooting arrow after arrow into my chosen target, I fought to calm my thoughts. The seeds or Bunny. There had to be another way. But if I went into the city to save her, I would likely die. What would that do to Granny? What would that do to Quinn? Then I thought of Bunny running through forest that night, more terrified of the flames than even of the Dixie bears. How could I break my promise to her? She gave us seeds. She gave me life. Any life I had left I owed to her.

Shoot another arrow, Deena. Just get through the next arrow.

How could a Josephite mean so much to me? How could a Josephite be the one to save my people? A woman, little more than a girl, who faced the most evil deeds of men with an innocent smile and a seed on a chain?

I reached for that same seed at my breast, much as she had done, and thought of the note for me she had left with it. *Plant your seeds, Deena. And remember, only God knows how many apples they hold.* Beside it, she had drawn a little bunny rabbit, complete with whiskers on its face and mountain daisies for its breakfast.

The sound of Tinker's ancient bailer rumbled from the meadow, and I knew the harvest would continue until it was too dark to go on. Nothing so small as human tragedy could stop the cycle of the seasons. The sun would rise, the sun would set, and the pain would carve new rivers of tears in my heart until I could mourn no more. Then I would be someone new. Someone different. Someone older.

I automatically reached for Daisy but found only air. Unreasonably, I looked to see if she had chased after my arrows, but the forest was empty of her spirit. She had not thought of the cost when she'd saved me. Thomas had not thought of the cost when he'd followed me into the Josephite camp. Could I be less and live with myself?

I can't. I'm sorry, Granny. I'm sorry, Quinn. But I can't.

A switch flipped in my brain. I had made my choice. I had to try, and there was nothing left to debate. I would find a way to save Bunny, or I would die trying.

I retrieved my arrows and continued to shoot, and my mind set to working through a plan. Atonement was Sunday, two days away. *Two days. It's not enough. Calm down and think.*

I sank into my repetitive motion and let my mind float without deliberate direction. Thunk. Thunk. Thunk.

There are tunnels under the city. Bunny knows where they are. If I can get in and get her away, she can get us to the tunnels.

I'll need a distraction. I can shoot Joseph. Bunny said he's always in Prophet's Plaza during the Atonement. Right under her window, lighting the altar with his own hand. I can shoot Joseph and whisk Bunny away during the confusion.

But shoot from where? Bunny's house. Bunny spoke of the screams and smells and how she was forced to watch. She lives on the plaza. Third-floor balcony. Three stories. Thirty feet or so. I could get in while they're in temple. I could take my shot from there.

And how could I pass for a Joe? One of Makenzie's dancing animal sweaters, my skirt, and Bunny's shoes. Risky, but if she could pass for a Sec, I can surely pass for a Joe.

But how to get into the city? Bunny said the readers are still working. Even if I find a weak spot in the wall, I have to have a chip. I won't make it a block without a chip.

Despair washed over me. It was impossible to get to Bunny without a tracking chip.

Just shoot.

I picked a new tree and started into the pile of arrows again, fighting down the panic and thinking no farther than my next shot. Thunk. Thunk. Thunk. But it was no good.

I stopped shooting and studied the meadow below me, tears filling my eyes just enough to sharpen my eyesight. It was ironic to me how much more clearly a person could see with a few tears in her eyes. A movement drew my attention to the graveyard. If only my ancestors could send me a message. Tell me what to do.

A small herd of deer foraged near the edge of the forest, boldly drawn to the slightly greener grass that pushed up from our loved ones' resting place. At first I thought it was only does and their young, but then I saw him in the shadows. The King of the Forest.

Oddly enough, I didn't even consider killing him. I'd had enough of death. He seemed to be confident of that. He grazed across the cemetery, occasionally shaking his head and his massive rack, as if practicing for the rutting battles that were sure to come soon. He nibbled only the choicest bites from the graves. So paradoxical that the richest life was born of death.

I couldn't help but think of Maverick's roses, pushing up in glorious beauty from the grave of the brave young woman who had helped Bunny and her mother. What was her name? Barbara Conway. She seemed a lovely girl from her smile.

While the buck enjoyed his dinner, I noticed that he preferred the pretty fall flowers to the grass, and I smiled to myself with the thought of turning him loose in Maverick's garden to eat the roses. As if the buck had heard my deliberations, he paused and looked up, staring my way.

And then, in a flash, I knew. I saw it all laid out before me—my ticket into the city.

I touched the tip of my arrow to my brow, saluting him. "Thank you, Deer King. I'll bring you a rose. And a Bunny."

CHAPTER 57

T HE WANING CRESCENT MOON dove in and out of wispy late-summer clouds when I reached Maverick's on Saturday evening, the night before Atonement.

The only person I told was Thomas. He was the only one who would understand. The only one who would do the same if he were in my shoes. I wrote letters for Granny and Quinn and left them with him in case I wasn't back with Bunny by Monday. Letters saying I was sorry, and that I hoped they could understand. That I couldn't live with myself if I didn't try to save her.

Mustering my courage to face Spooge, I entered the Arena. I had no idea if he would help me or spit on me. He might even shoot me if he was mad enough, but I had to find him. I needed him. Though I was bound to try my mission without him if I had to, I knew it would be near suicide, and I much preferred to succeed. I could only hope that his love for me outweighed his sense of betrayal.

Joes packed the Arena, busy behaving as Joes did when they thought no one who mattered would ever know. Slipping through the crowd as unobtrusively as I could, I swallowed my tension at being around so many people doing such bawdy things and took a seat at the bar near Marty. Things were hopping that night, so I waited politely for him to acknowledge me.

He finally glanced my way. "Hey, Archer. Glad you got out of the Homo House. I always thought you were too pretty for a boy." His wink and sincere smile were incongruous flashes of innocence in that playpen of iniquity. "Free the Cuban?"

"You know it." I suddenly felt self-conscious in my men's clothing, wondering if the whole world now knew I was a woman. When Marty handed me my rum, I slipped him a small piece of paper with a bow and arrow on it between two blinkers. It disappeared into his pocket, and I knew he would get it to Spooge.

"Pleasure doing business." Marty gave me a nod of thanks. "Oh, hey. I've got something for you."

He reached behind the counter and pulled out a coonskin hat—Flynx's coonskin hat. "I thought you'd want this."

I held it in my hands, a lump in my throat. "What happened?"

"He was in here about ten days or so ago when a patrol came in looking for him. He tried to fight his way out."

I swallowed hard. So Flynx was as good as his word. He hadn't been taken alive. My voice was hoarse when I finally spoke. "Thank you, Marty."

"You bet. Sorry about your friend." Marty patted me on the hand and then went to send a message boy to find Spooge.

I put the hat in my pack, took my drink, and slipped into the garden to wait in the quiet corner under the apple tree—the corner by the new rose garden. The Virgin Garden.

Accent lights lined the paths and highlighted a color burst of chrysanthemum blooms. Except for a whore on her knees in front of a john across the way, the sanctuary was empty. Shutting out the sound of their animalian pleasures, I breathed deeply, hoping to be filled with the beauty I had always known in that place, but all I could smell was the roses—the smell of death.

Full, heavy fruit burdened the boughs of the trees. While I waited on the stone bench, I had to restrain myself from stealing a ripe apple from a branch above me. The one Freefall saved me from the greenhouse had been the finest thing I'd ever tasted, but one killing offense was enough for the night.

My eyes studied those perfect roses still blooming in Maverick's agricultural utopia in spite of the night freezes on the plains around them. Maverick's pride. The price of a decent girl. The price of a girl like Bunny. What was it Spooge had told me? Pink at the legs, yellow at the arms, white at the privates, and red for the head. I tried not to think about the head.

Spooge took his time, but he came. Cold and closed, he stopped in front of me, his arms crossed, his eyes staring over my head into the full branches of the apple tree. The moon shone behind him, making a halo around his soft, golden curls. He was as sharp and polished as any man from a picture book in his fine white linen suit. A luminescent marble statue of a Greek god, and he stood in judgment over me. I had a lot of justifying to do, and I didn't know where to start.

Setting my drink by the bench, I took a hemp lollipop from my pocket and held it out. He looked away.

"I'm sorry." I said.

Even in the dim light, I saw him shake his head.

"I never liked lying to you, and I never lied about anything else. I love you, Spooge."

He rounded on me. "You love me? You bitch. You were all I had, and you're nothing but a skanky liar like the rest of them. You fucked me."

At his roar, the whore and her john hustled through the silo door, her blouse and his pants in their hands.

Spooge threw up his hands and stormed down the path. My heart sank. It had taken me nine years to fall from the pedestal he kept me on, and it broke my heart to land so low. I blinked back tears and took a deep breath, but as I let out the sigh, I heard steps coming back.

He stopped before me, arms still crossed, and in the moonlight, I saw his lower lip quiver. Neither of us knew what to say. I held out the candy again. This time, he took it and sat down beside me on the bench.

Neither of us spoke while he sucked on the treat. Finally he broke the silence. "Why didn't you trust me?"

"You were nine when I met you. I couldn't tell a nine year old. And after that, well, I was afraid to tell you. I was afraid you would hate me if I wasn't what you wanted to see, and I didn't want to lose you."

He stared at me, hard and searching. "You were afraid of losing me?" he asked. "Why?"

I knew he needed a real answer. I recalled the beautiful little boy left on the porch that day, his own father inside selling him to pay a gambling debt. He had leaned into me and cried, still young enough to trust a total stranger. I was the last stranger he trusted. I was the last one he *could* trust. He had given me the end of his innocence, and it was sacred to me.

"Because I love you. Because you're mine. You have been mine since the day I met you. I gave you a piece of my heart that day, and I was afraid you would break it if you knew my secret. I was afraid you wouldn't want me anymore."

He thought a moment. Then he took the sucker from his mouth and wrapped his arms around me, leaning into me as he had done when he was a child. I returned his embrace, stroking his soft curls, as I had then. "I'm still yours," he said.

I kissed the top of his head. "Thank you."

We enjoyed each other's presence, a little brother and a big sister, the issue of sex finally settled between us.

I truly wished I had no other agenda, but it could not be helped. I had to have his assistance, and soon. "There's something else I have to tell you. I hate to talk about it now, but I don't have any choice."

"What? You're not really a girl?"

I smiled. "No. Not that simple. I have to save Bunny from Atonement, and I need your help to do it."

He laughed until he realized I was serious. Then his eyes grew wide. "No. Fucking. Way."

CHAPTER 58

"**S**POOGE, I HAVE TO."

"You can't save her. What? Were you just going to walk in and snag her off the altar?"

I shrugged. "Sort of. I'm going to go to Prophet's Plaza, kill Joseph, and make off with her during the confusion."

"That's crazy. You can't even get into the city. You don't have a chip."

"That's why I need you."

"You think I've got a chip for you? What the hell?"

"No, I don't think you have one." I pointed to the red roses. "But she does."

It took him a moment to get my drift. "Are you crazy? You can't touch that. Maverick would kill us both. Slowly. And he'd laugh. He would. I've seen it."

"I only need you to keep everyone out of the garden for a little while. Please. I'd do it for you."

He started to say something and then stopped and shook his head thoughtfully. "You would, wouldn't you?"

I took his hand in my own. "Yes. I would."

He stroked my fingers a moment, thinking. "Do you know how many people came to your rescue?"

"No,. I guess I don't."

"Everyone. From me to Quinn to that little rude kid who came down here with Freefall to make the deal. All of us, Archer. We all put it down for you. How can you turn around and throw yourself back into their hands after what we did? There's no Bunny left to trade for you if they take you again."

"I know, and I will be forever grateful to all of you. But I promised her I would never let her die in the fire. She traded her life for my own to face the worst thing she could imagine. I can't just leave her. And if I fail, well, they won't take me alive again."

I kept my peace and gave Spooge time to think. The moonlight sifted down through the branches of the tree above us, the breeze stirring the shadows to dance up the path at our feet. I noticed the chill in the air at the same time I heard the hum of Maverick's climate control kick on.

Finally Spooge spoke. "I can give you forty-five minutes or so to get the chip, but don't get caught. If you do, I'll have to help Maverick kill you, and I don't want to have to do that."

I knew he meant it. "I forgive you now if it comes to that."

Spooge nodded and stood to go. "Forty-five minutes, max. You need anything else?"

"A ride to the city."

"Holy shit. Should I just do this thing for you?"

"I'm okay with that."

He put the back of his hand next to my cheek and slapped his other hand on it. I knew he wanted to slap me at that moment.

"Forty-five, and not one minute more."

"Got it."

Once he signaled me that the garden was secure, I spread a drop cloth around the rose bush and quickly assembled a flat spade. I scooped up the bark mulch and took care to slide it gently onto the cloth, sun-bleached side up. Once I had the dirt exposed, I spaded around the root ball in the shape of an isosceles triangle so I would be sure to get the bush back in the same direction. I popped out the root ball and set it on the cloth, taking care not to drop any dirt into the mulch.

I didn't have to dig far to find Barbara's head. It reeked, and even with my lifetime of hunting, my stomach turned over when I saw the decomposition. I had no time to search for her chip, so I grabbed her head and stuffed it unceremoniously into a plastic bag. Then I closed it in three more airtight bags to quell the stench before tucking it into my pack. Almost home. Quickly, I replaced the root ball, proud of myself for working so efficiently.

When I looked at it the ground, though, I realized I had a problem. The root ball sat several inches lower than the surrounding ground. *Oh, crap.* I had to put something in the hole where the head had been. Pulling the root ball back out, I took a quick mental inventory of my pack and came up empty. My palms started to sweat. *Think, Deena. It can't end here.* Looking around the garden, the ripe apples once more caught my eye.

I quickly picked a half dozen of them, careful to take them from different places around the tree, and I tossed them in the hole. Soon I had the bush in place, level with the ground around it, and the mulch replaced.

While I was blending the lines where the shovel-fulls of bark met up, I heard Spooge's voice carrying across the garden. "I don't think they're in here, sir. Perhaps over in the Main House."

"No. I'm sure I saw Salome come out here with her john over a good hour ago. I've had enough of her hiding out in the silos. It's time I put the fear of God into her. Bring that whip and come on." Maverick's voice was hard and cold. He was on the warpath.

I dropped to a crouch and slipped back to my seat on the bench, glad I had left my drink sitting on the ground beside it. Taking a sip, I tried to look like I was relaxing, though my heart raced.

Maverick rounded a pear tree at the curve in the path and stopped to inspect his roses. Spooge, his brow wrinkled, glanced from the flowers to me, and back again. I took another sip.

Maverick put his hands on his narrow hips and shook his head, the moonlight reflecting off his bald head. Then he studied the apple tree above my head and growled. "Somebody's going to hurt for this one."

CHAPTER 59

H E POINTED TO THE rose bed. "Look at that. Just look at that."

"Sorry, but look at what, sir?" Spooge asked, his fearful eyes meeting mine behind Maverick's back.

"Are you blind? That." He pointed to the mulch.

As unobtrusively as possible, I set my drink down and reached for my pack, calculating how I would jump to clear the garden wall. Then, with the delicacy of a mother bird turning an egg, Maverick bent and picked up a fallen apple tree leaf from the top of the mulch and held it up in the dim light. "This tree shouldn't start shedding leaves for another week. I want the climate control checked immediately."

"Yes, sir. I'll get Ricki right on it," Spooge said.

I hoped Maverick didn't hear the same relief in his voice that I did. Turning, Maverick seemed to see me for the first time. Pursing his mouth, his hands still on his hips, he leered at me. I stared back boldly, refusing to show my discomfort with his assessment. It seemed like forever before he came to his conclusion. "Huh. You'd be like screwing a pile of coat hangers. Don't know what Quinn's thinking."

Maverick turned on his heel and strode back the way he had

come. "I don't have time for this. Spooge, you find that bitch and get her back on the floor."

Spooge ran to keep up with him, but not before bending down to whisper, "Stay put."

For a change, I did as I was told.

Spooge returned when the half moon was tipping behind the mountains. He shook me awake where I slept on the bench. "Did you find a car?" I asked.

"I did you one better." He threw a bundle at me. "Follow me. Quick. We'll get you ready, and I can drive you as far as a store that's inside the Dome. The plaza where they'll torch her is about a mile away. It's the best I can do."

"Spooge, it's above and beyond. I'll owe you forever," I said.

"Yes, you will. Let's go."

CHAPTER 60

I FOUGHT MY URGE to slouch in the passenger seat of the armored Humvee when we passed through the gates of Promise City. Though we weren't positive the chip would work in the readers, any sign of trepidation on my part could draw unwelcome questions.

"Breathe," Spooge said, sounding exactly like Granny. "If we were going to have a problem, it would have been right there. The chip's good."

I exhaled but didn't speak.

Ash spit down from the sky, and a thick layer of brown cloud masked the dawn. But it didn't mask the people. People everywhere. Tall, short, brown, black, and white. All of them gaunt. All of them tense, their faces a mixture of anger and fear. Some of them stopped to glare at us, the only moving vehicle on the road. Overwhelmed by the press of them, I closed my eyes and took a deep breath to prove to myself that I still could.

"This is nothing," Spooge said. "Just wait an hour or two. These streets will be packed."

"You mean they're not already?"

Spooge shook his head. "Oh, Archer. You are truly a babe in the woods."

I shifted in my seat, uncomfortable in the short skirt, stockings, shiny black shoes, and dancing squirrel sweater that Spooge had given me to wear. After I had showered and "shaved everything below the eyebrows," as he put it, he had dried and curled my hair, applied my makeup, and hidden my duct-taped chip behind my ear with a red bow. I looked so much like Barbara Conway when he was finished with me that my own reflection in his mirror made me break out in a cold sweat.

I checked the knife in the sheath I had taped to my arm under my sleeve and then touched Barbara's chip at my neck, making sure it was still firmly in place.

Spooge reached over and pulled my hand down. "Stop fiddling with that."

I put my hands in my lap and laced my fingers together to make them behave.

Looking up, I saw a sight I didn't comprehend—a narrow metal road with a huge machine sitting on top that resembled nothing more than an enormous metal snake. "What is that?"

Spooge glanced where I was pointing. "That? That's a maglev train. It froze in place when the power went down. People ride on them to get around the city. See? There's another one over there."

Sure enough, every couple of blocks a train perched on rails that seemed far too small to me to support their weight. Were there enough people to fill that many of them? Enough people who wanted to go one place at one time? I shuddered at the thought. How could so many of them live together without going crazy?

The buildings grew taller the further we drove into the city—so high I only knew the sun was rising from the growing glow in the smoky sky. Finally the high rises opened to frame a large square. A concrete plaza.

Shops lined the west side with apartments above them stretching ten stories high. Across from us, a vertical farm rose up, almost as high as the apartments and heavily guarded by soldiers. No one looked at them or walked near them.

Next to the farm, on the north side of the plaza, a large Sword of Michael distinguished the temple from the storefronts surrounding it. Several people crowded the sidewalk in front of it, many of them on their knees in prayer. A massive holoscreen framed three stories of the apartments overhead, flanked on each side by banners of Joseph's face rising from a ripe cornfield. The holoscreen was empty.

I thought about Bunny's holowafer and how those people might react if they saw the recording. Would they hate Joseph? Would they refuse to believe? Would they turn to the Underground, looking for new leaders to guide them through their bleak existence?

Following the street around, my gaze froze, riveted to a concrete platform that filled the eastern side of the square. A tall metal rectangle stood in its center. I could not tell if the stains on the shackles hanging down from its top bar were rust or blood, but the blackened concrete moat stretching ten feet wide around the platform left no doubt as to its purpose.

The area smelled vaguely of trash smoke and burned flesh, and I willed my stomach to stay put. Then I realized what filled the moat and where the smell of burned trash had come from. I was shocked that even Josephites would go so far. "Trash? They burn the women in trash?"

Spooge glanced toward the plaza and then back to the road. He swerved to miss a man on a bicycle. "It's practical, if you think about it. Trash needs disposing, and sinners need burning. But don't worry, your cousin's the main event. They'll use real wood for her."

I was not comforted.

Behind the altar gaped the blackened hole of a burned- out building.

"I see one of their purifications got a bit out of hand."

Spooge rolled his eyes. "No, that was the work of your little rebellion. There used to be a small grocery in that building. Vandals broke in the day the power went down the second time. They started a fire on their way out."

I wasn't sure how I should react to that. He wasn't supposed to know it was us. My hesitance must have shown on my face.

"I thought the days of you thinking I was stupid were over." Spooge shook his head. "How long do you think it took me to put that together anyway? You people really didn't know what you were getting into, did you?"

Remembering the force of the soldiers and the Godfire, I had no defense. "No. But we know now."

Now we had fertile seeds waiting to be planted in a new meadow the following spring. Granny was right. There were other ways to fight them. "We know now," I repeated.

We drove deeper into the press of people, buildings, and trains, and I was surprised to find that Promise City was not one city at all, but a conglomeration of towns, each with its own flavor. Most were oceans of barren concrete. Spartan, functional, and devoid of any art or vegetation. Some were a squalor of dirt and graffiti in all opposition to the proclaimed Josephite values of cleanliness and order. But all had a plaza with four things—a vertical farm, a temple, a holoscreen, and an altar.

I forced myself to study the people around me. The people I would have to use as cover once I had Bunny with me and we were running for a tunnel.

The women all wore skirts and brightly colored sweaters, many with dancing forest animals on them like the one Bunny had worn. Like the one I wore. The amount of leg they displayed varied with age. There seemed to be two outfits for the men. Most wore white button-down shirts with blue slacks and suspenders, but a very few were in black suits with stiff white collars. The ones in black didn't seem to be going anywhere, and they appeared to be stopping random people to pray with them.

"What are those men doing?"

Spooge looked where I was pointing. "Huh? Oh. Those aren't men. Those are prayerbots." He glanced at me sharply. "Please tell me you knew about the prayerbots before you cooked up this scheme."

I shrugged, suddenly overwhelmed with the task before me. "Maybe you'd better fill me in."

"Oh, God. Don't you ever think before you do anything? Prayerbots are the thought police. There are four Readers embedded in each block. If twenty of them in a row read that you're stressed, Central downloads an order to the closest Prayerbot to stop you. Then the Readers download the last thirty minutes of info to your chip. The Prayerbot reads the chip and knows where you've been and what you've done. If there's anything suspicious, it detains you until the correct ministry arrives. Archer, I thought you'd accounted for that."

"Okay. Don't freak out on me." I was saying it as much to myself as to him. "I'll keep my heartbeat slow on the way, and Bunny and I will be down a tunnel in less than thirty minutes once I have her."

A thump on my window made me jump. Then came two more.

"Oh, crap." Spooge sped up as much as he could while rocks, hemp balls, and even a boot crashed into our vehicle. A man with a metal pipe ran at us and slammed it into my window. I jumped. Spooge swerved, barely missing a small boy with a bat in his hands. The people had found a target for their anger, and it was us.

CHAPTER 61

T WO MEN JUMPED ON the hood of the vehicle, and Spooge hit a button on the dashboard. A gray/green gas sprayed out from under our windshield. The two men fell away, writhing in agony. The tire bumped, and I didn't want to think about what had been under it. The gas did its work, and people backed off.

A motion caught my eye. We were approaching the wall of the Dome. Three stories tall. Dark gray cement with bright yellow geodesic dome triangles rose above the walls to enclose the city within the city. The heart of Joseph's kingdom. A dozen human-sized dolls swung on either side of the two-story opening.

"Spooge, what are . . ."

And then I knew. Bodies. They were bodies. They had been hung by the neck, their torsos split open and charred. My stomach flipped, and I swallowed hard.

"You might not want to look at that," Spooge said. "They were drawn and their entrails burned. Tried to break into the Dome for food. That was last week. Joseph had them hung there for a warning."

Message received. I noticed even Spooge was pale.

I looked straight ahead when we stopped at the gate, and Spooge handed the guard a fistful of blinkers. He waved us through.

Entering the Dome was like flying to another planet. The air was clean and free of ash and smoke, and a sun-like luminescence mimicked a clear day. I looked up to find a blue sky above me.

"Spooge, how do they do this?"

"The top of the Dome is a holoscreen. During the day, it mimics the daytime, and at night, it projects whatever stars are overhead."

Beautiful buildings surrounded me, built in the old style— red brick, two or three stories, and revealing true art in their architecture. They reminded me of the ruins of Gap, and I wondered if they had been preserved from before the war.

And there were plants. Grass in yards, trees with leaves in every shade of green, and bushes bursting with orange flowers next to others with leaves the color of fire. Even some of the junipers and pines of my own forest rose through the city, looking to me like caged animals out of their element.

Was this what Gap had looked like before the war? Was this the world Granny came from?

The effect was surreal. It was like driving through an enormous garden that people lived in. Like something out of one of Granny's books. No wonder people like Harmony could never really adjust to losing it.

I studied the people. They looked like Bunny had when she'd arrived. The men wore tailored two-piece suits, and the women had much finer quality skirts and sweaters. Clean and orderly, they looked as different from those outside the Dome as their sky did except for one thing. They had the same grim looks of anger and fear.

"What do these people have to be mad about?"

"Them? Oh, they've been going hungry too. Joseph locked down the vertical farms right away and put them on a ration.

They're lucky he needs them."

"He needs them?"

"Most of these people, the ruling class, they don't believe in anything. Their power lies in the current regime. A lot of them sympathize with the Underground because it's a pacifist movement, and peace brings prosperity, but they won't actually act until they think the movement will be successful. They'd be just as happy to put a blow-up doll in charge if it didn't interrupt their flow of power."

At first, the image of a blow-up doll in Joseph's toga sounded amusing, but then something struck me. What would these people have done if Maverick had let us broadcast the holowafer? If they had proof for the people outside the Dome that Joseph was a fraud?

I remembered Bunny saying the Underground needed a focus. Some momentum. Something or someone to give the people confidence that they could take control from Joseph and make a more positive, productive world.

I looked at these people around me with new eyes. They were people who only wanted a place to put their hope, even if it was for self-serving reasons. Maybe some day, with the right motive and focus, these would be people we Secs could deal with.

When we drew toward the center of the Dome, buildings became taller and longer. They were similar in size to those outside the protective shell, but each had its own personality and design, as if they were competing art projects lined up side by side.

A flock of crows passed and settled on the blank frame of a holoscreen stationed above a street corner. "Spooge, if the Dome holoscreen is working, why aren't these little ones working?"

"All of the transmission holoscreens are on the same system, but the Dome screen has its own power sources separate from the city's."

I thought about the holoscreens and how Joseph was planning to bring them up while Bunny burned. I wondered if someone would give the order once I killed him.

A large door opened up at street level in the middle of a building, and Spooge drove inside it into a parking lot that was similar to Maverick's but underground.

"What's this?"

"The Rapture Ecstasy Book Store."

"A book store? Seriously, why are we at a book store?"

"This is as far as we can drive. I only have auto clearance to this building." He got out of the car and opened my door. "Make yourself useful and grab a box."

He opened the compartment in the back of the vehicle, and I took out a box labeled "Inspirational Accessories" and followed him inside. We went up a flight of stairs to the first floor where a tall, thin man with short, brown, slicked-back hair immediately showed us through a locked door and into a back room.

I set down the box, took off my pack, and looked around. My mouth dropped open. The small room had a seedy feel to it, and it was stuffed wall to wall with shelves full of . . . things. All kinds of things. Many things I did not recognize and could not imagine their purpose. Many others, though of different sizes and textures were clearly designed to evoke images of male anatomy. I felt the heat rising in my face.

"You're blushing? Really? After all the time you've spent at Maverick's? That's kind of cute, Archer. Quinn should get you out more."

I set the box down, feeling anything but cute. "Focus, Spooge. Tell me what I need to know.

"Okay. Out the back, into the alley and . . ."

"What's an alley?"

Spooge smacked the palm of his hand to his head and shook it before explaining.

An idea popped into my mind. "Are there readers in the

alleys?"

"Only half as many."

"So Bunny and I would be safer in the alleys?"

"No. They'll stop you if you go down two in a row and you're not collecting trash."

"Damn. Where are the nearest tunnels to the square?"

"I don't know them all. But I do know there's one under this garage, so try and get here if Bunny doesn't know of one closer. Archer, this is crazy. You can't save her."

I set my jaw. "It's the right thing to do."

Sadness filled his eyes, and he took me in his arms for a warm hug. When he released me, he stared at me a long moment. Then he pulled out a lipstick and touched up my lips. With a quick twist on my hair bow and a flick at my skirt hem, he stepped back.

"Last chance," he said, his hands on his hips.

"I'm doing this." I put on my pack and checked the knife at my wrist. Still secure.

Spooge shook his head, sighed, and then took inventory of his own weapons—a knife in his boot and a tiny, two-shot revolver at his waistband. He opened a door for me and signaled the way. "All right, then. Let's go."

"What do you mean 'us'? What are you doing?"

"You don't even know what an alley is. You honestly think I'm going to let you go alone?"

"You don't have to do this. This is my burden."

"Archer, lots of people love you, but you're the only one who loves me. Now shut up and let's go."

Moved to silence, I thanked him with a kiss on the cheek, leaving a red print of my lips behind.

"Oh, for Michael's sake." He quickly cleaned his face with a kerchief and pulled out the lipstick again to perfect my lips once more. "Now get out of here before you ruin the rest of it." His voice was harsh, but I saw the adoration in his eyes.

"Whatever lies ahead, Spooge, I'll always love you."

"Get out."

CHAPTER 62

W E WERE IN A dirty, man-made crevasse between two five-story buildings. Several metal staircases zigzagged up walls, and large, rectangular containers stood outside each door. Looking inside of the one next to me, I found trash and closed it, accidentally dropping the lid the last inch. At the clang of metal, a strange-looking lion cub darted from behind the metal box and up the alley. Fear surged through me. Backing against the wall, my hand on my knife, I sought its mother.

Spooge grabbed my arm and pulled me into the alley. "Good God, Archer. That was a house cat. You see? I couldn't possibly let you do this alone."

While I was miffed at his words, I knew the truth of them. I was exactly like a Josephite in my forest.

The crowd flowed past at the end of the alley, and we blended into the stream. Looking like a young couple surrounded by families, no one noticed us. Spooge guided me toward a large family—a grandmother, two parents, a young blonde woman, and her seven siblings—and we put them between ourselves and the readers. I suddenly understood how elk felt, seeking security in numbers.

I noticed a prayerbot from the corner of my eye. It stared straight at me, and my heart raced.

Spooge either saw it or felt the sweat on my palms. He made sure his voice was loud enough to register. "No need to be nervous, dear. I'm sure our prayer leader will think you're charming."

I squeezed Spooge's hand and took a deep breath, willing my heart to slow.

Delicious, unidentifiable food smells filled my nostrils, and I remembered Bunny telling me once about Atonement Sunday—morning service, potluck, burning, and then a communion ceremony to celebrate the purification and unification of the Temple. A perverse ritual of life and death, and all of it centered around food.

"I thought you said these people weren't eating either." I was curious as to where they got their potluck fare.

He whispered. "I said it was rationed. Some of them nearly starve all week rather than show up to Atonement empty handed. It's their way."

I suddenly felt self conscious that I didn't have anything in my hands, and I almost laughed out loud at the thought of carrying a pot of hemp gruel into their service. I wondered if they would all wrinkle their noses as Bunny had.

Bunny. Were they feeding her? Were they torturing her? Did they try to map her brain in spite of their agreement? Did they find out about the seeds?

I forced myself to study my area, going through the motions of my mission. I would shoot Joseph at his podium in front of the altar before he could light the fire. Then in the confusion, I would get to Bunny, and we'd head through the distracted crowd for the nearest tunnel. In and out.

Breathe, Deena.

The young blonde woman in the family we tagged along with caught my eye and looked away. Was she suspicious?

I tried to concentrate on the beat of my heart, the feel of

Spooge's hand, and the pattern of the streets around me, but the press of people was overwhelming. It was all I could do not to start physically pushing them away, and their voices crowded in on me.

"Thank Michael they caught that heretic. Now maybe we can get some lights back on." A fat man pushed his wife past us, steering her by the elbow while she tugged a child by the hand.

The child was skipping. "Mom, will it smell bad? James told me it smells bad."

The young blonde woman who had worked her way next to us dropped her purse directly at our feet, scattering its contents. We could either help her pick it up, or we could make a spectacle of ourselves by picking our way around it. At a nod from Spooge, we squatted down and started grabbing what I now recognized as makeup.

She smiled. "Thank you, sister. God at your shoulder." And then, when I handed her her wallet, she leaned in close and whispered, "You are too bold."

Confused, I questioned her with a look. She stared straight at the seed pendant at my breast, and made the motion of tucking something into her dancing chipmunk sweater. That's when I noticed the glint of a gold chain at her neck. I quickly tucked the necklace inside my top. "Thank you, sister. God at your shoulder," I said. I hoped the words didn't sound as awkward as they felt on my tongue, but I thought it was something Bunny might say.

"Michael at your side." She didn't look at me while she scooped up the remainder of her belongings. I watched her catch up to her family, and I warmed a bit, realizing that I wasn't alone. That there would be some people in that crowd who would want Bunny and me to succeed.

Spooge pulled at my hand. "Heads up."

I looked over the top of the crowd to see them turning through a tall wrought-iron gate in the next block. It led into a five-acre garden, impeccably groomed and occupied by an old, majestic stone structure with a spire and a sword of Michael on top. A few people entered the building, but most took up positions on the grounds.

I checked the watch I wore. Bunny's watch. 9:49 a.m. Only eleven minutes to get safely into Bunny's house before the service began.

Once we passed the temple I found, to my dismay, that we were moving against the crowd. "Spooge, we're swimming upstream."

He squeezed my hand without looking at me. I could barely hear his words. "Just be cool and own it. Like you do it all the time."

I nodded and held my head up, but I felt the sweat on my brow, and try as I would, I could not calm my heartbeat. We stayed at the center of the crowd as much as possible, but there wasn't much crowd left. 9:51. Five blocks left. I lengthened my stride, practically dragging Spooge with me. He tugged me back.

Two blocks. The buildings were down to four stories, and only a few straggling worshippers remained on the street. I felt like a rabbit on an open hillside.

Then a man's voice cut through me, chilling my spine. "Miss Conway. Miss Barbara Conway." I glanced back to see the prayerbot coming directly my way.

CHAPTER 63

I SPED UP, WANTING to run, but Spooge tightened his grip. "Oh, crap. Don't panic, and *don't* try to kill it," he said. Then he turned and smiled at the approaching robot.

The creepiest thing about the prayerbot was how very human it sounded. "God at your shoulder, Darryl Jenkins."

"And Michael at your side," responded Spooge. It had never occurred to me that he had another name. I wondered if it was his real one.

The prayerbot studied us with lifeless eyes. "I must question your companion, Mr. Jenkins. Miss Conway, my sensors have been alerted that you are in distress. Please hold still, Miss Conway, while I pray with you." The robot held its hand over my head as if to bless me and then closed its blank eyes and prayed over me, downloading data from the chip taped to my neck.

My pulse raced, and I looked to Spooge. *Should I attack it? Should I run? Should I take out my knife and kill myself now?* But Spooge smiled back, his face relaxed, giving me no clue.

The prayerbot lowered its hand and opened its eyes. "Miss Conway, you are assigned to the 10:00 a.m. temple service. You passed your designated temple. Why did you pass your temple, Miss Conway?"

"She . . ." started Spooge, but the robot cut him off with a raised hand.

"The question is for Miss Conway."

Why did I pass the temple? Nonsensically, I searched the street for an answer. One family hurried by, the mother carrying a small covered dish, and the father pulling the children along.

"My dish. I forgot my dish at home. I have to hurry."

The robot looked unconvinced. "Miss Conway, you passed your designated temple twice. Why did you pass your temple for the book store, Miss Conway?"

Why did I pass my temple?

Before I could answer, Spooge pulled a copy of The Book of Joseph from his suit pocket. The price tag was prominent, and he made sure I saw it.

I understood. "A gift. We were buying a gift. To commemorate this great day when our society shall be cleansed of the demon seed." I straightened my back and stared at the robot straight on, as Bunny would have done. "Praise Michael, I need to hurry and get my dish if I'm going to make the service."

The prayerbot processed a moment longer and then released my arm. "God at your shoulder, daughter. I will record your errand. You may proceed."

"Thank you," Spooge said, stashing away the book and taking my hand once more. It was all I could do not to run up the street.

"So what would have happened if I had tried to kill it?" I looked forward, pretending to smile in case any robots were looking.

"It would have sent its friends." Spooge winked as if he'd told me a joke, and I nodded.

Two minutes. We finally reached the alley behind Bunny's home, which was three stories high and stretched the entire block. Unlike the alley outside the bookstore, the trashcans were fancier, large and square, and painted with scenes of

Joseph receiving the seeds.

Spooge stopped. "Which door, Archer?"

I looked up the block and counted no less than four doors. "The one to the women's quarters."

In his first display of nerves, Spooge smacked his palm against his forehead. "Oh, that's helpful. Can you give me a clue?"

I blocked out his irritation and thought back to the trip to the Big Box. Bunny talked about coming home from school when she was a girl and laying beneath a stained glass window with her strawberry smoothie. What did the window have? *Think, Deena.* The Josephites and the Secs. "Look for a window with a lamb and a lion," I said.

We walked the alley twice, and I searched for a bright green window with a lion and a lamb on it, but no luck. Then I realized that stained glass would be dark from the outside, not bright. I looked again, and there, near the roof of the third floor, I saw it—round and lined with silver, the pieces forming the outline of a large cat and a lamb.

"This one. It's this one."

Spooge pointed up the alley. "You'd better be right, 'cause we're out of time."

I glanced where he pointed, and my stomach flipped. A prayerbot had stopped and was watching from the street.

I pounded on the door, waiting for Bunny's maid.

"Keep it smooth. If you stay calm, it might not come our way."

"God, Spooge, how do you live like this all the time?" I glanced back up the alley and sighed in relief. The prayerbot had moved on.

I jerked out my lockpicker I'd gotten from Thomas and hooked it on, but nothing happened. I tried it again.

"Crap. What's happening?"

He rolled his eyes. "You didn't think they might have a security system that was a little better than a gate on a transformer station? Now what?"

I looked around, knowing nothing except that there was no way I was getting this close and giving up.

I noticed the metal staircases leading to the top of the building. Reaching up, I could just grasp a ladder and pull it down. "Come on." I climbed.

When I got to the top, I turned around and gave Spooge a hand up. To my surprise, he was puffing with exertion. "Great idea. You'll have a better shot from up here anyway."

I wasn't so sure. We crossed to the front of the building, passing what appeared to be large metal vents and a small shack or two. Crouching down, I peered over the top of the roof and down into the plaza.

Trees and lawn stretched out in front of me like a park of old. There was even a playground with metal climbing bars and sand, and each surrounding three-story building had half a dozen balconies, all of them decorated with bright paper roses and large white ribbons. I heard a slight tinkling of chimes and noticed garlands of bells woven through the bars of the balconies, singing as if this were a fiesta.

Directly across the plaza hung the typical blank holoscreen with its banners on either side. The angelic glow about Joseph's visage did not keep me from noticing the bright light in his blue eyes—a light I had seen once in the eyes of a man from South shortly before he killed his family.

"Where's their vertical farm?" I asked.

Spooge pointed to a building a few blocks away. "The Dome's the only place that doesn't have it on the plaza. I've heard that Joseph doesn't like his view of the sky blocked."

A spacious gazebo stood in the center of the park, filled to bursting with band equipment and flanked by choir risers. Beneath me, bizarre in the serene opulence, a large cement platform had been erected like a giant's altar. The trench around it was stacked high with wood, and its centered metal frame and shackles starkly proclaimed its purpose.

In front of the altar stoodpoised a large metal bowl on a tripod, and below it stood a speaking podium and candelabras, fronted by several decorative flower arrangements. Colorful streamers roped off twenty-five chairs directly below the podium. The combination of festive beauty and deadly intent was macabre. The trees, the playground, the bells, the flowers . . . and the pyre where they would burn my sister.

Vendors' booths lined the rest of the plaza. They were closed, but a few people already formed a line in front of them. A small group cut in front of a young man, crowding him into the older man beside him. The older man cuffed the young one, and I didn't need to hear what he said. His red, angry face was enough to tell me.

A few dozen others milled about the playground equipment or spread blankets under the trees, their grim faces as much a contrast to the festive decorations as the altar was.

I was confused. "Why aren't those people in a temple?"

"They've already been to the early service. They couldn't have everyone get here at the same time. That would jam up the streets."

As long as it doesn't interfere with my shot.

Without thinking, I licked my finger and held it up to find the wind. Then a thought occurred to me. "Why is there wind in here? We're in a dome."

"Joseph likes it this way. Reminds him of his childhood home in the Texas panhandle. Just be glad it isn't spring. He likes it storm force then."

I shook my head and then mentally measured my distance. About sixty yards, barely out of good range. I visualized the ugly little prophet behind the podium below me and how his life would end with my arrow and a spray of blood. And it wasn't working. "I have to get closer. Even one floor would make a difference. We've got to go in."

"Damn. Did you ever think that maybe you can't do this at all? That maybe you can't save her? I keep waiting for you to figure that out."

"I promised her I wouldn't let her die in the fire. I'm going in. Stay out here if you like."

"Look. Could you do it if the wind dies down? Let's wait a while and see if the wind calms."

Fair enough. We waited and watched more people flow into the plaza below. After another forty-five minutes, though, it was clear that not only was the wind not dying down, it was picking up.

"It's no good, Spooge. I'm going in."

Shaking his head, Spooge followed me. Within two minutes we had located the door on the roof above the area with the stained glass window. I took out my lockpicker, but it wasn't necessary. The door was unlocked. I remembered Bunny telling me how much she loved lying out on the roof, gazing up at the stars. I hadn't realized at the time that they weren't real stars. No wonder she was so frightened of the outdoors.

I tiptoed down the stairs, Spooge behind me, and I cracked open a door. We were in a short, blue-carpeted hallway at the back of the house, looking onto a square balcony that appeared, from my vantage point, to drop down to the first floor. There were doors on each side of the square. I studied them, but I couldn't see a clue as to which one was Bunny's.

Spooge started forward, but I blocked him with my arm, listening. The only thing I heard was the sound of running water, like a small stream, uninterrupted by hands, bodies, or dishes. It baffled me, but I didn't sense danger in it.

Sniffing the air, I found it humid, and I wondered if the water I heard was enough to make it that way. From somewhere, kitchen smells wafted up. I did not recognize them, but there was another odor underneath them that niggled at my memory. Something not Sec, but something I somehow knew.

Then it hit me. Bunny. Soap and cleaners. It smelled like Bunny the night I met her, before I dumped her down the latrine. It was strongest to my right.

I motioned Spooge to stay back, and I crept that direction—toward the front of the house. I wanted him to have a quick exit if he needed it. He ignored me, but he at least lagged a few feet behind me. Reaching out, I tried the knob, and it turned. We slipped inside, shutting the door behind us.

Bunny's presence permeated the large, luxurious room, and everything in it contributed to an atmosphere of privilege, grace, and class. A painting of Jesus in the Garden of Gethsemane hung over a natural sandstone hearth surrounded by plush blue and green chairs. Across from the door stood a baby grand piano, and beside us was an exquisitely inlaid wooden secretary desk.

Two books lay out on top of the antique. One was a Josephite Bible, and the other was a stack of papers labeled *Gospel of Joseph*. It only took me a moment to register that it was hand written, with Joseph's signature scrawled across the front. A priceless artifact of Bunny's civilization.

Spooge reached out for it. I grabbed his hand back and hissed at him. "That's not what we're here for."

That's when I noticed them—the fresh flowers by the plush chairs. Bunny had been gone a long time for anyone to be keeping fresh flowers in her room.

Just then a movement to my left caught my eye, and a man said calm and low, "Seize them."

CHAPTER 64

WHEN THE MAN ROLLED his wheelchair in from the balcony, I knew right away who he was. Thick gray hair, glasses, and a button-down shirt. Strong arms and shoulders, and careful consideration in every move. Bunny's father. I immediately put up my hands.

"It's okay, Spooge, do what they say."

Clearly skeptical, Spooge took his hand off the tiny pistol at his belt and followed my lead. Two men immediately searched us and took our weapons and packs before stepping back, their guns still trained on us.

"Who are you, and why have you come here?" asked the man in the wheelchair.

"You must be Joshua. My name is Deena Sprague. I'm your cousin. Bunny . . . I mean Tamar—we called her Bunny—she's been staying with me." I nodded toward Spooge. "This is my friend, Spooge. We've come to save her."

The man's eyes were swirling pools of grief, and his face bore the sorrow of ages. He silently considered my words. Finally he signaled to his men to lower their weapons. "What do you propose?"

I put my hands down but did not step any closer. "I've

brought my bow. It's in the pack with my arrows. I plan to . .
." *Do I trust him that much?* "I plan to kill Joseph and escape
from the city with Bunny through the underground tunnels."

The corners of Joshua's mouth turned up in a sad smile,
"And where will you take her? Back to your meadow?"

I shrugged. "We have tunnels, too, and in the spring, we'll
be starting a new meadow. She can come with us. They can't
tell one Sec from another. They'll never know."

Joshua slowly shook his head and then turned his wheelchair
toward the balcony, waving us to follow. I stepped out behind
him, staying behind a latticework that framed the edges of the
platform. When I gazed through it into the plaza, I gasped.
I had never seen so many people, and now that the second
service was out, they were flowing in from every direction.

The vendors' booths were open and turning a brisk trade
in T-shirts with the image of a woman burning on an altar and
banners with the slogan, "God loves the smell of a burning
sinner," and small hemp balls in baskets labeled "Satan Stones."

A balloon escaped the grip of a pretty little girl in a pink
dress, and she cried, pointing at it as it floated toward heaven—a
balloon with the face of a woman over flaming letters that
spelled out one word. *Atone.*

I shuddered.

Joshua gave me a moment to soak it in before he spoke, the
power of grief in his every word. "Your loyalty is commendable,
but you seem to think we are only one despotic dictator away
from a free society. Do you see now that you are mistaken?"

I said nothing, and he continued. "Our movement has some
momentum, it's true. But we need more than momentum.
We cannot remove a prophet without replacing him with
one equally as mystical. Equally as commanding of loyalty.
Religion abhors a vacuum."

Spooge stepped to my side and took hold of my elbow.
"Archer, all of these people want Bunny dead, not just Joseph.
You. Can't. Save. Her."

I wasn't ready to give up. "But she's so afraid. I promised I wouldn't let her suffer in the flames. I have to try."

Joshua's heavy tones cut through me. "There is another way to keep your promise."

Spooge turned to him, and they exchanged a knowing glance. Then Spooge said it out loud. "You could kill Bunny."

My mouth dropped open. I couldn't believe what they were suggesting. Stunned, I could only form one word. "No."

Spooge's eyes lit up. "No, listen to me. These people are all here for Atonement. The screams of their sins released through a burning woman. What if she didn't scream?"

Anger flared inside me. "It doesn't matter. I'm not here to kill her."

Joshua's voice commanded my attention. "According to the Doctrine of Atonement, if there are no screams, the woman is innocent. There is no Atonement, and the price of an innocent life will be on the heads of the people. Obviously, that has never happened before."

Spooge became agitated. "You see? No Atonement. Joseph was going to bring up the power while Bunny burned, proving that God accepts the sacrifice of his own seed and that he is still the Prophet. But if she doesn't scream, there's no Atonement. There's no restoration of grace."

Joshua finished his thought. "Joseph can't turn the power back on without looking like a fraud, and as angry as these people are, there's no telling what they will do."

Spooge put his hand on my elbow. "Bunny's getting burned, with or without a Joseph, but this way, you can make her death count for something."

Everything inside me rebelled against it. I sought a kernel of hope. *If I kill Joseph, they will let her go.* I looked down into the Prophet's Plaza. A group of teens were raising a long banner. Written in flames across it was their plea—*Atone the Sinner*. When they lifted it, the crowd broke out in a single cheer, and I saw that Joshua was right. These people wanted blood, and one woman could not stop them from getting it.

A profound grief split my heart. The only way I could save Bunny from the pain was to kill her myself. Deprive them of their Atonement.

I met Joshua's eye. "This is what you want?"

He reached out for my hand, a tear tracing his cheek. "You think I haven't thought these things? She is the child of my heart." He dropped his head to his hand, wiping the tears away before raising his eyes to me again. "Please, don't let her suffer."

I glanced back at the men behind me, their rifles now on their shoulders. "Why not have one of them do it?"

"Because people would hear a gunshot and know this was not an act of God. You said you had a bow. She must die silently if they are to believe."

I thought about that a moment. "Doesn't that make you sort of like Joseph? Leading the people with lies?"

"Those who see the truth will understand. For those who cannot see, their faith matters more than the truth. In pretense or in truth, so long as the path leads to Christ."

I studied the altar through the lattice. It was closer than the podium. A better shot. But the lattice could be annoying. The sun would drop lower in the next hour, and that could be a problem, even with my shades. I tested the wind again. The breeze was still strong, but it was not unmanageable at that distance.

Then I studied the crowd. More banners had gone up proclaiming the Josephite adage "God loves the smell of a burning sinner." Children wore T-shirts over their Sunday clothes with the image of a woman surrounded by flames. That same image adorned more balloons, and there were balloons everywhere, ready to launch with her screams.

I swallowed hard and nodded my assent. I would deprive Joseph of his miracle. I would kill her myself. My friend. My sister. And then I would kill Joseph.

CHAPTER 65

T HE BAND STRUCK UP in the gazebo, and a choir rustled out of the temple and onto the risers. The embroidered flames licking up from the hemlines of their white robes gave them the appearance of a fast-burning fire. When they were in place, the drummer struck up the beat, and they burst forth in song. "Pur—i—fi—ca—tion!"

By this time, parties filled the festive balconies, and the crowd packed the plaza to standing room only with streets overflowing in every direction. Not hundreds. Not thousands. Millions. Bodies everywhere, dipping, swaying, and stomping to the rhythm of the band. The cacophony jolted me back to the Program, threatening to overwhelm my senses.

Focus.

Retrieving my backpack from the soldier behind me, I took out my bow and put it together. Then I inspected the five arrows I had brought with me—the broadhead tips, the eagle feather fletching, and the carbon shafts. Choosing one, I set the rest into my quiver where I could snatch them quickly. Finally I strung my bow, tested it, and hunkered down to wait, moving into that place inside myself that I went to when I hunted my prey.

The band played song after song while I held my post, finally ending with a tumultuous chorus of "Let the Damned Burn in Hell!" The crowd, caught up, stomped and cheered, their mob ecstasy rising as one focused energy, chilling my skin and raising the hair on the back of my neck.

One times one is one. One times two is two. . . .

An abrupt hush deafened me. Beneath the Sword of Michael, the temple door opened, and a triangle of three boys wearing white and orange robes stepped from the darkness. The first carried a torch, and the two behind him held shining brass poles with candles at the top. The torch proceeded past the crowd, and the people dipped and bowed their reverences.

Once at the altar, the middle boy faced the crowd, holding the fire high while the other boys lit the candelabras on either side of the podium. Then he ceremoniously mounted two stairs to the large metal bowl perched on the tripod. Slowly, he lowered his torch. Flame burst from the bowl like a flare, and the crowd exploded with it, cheering and pounding their rapture in one voice, as if writhing in spiritual sex, working their way toward a frantic climax.

Two times six is twelve . . .

The crowd calmed, and the boys stationed themselves at the corner of the altar. Then the temple door opened again. A little man in orange robes with a tall, pointed hat stepped into the doorway. As one, the crowd knelt and bowed their heads. I took out my binoculars and focused in on him.

He was smaller than I expected. Lean and old, but with an aura of strength. In his left hand he held a staff topped with the Cross of Michael, and in his right he held a transparent orb with seven seeds suspended inside—the seven seeds given to him straight from Heaven by the Archangel Michael, or so he said. He ceremoniously paraded past his followers, moving like a man confident in his position. I wondered if he had even see the anger and doubt in his people's eyes.

I watched this little man who was responsible for so much,

and a coldness crept through me. The burnings. The starvation. The persecution of my people. But also the seeds that kept us alive after the volcano blew and covered the earth in the cold and dark. There was no way to estimate his effect on life as I knew it. What would the world have been like without him? I didn't know, but I was ready to find out what it could be.

A line of two dozen men in dress suits followed him. I recognized three of them as Maverick's customers before my eyes riveted to the man in front. My heart stopped, and I sucked in my breath. Norris. I'd known he would be there, but nothing prepared me for seeing him so proud, smiling at the bowing crowd. He waved his one good hand, the other bandaged and low at his side. He had told Bunny he would be glad to see her burn, and it showed.

Joseph handed off his staff and orb to an altar boy and mounted the podium. The men in suits took their chairs in front of the altar with Norris in the front row. I glanced at my arrows. There were more than enough to make it personal once my duty was done. Let him follow his master.

At Joseph's signal, the people rose as one. Every eye was trained on him. Angry, hopeful, waiting eyes. Waiting for the miracle he promised. Waiting for God to accept Joseph's own seed in Atonement and restore their power.

Joseph held up his hands as if to bless the people, and his high, thin voice carried over their bowed heads. "Beloved lambs, let us pray. Dear God. On the day I fought and conquered the Archangel Michael—on that first Ash Wednesday—you tested me, and I proved myself your worthy servant. You humbled me, Lord, and rewarded my faith with the Seeds of Heaven. Since that day, my people have faced many trials . . ."

While he enumerated the trials of the Josephite people, I searched for some sign of Bunny but saw none. Joshua sat frozen near me, tears streaming down his face, helpless to keep his own father from killing his daughter. His head was not bowed.

"And today, my people, God shall reward us for our perseverance and faith, for today I offer up to him my own seed for Atonement. I do this for you, my beloved lambs. Bring forth the sinner!"

The double doors of the temple flew open, and the crowd erupted. Bunny appeared in the doorway, standing alone in a wooden wagon being rolled by four men in orange robes. She looked small and frail in a plain white dress, white flowers adorning her long hair. Roses.

Her eyes grew wild when she saw the bloodthirsty crowd, and she awkwardly clutched at her dress with her bound hands, searching for something that was not there. I took hold of her pendant for her.

Joshua leaned forward in his wheelchair, as if to run to her. "She's so afraid. Dear God, help her."

Satan Stones flew toward Bunny from the crowd, and she ducked.

Millions of separate voices cried their outrage and demanded justice, each making its own plea unto heaven, until gradually they coalesced into a single voice. A single entreaty. "Atone us. Atone us. Atone us."

Louder and louder it grew, and the city of millions joined into one focus, one purpose—demanding the life of one innocent girl. One whom I had sworn to save from their fire.

Joseph raised his hands and his face toward heaven while his people cried out. Stomping and clapping in unison, demanding Atonement, the focused force of millions threatened to lift me up from my body and break me on its wave. A force I could never have imagined, it was an entity of its own that drove me to my knees and pounded through my brain, my heart beating with its rhythm.

The mob spit and shook their fists at Bunny, throwing whatever was in their hands, and guards fought to hold them back. She crouched in the corner of the wagon, her terrified eyes pinned to her father. I could not save her from the crowd, but I could let her know she was not facing this alone.

Without considering the cost, I set down my bow and stepped up behind Joshua's wheelchair where Bunny could see me. At first she looked confused, and then, as realization dawned on her, her rigid body relaxed. Her face took on a glow of peace, oblivious to the screaming crowd around her, and she bowed her head in prayer. She had seen me. She knew I would not let her feel the flames.

"Archer, no!" Spooge grabbed my arm and pulled me back. "That bastard saw you."

I looked down from behind the lattice to see Norris staring up past Joseph with a wicked gleam in his eye. Raising his crop with his bandaged hand, he saluted toward our balcony and smiled.

CHAPTER 66

NORRIS SIGNALED TOWARD THE guards at the edge of the altar and tapped on a device at his wrist. Through my binoculars it looked like some kind of small alphabet screen. They slipped out the side and discreetly made for the front of the house.

"Archer, we have to go," Spooge said, handing me my pack.

"No. I won't leave her."

"Well, we can't stay here."

Joshua interrupted. "Go to the roof. We will keep them occupied."

I scooped up my belongings and rushed for the door, but Spooge held me back. "You said you couldn't make a shot from there. You have to give it up."

I shook him off and ran for the stairs. "Lock the door behind me. I'll meet you back at the store."

In spite of his continued protests, Spooge followed me up to the roof, and as soon as I was through the door, he slammed the deadbolt into place. Then a hammering noise told me he had done one better. He was breaking the handle off the lock.

Crouching behind the parapet, I watched the wagon roll up to the altar. At least at that angle, most of the Satan Stones fell short. By this time, Bunny was standing again, her head still bowed in prayer. The guards reached for her to lift her from the wagon, but she shook them off. Her bearing regal, more like a queen than a condemned woman, she mounted the steps of the platform alone, with only a glance at her father. The guards followed behind.

I measured my shot to the altar, a very different shot from the one on the balcony. She was six yards closer to me than Joseph's podium was, but the breeze still gusted from the west. *Aim low to adjust for the angle. Take the spine at the base of the neck to make sure she feels no pain.*

The sun angled into my eyes, and I put on my Maui Jims. They helped, but they were not a perfect solution. I heard pounding on the door of the roof. My heart raced, and I fought to slow it to give me every advantage.

Bunny stepped up to the rectangular frame, and the guards took her by the arms, stretching them up and shackling her wrists above her head. Then one of them knelt and shackled her ankles.

A flicker from across the plaza caught my eye. It was the holoscreen. With another flash, it came up and stayed, filled with an image of . . . Dave the Engineer? Sure enough. He stood in front of the repaired transformer station. Behind him, none other than Maverick held a man at gunpoint, and Dave was talking.

No. Not the seeds. You didn't give him the seeds.

Then the sunlight flashed off Maverick's gold chains, and I saw it. The price. The only thing Maverick would want as much as the seeds—Granny's Bucellati necklace.

At first, I couldn't hear Dave's words over the crowd, but then the people seemed to quiet, pointing and turning around to see the image.

Finally the words themselves came through. "I worked on this project for four weeks, and I can tell you, this station has been in perfect condition and ready to go since the day after

Joseph captured his granddaughter, Tamar. So this is your miracle, folks. It's nothing but a dog and pony show."

Joseph roared, "Turn that off now. This is Satan among us."

Norris jumped up and spoke with two soldiers, who then rushed toward the temple. Then he put one hand under his suit coat and moved closer to Joseph.

The people milled in confusion. Dave continued. "Here's the real reason our fake prophet wants to kill his own granddaughter. Check it out."

With that, Mary appeared on the screen with her plants. Her lush, green, viable, fertile plants that weren't made by Joseph.

Now red in the face, Joseph jumped out from behind his podium. "Turn it off!" Norris grabbed his arm and tried to pull him away.

Hope burst within me. It was happening as I had said it would. The crowd, ready to turn after weeks of deprivation, saw the truth in what Dave said, and they were forgetting all about Bunny. They would surely riot by the time the recording finished. If I could get Bunny out of the shackles, we could make our escape. I could save her.

Then, turning toward Bunny, Joseph cried out, "You'll see she's guilty. Hear her screams." Grabbing the torch from the altar boy, he threw it on the pyre.

Fire exploded upward, and I took my shot. The last I saw of my dear sister was her head sagging. Then the flames engulfed her body.

CHAPTER 67

INOCKED ANOTHER ARROW for Joseph, but before I could shoot, a bullet whistled past my ear. Wheeling, I instead dropped the soldier who had broken through the door. Two more came out shooting behind him. I ran for cover, dodging behind the shoulder-high metal vents, but there was nowhere solid to make my stand.

Spotting the ladder to the fire escape, I jumped over the edge, half climbing and half falling to the first landing. Taking the stairs three at a time, I reached the ground and ran up the center of the alley, taking down my bow. I hurried toward the street and the security in numbers.

The people were frozen, and I was forced to slow down to cut through them discreetly while they stood dumbfounded, watching. Silent, they were transfixed by the fiery figure of the woman on the altar and the holoscreen above the plaza.

The recording ended with the Prophet's outburst in the laboratory, and then the image on the screen was replaced with the vision of Joseph, wide-eyed, searching the faces of his followers. Norris was at his side, his gun drawn and ready.

A woman wailed across the crowd. "No Atonement. The girl was innocent."

Then it happened. A Satan Stone flew through the air and hit Joseph on the temple. Then another, and another. The crowd surged forward toward Joseph, and soldiers began shooting into them. People ran in every direction. I ran too.

The crowd was a whirlwind, forcing me first one direction and then another for what seemed like forever. Fighting with everything I had, I managed to get around a corner and into an alley. Still empty, there was nothing to impede me until I had to cross the next street.

Then a shot exploded into a dumpster next to me. Glancing back, I saw the two men from the roof, and I jumped back into the crowd. This time, the irresistible force of the current of people took me two blocks in the wrong direction before I was able to push my way back to an alley, but there was no sign of pursuit.

Heedless of the readers, I stuck to the alleys. Ahead I could see where the buildings opened up to the temple grounds, not far from the store.

Dodging into the street, I zigzagged through the crowd until I felt an iron grip on my arm. "Miss Conway, you are distressed. Let us pray."

CHAPTER 68

TURNING INTO ITS GRIP, I came down on the prayerbot's bent elbow with all the force of my weight, kicking up with a back sweep that landed him on the ground and broke his hold on my arm.

The robot flailed and emitted a horrible screeching. "Sinner, sinner, sinner . . ."

I backed away, glancing around to see if anyone heard or cared. I saw two more bots coming toward me. I had to get to ground.

Pushing my way through the throng, I ran up the alley behind the temple. It was lined with a heavily vined wrought iron fence. The prayerbots turned the corner, and I slipped between the bars. *How did they know?* They were tracking my chip. I needed to block the signal for a while and lie low.

Hiding in the vines on the fence, I ripped the duct tape off my neck, pulling the chip with it. What to do? I looked down the alley. No question about it. They were making a beeline for me.

I couldn't just toss the chip. I was too far from the store. I looked around on the ground to see if I could find a container. The cigarette butts surrounding me told me my hiding place was clearly where people came to smoke. Smoke. That was it.

I ripped open the Velcro on my pack pocket and pulled out my aluminum tin. The bots were only twenty feet away. Prying off the top, I stuffed the chip inside, duct tape and all, and put the lid back on.

The bots stopped in their tracks, turning their heads this way and that. Without the signal from my chip, they were too confused to act.

Quickly, I dodged behind a hedgerow and slipped through the empty garden to the temple door, hoping their security was as bad as the transformer station's. It was. Within a minute, the lockpicker had me inside.

I shut the door and stood with my back to it, my hand on the knife in my sleeve, ready to fight or flee.

Who's the bunny now?

I was in a large room with a kitchen at one end and two dozen round tables spread across the gray tile floor. It was empty, but it was big. The kind of place so open I felt like prey. I wanted someplace smaller and more defensible to wait out the half hour, and I wanted a different door to leave by.

I scampered to the exit across from me and peeked out. It was a long hallway of windows, all of them dark, with plaques denoting offices, classrooms, and a nursery. Checking each of them, I found them all locked.

When I reached the double doors at the end of the hall, I cracked one open and peeked inside. I was at the side of a large auditorium. Row after row of chairs, at least a thousand of them, led away to my left, and above them were three layers of balconies. To my right, across the entire front of the room, three blue-carpeted steps led up to a stage. On the far side stood several throne-like chairs and three podiums, and the near side held a grand piano and risers like the ones the choir had used in the plaza. Several small space heaters dotted the floor.

At the center of the stage stood a large altar, decked in white and gold cloth and bearing an imposing Cross of Michael with a bowl of holy oil on one side. A loaf of bread sat on the other. On the wall at the back, two large banners of Joseph framed a deep baptismal font, on each side of which stood a tripod with a bowl of flame, casting eerie shadows on the twin faces of Joseph and bringing his eyes alive. I felt watched.

I thought briefly about darting out and grabbing the loaf of bread off the altar, but those eyes convinced me that their bread wasn't worth the risk. I decided the door I came in wasn't so bad and returned to the kitchen.

Hunkering down by the exit, I checked my watch. Five more minutes until I could pass the prayerbots and get to the shop—such a short distance away. I closed my eyes and tried to relax, but the shape of a flaming woman filled my vision, and the smell of burning flesh assaulted my nostrils. I opened my eyes and looked around the empty room. *Life is now, Archer. No one is burning here.*

My mind strayed to Quinn, and I smiled to myself. Granny's necklace. Maverick's weakness. I had not been able to save Bunny, but she sure went out with a bang.

Would Quinn be angry with me? Would he be proud? It didn't matter. All I wanted in that moment was his strong arms around me.

The minutes slid by so very slowly, but they finally passed. I took the chip out of my aluminum tin and taped it back under my collar. Smoothing my skirt and sweater, I shouldered my pack and cautiously cracked open the door.

Seeing nothing, I opened it wider to slip out, and I gasped. Norris stood an arm's length from the temple door, and Joseph was right behind him.

CHAPTER 69

NORRIS RECOGNIZED ME INSTANTLY. "Hah!" He grabbed the door with his good hand, and I slammed it shut. Hearing the crunch of bones, I gave it a vicious tug and turned to flee.

I dashed toward the opposite door, his screams and cursing following me.

Halfway down the long hall he tackled me, and we both went flying. His bandaged fist smashed toward me, narrowly missing. I rolled to my feet and ran toward the sanctuary. There had to be another way out from there.

Norris grabbed me by my pack and jerked hard. I fell back and then pulled forward, slipping my arms from my pack straps and dashing for the double doors. I fumbled for the knife in my sleeve while I ran, but in my haste, I couldn't get a grip.

Once in the sanctuary, I tore toward the altar with Norris hard on my heels. Grabbing the silver Cross of Michael, I swung around, aiming at his head with a braining blow. He was ready. He blocked with his left arm and slammed my temple with the butt of his right hand. The blow literally lifted me from my feet. I flew backwards, dropping the holy symbol and crashing into a flaming sconce. The fire pot sailed into the banner of Joseph, and flames engulfed the cloth.

My ears rang, and my world spun. I rolled, hoping it was away from the flames, but not certain. Jumping to my feet, I felt darkness close in. I almost collapsed. Norris reached for me. I grabbed a podium and slammed him with it.

Behind him, Joseph pushed on a corner of the altar. "Help me, you fool."

Norris ignored him and kept coming for me. I tried to dodge, but in my confusion, he was faster. His kick caught me in my bad knee, and I went down. Grabbing my neck, he pulled me up and banged me against a podium, his grip closing around my throat.

The ringing in my ears intensified, and my field of vision narrowed. I fought the black for all I was worth, knowing that to surrender was certain death.

Norris towered over me. "Where's your fire now?"

The ceiling of the temple swam above me. I tried to kick him, but the effort only hastened the darkness.

Norris pinned me harder with his weight. "Once I kill you, you filthy Sec, I'll clean your seed from the hills."

Primal terror flooded my veins. I was drowning. Helpless. Almost gone.

And then he laughed. The same laugh as when he killed Iain. The same laugh as when he incinerated my people with the Godfire.

Anger exploded within me. I refused to die without taking this bastard with me. With the strength only pure fury supplies, I grabbed the hand around my throat, the one I had smashed in the door, and I twisted it backward, cranking his wrist and arm with all my might. He screamed in pain, shifting just enough to allow me to roll away from him.

The fire from the banner reached the podiums, and they went up like Ash Wednesday tinder. I staggered back toward the altar, which Joseph was still pushing aside to reveal an opening to the tunnels below. Norris charged me, and Joseph jumped aside.

I tripped on the cord of a space heater. I grabbed its handle on my way down and rolled, swinging it toward Norris's incoming hand. His fist went straight through the grill and into the heating element.

Norris's roar of pain shook the auditorium. I crawled away as fast as I could and crouched on the far side of the altar. Finding my knife, I took two deep breaths to clear my head while he extricated his hand from the heater.

"I'll kill you, you bitch!"

Pulling myself up on my good leg, I paused for a split second to take aim, and I threw. The knife buried to the hilt in Norris's chest. He staggered backwards and went down, his eyes wide with surprise and his hands groping at the knife.

From the corner of my eye, I saw Joseph sling the tripod with the second fire sconce in my direction. The flaming bowl flew toward me, and I spun out of the way, falling to my hands and knees. It crashed into the altar with a shower of sparks, lighting the altar cloth.

My world swirled around me, and I fought to stay conscious. Beside me, the silver Sword of Michael glinted, reflecting the blaze around me. I closed my hand on it, and when Joseph rushed toward me, I threw it with all my might. He jumped out of its way, but right into the flaming banner.

His robes caught fire, and he screamed, ripping them open to take them off. But he wasn't fast enough. I grabbed the bowl of holy oil and threw it on him. Joseph burst into flames, screaming and flailing his way toward the baptismal font, only to miss it by inches and fall into the other banner. It came down around him, burying him in its folds before itself catching fire.

My good leg went out from under me, and I crashed to the floor. Norris, on his knees, the knife still protruding from his chest, had hold of my ankle with his four-fingered hand, pulling me with all his might toward the gaping hole under the altar.

Horror consumed me. I grappled for a hold but found

nothing to keep me from sliding ever closer to the drop. Small pieces of flaming ceiling showered down. Without thinking, I grabbed a handful of fiery debris. Then, twisting my own knee, I flipped and threw it into Norris's face.

Crying out, he released my ankle. I scrambled to him and grabbed the knife from his chest. He fell backward. His hand shot out and snatched a burning chair, and he flung it blindly in my direction. I rolled and scrabbled onto my good leg. Then he reached toward me, and I jumped behind him. With my hand on his forehead, I bent his head backward and slashed hard, severing his jugular and windpipe and baptizing the flaming altar with his blood.

A timber of burning ceiling crashed down, and I leapt back. Unable to put weight on my twisted knee, I limped away as quickly as I could, my burnt hand screaming in pain. Scooping up my pack from the hallway, I bolted through the kitchen door.

The streets were a roiling chaos of humanity. The common people had breached the gates and were filling the Dome, breaking windows, smashing prayerbots, and looting all they could hold, releasing the anger born of weeks of hunger and years of oppression.

My ears rang, and my brain clouded. Darkness threatened at the edges of my vision while I stumbled through the street. Somehow, I found the store.

Spooge waited for me in the alley. His worried look grew deeper when he saw me. "You look like hell. Get in here."

He pulled me into the back room of the store. "Dear God, what have you done?"

Trembling, I collapsed into his arms. "I don't know, but it's done. Joseph is dead." Then I surrendered to the pain and the darkness.

EPILOGUE

Q UINN DROPPED HIS PACK, careful to avoid setting it
on the first show of spring green. "What do you think of
this one? It looks like home to me."

"That's what you said about the last four places we looked
at." We had already hiked five days through the foothills,
searching for a new meadow—a proper home for our seeds.

I limped slightly, shepherding Ruth in front of me. It had
been seven months, and my knee still bothered me. Granny
said it always would in spite of her devoted ministrations, just
as my hand would always be scarred from the burns of that last
fight. I was learning to live with the changes within me and
find my new normal.

Quinn put his hands on his hips and shook his head. "Come
on, Archer. A meadow is a meadow."

I caught up to him and kissed him on the cheek. "Spoken
like a city boy." Opening my canteen, I passed it around.

Ruth tugged at the hem of my shirt. "I'm hungry, Mommy."

I smiled, still not used to her calling me that. It was
something she'd started doing since the spring solstice, and
I wondered if she somehow knew what was happening inside
me. I gave her a bear bar and some water and then set myself

to assessing the place.

This meadow wasn't as large as the others had been—only about forty acres—but it was flat and wide and at a lower altitude. Zander had said the lower altitude would be better for the new seeds but most importantly, that they had to be planted in isolation to keep them pure. Fortunately, there were enough refugees from North to start a new colony with us.

Quinn sat down and took Ruth into his lap. "Well, it's hard to access," he said, "Which is a mixed blessing. And we'll need to clear a lot of trees and deadfall."

"That's a 'you' we," I said. "I didn't get married to cut trees by myself." I gave him my sweetest smile. "And I do appreciate that."

A twinkle shone from his eye. "Yeah, well, there are things I appreciate not doing by myself too."

I shot him a sidelong glance, hoping he could see in my eyes what I had planned for him as soon as Ruth was asleep.

Quinn leaned back against a tree and closed his eyes, and I began to circumnavigate the area. Ruth took her little bow from her pack, the one my father had made for me at her age, and she followed me, collecting straight sticks to use for arrows.

I scratched a circle on a piece of dead bark for her and set it up as a target. "Aim right here, sweetie. Chin down. That's it." I loved it that she had a natural ability and interest. I had tried to teach a few of Tinker's kids, and while they were terrific farmers, they had never been much in the way of hunting material.

"You stay here and practice. I'm going to keep looking around."

She was concentrating and didn't answer, but I knew she heard me.

I put my hand in my pocket and felt Daisy's bone, the one she always gnawed on with such glee. I would bury it in our new home to keep her spirit near me.

While I walked, I imagined where our cabin might be. I

studied the patterns of the wind and sunlight, and I thought about what we would move up with us and what we would leave at Granny's. I closed my eyes, breathing in the feel of the place, its spirits and its mysteries.

Lacing my fingers across my belly, I focused on the life inside me. The first sign had been in my dreams. Instead of nightmares of fire and the faces of the dead each night, I had started dreaming of water, and of travel, and of people I didn't know. And I dreamed of a baby with black hair and Quinn's eyes.

Is that you? Will you be little Maerina Tamar or our Darryl Tamas? Will you be like her?

She's becoming a legend, you know. Your Uncle Spooge tells me there's a new cult growing up around her. They call themselves the Tamarites. I'm sure Joshua and the Underground are behind it. Perhaps one day they will lead the new Temple Council and bring the Josephites to a renaissance. At least for now the Atonements have stopped while they try to re-create Mary's work.

I smiled to myself.

But we have Mary's work. Some day, when you are old enough, I will tell you of Bunny and of her gift. Mary's seeds. The seeds we will plant here. The seeds you will help us protect. And maybe, some day, we will even be free to write about Bunny so that our people will never forget what she did for us.

"Mommy, Mommy." Ruth's excitement brought me back to the moment. I opened my eyes and saw him—the majestic buck I had seen for the first time almost a year ago. Was it only a year?

Stock-still and relaxed, he stared at me with wise and ancient eyes.

Ruth valiantly shot toward him, and her little stick reached me before she did. I held out my hand and whispered. "No, Ruth. Not this one. We never shoot this one."

"Is he special?"

"Yes, sweetie. He's special. He is under my protection, and I am under his."

The buck turned his head, unconcerned with our presence, and meandered into the forest.

And then I saw it. Right where he had been standing. A tiny white thing, its bright yellow center was framed in the afternoon sun. A mountain daisy. The flower Bunny and I loved. The flower we thought was gone forever.

I grinned, and joy filled my soul. Taking hold of my pendant, I said, "This is it, Quinn. Bring up the seeds. We're home."

THE BEGINNING

ABOUT THE AUTHOR

Piper Bayard is an author and a recovering attorney with a college degree or two. She's also a belly dancer from way back and a former hospice volunteer. She is currently an instructor for WANA International and the managing editor of Social In Worldwide, Inc. She pens post-apocalyptic science fiction and spy thrillers when she isn't shooting, baking cookies, or chauffeuring her children.

Her spy thriller writing partner, Jay Holmes, is a veteran field intelligence operative with experience spanning from the Cold War fight against the Soviets, the East Germans, and the various terrorist organizations they sponsored to the present Global War on Terror. He is still an anonymous senior member of the intelligence community and unwilling to admit to much more than that. Piper is the public face of their partnership.

Come to BayardandHolmes.com and click on "Subscribe Newsletter" at the bottom of the page to receive infrequent news about upcoming releases. We hold our readers in the highest regard and promise to protect your information from any and all foreign agents, marketing vultures, and phone solicitors.

You can contact Piper at BayardandHolmes.com in comments, on Twitter at @piperbayard, on Facebook at Piper Bayard or at Bayard & Holmes, or by email at BH@BayardandHolmes.com. You can also meet Piper at the conferences she presents at throughout the year, and, if time permits, she is happy to join your book club discussions of Piper Bayard and Bayard & Holmes books over the phone or via the computer.

Made in the USA
Lexington, KY
25 May 2015